About the editor

Brian J. Frost is a young fantasy historian whose essays on weird fiction and fantasy art have been published in several amateur journals devoted to fantastic literature. He is an avid reader and collector of weird fantasy stories and his large personal collection of books boasts a sizable run of the legendary American magazine *Weird Tales*. He works as a typographic designer but in his leisure time he prefers to utilise his artistic talents drawing fantasy illustrations to decorate the covers of his favourite fanzines. Currently he is associated with *Shadow*, a fantasy literature review. He is also a member of the newly-formed British Fantasy Society which aims to attract people with a common interest in fantasy and horror literature.

Book of the Werewolf
Edited by BRIAN J. FROST

SPHERE BOOKS LIMITED
30/32 Gray's Inn Road, London WC1X 8JL

First published in Great Britain
by Sphere Books Ltd 1973
Anthology copyright © Sphere Books Ltd 1973
Introduction copyright © Brian J. Frost

TRADE
MARK

This book is sold subject to the condition that
it shall not, by way of trade or otherwise, be lent,
re-sold, hired out or otherwise circulated without
the publisher's prior consent in any form of
binding or cover other than that in which it is
published and without a similar condition
including this condition being imposed on the
subsequent purchaser.

Set in Times Roman

Printed in Great Britain by
Hazell Watson & Viney Ltd
Aylesbury, Bucks

ISBN 0 7221 3688 9

ACKNOWLEDGEMENTS

HUGUES, THE WER-WOLF by Sutherland Menzies from *Victorian Ghost Stories* (1934), Ed. Montague Summers; THE WHITE WOLF OF KOSTOPCHIN by Sir Gilbert Campbell, Bart., from *Wild & Weird* (1889); THE EYES OF THE PANTHER by Ambrose Bierce from *In the Midst of Life* (1961), Signet; THE WERE-WOLF by Clemence Houseman from *Atalanta* (1895); MERE MAXIM by Elliott O'Donnell from *Werewolves* (1912), copyright © 1965 by Longvue Press; THE WEREWOLF OF PONKERT by H. Warner Munn, copyright 1925 The Popular Fiction Publishing Company; THE WOLF OF ST. BONNOT by Seabury Quinn, copyright 1930 The Popular Fiction Publishing Company; THE KILL by Peter Fleming, copyright 1942 by the author; THE DRONE by A. Merritt, copyright 1934 by the author; EENA by Manly Banister from *Weird Tales*, copyright 1947; THE ADVENTURE OF THE TOTTENHAM WEREWOLF by August Derleth, copyright the author 1951; MRS. KAYE by Beverly Haaf, copyright © 1968 by Beverly Haaf; PIA! by John Donaldson, copyright © 1969 by John Donaldson.

CONTENTS

Introduction	11
The Werewolf Theme in Weird Fiction	23
Hugues, The Wer-Wolf *by Sutherland Menzies*	53
The White Wolf of Kostopchin *by Sir Gilbert Campbell, Bart.*	75
The Eyes of the Panther *by Ambrose Bierce*	107
The Were-Wolf *by Clemence Houseman*	117
Mère Maxim *by Elliott O'Donnell*	155
The Werewolf of Ponkert *by H. Warner Munn*	161
The Wolf of St. Bonnot *by Seabury Quinn*	197
The Kill *by Peter Fleming*	238
Eena *by Manly Banister*	251
The Drone *by A. Merritt*	267
The Adventure of the Tottenham Werewolf *by August Derleth*	279
Mrs. Kaye *by Beverly Haaf*	301
Pia! *by Dale C. Donaldson*	311

BOOK OF THE WEREWOLF

INTRODUCTION

IMAGES OF THE WEREWOLF

The realm of the supernatural is the natural habitat of all manner of fearsome entities but none are quite as bizarre, or enjoy as much popular appeal, as the werewolf. With all due respect to the other monsters of the occult, I believe it is no exaggeration to claim that of all the half-human creatures inhabiting the night side of nature the werewolf dominates, both in its dreadful lore and in the depth of terror its diabolical practices can inspire.

From time immemorial men's minds and imaginations have been intrigued by the idea of shapeshifting and animal metamorphosis, but though many and wonderful were the 'man-into-beast' transformations man envisaged in the past, the werewolf remains the only one whose power to terrify has lost none of its potency. The legends surrounding this phenomenon are immeasurably ancient and can be traced back to the earliest records of civilisation, persisting all through Antiquity and the Middle Ages. Even today, in this ultra-sophisticated age of ours, the superstition is still preserved by isolated communities in remote parts of eastern Europe and Asia.

Over the years a copious literature has accumulated on the subject of werewolfism, including scholarly treatises on the origin of the legend and countless fictional stories. In fiction the werewolf theme still holds as great a fascination for the modern reader as it did for his ancestors. A tale of metamorphosistry can still chill the marrow with its blood-curdling horrors as much as it did in the far off days of the Middle Ages.

Traditionally the werewolf is depicted as the embodiment of evil, the most terrible and depraved of all the bond-slaves of Satan. In folk-lore he is ever the emblem of treachery, savagery, and bloodthirstness. In his wolf form the lycanthropist becomes a homicidal aggressor of superhuman strength whose bestial ferocity, sadistic cruelty, and ravening hunger, make him the very epitome of supernatural terror.

The term 'werewolf' literally means man-wolf, and is Anglo-Saxon in origin. In countries outside the northern hemisphere, where the wolf is not the predominant predator, the transformation is related to animals more familiar to the native population, e.g. were-tigers, were-leopards, and were-bears.

In the opinion of psycho-analysts the werewolf superstition is based on the same psychological facts as the vampire, the main elements being fear, hate, and sadism, and is probably a combination of man's archetypal fears and his age-old abhorrence of the wolf.

It is an accepted part of werewolf lore that a man who has been a werewolf during his lifetime will become a vampire after death, and so, on the face of it, there would appear to be a close link, both psychologically and supernaturally, between these two occult manifestations. For instance, in Ancient Rome, an outbreak of the birth of monsters, half human, half animal, following the calamitous reign of Nero, was believed to foreshadow disaster and to be the result of unions between vampires and women. However, it should be made clear from the outset that the vampire is altogether different from the werewolf in one major respect—the former is dead whilst the latter is fearfully *alive!* The one characteristic both these loathsome creatures do have in common is their unrelenting thirst for blood.

In a Freudian light the werewolf can be seen to represent the purely sadistic side of the sexual instinct. Unlike the vampire, who on occasions may display a perverted type of love for his chosen victim, showing all the refinement of an epicure when dining on his host's blood, the werewolf has only hate in his heart and a rapacious desire to destroy and mutilate his prey. In view of this, it is easy to see why the werewolf has become the ideal symbol of vicious, immoral mankind.

A common fallacy, perpetuated by weird fiction writers, is that the terms 'werewolf' and 'lycanthrope' are interchangeable—in fact there is an important difference. Strictly speaking a werewolf is a man or woman who, either voluntarily or involuntarily, changes or is transformed by sorcery into the shape of a wolf, and is then possessed of all the characteristics of that animal: i.e. a shaggy covering of fur, glaring eyes, long canine teeth, and razor sharp claws to ravish and rend its prey. A werewolf also exhibits all the fiendish traits associated with a wolf whilst still retaining his human intelligence.

On the other hand, Lycanthropy is a term best used to describe an authentic form of insanity in which the 'patient' imagines himself to be a wolf. In the case of a person suffering from this rare form of melancholia the following symptom complex is to be observed: The lycanthrope is weak and debilitated with a gaunt, emaciated body. His legs are covered in ulcerated sores caused by frequent falls and through grovelling on all fours in wolflike posture. His face is deathly pale, the eyes dry and hollow yet blazing with a demoniac fury mirroring the bestial thoughts within his soul. Though his mouth is parched he craves only for warm blood to quench his thirst, and exhibits a wolfish hunger for raw meat—often preferring it in a state of putrefaction. If not restrained by force he will indulge in violent sexual attacks on any female victim he can overpower. In rare cases lycanthropes have been known to violate graves and devour the corpses within like a ghoul.

There are several ways a person can become a werewolf. A voluntary metamorphosis is usually obtained through a pact with the devil, whilst an involuntary transformation is most likely to be the result of a curse, or may also be bestowed on someone as punishment for evil crimes.

In any voluntary metamorphosis there must initially be the will to do evil and the desire to exert power through fear. The sorcerer, or one who dabbles in the occult, is the sort of person most likely to wish for this power, though it is also possible that a man might wish to become a werewolf from sheer loneliness and dissatisfaction with life. In the latter case I have in mind the shunned outcast from society who falls into such a depressed state of mind that it leads to scorn and hatred for his fellow men and a burning desire to exact revenge. If, at the same time, he should develop a Satanist complex then bodily transference to animal shape becomes very desirable, especially with the complete disguise and total freedom that are implicit with the transformation. The logical conclusion to this chain of events is a pact with the devil.

In direct contrast the world of the involuntary werewolf is one of constant dread and agony. An involuntary metamorphosis is usually inflicted through a curse—witches were said to cast such enchantments over their enemies—or it may be the result of demonic possession. At night the 'innocent' werewolf will behave exactly like a ravening wolf, but during the day-time, when he is once more permitted to assume his human form, he is driven to utter desperation by contemplating the horror of his position. He longs to be slain and know the bliss of release from his enforced bondage.

The werewolf reached a peak of activity in the Middle Ages, and if we are to believe the accounts written at the time, approached the proportion of an epidemic. This infamous era of ignorance and depravity was riddled with every variety of auto-suggestion resulting in an excessive cultivation of crude fantasies among the ordinary people who abandoned themselves to a positive orgy of weird superstitions. The humble peasant, disappointed by the dull monotony of his daily life, and burdened by the oppressions of the Feudal System, tried to escape by giving his life the atmosphere of a wild fairy tale in which mystery dominated every aspect of existence.

In medieval England the demonic power to change shape was generally associated with witchcraft and Black Magic. The witch, that supreme symbol of feminine evil, was credited with many amazing powers. From old manuscripts we learn that the witch goes out on her nightly errand in the form of an invisible double; she can fly through the air and appears as a falling star; she can hear and smell at enormous distances, and she is endowed with sarcophagous propensities and feeds on corpses. Witches were also credited with the ability to change their shape at will, usually assuming the form of a wolf. Some accounts suggest that this was a corporeal and material change, whilst others were of the opinion that it was a hallucinatory or fantastical transformation. Those of the latter persuasion believed that by certain charms and spells witches could cause a certain subjective delusion or 'glamour' (now equated with mass hypnotism) which gave them the ability to appear as a wolf to all who gazed upon them, although no physical transformation actually occurred. Another belief current at that time was that witches knew how to prepare ointments which when rubbed on the body enabled them to take the form of wolves. In this fearsome guise they would range the countryside killing animals and lonely travellers. Then with gorged stomachs they would bear the warm offal of their victims' entrails to the notorious Black Sabbats as homage and foul sacrifice to the Monstrous Goat who sat upon the throne of worship, presiding over the proceedings as representative of his dark majesty, 'The Prince of Darkness'. In the case of sorcerers and warlocks, it was popularly believed that they possessed a two-sided skin, human on one side and wolf-like on the other.

The practice of witchcraft became so widespread that the Church set up an Inquisition to stamp it out. The witchhunters' 'Bible' was Sprenger and Kramer's *Malleus Maleficarum* (The Hammer of the Witches). It consists largely of a series of questions and answers on the nature and the practices of the witch. A passage of particular relevance to the subject under discussion reads as follows: —

"Question X deals with whether or not witches can by glamour change men into beasts, and with the question of Lycanthropy—whether ravening wolves are true wolves, or wolves possessed by devils. They may be either. But it is argued in another way, it may be an illusion caused by witches. For William of Paris tells of a certain man who thought that he was turned into a wolf, and at certain times went hiding among the caves. For there he went at a certain time, and though he remained there all the time stationary, he believed that he was a wolf which went about devouring children; and though the devil, having possessed a wolf, was really doing this, he erroneously thought that he was prowling about in his sleep. And he was for so long thus out of his senses that he was at last found in the wood raving. The devil delights in such things, and caused the illusion of the pagans who believed that men and old women were changed into beasts. From this is seen that such things only happen by the permission of God alone and through the operation of devils, and not through any natural defect; since by no art or strength can such wolves be injured or captured."

Another aspect of the werewolf syndrome is that animal metamorphosis, or more simply the possibility of assuming the skin of an animal, is closely linked with the desire to control a group of people by means of terror; indeed this was precisely the reason behind the panther men of West Africa who took on the aspect of formidable beasts of prey to defend their community against civilising influences.

A more sophisticated form of this idea was the 'Werewolf Organisation' formed by Adolph Hitler in pre-war Nazi Germany; the members of which were a gang of terrorists who hunted down their victims in the dark of the night. It has been suggested by certain alienists that there was a strong lycanthropic streak in Hitler's personality, and the following lines from a speech he made about education undoubtedly lend weight to this theory:— "Youth must be indifferent to pain. There must be no weakness or tenderness in it. I want to see once more in the eyes of a pitiless youth the gleam of pride and independence of the beast of prey, and to eradicate the thousands of years of human domestication." These terrifying words remind one how right Winston Churchill was to describe Hitler as 'the Nazi Beast'.

Theories about werewolfery vary widely in their content. Occultists support the theory that the werewolf form that wanders abroad at night is actually a spectral or astral projection of the body which they call the 'etheric double', and is of a quasi-material nature. Dion Fortune, the famous occultist and early student of psycho-analysis, relates in *Psychic Self Defence* how she accidentally formulated a werewolf when she had been brooding over revenge against someone who had wronged her. On drifting into a state of semi-consciousness, while resting one afternoon, there came to her mind the thought of going berserk; visions of the ancient Nordic myths of werewolves passed before her eyes and presently she felt a curious 'drawing-out' sensation from her solar plexus, and there materialised beside her the ectoplasmic form of a huge wolf. This visible manifestation, which had been energised by her malignant thoughts, was connected to her body by a psychic navel-cord. Eventually, by sheer will power Miss Fortune was able to draw the life out of the wolf, via the silver cord of ectoplasm, and back into her body—though at the precise point of absorption she experienced the most furious impulse to rend and tear anything and anybody near at hand. Fortunately, this proved only temporary, but the experience was a timely warning to her of the frightening forces trapped within ourselves, ever waiting to gain entry through the psychic door.

Theosophists believe that werewolves are inhabitants of the Astral Plane which is the lower part of the unseen world into which, so they say, man enters immediately after death. One of the remarkable characteristics of this 'realm of illusion', as it is sometimes called, is that many of its inhabitants have the power of changing their forms with Protean rapidity, and also of casting practically unlimited glamour over those with whom they wish to sport. The werewolf, along with other evil entities such as the vampire, dwells in the seventh and lowest subdivision of the Astral Plane. This section is indescribably loathsome and those frequenting it are usually people whose earth-lives have been brutal and sensual. In this infernal region they are liable to develop into terribly evil entities, inflamed with all kinds of horrible appetites.

Writing about werewolves, in *The Astral Plane: Its Inhabitants & Phenomena,* C. W. Leadbetter says: "It is always during a man's lifetime that he first manifests under this form. It invariably implies some knowledge of magical arts—sufficient at any rate to be able to project the astral body.

"When a perfectly cruel and brutal man does this, there are certain circumstances under which the body may be seized upon by other astral entities and materialized, not into the human form, but into that of some wild animal—usually the wolf; and in that condition it will range the surrounding country killing other animals, and even human beings, thus satisfying not only its own craving for blood, but that of the fiends who drive it on."

According to the sixteenth century occultist Theophras-

tus Paracelsus, man has in him two spirits—an animal
and a human spirit—and he claimed that a man in whom
the animal spirit is uppermost becomes a lunatic, and his
character resembles that of some savage animal. In after-
life he will appear in the shape of this animal, and if he
has given way to his carnal and bestial cravings, his
phantasm becomes earth-bound, usually in the guise of a
werewolf.

Eliphas Levi, the famous Victorian magician, wrote of
lycanthropy and the nocturnal transformation of men into
wolves in *The Mysteries of Magic* (1897). In this book
he claims that werewolfery is due to the 'astral body'
which, he says, is the mediator between the soul and the
material organism. Thus, in the case of a man whose instinct is savage and sanguinary, his phantom (or astral
projection) will wander abroad in lupine form whilst he
sleeps soundly in his bed dreaming he is a veritable wolf.
The body, being subject to nervous and magnetic influences, will receive blows and cuts dealt at the fantastical shape.

A modern psychological theory on lycanthropy was ex-
pounded by Carl Jung, the eminent psycho-analyst. He
put forward the idea that archetypal memories survive in
the ancestral subconscious strata of the human mind, and
that atavistic dreams of our lycanthropic ancestry can
sometimes break through into the consciousness of a person. In making this claim Jung was influenced by his discovery of the constant reappearance of ancient symbols
in the dreams of individuals who could not have had any
experience in the modern world that might have suggested
them.

The major sources of werewolf lore and legend available to us today are the numerous treatises that have been
written on the subject. The definitive work is Montague
Summers' *The Werewolf* (1933), which is the most
scholarly and detailed study of the werewolf ever attempted. Other important works examining the legend in depth
are: Sabine Baring-Gould's *The Book of Were-wolves*
1865); Elliott O'Donnell's *Werwolves* (1912); and Frank
Hamel's *Human Animals* (1915). Hamel's book is also a
comprehensive survey of every variety of human and
animal transformation.

The best modern study of lycanthropy is Robert Eisler's *Man into Wolf* (1947). This is an important work dealing with the anthropological interpretation of sadism, masochism, and lycanthropy. The author elaborates on the theme that there is a pre-historical, evolutionist derivation of all crimes of violence. Two modern studies of a less scholarly nature are: *Terror by Night* (1963) and *Vampires, Werewolves and Ghouls* (1968), both of which are compiled by Bernhardt J. Hurwood.

The werewolf theme in fiction has a long, fascinating history throughout which the werewolf's image has undergone a gradual evolution. In the traditional werewolf story the werewolf figure is usually depicted as a supernatural monster, but today this primitive image has largely been abandoned in favour of the 'innocent' werewolf (i.e. the dupe of malignant psychic forces, or the recipient of a curse) who is portrayed as a victim rather than as a criminal.

Looking back to the early exponents of the horror tale one observes that the Gothic novelists invariably capitalise on regional legends and their image of the werewolf corresponds closely to the medieval version. Symbolism, now accepted as an integral part of weird fiction, didn't enter the genre until the Victorian era when the principal sources of terror in everyday life were social fears and taboos. The Victorians' unnatural obsession with excessive prudery and religious fanaticism were mainly responsible for creating a repressed society which sought relief in the spate of sensational novels that flourished during the nineteenth century. As the secrets of passion were considered taboo they had to be translated into terms of bloodshed, and consequently the gruesome horror story became an allegory of these forbidden desires. The effect of this on the werewolf tale was that the werewolf's savage method of killing now became equated with rape and sexual possession.

In modern tales of metamorphosistry one constantly finds that the author visualises the werewolf as a psychical creature, more to be sympathised with than feared—a trend that has led to a marked diminuation in the supernatural content of the werewolf tale. Nowadays a weird fantasy writer can no longer count on a fair proportion of his readers believing in the reality, or at least the possibility of werewolves, so in order to establish some credibility for his narrative he has resorted to various ingenious methods of explaining the transformation from human to animal scientifically. Stimulated by the great advances being made in the study of hypnotism and abnormal psychology, the horror story writer has discerned that in dreams and madness is the very essence of the supernatural, and by probing the psychological aspect of lycanthropy he has been able to explore new and intriguing variations on the theme, without any lessening of the horror content.

Though modern science has destroyed many of man's most cherished myths, it is still hard for us to dismiss the werewolf as a mere figment of the imagination. Psychologists may try to reassure us that werewolves are merely monsters spawned in our unconscious—fanciful extensions of the symbolic monsters that haunt our dreams and waking fantasies—but, nevertheless, something deep within us cannot fully accept this idea. For, although man's evolution has made him separate from the other animals, there are still bestial instincts beneath his civilised exterior. Within our souls still smoulder the flames of our brute heritage. Sometimes the monsters trapped inside us escape vicariously in our dreams or manifest themselves in the raving madness of the lycanthrope. Yes, indeed, it is frightening to think that something of the werewolf's instincts may be in us all, crouching within our souls, still capable of leaping into conscious life.

In this anthology I have attempted to highlight the milestones in the long history of the werewolf story by offering a representative selection of short werewolf stories spanning over 130 years of supernatural fiction. The stories are arranged in chronological order, and so that the literary development of the werewolf tale can be outlined more fully, I have written a concise historical survey of the theme in fiction. In compiling this anthology I have felt it my duty to search out those stories which will be unknown to the average reader either because the originals are in scarce out-of-print collections, or only available in expensive hardcover editions. The stories are varied in style, ranging from Victorian tales of physical horror to modern stories of psychological terror, So, whatever your tastes in weird fiction may be, I am confident that if you have a taste for the ultimate in horror you will find the subject matter of this volume to be just your cup of tea ... but beware, it's a strong brew!

BRIAN J. FROST

1972

THE WEREWOLF THEME IN WEIRD FICTION

The werewolf motif was introduced into English fiction by Marie de France in her 13th century court romance *Lay of the Bisclavaret*. Equally well-known in medieval times was the French romance *William & the Werewolf*, which was translated into English in 1350. Although both works have a minor historical significance they are rather insipid when compared with the werewolf tales of more recent vintage.

The werewolf theme, though common enough in folklore, does not reappear in fiction until the early nineteenth century, with the advent of the Gothic novel. The Gothic novelists, those arch-purveyors of supernatural horror, took up the theme once more and adapted it to their own particular requirements. Their sources of inspiration were the gruesome legends of the Middle Ages, and their narratives abound with sensational events making full use of the werewolf's animal glamour and bestial phantasmagory. A typical werewolf novel of the period is Weber's *Wolf: or The Tribunal of Blood* (1806).

Charles Maturin, the last great exponent of the Gothic novel, utilised the werewolf motif to great effect in his last romance *The Albigenses* (1824). In one episode, in the dungeon of his castle, the hero Sir Paladour is confronted with an amorphous form howling and yelling "I am a mad wolf . . . the hair grows inwards—the wolfish coat is within—the wolfish heart is within—the wolfish fangs are within!" Maturin then proceeds with great relish to describe the horrors of the werewolf's den.

In the authentic Gothic novel the werewolf figure is only rarely encountered, but the prolific hacks employed by Edward Lloyd for his 'penny dreadfuls' frequently introduced the werewolf into their outrageous yarns to add even more horror to their gory plots. G. W. Reynolds, who wrote many popular Gothic thrillers, is credited with the novel, *Wagner: The Wehr-Wolf* (1846), which before book publication was run as a serial in no less than seventy-seven episodes. An essential ingredient of any traditional werewolf tale is the transformation scene, and Reynolds' own graphic description, given below, has served as the prototype for many subsequent versions:—

"The young man, handsome, and splendidly attired has thrown himself upon the ground, where he writhes like a stricken serpent. He is the prey of a demoniac excitement; an appalling consternation is on him . . . madness is in his brain . . . his mind is on fire. Lightnings appear to gleam from his eyes . . . as if his soul were dismayed, and withering within his breast.

"Oh no! . . . No!" He cries, with a piercing shriek, as if wrestling madly, furiously, but vainly, against some unseen fiend that holds him in his grasp. And the wood echoes to that terrible wail, and the startled bird flies fluttering from its bough. But lo! What awful change is taking place in the form of that doomed being? His handsome countenance elongates into one of savage and brute-like shape; the rich garment which he wears becomes a rough, shaggy, and wiry skin; his body loses its human contours, his arms and limbs take another form, and, with a frantic howl of misery, to which the woods give horribly faithful reverberations, and with a rush like a hurling wind, the wretch starts wildly away . . . no longer a man, but a monstrous wolf!"

The excesses of this novel are not so evident in the short stories of the period. Captain Marryat's *The White Wolf of the Hartz Mountains,* from *The Phantom Ship* (1839), is a classic story which has been anthologised many times, usually under the abbreviated title 'The Werewolf', and is probably the best known of all werewolf tales. Equally effective is Mrs. Crowe's *A Story of a Weir-Wolf* (1846) in which suspected lycanthropy and witchcraft are the main motifs. The author is chiefly noted for her collections of true ghost stories, and in Victorian times was considered a leading authority on the supernatural. Her two most famous works are: *The Night Side of Nature* (1848) and *Light and Darkness* (1850). In the latter volume the subject of wolfomania is discussed in a chapter entitled 'The Lycanthropist'.

For the opening story in this anthology I have chosen a typical example of the Gothic romance, *Hugues, the Wer-Wolf* by Sutherland Menzies, which was written in 1838 when the Gothic influence was still prevalent in supernatural fiction. Although it displays all the stock features associated with this style of writing, it is nevertheless fast-paced and more than just a curiosity piece.

On the Continent, during the mid-nineteenth century, the colourful novels of Alexandre Dumas were all the rage; one of his lesser known works is a Gothic romance of Satanism and werewolfery entitled *The Wolf-Leader*, published in 1857. This tells the story of Thibault, a French peasant of the eighteenth century, who is dissatisfied with his humble status and calls upon the devil for aid. His pleas are answered when he is visited by the arch-fiend in the guise of a huge black wolf. As a result of this meeting he is tricked into a pact with the devil by which he is granted his every wish in return for hairs from his head, one for the first wish, two for the second, four for the third, and so on, doubling the number for each wish granted. At first the greedy peasant considers that this is a very fair bargain, but discovers to his horror that the hairs, instead of disappearing, turn flame-red, and thus brand him as a Satanist. Thibault, however, is a cunning rogue and initially tries not to abuse his unholy gifts, but his envy of the nobility, and their rejection of him, make him resolve to use his magical powers to the utmost, even though all of his hair will eventually be claimed by the devil's colour. Finally, when all the wishes are used up, and his hair has become one mass of flame, the devil claims his soul and transforms him into a werewolf.

Another fine werewolf tale originating from the Continent is Erckmann-Chatrian's *Hugues-le-Loup* (1869).

This was later translated into English for the collection *The Man-Wolf and Other Tales* (1872).

A phenomenon of the Victorian era in England was the rise to prominence of women writers, especially in the realm of the macabre, where they showed a great facility for fashioning tales of terror. One such 'gentlewoman of evil' was the Hon. Mrs. Greene who wrote the novel *Bound by a Spell; or The Hunted Witch of the Forest* (1885); a neo-Gothic romance in which the classic motifs of witchcraft, Satanism, and werewolfism are combined.

Robert Louis Stevenson, besides writing such timeless classics as 'Treasure Island' and 'Kidnapped', was also expert at composing tales of the supernatural. His masterpiece in the genre is undoubtedly *The Strange Case of Dr. Jekyll and Mr. Hyde* (1886), which, in my opinion, qualifies for discussion here as a brilliant extension of the werewolf theme. Although Hyde retains his human form he still has all the qualities of a lycanthrope. The idea for this story is supposed to have come to the author in a dream, and even in his waking life the idea of the double life seems to have haunted Stevenson's imagination, as he penned several stories with this particular theme. A year after the publication of 'Jekyll & Hyde' Stevenson wrote *Ollala*, an intensely atmospheric novelette about hereditary lycanthropy. It is also one of the earliest stories to deal accurately with this form of insanity, and as a result makes a most convincing narrative.

Stories of female werewolves are perhaps even more intriguing than those about their male counterparts. The undercurrent of eroticism in such tales is probably a major factor in their popularity, as is also the sharp contrast provided between the attraction of a mysteriously beautiful woman and the repulsion of that same personality when it reveals its true nature and assumes the hideous form of a wolf. The next story, Sir Gilbert Campbell's *The White Wolf of Kostopchin*, is from a rare collection entitled *Wild and Weird* which was published in 1889. As far as I am aware this will be its first appearance in a paperback.

The Victorian periodicals from the late nineteenth century contain some of the best supernatural stories ever written. From *The Spirit Lamp,* an occult magazine edited by Lord Alfred Douglas, comes a noted werewolf tale, *The Other Side* by Count Eric Stenbock. This lurid nightmare of diablery and Black Magic is based on an old French legend of werewolfery and features a lycanthropous brook which carries the hero over the other side into the dread 'dominion of darkness'. The following brief passage will serve to illustrate the story's sombre power.

"And through the darkness he heard wolves howling and shrieking in the hideous ardour of the chase, and there passed before him a terrible procession of wolves (black wolves with red fiery eyes) and with them men that had the heads of wolves and wolves that had the heads of men, . . . and last of all seated on an enormous black ram with hideous human face the wolf-keeper, on whose face was eternal shadow".

The author of this controversial piece was a Russian nobleman, domiciled in England, whose sole claim to fame is as the author of a handful of stories on witchcraft, demonology, and werewolves, the best of which were collected in *Studies of Death* (1894). Literary biographers describe Stenbock as an eccentric and a pervert who led an extremely dissolute life, finally killing himself with drink and drugs at the age of thirty-five. Stenbock's obsession with the dark side of life eventually brought on fits of madness which gave him such an evil disposition that a contemporary of his is reported to have described him as "one of the most inhuman beings I have ever met".

Stories of shapeshifting, other than the lupine variety, are not all that plentiful in modern European literature. Generally such stories are linked with an allied theme known as metempsychosis (the transmigration of souls). Rudyard Kipling wrote a particularly gruesome tale about this phenomenon in *The Mark of the Beast* (from 'Life's Handicap', 1891). This describes the macabre results of an Indian leper priest's curse through which a beast's soul is put into the body of an Englishman. Another unusual shapeshifting story is *A Vendetta of the Jungle* by Sidney Warwick and Arthur Applier. The wife of an Englishman living in India is devoured by a tiger. Instead of leaving the world her soul enters the body of the savage beast which comes back (later in the story) and slays her rival. When the husband realises the truth and tries to kill the animal he sees the eyes of his former wife staring at him from the tiger's face.

Human transformation into leopards or panthers is another popular variant on the shapeshifting theme. Preeminent among such tales is Ambrose Bierce's *The Eyes of the Panther*, which is the next course on our menu of terror. Bierce ranks highly among nineteenth century American horror writers, perhaps second only to Edgar Allan Poe. His horror tales usually have natural settings but harken back to the sombre style of Poe with their obsession with violent and unnatural death. The late H. P. Lovecraft was of the opinion that Bierce's stories, particularly those about the American Civil War, "come close to real genius".

The golden age of English supernatural fiction, which began in the 1890's and continued through to the outbreak of the Great War, produced hundreds of stories about the more outré forms of the supernatural. Two minor stories of werewolfery from this period are: H. Beaugrand's *The Werwolves* (1898), and Eden Phillpotts' *Loup-Garou!* (1899). The latter is set in the West Indies, home of loup-garous and jumbies—monsters of the night akin to both the vampire and werewolf. Also deserving of mention here is S. R. Crockett's stirring historical romance *The Black Douglas* (1899). This incident-packed novel features the great Satanist Gilles de Rais and his constant companion Astarle, a huge she-wolf, which is the beast form taken by an evil female lycanthropist.

The old saw about the female of the species being deadlier than the male is highly appropriate in the case of the werewolf. Female werewolves often appear in the guise of beautiful, seductive young women in order to ensnare young men into their cruel embrace. After satisfying her carnal desires the werewoman resumes her lupine form and destroys her victim without mercy. Her image is superbly realised in our next story, Clemence Housman's *The Were-wolf*, which was initially published in 1896, and has enjoyed critical acclaim ever since. Sam Moskowitz, a leading expert on supernatural fiction, has written: "It may quite likely be the single greatest work of fiction on the theme of lycanthropy . . . it carries the reader with dramatic intensity toward an ultimate horror that threatens both the body and the soul".

The evil protagonist of this exquisite prose-poem is a beautiful female lycanthropist who brings death to all who receive her deadly kiss. True to the image of the fatal woman she is heartless and destructive—a creature whose beautiful face masks the deepest depravity and the subtlest vice. Here, for your assured approval is an unforgettable tale of beauty, suspense, and horror that is unequalled, both for literary quality and dramatic power.

The Edwardian era produced a spate of neo-Gothic novels which followed in the wake of Bram Stoker's *Dracula*. One of the most successful of these, *The Door of the Unreal* by Gerald Biss, is a werewolf story of uncommon power. Of course, not every story on the theme is a classic: Fred Whishaw's *The Were-Wolf* (1902), besides having the most unoriginal of titles, is also of minor significance plot-wise, being another of those tales of imposture where a villainous rogue uses the legend of the werewolf to frighten a group of gullible peasants. Saki's *Gabriel Ernest* (1910) is a much anthologised piece, mainly I suspect on account of this author's substantial reputation rather than for any merit the story possesses, as it is extremely slight. Just as insipid is Eugene Field's *The Werewolf* (1911) in which the metamorphosis is due to an ancestral curse. A much more naturalistic treatment of the theme occurs in *Vandover and the Brute* by Frank Norris. In this novel the author has divested the werewolf motif of all its supernatural trappings to give us a fascinating study of the moral degeneration of the soul. The hero of the story falls to such utter degradation that he imagines himself transformed into the beast his soul symbolises, and runs about on his hands and knees howling like a wolf.

Algernon Blackwood, the leading exponent of the supernatural story this century, has a number of werewolf stories to his credit. In *The Camp of the Dog* (1908), an adventure of Dr. John Silence, the famous psychic sleuth, Blackwood envisages the werewolf in the role of a victim rather than a criminal. A young man, gentle by day, leaves his body at night by astral projection and assumes the shape of a wolf. During the hours of sleep when his subconscious takes over the brutish instincts buried deep within his soul come to the surface, and in a frantic fit of lycanthropy his 'etheric double' violently assaults his fiancée.

Blackwood was a dedicated writer who took the supernatural seriously; he was continually searching for signs and proof of hitherto unknown powers that lie hidden in us all, particularly the extension of consciousness and the benefits—or dangers—involved. He expressed a firm belief in the 'psychical' werewolf, seeing it as the projection of the slumbering, untamed, sanguinary instincts in men, strong enough to materialise and assume what he called 'the body of desire'. One of his short stories that is based on this theory is *The Empty Sleeve* (from *The Wolves of God and other Fey Stories*, (1921). This is a highly provocative extension of the werewolf theme in which the 'desire body' of a violent man assumes the shape of an enormous cat. From the same collection of stories comes the well-known *Running Wolf*, which is based on Red Indian folk-lore. A young brave kills a wolf, the sacred totem animal of his tribe, and for this outrage he is doomed, after death, to appear in the form of a wolf until he has fully atoned for his crime.

Excellent though this, and the other Blackwood stories are, I have decided not to include any of them here due to their easy access in other anthologies. Instead, I have chosen as representative of the Edwardian era a short extract from Elliott O'Donnell's *Werwolves* (1912). This famous work is supposedly a non-fiction study of werewolves but throughout its pages the scholar and novelist often merge. The following story of witchcraft and werewolfery is reputed to be a French legend but it is patently obvious that the author has done quite a lot of fictional embroidery around the original anecdote. The setting for this tale is the Middle Ages when witchcraft cast its dark shadow over the lives of the superstitious peasantry. The witch in this story is not the usual ugly old crone but a sensuous beauty in the great tradition of the fatal women of European romantic literature.

Apart from the Blackwood stories, the 1920s was not a particularly vintage decade for British tales of metamorphosistry; the only outstanding novel is David Garnett's amusing fantasy *Lady into Fox*. Since its publication in 1922 several authors have adopted this motif for their stories—notably A. Meritt in his *The Fox Woman*. E. O. Carolin's novel *The Soul of the Wolf* (1923) has little to commend it and Charles Lee Swem's *Were Wolf* (1929) is only slightly more interesting. The latter, an unpretentious thriller, features a bedridden invalid who suffers from spasmodic attacks of insanity during which he regains his strength and roams abroad at night dressed in a wolf's skin, causing havoc among the village community. Of the American werewolf novels written during this decade only R. W. Service's *The House of Fear* (1927) has achieved any lasting popularity. In this exciting yarn a descendant of Gilles de Rais controls a wolf-like monster which he sends out at night to attack his chosen victims. The two most notable short stories with a werewolf theme published in the 1920s are: Arthur Salmon's *The Were-Wolf*

(1927), and Oliver Onions' *The Master of the House* (1929). In the latter a varlet who has learned oriental magic is able to shift his shape to that of an alsatian dog.

Toward the end of the 1920s, as the traditional English expertise at horror writing fell into decline, new writers from America began to emerge as the leaders in the horror field, particularly in the art of short story writing. This minor literary revolution was mainly brought about by the creation of a new market for fantasy fiction with the advent of the American 'pulp' magazines. The greatest of these periodicals was *Weird Tales* which, as the first all-fantasy magazine in the world, pioneered the development of the weird fantasy story as a specialised form of popular fiction. For more than thirty years it provided a perfect showcase, not only for established authors, but for new talents of the calibre of H. P. Lovecraft, Clark Ashton Smith, and Robert E. Howard.

When *Weird Tales* first appeared on the news-stands in March 1923 it promised its readers "fantastic, extraordinary, grotesque stories; stories of strange and bizarre adventure . . . that will startle and amaze you". This, as all lovers of weird fiction will affirm, was a pledge well kept. Many of the stories in 'the unique magazine', as it was subtitled, were incomparably written; others, while not written with the style of a master, displayed the fertile imagination of aspiring young authors eager to experiment with new ideas.

The 'Weird Tales' author whose name is virtually synonymous with werewolf tales is H. Warner Munn. During the late 1920s and early years of the following decade he related, in a series of connected stories, the sanguinary career of a 1,000-year old warlock called 'The Master'. The first story in the series, now presented here for the first time in paperback, is *The Werewolf of Ponkert* (from the issue for July 1925). The unusual feature about this tale is the way it is told from the point of view of one of the werewolves, giving the reader an insight into the horror of such an existence. Encouraged by the success of his grim tale Munn went on to pen a sequel, *The Return of The Master* (July 1927), and a third story featuring the offspring of the Werewolf of Ponkert entitled *The Werewolf's Daughter* (serialised in three parts, commencing

October 1928). After a gap of two years the same author brought out a further series of stories featuring 'The Master' under the group heading 'Tales of the Werewolf Clan'. The story titles are: *The Master Strikes* (November 1930), *The Master Fights* (December 1930), and *The Master Has A Narrow Escape* (January 1931). They each narrate the adventures of the progeny of the Werewolf of Ponkert, showing how the hereditary curse of lycanthropy affected the family in different generations and locales. For all their ingenuity the stories in this second trilogy lack the sombre power of the earlier ones and never achieve any great heights of horror. This charge cannot be levelled at the next story which, while not likely to win any plaudits for its literary style, has many moments of real horror, both physical and mental.

One of the most productive policies of *Weird Tales* was its readiness to introduce new talent to its pages. This paid an early dividend with the discovery, in the first year of publication, of Seabury Quinn, who at the time of his debut was a struggling young writer just out of law school. His first story for the magazine was the werewolf tale *The Phantom Farmhouse* (October 1923) which today is recognised as a classic of its kind. For Quinn this was the start of a long association with *Weird Tales* during which he established himself as the magazine's most popular author.

The Phantom Farmhouse is a story of poignant, pathetic beauty, set in the sylvan atmosphere of the American countryside, through which flit shapes of horror. While convalescing at a sanitorium, a young clergyman hears strange rumours circulating among the patients that loup-garous are infesting the neighbouring countryside. Unperturbed by these wild stories he ventures one night into the woods where he discovers a secluded farmhouse, and makes friends with the mysterious occupants—an old man and his wife and their beautiful young daughter. Unbeknown to him the strange trio are in reality werewolves, and the farmhouse merely an illusion created by sorcery. During the day the werewolves must repose in their graves, but at night they are free to roam abroad. When the moon is shining they are obliged to appear in their human shapes but when the moon hides its light they have the power to assume their wolfish form.

The hero falls in love with the girl who returns his affection and at the same time protects him from the enmity of her parents. However, she comes to realise that her affliction makes impossible any normal relationship between herself and her lover, and decides upon a plan to bring about her own, and her parents', salvation. At a final midnight tryst with the young clergyman she makes him promise to come early the next morning and read the office for the burial of the dead over their graves so that they may finally be released from their unholy bondage. Although the author has diverged from accepted werewolf lore by suggesting that werewolves are members of the 'Undead' there is no reason why this small technicality should detract from this highly entertaining narrative which, with the possible exception of *Roads*, was Quinn's most popular story.

For the October 1925 issue of *Weird Tales* Quinn penned a story entitled *The Horror on the Links* which introduced his most famous character, the ubiquitous Jules de Grandin—psychic investigator extraordinary. The mercurial Frenchman, assisted by the faithful Dr. Trowbridge, was to appear in more than ninety stories chronicling his daring exploits. During his long, successful career Jules fought every conceivable denizen of the phantom world, but it was his dramatic encounters with vampires and werewolves that were the most memorable.

One of de Grandin's earliest appearances was in a werewolf story entitled *The Blood Flower* (March 1927). In this thrill-packed tale a young woman comes under an evil spell by wearing a hellish bloom which has the property of changing her into a wolf. The flower is given to her by an evil relative who is himself a werewolf and wants her for his mate. A highlight of the narrative is the chilling description of the man-wolf:—

"Not human, nor yet wholly bestial it was, but partook grotesquely of both, so that it was at once a foul caricature of each. The forehead was low and narrow and sloped back to a thatch of short, nondescript-coloured hair resembling animal's fur. The nose was elongated out of all semblance to a human feature and resembled the pointed snout of some animal of the canine tribe except that it curved sharply down at the tip like the beak of some unclean bird of prey. The cruel lips were drawn sneeringly back from a double row of tusklike teeth which gleamed horridly in the dim reflection of the open fire, and a pair of round baleful eyes, green as the luminescence from a rotting carcass in a midnight swamp glared at us from the window."

Fortune's Fools (July 1938), another tremendous werewolf story by Seabury Quinn, features the illustrious ancestor of Jules de Grandin and is a werewolf tale that literally has everything a good weird yarn should have: action, thrills, and shudders galore, with a lacing of eroticism for good measure. Like many of the best tales of metamorphosistry it is set against the romantic background of medieval Europe.

In the opening sequence the hero, Ramon de Grandin, rescues a beautiful young woman from a pack of werewolves. The couple then seek shelter for the night at the nearby castle of Otto von Wolfsberg, little realising that they have stumbled into the werewolves' den. They are immediately made prisoners by the brutish baron and his henchmen who are in fact a pack of werewolves that maraud the surrounding countryside, preying upon the local inhabitants. How the hero and his beautiful companion effect their escape, and the eventual destruction of the werewolves, is the thrilling denouement to this exciting and thoroughly entertaining narrative. One enthusiastic reader of *Weird Tales* described it as "another of those word-faceted jewel carvings of phrases which we owe to the genius of Seabury Quinn." This was typical of the sort of praise lavished upon his work during the hey-day of the magazine.

A year later Quinn came up with another mediaeval werewolf tale entitled *Uncanonized* (November 1939). In this story he abandoned his swashbuckling style for a more sensitive treatment. His *Glamour* (December 1939) in the next issue of *Weird Tales* is another clever twist on the transformation theme. This deals with the hypnotic power that certain witches possess; the plot revolving around the way a witch uses this ability to create an illusion to delude her victims. The hag-like enchantress of the story is not only able to transform herself into various animals but also into a ravishingly beautiful woman. Quinn's other excursions into the realm of the werewolf are: *The Wolf of St. Bonnot* (December 1930), *The Thing in the Fog* (March 1933), and *The Gentle Werewolf* (July 1940).

Seabury Quinn's popularity as an author continues right up to the present day, and the reprinting of his tales in *The Magazine of Horror* and *Startling Mystery Stories* has brought him a host of new fans from today's younger generation. His death, at the age of eighty on Christmas Eve 1969, ended an illustrious career during which he penned over 500 short stories.

Because Quinn wrote so many fine werewolf tales it has been a difficult task to select just one for this anthology. *The Phantom Farmhouse* is his most famous story but as this has been reprinted many times I have chosen instead *The Wolf of St. Bonnot* which was inspired by the real-life case of Gilles Garnier. This will also serve as an introduction to the captivating Jules de Grandin for those who have not previously made his acquaintance.

There was always a steady demand for werewolf stories from the readers of *Weird Tales* and there were always plenty of authors willing to supply them with this gruesome fare. Robert E. Howard, famed creator of Conan, had two fine werewolf yarns to his credit. The first to be accepted by *Weird Tales* was a short piece called *In The Forest of Villefere* (August 1925), and the following year appeared his tale of swordplay and werewolfery, *Wolfshead* (April 1926). Both stories, though immature, were evidence of an embryo talent that would later mature into full stature in the adventures of the mighty barbarian hero, Conan.

A stalwart of *Weird Tales* during most of its lifetime was the popular author Manly Wade Wellman. He made his debut in 1927 with *Back To The Beast* and was still writing for the magazine in the early fifties. His initial foray into the dark world of the werewolf was with *The Horror Undying* (May 1936). Here Wellman utilises the superstition that if a werewolf dies painlessly and his body is left whole he can still live on as a vampire. The other werewolf yarns from his pen are: *The Werewolf Snarls* (March 1937) and *The Last Grave of Lill Warran* (May 1951). The latter is another variation on the idea of a werewolf becoming a vampire after death.

Under the pseudonym 'Gans T. Field' Wellman wrote *The Hairy Ones Shall Dance* which was the first of a quartet of novelettes featuring the psychic investigator, Judge Pursuivant. (It was serialised in three parts, commencing January 1938). The story opens sensationally with a seance at which all the participants are hand-cuffed together. During the eerie proceedings a strange wolf-like shape materialises in the darkened room and springs upon one of the guests and rends him to death. It is later discovered that this terrible crime was perpetrated by no ordinary flesh and blood creature but by an ectoplasmic materialisation emanating from the body of the medium. Here the author has drawn his inspiration from the theory put forward by spiritualists that certain mediums can exude an unclassified material called ectoplasm. This substance, at first light and vaporescent, becomes firm and takes shape either upon the body of the medium or as a separate and 'living' creature—in this case as a werewolf. Throughout the narrative there are many references and quotations from Montague Summers' 'The Werewolf' and other occult treatises, so it is obvious that a lot of research had been done before the author commenced the story. This added touch of authenticity obviously appealed to the readers of *Weird Tales* who voiced their approval of the story in the readers column—even Seabury Quinn was moved to add his own personal congratulations.

Another highly rated werewolf serial is Greye La Spina's *Invaders from the Dark* (published in three parts, commencing April 1925). The young heroine, a psychic investigator, suspects the presence of malign forces when her fiancé is enticed away from her by a glamorous Russian princess who has recently taken up residence in their small American town. The evil femme fatale, who is eventually exposed as a werewolf, plans to install the heroine's boy-friend as her mate. This serial was later published as a novel by Arkham House and was also reissued by Paperback Library in 1966 under the title *Shadow of Evil*.

In my opinion, a much superior werewolf tale by Miss La Spina is *The Devil's Pool* (June 1932). It was the featured story of the issue and inspired a fine cover painting by Allen St. John. This shows a scene where the werewolf is staring into a full-length mirror with the reflection showing, not a wolf, but a naked woman crouching on all fours. The readers voted it the best story in that issue, thus confirming editor Farnsworth Wright's opinion of it as "a tremendous werewolf story full of eerie thrills and shudders."

Another popular female writer contributing to *Weird Tales* was G. G. Pendarves (pseudonym of British author Gladys Gordon Trenery). Her best remembered stories are: *The Eighth Green Man* (March 1928); *Thing of Darkness* (August 1937); and a werewolf yarn improbably entitled *Werewolf of the Sahara* (August/September 1936). This last piece is the story of Gunnar the Werewolf and the evil arab Sheikh El Shabur, and the dreadful occult forces that were unleashed in a desperate struggle for the soul of a beautiful girl. A typical 'pulp type' potboiler but entertaining none the less.

Probably the best werewolf tale by a lady writer is Lireve Monet's *Norn* (February 1936). It features both male and female werewolves and is told from the point of view of a young girl who is an innocent bystander to an unfolding tragedy that ends in stark terror. This is not only a gripping story but also a fascinating study of human emotions. *The House of the Golden Eyes:* Theda Kenyon

(September 1930) is by the author of the book *Witches Still Live* and tells of werewolves and a dreadful night in rural Ireland.

An excellent example of the inventiveness of the 'Weird Tales' school of writers is Arlton Eadie's novelette *The Wolf-Girl of Josselin* (August 1938) which relates the tragic consequences of a young man's love for a female werewolf. The hero marries a startlingly beautiful girl, unaware that she is descended from the legendary 'Barking Women of Josselin' who were put under a curse which caused them to change into wolves and devour their newborn offspring.

The most unusual story about a female werewolf to appear in *Weird Tales* is Howard Wandrei's *The Hand of the O'Mecca* (April 1935) in which a farmer courts Kate O'Mecca, a strange girl from his village, and asks for her hand in marriage. Later on in the story he receives it literally when he chops it off during a fierce struggle with her when she attacks him in her lupine form.

An above-average story of hereditary lycanthropy is Captain S. P. Meek's *The Curse of the Valedi* (July 1935). This is a traditional tale set in Romania and tells of the dark powers that infest the slopes of the Carpathian mountains.

Lesser tales of lycanthropy were fairly numerous in *Weird Tales;* most were short 'fillers' tucked away at the back of the magazine. Into this category fall stories like: *Silver Bullets* by Jeremy Ellis (April 1930); *The Silver Knife* by Ralph Allen Lang (January 1932); *The Werewolf's Howl* by Brooke Byrne (December 1934); *The Woman at Loon Point* by August Derleth (December 1936); *The Werewolf Howls* by Clifford Ball (November 1941); and *Loup Garou* by Manly Banister (May 1947).

The theme of bodily transference from human to animal form is not, of course, restricted to the lupine variety. *Weird Tales* published many variations on the theme of shapeshifting with stories that described every conceivable type of metamorphosis. Bassett Morgan's *Tiger-Dust* (April 1933) is generally acknowledged as the best weretiger story ever published in the entire history of the magazine, and the best story about a were-leopard is, in my opinion, John Horne's *The Speared Leopard* (August

1929). A feline metamorphosis occurs in Mary E. Counselman's *The Cat Woman* (October 1933), while Frank Belknap Long's *The Were-Snake* (September 1925) has an even more formidable horror, the nature of which is evident from the title. Robert Bloch's best contribution to the mythos is *The Black Kiss* (June 1937) which was written in collaboration with Henry Kuttner. This cleverly plotted tale of bodily transference gives the legend of the mermaid a new and frightening twist; being based on the premise that mermaids are not the beautiful creatures of mythology but foul monstrosities who steal the souls of men, which they draw out by means of a kiss. In the story the doomed hero eventually meets his fate and finds himself looking out from the eyes of the evil sea-dweller, his soul trapped within her loathsome body.

In summarising the contribution to the werewolf theme made by *Weird Tales* one must acknowledge that, although a large number of the stories were hack work of an ephemeral nature, quite a fair percentage rank as minor classics of their kind. And in the final analysis it is the good stories one remembers; stories such as those penned by Seabury Quinn or H. Warner Munn which show a profound knowledge of the werewolf theme and which have a virginity of conception and a weird, unhackneyed, fully satisfying depth of colourful imagery.

Peter Fleming's *The Kill*, though not actually from *Weird Tales* would certainly have graced its pages had it been featured therein. The famous tale, originally published in 1931, is in the great British tradition of horror stories, and for weird atmosphere and mounting suspense could hardly be bettered.

Outstanding contributions to the werewolf mythos have also been made by pre-war pulps other than *Weird Tales*. A short-lived rival to *Weird Tales* in the early 1930s was *Strange Tales* edited by Harry Bates. The best werewolf tale it ever published was undoubtedly Jack Williamson's *Wolves of Darkness* (January 1932). This chilling novelette, a curious mixture of pseudo-science and stark horror, is among the most gruesome werewolf stories ever penned. Although this was Williamson's debut in a weird fiction magazine he managed the transition from science fiction quite successfully as the following extract ably demonstrates.

"I saw them. The pinnacle of horror! Grey wolves, leaping, green-eyed and gaunt. And strange human figures among them, racing with them. Chill soulless emerald orbs staring. Bodies ghastly pallid, clad only in tattered rags. One had no head. A black mist seemed gathered above the jutting, lividly white stump of his neck, and in it glowed malevolently—two green eyes! A woman ran with them, one arm was torn off, her naked breasts were in ribbons. She ran with the rest, green eyes glowing, mouth wide open, baying with other members of the pack."

This wildly sensational sequence is just one of many in a story that, while never likely to win any literary prizes, is nevertheless vastly entertaining. Also from *Strange Tales* comes Bassett Morgan's *Tiger* (March 1932) which is another of his tales about were-tigers.

A magazine which even predated *Weird Tales* was *The Thrill Book*. Although it was published as early as 1919 it missed out on the honour of being the first all-fantasy magazine because it was not solely devoted to this type of fiction. The featured story of the first issue was Greye La Spina's *Wolf of the Steppes* (March 1919). Another werewolf story from this magazine is Ada Louvie Evans' *Between Two Worlds* (October 1919).

Ghost Stories, another early competitor of *Weird Tales*, featured 'true' stories of psychic phenomena as well as fictional items. Werewolf stories from its pages include: *Werewolf* by Cassie H. MacLaury (March 1927); *The Wolf Man* by Mont Hurst (July 1928); and *The Wolf in the Dark* by J. Paul Suter (February 1931). Besides these three there were shapeshifting stories such as: *The Tiger Woman of the Punjab* by Allen Van Hoesan (October 1927); *The Leopard Woman* by Edith Ross (January 1929); and *Curse of the Jungle* by Vivma (December 1930).

Two other interesting items from pre-war magazines are: Max Brand's *The Werewolf* (from *Western Story Magazine*, December 1926), and C. L. Moore's *Werewoman* (from *Leaves*, Winter 1938-39). The latter is from the pen of fantasy's leading female writer and features her famous hero Northwest Smith. It was originally intended for *Weird Tales* as a sequel to her much-acclaimed *Shambleau*, but was surprisingly rejected by the editor.

The next story in this anthology is, in my opinion, one of the gems of the collection. This is A. Merritt's *The Drone*, a scarce fantasy classic which is very much out of the ordinary as far as shapeshifting stories are concerned. Abraham Merritt was the possessor of one of the richest imaginations in the whole of fantasy literature, and during the period of his greatest popularity was known affectionately as 'The Lord of Fantasy'. An American, he was born in Beverly, New Jersey, in 1884. He studied law after leaving school and entered Journalism at the age of eighteen as a newspaper reporter, eventually rising to the position of editor of 'The American Weekly'. Writing fiction was more of a hobby with Merritt and due to his other commitments he was never a prolific writer; nor was he a hasty writer but rather a true literary craftsman whose entire output shows a degree of care and thought so lacking in many other authors working in the fantasy field. This facet of his talent is undoubtedly the main reason for his continued popularity among fantasy enthusiasts, many of whom are persistently clamouring for the reprinting of his famous fantasy novels which are noted for their vivid action and unparalleled beauty. The author of these marvellous tales may have long since passed from this world but his stories live on as testimony to his genius.

The Drone, written towards the end of his career, was originally published in *Thrilling Wonder Stories* (August 1936). The opening paragraphs reveal the author's considerable knowledge of the subject of shapeshifting whilst the final sequence is a delightful piece of pure fantasy. So, if this is your first encounter with a Merritt tale, read on and be prepared to be enthralled as so many have been before you.

The 1930s, besides being a prestigious decade for the pulp magazines, was also a vintage era for hardcover novels about werewolves and shapeshifting. In 1931 appeared Alfred H. Bill's horror classic *The Wolf in the Garden*. Set in the early nineteenth century, it tells the story of the Comte de Saint Loup, a fugitive nobleman from revolutionary France who flees to America and proceeds to carry out his own 'reign of terror' in the form of a huge werewolf. He is eventually brought to bay and destroyed by the use of silver bullets—a somewhat hackneyed ending to an otherwise excellent story. A paperback edition of this novel was published in 1972.

The most famous novel about lycanthropy written this century is undoubtedly Guy Endore's *The Werewolf of Paris* (1933). This classic of the macabre is based on the real-life story of Sergeant Bertrand of the French army, who enjoyed digging up corpses from their graves and devouring the rotting flesh like a ghoul. At his trial he claimed he turned into a wolf when committing his bestial acts. American author, Guy Endore, who was a keen disciple of Hanns Heinz Ewers, has divested his story of any supernatural quality and imparts credibility to his narrative by skilfully blending lycanthropy with sexual pathology. He also incorporates many ideas first expressed in Ewers' novel *Vampire*.

The hero of the Endore novel is Bertrand Caillet whose existence is an unnatural one from birth. Born on Christmas Eve, his appearance shows a strange canine resemblance, which later in childhood manifests itself in several acts of cruelty. Bertrand shows a particular delight in killing the neighbourhood animals, and soon comes to experience realistic dreams in which he assumes lupine form. His guardian learns of his lycanthropic ways and tries to hide him away from society—but he escapes and flees to Paris. There his affliction gets worse and soon his wholesale killings terrorise all Paris, Then, at the point where it seems his excesses must bring about his detection, he meets and falls in love with the beautiful Sophie de Blumenburg. This is the beginning of a strange sado-masochistic relationship in which the young girl gladly yields some of her blood each night resulting in the temporary cessation of Bertrand's lycanthropic atrocities. Through this partial cure is revealed the true nature of Caillet's illness. He is shown as the type of person in whom the soul of man and beast are continually at war. Whatever weakens his human soul, either sin or darkness, brings the wolf to the fore, and whatever weakens the beastly soul, either virtue or daylight, raises up the human soul. For a while Sophie's love is the means of his salvation but eventually she leaves him when his incessant demands for larger quantities of her life's blood prove too great a sacrifice for her to make. The story ends with Bertrand's capture and internment in a lunatic asylum, where he ends his life in suicide.

The most intriguing aspect of this novel is the way cruelty is linked with sexuality. The author gives an accurate picture of the sadist, showing how his desire to dominate becomes the desire to injure, to torture—to inflict pain. On the other hand, Sophie shows masochistic tendencies and derives pleasure from pain. This is brilliantly expressed in the passage describing the lovers' first clandestine meeting. At Bertrand's first tentative attempt to show affection Sophie rebukes him: "Don't hurt me! Oh, please don't hurt me!" But when he releases her from his embrace she is filled with contrition and implores him to embrace her once more: "You must hold me tighter," she said. "Tighter still," she whispered. Such a bliss flowed through her from his body pressed close to hers that her head grew dizzy, her breath came and went. Her body tensed and then seemed to dissolve in liquid. If only he would press harder. If only he would crush her. Tear her! Mutilate her! In desperation she cried out: "Hurt me! Bertrand, hurt me!".

As a prelude to their love making, Bertrand makes small incisions in Sophie's naked body with a sharp knife and drains small quantities of her blood. Later this lust for blood becomes almost vampiric in its intensity. The narrative reads thus: "He bent over her body ... the sharp blade of the knife flashed orange. The blood welled up, ruby-red. He put his mouth to it at once and drank greedily. His lips made ugly sucking noises, as he strove to extract all the blood he could."

On reflection it seems strange that, prior to this great classic, so few werewolf stories stress the psycho-erotic nature of lycanthropy. Endore's novel ably demonstrates that the Marquis de Sade's philosophy of total freedom through cruelty lends itself perfectly to this type of story in which brute sensation and animal pleasure alone possess reality. In such stories the homicidal psychopath, his senses blunted by the habits and excesses of the most monstrous debauchery, can no longer find any means of excitement or stimulation except in the images of terror, suffering, and destruction, with which a crime-stained soul furnishes him only too easily.

A highly rated novel, which was first published in Britain in 1936, is *The Undying Monster* by Jessie Douglas Kerruish. The plot revolves around a family curse which destroys a member of the Hammond family each generation. The curse manifests itself in the form of an unknown monster-form which attacks and horribly kills its chosen victims. A psychic investigator, Luna Bartendale, is employed to explain the curse. However, the path to the solution is studded with terrors, involving satanic ghosts, a long dead witch whose nightmare magic still holds sway, and a gloomy room that keeps disappearing and reappearing before the occupant's eyes. By deciphering ancient inscriptions and applying her knowledge of witchcraft and Norse mythology, Luna learns the exact nature of the monster. Apparently the curse causes hereditary attacks to manifest themselves in the mind of a member of the family who, unknowingly, assumes werewolf form as a result of an ancient vow. Miss Bartendale eventually lifts the curse by hypnotism.

Another entertaining werewolf novel published during the 1930's is *Grey Shapes* by British author Jack Mann.

This is one of his famous 'Gees' novels much sought after by collectors. Special investigator Gregory George Gordon Green, alias Gees, is called in to investigate wolf-like creatures which are destroying a farmer's sheep. This turns out to be a greater mystery that at first sight, leading to some hair-raising moments before the case is eventually solved. Gees becomes suspicious of a strange pair of neighbours, Diarmid and Gyda McCoul, whose actions arouse his interests. He investigates them and learns the strange history of their home, a half-ruined castle. When further killings occur, including that of a shepherd, Green arranges a trap for the werewolves, and they are killed. The dead forms then assume human shape, and are identified as the McCouls. Further investigations reveal that the two werewolves were seven hundred years old, and had lived at their ancestral home since the reign of Henry III.

A lesser novel with a werewolf theme is F. Layland Barratt's *Lycanthia* (1935)—a rather routine story about a female werewolf. Eden Phillpotts' novel, *Lycanthrope* (1937), is an entertaining potboiler but nothing out of the ordinary. A further novel worth a mention is Virginia Swain's *The Hollow Skin* (1938) which features a reptilian metamorphosis.

As far as short stories with a 'man-into-beast' theme are concerned, the bulk of the 1930's crop were published in the American pulps, but several stories from hardcover collections are also worthy of mention. A fine story about a female werewolf is *The Wolf's Bride* by Madame Aino Kallas, published in 1930. The heroine is the victim of a curse which brings the evil of lycanthropy into her life so that by day she is a gentle and loving wife but at night is obliged to change into a marauding werewolf. Hugh Walpole's *Tarnhelm* (1933) is a masterly tale of shape-shifting in which an old man is able to transform himself into an evil-looking dog. Also of more than usual interest is a rare story of werewolfery by Mrs. Baillie Reynolds entitled *The Terrible Baron* (from the collection of the same name, published in 1933). An above-average were-tiger story is *The Beauty and the Beast* by C. H. B. Kitchin, from the pre-war anthology *A Century of Creepy Stories* (1935). Geoffrey Household's *Taboo*, another notable story of the period, is a bizarre crime story which deals with lycanthropy as a mental disease. It was probably inspired by the real-life case of Denke the Butcher which scandalised all Europe in the years immediately following the First World War. A factual account of this case can be found in Bernhardt J. Hurwood's *Vampires, Werewolves & Ghouls*.

The outstanding werewolf novel of the 1940s is Franklin Gregory's *The White Wolf* (1941). Written on traditional lines, it tells the story of a cruel young woman who comes under the influence of a disguised Satan. She exchanges her soul for the power to change her shape at will, and enters into a dread covenant that gives her other powers of sorcery. Her fiancé is hypnotised into joining her on her nightly orgies of killing which are only terminated through the intervention of her father. He is also steeped in the lore of the occult and uses this knowledge to bring about her destruction.

The humorous tale of shape-shifting is rarely encountered in modern fiction but one of considerable merit is Ewart C. Jones's *How Now, Brown Cow* (1947). This amusing novel of metamorphosistry is about a village 'tart' who is transformed into a bovine—a clever twist on an old Greek legend.

Perhaps the best known of modern werewolf novels is Jack Williamson's *Darker Than You Think* (Fantasy Press, 1948). Although written in a slick magazine style and lacking depth, the plot of the story is quite unusual. It features the beautiful red-head, April Kane, who is a surviving member of were-folk called 'Homo Lycanthropus'. They were an ancient race who had the power to assume the shape of any animal, to pass through obstacles, and to foresee and manipulate the future. However, because of their habit of dining on human flesh they are exterminated by the other human races. One of the more eccentric habits of the story's heroine is to ride about the countryside, in the nude, on the back of a sabre-toothed tiger. She eventually teams up with Will Barbee who discovers that he, too, is a member of her race, and he cultivates his hereditary powers under April's guidance. Together they set out to revive their centuries-old race.

Anthologies of werewolf tales are few and far between; the earliest post-war title is *Man into Beast: Strange Tales of Transformation* edited by A. C. Spectorsky, published in 1948.

The only weird fantasy magazine to seriously challenge *Weird Tales* in the 1940s was *Unknown Worlds,* a quality pulp which presented mostly off-trail stories in which popular weird themes were satirised or parodied. It flourished briefly in the late 1930s and early 40s but came to a premature end when it became a victim of the war-time paper shortage. Two memorable werewolf stories from its pages are: Anthony Boucher's *The Compleat Werewolf* (April 1942), and Jane Rice's *The Refugee* (October 1943). The latter has been anthologised in Douglas Hill's *Way of the Werewolf.* From *Thrilling Wonder Stories,* a cheap pulp that catered for science fantasy addicts, comes James Blish's novelette *There Shall Be No Darkness* (April 1950), which many critics have acclaimed for its originality.

The immediate post-war era marked the beginning of the end for the pulp magazines; one by one they expired to be replaced by slick, characterless, digest magazines which were mainly orientated towards the science fiction fan. Occasionally they ran a few stories with weird themes, including the odd werewolf tale. One of the best of these is *Frontier of the Dark* by B. Chandler (*Astounding Science Fiction,* September 1952). And for *Magazine of Fantasy & Science Fiction,* October, 1954, the great Clark Ashton Smith donated a short satirical werewolf tale called *A Prophecy of Monsters.* This has also been included in *Other Dimensions* (1970), a final collection of Smith's tales published by Arkham House, where it appears under the title of *Monsters in the Night.* My researches into *Fantastic,* another digest magazine for fantasy enthusiasts, have not unearthed any gems but the following three titles are passably good werewolf yarns:

The Young One by Jerome Bixby (April 1954); *The Girl Who Played Wolf* by Gordon Dickson (August 1958); and *The Wolf Woman* by H. Bedford Jones (October 1963). One of the most original werewolf stories of recent years is *Wolves Don't Cry* by Bruce Elliott (*Magazine of Fantasy & Science Fiction*, 1953). This was probably the first story to speculate on what would happen if a wolf was suddenly transformed into a man.

August Derleth's hardcover collection *The Memoirs of Solar Pons* (1951) provides our next story, *The Adventure of the Tottenham Werewolf*, which is one of this author's enjoyable Sherlock Holmes pastiches. Derleth who died in 1971, was a prolific author who, besides his tally of over a hundred stories for *Weird Tales*, wrote over one hundred books (including novels, collections, biographies, and anthologies). Besides this he also found time to run Arkham House, the renowned publishing firm, which was initially inaugurated for the purpose of perpetuating the work of H. P. Lovecraft.

The past ten or twelve years have seen a gradual diminuation of the werewolf motif in weird fiction. Novels with a 'man-into-beast' theme have been at a premium, and those that have appeared are of little consequence. Better than most is Vercors' *Sylva* (1963), which has a 'lady-into-fox' motif but reverses the usual formula to tell how a fox is metamorphosed into a beautiful, sensuous young woman. The only werewolf novel from the recent past worth mentioning is Bruce Lowery's *Werewolf* (1969).

This dearth of werewolf novels is very disappointing for the horror fan and one hopes that the theme will not die out completely. Perhaps there is some hope for its survival, in a slightly different form, in the realms of science fiction. One author working in this sub-genre who has already discovered its potential is Clifford Simak, in his novel *The Werewolf Principle*—an ingenious story about an 'adapted' human who can change his shape at will. Adam Lukens' *Sons of the Wolf* is a further example of the werewolf theme being given a science-fictional treatment.

The most recent anthology devoted exclusively to werewolf stories is *Way of the Werewolf* edited by Douglas Hill (1966). Although half of the eight stories are 'old favourites' that have been anthologised countless times, it does contain two stories which, to my knowledge, have not appeared in an anthology before. The more intriguing of the two, and destined to become a classic of its kind, is Claude Seignolle's *The Gâloup*. This brilliant tour-de-force is told from the point of view of a werewolf, and is by far the most successful use of this particular technique of narration. The other story original to this anthology is a black comedy called *Canis Lupus Sapiens* by Alex Hamilton. Two other anthologies that contain a number of werewolf stories are: *Witches, Warlocks and Werewolves*, edited by Rod Serling (1963), and *Monsters Galore*, edited by Bernhardt J. Hurwood (1965). Another interesting anthology is *A Walk with the Beast*, edited by Charles M. Collins (1969). With its intriguing selection of stories about were-beasts, it attempts to show the image of the beast in its many literary variations, both human and supernatural.

Startling Mystery Stories, a recently defunct digest-size magazine which specialised in weird mystery stories, provides the penultimate story in this anthology.

The werewolf of today, stripped of its former symbolism and Gothic trappings, is hardly recognisable from the old-fashioned stories of werewolfery and shape-shifting. Nowadays the werewolf story is little more than a vehicle for violence and sadism. The protagonists are not supernatural monsters but homicidal maniacs or sexually deviated psychopaths who perform their bestial acts of sadism without the necessity to assume the form of a wolf. Invariably the lycanthrope is depicted as an ascetic, repressed to such an extent that he can no longer enjoy normal instinctual satisfaction. Therefore, any sensual impulse is, to his warped mind, an act of evil, and can only be performed if he imagines himself as a beast. Raymond Rudorff's *Monsters: Studies in Ferocity*, a series of essays on perverts and psychopathic killers, is a likely source of inspiration for such stories.

The future development of the werewolf tale has yet to be decided but I believe it will continue to flourish as long as writers find it useful as a means of sublimating unpleasant neurotic tendencies. And there will always be readers who welcome such an expression in literature of their hidden aggressiveness.

To conclude this survey, I turn once more to the American horror magazines, which are still the major market for new stories of terror and the supernatural, and thus provide the best guide to the latest trends in weird fiction. If *Adventures in Horror*, one of the more recent titles, is an accurate barometer of public taste it looks like horror fans are in for a rash of highly sensational, semi-pornographic stories. Two lurid werewolf tales from the magazine's early issues are: *Howl, Wolf, Howl!* by William Cornish (issue No. 1, 1970), and *It Takes Two for Terror* by Obadiah Kemp (issue No. 2, 1970).

A factor common to most periodicals specialising in weird fiction is that they tend to have a brief existence, which coupled with the annoying habit of changing their titles after only a few issues, means that only the well-informed fan can keep track of them. At the time of writing, the forerunner in the field is *Witchcraft & Sorcery*. This has featured several werewolf stories, mainly in its earlier issues when it was called *Coven 13*. The second issue featured *Once Upon a Werewolf* by Ronald I. Davis and the fourth had Lee Chater's splendid black comedy, *The Thing on the Stairs*, a story that has equal shares of caustic wit and pure grue. However, to my mind, the best werewolf story from this publication is *Pia* by Dale C. Donaldson; perhaps the most gruesome werewolf story ever written. I am pleased to be able to include it here as the final story in this anthology.

SUTHERLAND MENZIES

HUGUES, THE WER-WOLF

A KENTISH LEGEND OF THE MIDDLE AGES

I

"Ye hallowed bells whose voices thro' the air
The awful summons of afflictions bare."
Honoria, or the Day of All Souls.

On the confines of that extensive forest-tract formerly spreading over so large a portion of the county of Kent, a remnant of which, to this day, is known as the weald* of Kent, and where it stretched its almost impervious covert midway between Ashford and Canterbury during the prolonged reign of our second Henry, a family of Norman extraction, by name Hughes (or Wulfric, as they were commonly called by the Saxon inhabitants of that district) had, under protection of the ancient forest laws, furtively erected for themselves a lone and miserable habitation. And amidst those sylvan fastnesses, ostensibly following the occupation of woodcutters, the wretched outcasts, for such, from some cause or other, they evi-

* That woody district, at the period to which our tale belongs, was an immense forest, desolate of inhabitants, and only occupied by wild swine and deer; and though it is now filled with towns and villages and well peopled, the woods that remain sufficiently indicate its former extent. "And being at first," says Hasted, "neither peopled nor cultivated, and only filled with herds of deer and droves of swine, belonged wholly to the king, for there is no mention of it but in royal grants and donations. And it may be presumed that when the weald was first made to belong to certain known owners, as well as the rest of the country, it was not then allotted into tenancies, nor manured like the rest of it; but only as men were contented to inhabit it, and by piecemeal to clear it of the wood, and convert it into tillage."—*Hasted's Kent*, vol. 1, p. 134.

53

dently were, had for many years maintained a secluded and precarious existence. Whether from the rooted antipathy still actively cherished against all of that usurping nation from which they derived their origin, or from recorded malpractice by their superstitious Anglo-Saxon neighbours, they had long been looked upon as belonging to the accursed race of wer-wolves, and as such churlishly refused work on the domains of the surrounding franklins or proprietors, so thoroughly was accredited the descent of the original lycanthropic stain transmitted from father to son through several generations. That the Hugues Wulfric reckoned not a single friend among the adjacent homesteads of serf or freedman was not to be wondered at, possessing as they did so unenviable a reputation; for to them was invariably attributed even the misfortunes which chance alone might seem to have given birth. Did midnight fire consume the grange;—did the time-decayed barn, over-stored with an abundant harvest, tumble into ruins;—were the shocks of wheat laid prostrate over the fields by a tempest;—did the smut destroy the grain;—or the cattle perish, decimated by a murrain;—a child sink under some wasting malady;—or a woman give premature birth to her offspring; it was ever the Hugues Wulfric who were openly accused, eyes askaunt with mingled fear and detestation, the finger of young and old pointing them out with bitter execrations—in fine, they were almost as nearly classed *feræ natura* as their fabled prototype, and dealt with accordingly.*

Terrible, indeed, were the tales told of them round the glowing hearth at eventide, whilst spinning the flax, or plucking the geese; equally affirmed, too, in broad daylight, whilst driving the cows to pasturage, and most circumstantially discussed on Sundays between mass and vespers, by the gossip groups collected within Ashford parvyse, with most seasonable admixture of anathema

* King Edgar is said to have been the first who attempted to rid England of these animals; criminals even being pardoned by producing a stated number of these creatures' tongues. Some centuries after they increased to such a degree as to become again the object of royal attention; and Edward I appointed persons to extirpate this obnoxious race. It is one of the principal bearings in armoury. Hugh, surnamed *Lupus,* the first Earl of Kent, bore for his crest a wolf's head.

and devout crossings. Witchcraft, larceny, murther, and sacrilege, formed prominent features in the bloody and mysterious scenes of which the Hugues Wulfric were the alleged actors: sometimes they were ascribed to the father, at others to the mother, and even the sister escaped not her share of vilification; fain would they have attributed an atrocious disposition to the unweaned babe, so great, so universal was the horror in which they held that race of Cain! The churchyard at Ashford, and the stone cross, from whence diverged the several roads to London, Canterbury, and Ashford, situated midway between the two latter places, served, so tradition avouched, as nocturnal theatres for the unhallowed deeds of the Wulfrics, who thither prowled by moonlight, it was said, to batten on the freshly-buried dead, or drain the blood of any living wight who might be rash enough to venture among those solitary spots. True it was that the wolves had, during some of the severe winters, emerged from their forest lairs, and, entering the cemetery by a breach in its walls, goaded by famine, had actually disinterred the dead; true was it, also, that the Wolf's Cross, as the hinds commonly designated it, had been stained with gore on one occasion through the fall of a drunken mendicant, who chanced to fracture his skull against a pointed angle of its basement. But these accidents, as well as a multitude of others, were attributed to the guilty intervention of the Wulfrics, under their fiendish guise of wer-wolves.

These poor people, moreover, took no pains to justify themselves from a prejudice so monstrous: full well apprised of what calumny they were the victims, but alike conscious of their impotence to contradict it, they tacitly suffered its infliction, and fled all contact with those to whom they knew themselves repulsive. Shunning the highways, and never venturing to pass through the town of Ashford in open day, they pursued such labour as might occupy them within doors, or in unfrequented places. They appeared not at Canterbury market, never numbered themselves amongst the pilgrims at Becket's farfamed shrine, or assisted at any sport, merry-making, haycutting, or harvest home: the priest had interdicted them from all communion with the church—the ale-bibbers from the hostelry.

The primitive cabin which they inhabited was built of chalk and clay, with a thatch of straw, in which the high winds had made huge rents, and closed up by a rotten door, exhibiting wide gaps, through which the gusts had free ingress. As this wretched abode was situated at considerable distance from any other, if, perchance, any of the neighbouring serfs strayed within its precincts towards nightfall, their credulous fears made them shun near approach so soon as the vapours of the marsh were seen to blend their ghastly wreaths with the twilight; and as that darkling time drew on which explains the diabolical sense of the old saying, " 'Tween dog and wolf," " 'twixt hawk and buzzard," at that hour the will-o'-wisps began to glimmer around the dwelling of the Wulfrics, who patriarchally supped—whenever they had a supper— and forthwith betook themselves to their rest.

Sorrow, misery, and the putrid exhalations of the steeped hemp, from which they manufactured a rude and scanty attire, combined eventually to bring sickness and death into the bosom of this wretched family, who, in their utmost extremity, could neither hope for pity or succour. The father was first attacked, and his corpse was scarce cold ere the mother rendered up her breath. Thus passed that fated couple to their account, unsolaced by the consolation of the confessor, or the medicaments of the leech. Hugues Wulfric, their eldest son, himself dug their grave, laid their bodies within it swathed with hempen shreds for grave cloths, and raised a few clods of earth to mark their last resting-place. A hind, who chanced to see him fulfilling this pious duty in the dusk of evening, crossed himself, and fled as fast as his legs would carry him, fully believing that he had assisted at some hellish incantation. When the real event transpired, the neighbouring gossips congratulated one another upon the double mortality, which they looked upon as the tardy chastisement of heaven: they spoke of ringing the bells, and singing masses of thanks for such an action of grace.

It was All Souls' eve, and the wind howled along the bleak hillside, whistling drearily through the naked branches of the forest trees, whose last leaves it had long since stripped; the sun had disappeared; a dense and chilling fog spread through the air like the mourning veil of the widowed, whose day of love hath early fled. No star shone in the still and murky sky. In that lonely hut, through which death had so lately passed, the orphan survivors held their lonely vigil by the fitful blaze emitted by the reeking logs upon their hearth. Several days had passed since their lips had been imprinted for the last time upon the cold hands of their parents; several dreary nights had passed since the sad hour in which their eternal farewell had left them desolate on earth.

Poor lone ones! Both, too, in the flower of their youth —how sad, yet how serene did they appear amid their grief! But what sudden and mysterious terror is it that seems to overcome them? It is not, alas! the first time since they were left alone upon earth that they have found themselves at this hour of the night by their deserted hearth, enlivened of old by the cheerful tales of their mother. Full often had they wept together over her memory, but never yet had their solitude proved so appalling; and, pallid as very spectres, they tremblingly gazed upon one another as the flickering ray from the wood-fire played over their features.

"Brother! heard you not that loud shriek which every echo of the forest repeated? It sounds to me as if the ground were ringing with the tread of some gigantic phantom, and whose breath seems to have shaken the door of our hut. The breath of the dead they say is icy cold. A mortal shivering has come over me."

"And I, too, sister, thought I heard voices as it were at a distance, murmuring strange words. Tremble not thus— am I not beside you?"

"Oh, brother! let us pray the Holy Virgin, to the end that she may restrain the departed from haunting our dwelling."

"But, perhaps, our mother is amongst them: she comes, unshrived and unshrouded, to visit her forlorn offspring— her well-beloved! For, knowest thou not, sister, 'tis the eve on which the dead forsake their tombs. Let us open the door, that our mother may enter and resume her wonted place by the hearthstone."

"Oh, brother, how gloomy is all without doors, how damp and cold the gust sweeps by. Hearest thou, what groans the dead are uttering round our hut? Oh, close the door, in heaven's name!"

"Take courage, sister, I have thrown upon the fire that holy branch, plucked as it flowered on last Palm Sunday, which thou knowest will drive away all evil spirits, and now our mother can enter alone."

"But how will she look, brother? They say the dead are horrible to gaze upon; that their hair has fallen away; their eyes become hollow; and that, in walking, their bones rattle hideously. Will our mother, then, be thus?"

"No; she will appear with the features we loved to behold; with the affectionate smile that welcomed us home from our perilous labours; with the voice which, in early youth, sought us when, belated, the closing night surprised us far from our dwelling."

The poor girl busied herself awhile in arranging a few platters of scanty fare upon the tottering board which served them for a table; and this last pious offering of filial love, as she deemed it, appeared accomplished only by the greatest and last effort, so enfeebled had her frame become.

"Let our dearly-loved mother enter then," she exclaimed, sinking exhausted upon the settle. "I have prepared her evening meal, that she may not be angry with me, and all is arranged as she was wont to have it. But what ails thee, my brother, for now thou tremblest as I did a while agone?"

"See'st thou not, sister, those pale lights which are rising at a distance across the marsh? They are the dead, coming to seat themselves before the repast prepared for them. Hark! list to the funeral tones of the Allhallowtide* bells, as they come upon the gale, blended with their hollow voices.—Listen, listen!"

"Brother, this horror grows insupportable. This, I feel, of a verity, will be my last night upon earth! And is there no word of hope to cheer me, mingling with those fearful sounds? Oh, mother! mother!"

"Hush, sister, hush! see'st thou now the ghastly lights which herald the dead, gleaming athwart the horizon?

---

* On this eve formerly the Catholic church performed a most solemn office for the repose of the dead.

Hearest thou the prolonged tolling of the bell? They come! they come!"

"Eternal repose to their ashes!" exclaimed the bereaved ones, sinking upon their knees, and bowing down their heads in the extremity of terror and lamentation; and as they uttered the words, the door was at the same moment closed with violence, as though it had been slammed by a vigorous hand. Hugues started to his feet, for the cracking of the timber which supported the roof seemed to announce the fall of the frail tenement; the fire was suddenly extinguished, and a plaintive groan mingled itself with the blast that whistled through the crevices of the door. On raising his sister, Hugues found that she too was no longer to be numbered among the living.

II

Hugues, on becoming head of his family, composed of two sisters younger than himself, saw them likewise descend into the grave in the short space of a fortnight; and when he had laid the last within her parent earth, he hesitated whether he should not extend himself beside them, and share their peaceful slumber. It was not by tears and sobs that grief so profound as this manifested itself, but in a mute and sullen contemplation over the sepulture of his kindred and his own future happiness. During three consecutive nights he wandered, pale and haggard, from his solitary hut, to prostrate himself and kneel by turns upon the funereal turf. For three days food had not passed his lips.

Winter had interrupted the labours of the woods and fields, and Hugues had presented himself in vain among the neighbouring domains to obtain a few days' employment to thresh grain, cut wood, or drive the plough; no one would employ him from fear of drawing upon himself the fallity attached to all bearing the name of Wulfric. He met with brutal denials at all hands, and not only were these accompanied by taunts and menace, but dogs were let loose upon him to rend his limbs; they deprived him even of the alms accorded to beggars by profession; in short, he found himself overwhelmed with injuries and scorn.

Was he, then, to expire of inanition or deliver himself from the tortures of hunger by suicide? He would have embraced that means, as a last and only consolation, had he not been retained earthward to struggle with his dark fate by a feeling of love. Yes, that abject being, forced in very desperation, against his better self, to abhor the human species in the abstract, and to feel a savage joy in waging war against it; that *paria* who scarce longer felt confidence in that heaven which seemed an apathetic witness of his woes; that man so isolated from those social relations which alone compensate us for the toils and troubles of life, without other stay than that afforded by his conscience, with no other fortune in prospect than the bitter existence and miserable death of his departed kin: worn to the bone by privation and sorrow, swelling with rage and resentment, he yet consented to live—to cling to life; for, strange—he loved! But for that heaven-sent ray gleaming across his thorny path, a pilgrimage so lone and wearisome would he have gladly exchanged for the peaceful slumber of the grave.

Hugues Wulfric would have been the finest youth in all that part of Kent, were it not that the outrages with which he had so unceasingly to contend, and the privations he was forced to undergo, had effaced the colour from his cheeks, and sunk his eyes deep in their orbits: his brows were habitually contracted, and his glance oblique and fierce. Yet, despite that recklessness and anguish which clouded his features, one, incredulous of his atrocities, could not have failed to admire the savage beauty of his head, cast in nature's noblest mould, crowned with a profusion of waving hair, and set upon shoulders whose robust and harmonious proportions were discoverable through the tattered attire investing them. His carriage was firm and majestic; his motions were not without a species of rustic grace, and the tone of his naturally soft voice accorded admirably with the purity in which he spoke his ancestral language—the Norman-French: in short, he differed so widely from people of his imputed condition that one is constrained to believe that jealousy or prejudice must originally have been no stranger to the malicious persecution of which he was the object. The women alone ventured first to pity his forlorn condition, and endeavoured to think of him in a more favourable light.

Branda, niece of Willieblud, the flesher of Ashford, had, among other of the town maidens, noticed Hugues with a not unsavouring eye, as she chanced to pass one day on horseback, through a coppice near the outskirts of the town, into which the latter had been led by the eager chase of a wild hog, and which animal, from the nature of the country was, single-handed, exceedingly difficult of capture. The malignant falsehoods of the ancient crones, continually buzzed in her ears, in nowise diminished the advantageous opinion she had conceived of this ill-treated and good-looking wer-wolf. She sometimes, indeed, went so far as to turn considerably out of her way, in order to meet and exchange his cordial greeting: for Hugues, recognizing the attention of which he had now become the object, had, in turn, at last summoned up courage to survey more leisurely the pretty Branda; and the result was that he found her as buxom and pretty a lass as, in his hitherto restricted rambles out of the forest, his timorous gaze had ever encountered. His gratitude increased proportionally; and at the moment when his domestic losses came one after another to overwhelm him, he was actually on the eve of making Branda, on the first opportunity presenting itself, an avowal of the love he bore her.

It was chill winter—Christmas-tide—the distant roll of the curfew had long ceased, and all the inhabitants of Ashford were safe housed in their tenements for the night. Hugues, solitary, motionless, silent, his forehead grasped between his hands, his gaze dully fixed upon the decaying brands that feebly glimmered upon his hearth; he heeded not the cutting north wind, whose sweeping gusts shook the crazy roof, and whistled through the chinks of the door; he started not at the harsh cries of the herons fighting for prey in the marsh, nor at the dismal croaking of the ravens perched over his smoke-vent. He thought of his departed kindred, and imagined that his hour to join them would soon be at hand; for the intense cold congealed the marrow of his bones, and fell hunger gnawed and twisted his entrails. Yet, at intervals, would a recollection of nascent love, of Branda, suddenly appease his else intolerable anguish, and cause a faint smile to gleam across his wan features.

"Oh, blessed Virgin! grant that my sufferings may speedily cease!" murmured he, despairingly. "Oh, would I might be a wer-wolf, as they call me! I could then requite them for all the foul wrong done me. True, I could not nourish myself with their flesh; I would not shed their blood; but I would be able to terrify and torment those who have wrought my parents' and sisters' death—who have persecuted our family even to extermination! Why have I not the power to change my nature into that of a wolf, if, of a verity, my ancestors possessed it, as they avouch? I should at least find carrion to devour,* and not die thus horribly. Branda is the sole being in this world who cares for me; and that conviction alone reconciles me to life!"

Hugues gave free current to these gloomy reflections. The smouldering embers now emitted but a feeble and vacillating light, faintly struggling with the surrounding gloom, and Hugues felt the horror of darkness coming strong upon him; frozen with the ague-fit one instant, and troubled the next by the hurried pulsation of his veins, he arose, at last, to seek some fuel, and threw upon the fire a heap of faggot-chips, heath and straw, which soon raised a clear and crackling flame. His stock of wood had become exhausted, and, seeking to replenish his dying hearth-light, whilst foraging under the rude oven amongst a pile of rubbish placed there by his mother wherewith to bake bread—handles of tools, fractured joint-stools, and cracked platters, he discovered a chest rudely covered with a dressed hide, and which he had never seen before; and seizing upon it as though he had discovered a treasure, broke open the lid, strongly secured by a string.

This chest, which had evidently remained long unopened, contained the complete disguise of a wer-wolf:— a dyed sheepskin, with gloves in the form of paws, a tail, a mask with an elongated muzzle, and furnished with formidable rows of yellow horse-teeth.

Hugues started backwards, terrified at his discovery—so

---

* Horseflesh was an article of food among our Saxon forefathers in England.

opportune, that it seemed to him the work of sorcery; then, on recovering from his surprise, he drew forth one by one the several pieces of this strange envelope, which had evidently seen some service, and from long neglect had become somewhat damaged. Then rushed confusedly upon his mind the marvellous recitals made him by his grandfather, as he nursed him upon his knees during earliest childhood; tales, during the narration of which his mother wept silently, as he laughed heartily. In his mind there was a mingled strife of feelings and purposes alike undefinable. He continued his silent examination of this criminal heritage, and by degrees his imagination grew bewildered with vague and extravagant projects.

Hunger and despair conjointly hurried him away: he saw objects no longer save through a bloody prism: he felt his very teeth on edge with an avidity for biting: he experienced an inconceivable desire to run: he set himself to howl as though he had practised wer-wolfery all his life, and began thoroughly to invest himself with the guise and attributes of his novel vocation. A more startling change could scarcely have been wrought in him, had that so horribly grotesque metamorphosis really been the effect of enchantment; aided, too, as it was, by the fever which generated a temporary insanity in his frenzied brain.

Scarcely did he thus find himself travestied into a werwolf through the influence of his vestment, ere he darted forth from the hut, through the forest and into the open country, white with hoar frost, and across which the bitter north wind swept, howling in a frightful manner and traversing the meadows, fallows, plains, and marshes, like a shadow. But at that hour, and during such a season, not a single belated wayfarer was there to encounter Hugues, whom the sharpness of the air, and the excitation of his course, had worked up to the highest pitch of extravagance and audacity: he howled the louder proportionally as his hunger increased.

Suddenly the heavy rumbling of an approaching vehicle arrested his attention; at first with indecision, then with a stupid fixity, he struggled with two suggestions, counselling him at one and the same time to fly and to advance. The carriage, or whatever it might be, continued, rolling towards him; the night was not so obscure but that he was enabled to distinguish the tower of Ashford church at a short distance off, and hard by which stood a pile of unhewn stone, destined either for the execution of some repair, or addition to the saintly edifice, in the shade of which he ran to crouch himself down, and so await the arrival of his prey.

It proved to be the covered cart of Willieblud, the Ashford flesher, who was wont twice a week to carry meat to Canterbury, and travelled by night in order that he might be among the first at market-opening. Of this Hugues was fully aware, and the departure of the flesher naturally suggested to him the inference that his niece must be keeping house by herself, for our lusty flesher had been long a widower. For an instant he hesitated whether he should introduce himself there, so favourable an opportunity thus presenting itself, or whether he should attack the uncle and seize upon his viands. Hunger got the better of love this once, and the monotonous whistle with which the driver was accustomed to urge forward his sorry jade warning him to be in readiness, he howled in a plaintive tone, and, rushing forward, seized the horse by the bit.

"Willieblud, flesher," said he, disguising his voice, and speaking to him in the *lingua Franca* of that period, "I hunger; throw me two pounds of meat if thou would'st have me live."

"St. Willifred have mercy on me!" cried the terrified flesher, "is it thou, Hugues Wulfric, of Wealdmarsh, the born wer-wolf?"

"Thou say'st sooth—it is I," replied Hugues, who had sufficient address to avail himself of the credulous superstition of Willieblud; "I would rather have raw meat than eat of thy flesh, plump as thou art. Throw me, therefore, what I crave, and forget not to be ready with the like portion each time thou settest out for Canterbury market; or, failing thereof, I tear thee limb from limb."

Hugues, to display his attributes of a wer-wolf before the gaze of the confounded flesher, had mounted himself upon the spokes of the wheel, and placed his forepaw upon the edge of the cart, which he made semblance of snuffing at with his snout. Willieblud, who believed in werwolves as devoutly as he did in his patron saint, had no sooner perceived this monstrous paw, than, uttering a fervent invocation to the latter, he seized upon his daintiest joint of meat, let it fall to the ground, and whilst Hugues sprung eagerly down to pick it up, the butcher at the same instant having bestowed a sudden and violent blow upon the flank of his beast, the latter set off at a round gallop without waiting for any reiterated invitation from the lash.

Hugues, so satisfied with a repast which had cost him far less trouble to procure than any he had long remembered, readily promised himself the renewal of an expedient, the execution of which was at once easy and diverting; for though smitten with the charms of the fair-haired Branda, he not the less found a malicious pleasure in augmenting the terror of her uncle Willieblud. The for a long while, revealed not to a living being the tale of his terrible encounter and strange compact, which had varied according to circumstances, and he submitted unmurmuringly to the imposts levied each time the wer-wolf presented himself before him, without being very nice about either the weight or quality of the meat; he no longer even waited to be asked for it, anything to avoid the sight of that fiend-like form clinging to the side of his cart, or being brought into such immediate contact with that hideous mis-shapen paw stretched forth, as it were to strangle him, that paw too, which had once been a human hand. He had become dull and thoughtful of late; he set out to market unwillingly, and seemed to dread the hour of departure as it approached, and no longer beguiled the tedium of his nocturnal journey by whistling to his horse, or trolling snatches of ballads, as was his wont formerly; he now invariably returned in a melancholy and restless mood.

Branda, at loss to conceive what had given birth to this new and permanent depression which had taken possession of her uncle's mind, after in vain exhausting conjecture, proceeded to interrogate, importune, and supplicate him by turns, until the unhappy flesher, no longer proof against such continued appeals, at last disburthened himself of the load which he had at heart, by recounting the history of his adventure with the wer-wolf.

Branda listened to the whole of the recital without offering interruption or comment; but, at its close—

"Hugues is no more a wer-wolf than thou or I," exclaimed she, offended that such unjust suspicion should be cherished against one for whom she had long felt more than an interest: "'tis an idle tale, or some juggling device; I fear me thou must needs dream these sorceries, uncle Willieblud, for Hugues of the Wealdmarsh, or Wulfric, as the silly fools call him, is worth far more, I trow, than his reputation."

"Girl, it boots not saying me nay, in this matter," replied Willieblud, pertinaciously urging the truth of his story; "the family of Hugues, as everybody knows, were werwolves born, and, since they are all of late, by the blessing of heaven, defunct, save one, Hugues now inherits the wolf's paw."

"I tell thee, and will avouch it openly, uncle, that Hugues is of too gentle and seemly a nature to serve Satan, and turn himself into a wild beast, and that will I never believe until I have seen the like."

"Mass, and that thou shalt right speedily, if thou wilt but along with me. In very troth 'tis he, besides, he made confession of his name, and did I not recognize his voice, and am I not bethinking me of his knavish paw, which he places me on the shaft while he stays the horse. Girl, he is in league with the foul fiend."

Branda had, to a certain degree, imbibed the superstition in the abstract, equally with her uncle, and, excepting so far as it touched the hitherto, as she believed, traduced being on whom her affections, as if in feminine perversity, had so strangely lighted. Her woman's curiosity, in this instance, less determined her resolution to accompany the flesher on his next journey, than the desire to exculpate her lover, fully believing the strange tale of her kinsman's encounter with, and spoliation by the latter, to be the effect of some illusion, and of which to find him guilty, was the sole fear she experienced on mounting the rude vehicle laden with its ensanguined viands.

It was just midnight when they started from Ashford, the hour alike dear to wer-wolves as to spectres of every denomination. Hugues was punctual at the appointed spot; his howlings, as they drew nigh, though horrible enough, had still something human in them, and disconcerted not a little the doubts of Branda. Willieblud, however, trembled even more than she did, and sought for the wolf's portion; the latter raised himself upon his hind legs, and extended one of his forepaws to receive his pittance as soon as the cart stopped at the heap of stones.

"Uncle, I shall swoon with affright," exclaimed Branda, clinging closely to the flesher, and tremblingly pulling the coverchief over her eyes; "loose rein and smite thy beast, or evil will sure betide us."

"Thou are not alone, gossip," cried Hugues, fearful of a snare; "if thou essay'st to play me false, thou art at once undone."

"Harm us not friend Hugues, thou know'st I weigh not my pounds of meat with thee; I shall take care to keep my troth. It is Branda, my niece, who goes with me tonight to buy wares at Canterbury."

"Branda with thee? By the mass 'tis she indeed, more buxom and rosy too, than ever; come pretty one, descend and tarry awhile, that I may have speech with thee."

"I conjure thee, good Hugues, terrify not so cruelly my poor wench, who is wellnigh dead already with fear; suffer us to hold our way, for we have far to go, and the morrow is early market-day."

"Go thy ways then alone, uncle Willieblud, 'tis thy niece I would have speech with, in all courtesy and honour; the which, if thou permittest not readily, and of a good grace, I will rend thee both to death."

All in vain was it that Willieblud exhausted himself in prayers and lamentations in hopes of softening the bloodthirsty wer-wolf, as he believed him to be, refusing as the latter did, every sort of compromise in avoidance of his demand, and at last replying only by horrible threats, which froze the hearts of both. Branda, although especially interested in the debate, neither stirred foot, or opened her mouth, so greatly had terror and surprise overwhelmed her; she kept her eyes fixed upon the wolf, who peered at her likewise through his mask, and felt incapable of offering resistance when she found herself forcibly dragged out of the vehicle, and deposited by an invisible power, as it seemed to her, beside the piles of stones: she swooned without uttering a single scream.

The flesher was no less dumbfounded at the turn which the adventure had taken, and he, too, fell back among his meat as though stricken by a blinding blow; he fancied that the wolf had swept his bushy tail violently across his eyes, and on recovering the use of his senses found himself alone in the cart, which rolled joltingly at a swift pace towards Canterbury. At first he listened, but in vain, for the wind bringing him either the shrieks of his niece, or the howlings of the wolf; but stop his beast he could not, which, panic-stricken, kept trotting as though bewitched, or felt the spur of some fiend pricking her flanks. Willieblud, however, reached his journey's end in safety, sold his meat, and returned to Ashford, reckoning full sure upon having to say a *De Profundis* for his niece, whose fate he had not ceased to bemoan during the whole night. But how great was his astonishment to find her safe at home, a little pale, from recent fright and want of sleep, but without a scratch; still more was he astonished to hear that the wolf had done her no injury whatsoever, contenting himself, after she had recovered from her swoon, with conducting her back to their dwelling, and acting in every respect like a loyal suitor, rather than a sanguinary wer-wolf. Willieblud knew not what to think of it.

This nocturnal gallantry towards his niece had additionally irritated the burly Saxon against the wer-wolf, and although the fear of reprisals kept him from making a direct and public attack upon Hugues, he ruminated not the less upon taking some sure and secret revenge; but previous to putting his design into execution, it struck him that he could not do better than relate his misadventures to the ancient sacristan and parish grave-digger of St. Michael's, a worthy of profound sagacity in those sort of matters, endowed with a clerk-like erudition, and consulted as an oracle by all the old crones and love-lorn maidens throughout the township of Ashford and its vicinity.

"Slay a were-wolf thou canst not," was the repeated rejoinder of the wiseacre to the earnest queries of the tormented flesher; "for his hide is proof against spear or arrow, though vulnerable to the edge of a cutting weapon of steel. I counsel thee to deal him a slight flesh wound, or cut him over the paw, in order to know of a surety whether it really be Hugues or no; thou'lt run no danger, save thou strikest him a blow from which blood flows not therefrom, for, so soon as his skin is severed he taketh flight."

Resolving implicitly to follow the advice of the sacristan, Willieblud that same evening determined to know with what wer-wolf it was with whom he had to do, and with that view hid his cleaver, newly sharpened for the occasion, under the load in his cart, and resolutely prepared to make use of it as a preparatory step towards proving the identity of Hugues with the audacious spoiler of his meat, and eke his peace. The wolf presented himself as usual, and anxiously enquired after Branda, which stimulated the flesher the more firmly to follow out his design.

"Here, Wolf," said Willieblud, stooping down as if to choose a piece of meat; "I give thee double portion tonight; up with thy paw, take toll, and be mindful of my frank alms."

"Sooth, I will remember me, gossip," rejoined our werwolf; "but when shall the marriage be solemnized for certain, betwixt the fair Branda and myself?"

Hugues believing he had nothing to fear from the flesher, whose meats he so readily appropriated to himself, and of whose fair niece he hoped shortly no less to make lawful possession; both that he really loved, and viewed his union with her as the surest means of placing him within the pale of that sociality from which he had been so unjustly exiled, could he but succeed in making intercession with the holy fathers of the church to remove their interdict. Hugues placed his extended paw upon the edge of the cart; but instead of handing him his joint of beef, or mutton, Willieblud raised his cleaver, and at a single blow lopped off the paw laid there as fittingly for the purpose as though upon a block. The flesher flung down his weapon, and belaboured his beast, the wer-wolf roared aloud with agony, and disappeared amid the dark shades of the forest, in which, aided by the wind, his howling was soon lost.

The next day, on his return, the flesher, chuckling and laughing, deposited a gory cloth upon the table, among the trenchers with which his niece was busied in preparing his noonday meal, and which, on being opened, displayed to her horrified gaze a freshly severed human hand enveloped in wolf-skin. Branda, comprehending what had occurred, shrieked aloud, shed a flood of tears, and then hurriedly throwing her mantle round her, whilst her uncle amused himself by turning and twitching the hand about with a ferocious delight, exclaiming, whilst he staunched the blood which still flowed:

"The sacristan said sooth; the wer-wolf has his need I trow, at last, and now I wot of his nature, I fear no more his witchcraft."

Although the day was far advanced, Hugues lay writhing in torture upon his couch, his coverings drenched with blood, as well also the floor of his habitation; his countenance of a ghastly pallor, expressed as much moral, as physical pain; tears gushed from beneath his reddened eyelids, and he listened to every noise without, with an increased inquietude, painfully visible upon his distorted features. Footsteps were heard rapidly approaching, the door was hurriedly flung open, and a female threw herself beside his couch, and with mingled sobs and imprecations sought tenderly for his mutilated arm, which, rudely bound round with hempen wrappings, no longer dissembled the absence of its wrist, and from which a crimson stream still trickled. At this piteous spectacle she grew loud in her denunciations against the sanguinary flesher, and sympathetically mingled her lamentations with those of his victim.

These effusions of love and dolour, however, were doomed to sudden interruption; some one knocked at the door. Branda ran to the window that she might recognize who the visitor was that had dared to penetrate the lair of a wer-wolf, and on perceiving who it was, she raised her eyes and hands on high, in token of her extremity of despair, whilst the knocking momentarily grew louder.

"'Tis my uncle," faltered she. "Ah! woes me, how shall I escape hence without his seeing me? Whither hide? Oh, here, here, nigh to thee, Hugues, and we will die together," and she crouched herself into an obscure recess behind his couch. "If Willieblud should raise his cleaver to slay thee, he shall first strike through his kinswoman's body."

Branda hastily concealed herself amidst a pile of hemp, whispering Hugues to summon all his courage, who, however, scarce found strength sufficient to raise himself to a sitting posture, whilst his eyes vainly sought around for some weapon of defence.

"A good morrow to thee, Wulfric!" exclaimed Willieblud, as he entered, holding in his hand a napkin tied in a knot, which he proceeded to place upon the coffer beside the sufferer. "I come to offer thee some work, to bind and stack me a faggot-pile, knowing that thou art no laggard at bill-hook and wattle. Wilt do it?"

"I am sick," replied Hugues, repressing the wrath which, despite of pain, sparkled in his wild glance; "I am not in fitting state to work."

"Sick, gossip, sick, art thou indeed? Or is it but a sloth fit? Come, what ails thee? Where lieth the evil? Your hand, that I may feel thy pulse."

Hugues reddened, and for an instant hesitated whether he should resist a solicitation, the bent of which he too readily comprehended; but in order to avoid exposing Branda to discovery, he thrust forth his left hand from beneath the coverlid, all imbued in dried gore.

"Not that hand, Hugues, but the other, the right one. Alack, and well-a-day, hast thou lost thy hand, and must I find it for thee?"

Hugues, whose purpling flush of rage changed quickly to a death-like hue, replied not to this taunt, nor testified by the slightest gesture or movement that he was preparing to satisfy a request as cruel in its preconception as the object of it was slenderly cloaked. Willieblud laughed, and ground his teeth in savage glee, maliciously revelling in the tortures he had inflicted upon the sufferer. He seemed already disposed to use violence, rather than allow himself to be baffled in the attainment of the decisive proof he aimed at. Already had he commenced untying the napkin, giving vent all the while to his implacable taunts; one hand alone displaying itself upon the coverlid, and which Hugues, wellnigh senseless with anguish, thought not of withdrawing.

"Why tender me that hand?" continued his unrelenting persecutor, as he imagined himself on the eve of arriving at the conviction he so ardently desired—"That I should lop it off? quick, quick, Master Wulfric, and do my bidding; I demanded to see your right hand."

"Behold it then!" ejaculated a suppressed voice, which belonged to no supernatural being, however it might seem appertaining to such; and Willieblud to his utter confusion and dismay saw a second hand, sound and unmutilated, extend itself towards him as though in silent accusation. He started back; he stammered out a cry for mercy, bent his knees for an instant, and raising himself, palsied with terror, fled from the hut, which he firmly believed under the possession of the foul fiend. He carried not with him the severed hand, which henceforward became a perpetual vision ever present before his eyes, and which all the potent exorcisms of the sacristan, at whose hands he continually sought council and consolation, signally failed to dispel.

"Oh, that hand! To whom then, belongs that accursed hand?" groaned he, continually. "Is it really the fiends, or that of some wer-wolf? Certain 'tis, that Hugues is innocent, for have I not seen both his hands? But wherefore was one bloody? There's sorcery at bottom of it."

The next morning, early, the first object that struck his sight on entering his stall, was the severed hand that he had left the preceding night upon the coffer in the forest hut; it was stripped of its wolf-skin covering, and lay among the viands. He dared no longer touch that hand, which now, he verily believed to be enchanted; but in hopes of getting rid of it for ever, he had it flung down a well, and it was with no small increase of despair that he found it shortly afterwards again lying upon his block. He buried it in his garden, but still without being able to rid himself of it; it returned livid and loathsome to infect his shop, and augment the remorse which was unceasingly revived by the reproaches of his niece.

At last, flattering himself to escape all further persecution from that fatal hand, it struck him that he would have it carried to the cemetery at Canterbury, and try whether exorcism, and sepulture in holy ground would effectually bar its return to the light of day. This was also done; but lo! on the following morning he perceived it nailed to his shutter. Disheartened by these dumb, yet awful reproaches, which wholly robbed him of his peace, and impatient to annihilate all trace of an action with which heaven itself seemed to upbraid him, he quitted

Ashford one morning without bidding adieu to his niece, and some days after was found drowned in the river Stour. They drew out his swollen and discoloured body, which was discovered floating on the surface among the sedge, and it was only by piecemeal that they succeeded in tearing away from his death-contracted clutch, the phantom hand, which, in his suicidal convulsions he had retained firmly grasped.

A year after this event, Hugues, although minus a hand, and consequently a confirmed wer-wolf, married Branda, sole heiress to the stock and chattels of the late unhappy flesher of Ashford.

SIR GILBERT CAMPBELL, BART.

THE WHITE WOLF OF KOSTOPCHIN

I

A wide sandy expanse of country, flat and uninteresting in appearance, with a great staring whitewashed house standing in the midst of wide fields of cultivated land; whilst far away were the low sand-hills and pine-forests to be met with in the district of Lithuania, in Russian Poland. Not far from the great white house was the village in which the serfs dwelt, with the large bakehouse and the public bath which are invariably to be found in all Russian villages, however humble. The fields were negligently cultivated, the hedges broken down and the fences in bad repair, shattered agricultural implements had been carelessly flung aside in remote corners, and the whole estate showed the want of the superintending eye of an energetic master. The great white house was no better looked after, the garden was an utter wilderness, great patches of plaster had fallen from the walls, and many of the Venetian shutters were almost off the hinges. Over all was the dark lowering sky of a Russian autumn, and there were no signs of life to be seen, save a few peasants lounging idly towards the vodki shop, and a gaunt half-starved cat creeping stealthily abroad in quest of a meal.

The estate, which was known by the name of Kostopchin, was the property of Paul Sergevitch, a gentleman of means, and the most discontented man in Russian Poland. Like most wealthy Muscovites, he had travelled much, and had spent the gold, which had been amassed by serf labour, like water, in all the dissolute revelries of the capitals of Europe. Paul's figure was as well known in the boudoirs of the *demi mondaines* as his face was familiar to the public gaming tables. He appeared to have no thought for the future, but only to live in the excitement of the mad career of dissipation which he was pursuing. His means, enormous as they were, were all forestalled, and he was continually sending to his intendant for fresh supplies of money. His fortune would not have held out long against the constant inroads that were being made upon it, when an unexpected circumstance took place which stopped his career like a flash of lightning. This was a fatal duel, in which a young man of great promise, the son of the prime minister of the country in which he then resided, fell by his hand. Representations were made to the Czar, and Paul Sergevitch was recalled, and, after receiving a severe reprimand, was ordered to return to his estates in Lithuania. Horribly discontented, yet not daring to disobey the Imperial mandate, Paul buried himself at Kostopchin, a place he had not visited since his boyhood. At first he endeavoured to interest himself in the workings of the vast estate; but agriculture had no charm for him, and the only result was that he quarrelled with and dismissed his German intendant, replacing him by an old serf, Michal Vassilitch, who had been his father's valet. Then he took to wandering about the country, gun in hand, and upon his return home would sit moodily drinking brandy and smoking innumerable cigarettes, as he cursed his lord and master, the emperor, for consigning him to such a course of dullness and *ennui*. For a couple of years he led this aimless life, and at last, hardly knowing the reason for so doing, he married the daughter of a neighbouring landed proprietor. The marriage was a most unhappy one; the girl had really never cared for Paul, but had married him in obedience to her father's mandates, and the man, whose temper was always brutal and violent, treated her, after a brief interval of contemptuous indifference, with savage cruelty. After three years the unhappy woman expired, leaving behind her two children—a boy, Alexis, and a girl, Katrina. Paul treated his wife's death with the most perfect indifference; but he did not put anyone in her place. He was very fond of the little Katrina, but did not take much notice of the boy, and resumed his lonely wanderings about the country with dog and gun. Five years had passed since the death of his wife. Alexis was a fine, healthy boy of seven, whilst Katrina was some eighteen months younger. Paul was lighting one of his eternal cigarettes at the door of his house, when the little girl came running up to him.

"You bad, wicked papa," said she. "How is it that you have never brought me the pretty grey squirrels that you promised I should have the next time you went to the forest?"

"Because I have never yet been able to find any, my treasure," returned her father, taking up the child in his arms and half smothering her with kisses. "Because I have not found them yet, my golden queen; but I am bound to find Ivanovitch, the poacher, smoking about the woods, and if he can't show me where they are, no one can."

"Ah, little father," broke in Old Michal, using the term of address with which a Russian of humble position usually accosts his superior; "Ah, little father, take care; you will go to those woods once too often."

"Do you think I am afraid of Ivanovitch?" returned his master, with a coarse laugh. "Why, he and I are the best of friends; at any rate, if he robs me, he does so openly, and keeps other poachers away from my woods."

"It is not of Ivanovitch that I am thinking," answered the old man. "But oh! Gospodin, do not go into these dark solitudes; there are terrible tales told about them, of witches that dance in the moonlight, of strange, shadowy forms that are seen amongst the trunks of the tall pines, and of whispered voices that tempt the listeners to eternal perdition."

Again the rude laugh of the lord of the manor rang out as Paul observed, "If you go on addling your brain, old man, with these nearly half-forgotten legends, I shall have to look out for a new intendant."

"But I was not thinking of these fearful creatures only," returned Michal, crossing himself piously. "It was against the wolves that I meant to warn you."

"Oh, father dear, I am frightened now," whimpered little Katrina, hiding her head on her father's shoulder. "Wolves are such cruel, wicked things."

"See there, greybearded dotard," cried Paul, furiously, "you have terrified this sweet angel by your farrago of lies; besides, who ever heard of wolves so early as this. You are dreaming, Michal Vassilitch, or have taken your morning dram of vodki too strong."

"As I hope for future happiness," answered the old man, solemnly, "as I came through the marsh last night from Kosma the herdsman's cottage—you know, my lord, that he has been bitten by a viper, and is seriously ill—as I came through the marsh, I repeat, I saw something like sparks of fire in the clump of alders on the right-hand side. I was anxious to know what they could be, and cautiously moved a little nearer, recommending my soul to the protection of Saint Vladamir. I had not gone a couple of paces when a wild howl came that chilled the very marrow in my bones, and a pack of some ten or a dozen wolves, gaunt and famished as you see them, my lord, in the winter, rushed out. At their head was a white she-wolf, as big as any of the male ones, with gleaming tusks and a pair of yellow eyes that blazed with lurid fire. I had round my neck a crucifix that had been given me by the priest of Streletza, and the savage beasts knew this and broke away across the marsh, sending up the mud and water in showers in the air; but the white she-wolf, little father, circled round me three times as though endeavouring to find some place from which to attack me. Three times she did this, and then, with a snap of her teeth and a howl of impotent malice, she galloped away some fifty yards and sat down, watching my every movement with her fiery eyes. I did not delay any longer in so dangerous a spot, as you may well imagine, Gospodin, but walked hurriedly home, crossing myself at every step; but, as I am a living man, that white devil followed me the whole distance, keeping fifty paces in the rear, and every now and then licking her lips with a sound that made my flesh creep. When I got to the last fence before you come to the house I raised up my voice and shouted for the dogs, and soon I heard the deep bay of Troska and Branscöe as they came bounding towards me. The white devil heard it, too, and, giving a high bound into the air, she uttered a loud howl of disappointment, and trotted back leisurely towards the marsh."

"But why did you not set the dogs after her?" asked Paul, interested, in spite of himself, at the old man's narrative. "In the open Troska and Branscöe would run down any wolf that ever set foot to the ground in Lithuania."

"I tried to do so, little father," answered the old man, solemnly; "but directly they got up to the spot where the beast had executed her last devilish gambol, they put their tails between their legs and ran back to the house as fast as their legs could carry them."

"Strange," muttered Paul, thoughtfully, "that is, if it is truth and not vodki that is speaking."

"My lord," returned the old man, reproachfully, "man and boy, I have served you and my lord your father for fifty years, and no one can say that they ever saw Michal Vassilitch the worse for liquor."

"No one doubts that you are a sly old thief, Michal," returned his master, with his coarse, jarring laugh; "but for all that, your long stories of having been followed by white wolves won't prevent me from going to the forest today. A couple of good buckshot cartridges will break any spell, though I don't think that the she-wolf, if she existed anywhere than in your own imagination, has anything to do with magic. Don't be frightened, Katrina, my pet; you shall have a fine white wolf's-skin to put your feet on, if what this old fool says is right."

"Michal is not a fool," pouted the child, "and it is very wicked of you to call him so. I don't want any nasty wolf-skins, I want the grey squirrels."

"And you shall have them, my precious," returned her father, setting her down upon the ground. "Be a good girl, and I will not be long anyway."

"Father," said the little Alexis, suddenly, "let me go with you. I should like to see you kill a wolf, and then I should know how to do so, when I am older and taller."

"Pshaw," returned his father, irritably. "Boys are always in the way. Take the lad away, Michal; don't you see that he is worrying his sweet little sister."

"No, no, he does not worry me at all," answered the impetuous little lady, as she flew to her brother and covered him with kisses. "Michal, you shan't take him away, do you hear?"

"There, there, leave the children together," returned Paul, as he shouldered his gun, and kissing the tips of his fingers to Katrina, stepped away rapidly in the direction of the dark pine woods. Paul walked on, humming the fragment of an air that he had heard in a very different

place many years ago. A strange feeling of elation crept
over him, very different to the false excitement which his
solitary drinking bouts were wont to produce. A change
seemed to have come over his whole life, the skies looked
brighter, the *spiculae* of the pine-trees of a more vivid
green, and the landscape seemed to have lost that dull
cloud of depression which had for years appeared to hang
over it. And beneath all this exaltation of the mind,
beneath all this unlooked-for promise of a more happy
future, lurked a heavy, inexplicable feeling of a power to
come, a something without form or shape, and yet the
more terrible because it was shrouded by that thick veil
which conceals from the eyes of the soul the strange
fantastic designs of the dwellers beyond the line of earthly
influences.

There were no signs of the poacher, and wearied with
searching for him, Paul made the woods re-echo with his
name. The great dog Troska, who had followed his
master, looked up wistfully into his face, and at a second
repetition of the name "Ivanovitch," uttered a long
plaintive howl, and then, looking round at Paul as though
entreating him to follow, moved slowly ahead towards a
denser portion of the forest. A little mystified at the
hound's unusual proceedings, Paul followed, keeping his
gun ready to fire at the least sign of danger. He thought
that he knew the forest well, but the dog led the way to
a portion which he never remembered to have visited
before. He had got away from the pine trees now, and had
entered a dense thicket formed of stunted oaks and hollies.
The great dog only kept a yard or so ahead, his lips were
drawn back, showing the strong white fangs, the hair upon
his neck and back was bristling, and his tail firmly
pressed between his hind legs. Evidently the animal was in
a state of the most extreme terror, and yet it proceeded
bravely forward. Struggling through the dense thicket,
Paul suddenly found himself in an open space of some
ten or twenty yards in diameter. At one end of it was a
slimy pool, into the waters of which several strange-
looking reptiles glided as the man and dog made their
appearance. Almost in the centre of the opening was a
shattered stone cross, and at its base lay a dark heap,
close to which Troska stopped, and again raising his head,

uttered a long melancholy howl. For an instant or two, Paul gazed hesitatingly at the shapeless heap that lay beneath the cross, and then, mustering up all his courage, he stepped forward and bent anxiously over it. One glance was enough, for he recognized the body of Ivanovitch the poacher, hideously mangled. With a cry of surprise, he turned over the body and shuddered as he gazed upon the terrible injuries that had been inflicted. The unfortunate man had evidently been attacked by some savage beast, for there were marks of teeth upon the throat, and the jugular vein had been almost torn out. The breast of the corpse had been torn open, evidently by long sharp claws, and there was a gaping orifice upon the left side, round which the blood had formed in a thick coagulated patch. The only animals to be found in the forests of Russia capable of inflicting such wounds are the bear or the wolf, and the question as to the class of the assailant was easily settled by a glance at the dank ground, which showed the prints of a wolf so entirely different from the plantegrade traces of the bear.

"Savage brutes," muttered Paul. "So, after all, there may have been some truth in Michal's story, and the old idiot may for once in his life have spoken the truth. Well, it is no concern of mine, and if a fellow chooses to wander about the woods at night to kill my game, instead of remaining in his own hovel, he must take his chance. The strange thing is that the brutes have not eaten him, though they have mauled him so terribly."

He turned away as he spoke, intending to return home and send out some of the serfs to bring in the body of the unhappy man, when his eye was caught by a small white object hanging from a bramble bush near the pond. He made towards the spot, and taking up the object, examined it curiously. It was a tuft of coarse white hair, evidently belonging to some animal.

"A wolf's hair, or I am much mistaken," muttered Paul, pressing the hair between his fingers, and then applying it to his nose. "And from its colour, I should think that it belonged to the white lady who so terribly alarmed old Michal on the occasion of his night walk through the marsh."

Paul found it no easy task to retrace his steps towards

those parts of the forest with which he was acquainted, and Troska seemed unable to render him the slightest assistance, but followed moodily behind. Many times Paul found his way blocked by impenetrable thicket or dangerous quagmire, and during his many wanderings he had the ever-present sensation that there was a something close to him, an invisible something, a noiseless something; but for all that, a presence which moved as he advanced, and halted as he stopped in vain to listen. The certainty that an impalpable thing of some shape or other was close at hand grew so strong, that as the short autumn day began to close, and darker shadows to fall between the trunks of the lofty trees, it made him hurry on at his utmost speed. At length, when he had grown almost mad with terror, he suddenly came upon a path he knew, and with a feeling of intense relief, he stepped briskly forward in the direction of Kostopchin. As he left the forest and came into the open country, a faint wail seemed to ring through the darkness; but Paul's nerves had been so much shaken that he did not know whether this was an actual fact or only the offspring of his own excited fancy. As he crossed the neglected lawn that lay in front of the house, old Michal came rushing out of the house with terror convulsing every feature.

"Oh, my lord, my lord!" gasped he, "is not this too terrible?"

"Nothing has happened to my Katrina?" cried the father, a sudden sickly feeling of terror passing through his heart.

"No, no, the little lady is quite safe, thanks to the Blessed Virgin and Saint Alexander of Nevskoi," returned Michal; "but oh, my lord, poor Marta, the herd's daughter——"

"Well, what of the slut?" demanded Paul, for now that his momentary fear for the safety of his daughter had passed away, he had but little sympathy to spare for so insignificant a creature as a serf girl.

"I told you that Kosma was dying," answered Michal. "Well, Marta went across the marsh this afternoon to fetch the priest, but alas! she never came back."

"What detained her, then?" asked his master.

"One of the neighbours, going in to see how Kosma

was getting on, found the poor old man dead, his face was terribly contorted, and he was half in the bed, and half out, as though he had striven to reach the door. The men ran to the village to give the alarm, and as the men returned to the herdsman's hut, they found the body of Marta in a thicket by the clump of alders on the marsh."

"Her body, she was dead then?" asked Paul.

"Dead, my lord, killed by wolves," answered the old man. "And oh, my lord, it is too horrible, her breast was horribly lacerated, and her heart had been taken out and eaten, for it was nowhere to be found."

Paul started, for the horrible mutilation of the body of Ivanovitch the poacher occurred to his recollection.

"And, my lord," continued the old man, "this is not all, on a bush close by was this tuft of hair," and, as he spoke, he took it from a piece of paper in which it was wrapped to his master.

Paul took it, and recognised a similar tuft of hair to that which he had seen upon the bramble bush beside the shattered cross.

"Surely, my lord," continued Michal, not heeding his master's look of surprise, "you will have out men and dogs to hunt down this terrible creature, or, better still, send for the priest and holy water, for I have my doubts whether the creature belongs to this earth."

Paul shuddered, and, after a short pause, he told Michal of the ghastly end of Ivanovitch the poacher.

The old man listened with the utmost excitement, crossing himself repeatedly, and muttering invocations to the Blessed Virgin and the saints every instant, but his master would no longer listen to him, and, ordering him to place brandy on the table, sat drinking moodily until daylight.

The next day a fresh horror awaited the inhabitants of Kostopchin. An old man, a confirmed drunkard, had staggered out of the vodki shop with the intention of returning home; three hours later he was found at a turn of the road, horribly scratched and mutilated, with the same gaping orifice, in the left side of the breast, from which the heart had been forcibly torn out.

Three several times in the course of the week the same ghastly tragedy occurred—a little child, an able-bodied labourer, and an old woman, were all found with the same terrible marks of mutilation upon them, and in every case the same tuft of white hair was found in the immediate vicinity of the bodies. A frightful panic ensued, and an excited crowd of serfs surrounded the house at Kostopchin, calling upon their master, Paul Sergevitch, to save them from the fiend that had been let loose upon them, and shouting out various remedies, which they insisted upon being carried into effect at once.

Paul felt a strange disinclination to adopt any active measures. A certain feeling which he could not account for urged him to remain quiescent, but the Russian serf when suffering under an excess of superstitious terror is a dangerous person to deal with, and, with extreme reluctance, Paul Sergevitch issued instructions for a thorough search through the estate, and a general *battue* of the pine woods.

CHAPTER II

The army of beaters convened by Michal was ready with the first dawn of sunrise, and formed a strange and almost grotesque-looking assemblage, armed with rusty old firelocks, heavy bludgeons, and scythes fastened on to the end of long poles. Paul, with his double-barrelled gun thrown across his shoulder and a keen hunting-knife thrust into his belt, marched at the head of the serfs, accompanied by the two great hounds, Troska and Branscöe. Every nook and corner of the hedgerows were examined, and the little out-lying clumps were thoroughly searched, but without success, and at last a circle was formed round the larger portion of the forest, and with loud shouts, blowing of horns and beating of copper cooking utensils, the crowd of eager serfs pushed their way through the brushwood. Frightened birds flew up, whirring through the pine branches; hares and rabbits darted from their hiding-places behind tufts and hummocks of grass, and skurried away in the utmost terror. Occasionly a roe deer rushed through the thicket, or a wild boar burst through the thin line of beaters, but no signs of wolves were to be seen. The circle grew narrower and yet more narrow, when all at once a wild shriek and a confused murmer of voices echoed through the pine trees. All rushed to the spot, and a young lad was discovered weltering in his blood and terribly mutilated, though life still lingered in the mangled frame. A few drops of vodki were poured down his throat, and he managed to gasp out that the white wolf had sprung upon him suddenly, and, throwing him to the ground, had commenced tearing at the flesh over his heart. He would inevitably have been killed, and not the animal quitted him, alarmed by the approach of the other beaters.

"The beast ran into that thicket," gasped the boy, and then once more relapsed into a state of insensibility.

But the words of the wounded boy had been eagerly passed round, and a hundred different propositions were made.

"Set fire to the thicket," exclaimed one.

"Fire a volley into it," suggested another.

"A bold dash in, and trample the beast's life out," shouted a third.

The first proposal was agreed to, and a hundred eager hands collected dried sticks and leaves, and then a light was kindled. Just as the fire was about to be applied, a soft, sweet voice issued from the centre of the thicket.

"Do not set fire to the forest, my dear friends; give me time to come out. Is it not enough for me to have been frightened to death by that awful creature?"

All started back in amazement, and Paul felt a strange, sudden thrill pass through his heart as those soft musical accents fell upon his ear.

There was a light rustling in the brushwood, and then a vision suddenly appeared, which filled the souls of the beholders with surprise. As the bushes divided, a fair woman, wrapped in a mantle of soft white fur, with a fantastically-shaped travelling cap of green velvet upon her head, stood before them. She was exquisitely fair, and her long Titian red hair hung in dishevelled masses over her shoulders.

"My good man," began she, with a certain tinge of aristocratic hauteur in her voice, "is your master here?"

As moved by a spring, Paul stepped forward and mechanically raised his cap.

"I am Paul Sergevitch," said he, "and these woods are on my estate of Kostopchin. A fearful wolf has been committing a series of terrible devastations upon my people, and we have been endeavouring to hunt it down. A boy whom he has just wounded says that he ran into the thicket from which you have just emerged, to the surprise of us all."

"I know," answered the lady, fixing her clear, steel-blue eyes keenly upon Paul's face. "The terrible beast rushed past me, and dived into a large cavity in the earth in the very centre of the thicket. It was a huge white wolf, and I greatly feared that it would devour me."

"Ho, my men," cried Paul, "take spade and mattock, dig out the monster, for she has come to the end of her tether at last. Madam, I do not know what chance has conducted you to this wild solitude, but the hospitality of Kostopchin is at your disposal, and I will, with your permission, conduct you there as soon as this scourge of the countryside has been dispatched."

He offered his hand with some remains of his former courtesy, but started back with an expression of horror on his face.

"Blood," cried he, "why, madam, your hand and fingers are stained with blood."

A faint colour rose to the lady's cheek, but it died away in an instant as she answered, with a faint smile:

"The dreadful creature was all covered with blood, and I suppose I must have stained my hands against the bushes through which it had passed, when I parted them in order to escape from the fiery death with which you threatened me."

There was a ring of suppressed irony in her voice, and Paul felt his eyes drop before the glance of those cold steel-blue eyes. Meanwhile, urged to the utmost exertion by their fears, the serfs plied spade and mattock with the utmost vigour. The cavity was speedily enlarged, but, when a depth of eight feet had been attained, it was found to terminate in a little burrow not large enough to admit a rabbit, much less a creature of the white wolf's size. There were none of the tufts of white hair which had hitherto been always found beside the bodies of the victims, nor did that peculiar rank odour which always indicates the presence of wild animals hang about the spot.

The superstitious Muscovites crossed themselves, and scrambled out of the hole with grotesque alacrity. The mysterious disappearance of the monster which had committed such frightful ravages had cast a chill over the hearts of the ignorant peasants, and, unheeding the shouts of their master, they left the forest, which seemed to be overcast with the gloom of some impending calamity.

"Forgive the ignorance of these boors, madam," said Paul, when he found himself alone with the strange lady, "and permit me to escort you to my poor house, for you must have need of rest and refreshment, and———"

Here Paul checked himself abruptly, and a dark flush of embarrassment passed over his face.

"And," said the lady, with the same faint smile," and you are dying of curiosity to know how I suddenly made my appearance from a thicket in your forest. You say that you are the lord of Kostopchin, then you are Paul Sergevitch, and should surely know how the ruler of Holy Russia takes upon himself to interfere with the doings of his children?"

"You know me, then?" exclaimed Paul in some surprise.

"Yes, I have lived in foreign lands, as you have, and have heard your name often. Did you not break the bank at Blankburg? Did you not carry off Isola Menuti, the dancer, from a host of competitors; and, as a last instance of my knowledge, shall I recall to your memory a certain morning, on a sandy shore, with two men facing each other, pistol in hand, the one young, fair, and boyish-looking, hardly twenty-two years of age, the other———"

"Hush!" exclaimed Paul, hoarsely; "you evidently know me, but who in the fiend's name are you?"

"Simply a woman who once moved in society and read the papers, and who is now a hunted fugitive."

"A fugitive!" returned Paul, hotly; "who dares to persecute you?"

The lady moved a little closer to him, and then whispered in his ear—

"The police!"

"The police!" repeated Paul, stepping back a pace or two. "The police!"

"Yes, Paul Sergevitch, the police," returned the lady, "that body at the mention of which it is said the very Emperor trembles as he sits in his gilded chambers in the Winter Palace. Yes, I have had the imprudence to speak my mind too freely, and—well, you know what women have to dread who fall into the hands of the police in Holy Russia. To avoid such infamous degradations I fled, accompanied by a faithful domestic. I fled in hopes of gaining the frontier, but a few versts from here a body of mounted police rode up. My poor old servant had the impudence to resist, and was shot dead. Half wild with terror I fled into the forest, and wandered about until I heard the noise your serfs made in beating the woods. I thought it was the police, who had organized a search for me, and I crept into the thicket for the purpose of concealment. The rest you know. And now, Paul Sergevitch, tell me whether you dare give shelter to a proscribed fugitive such as I am?"

"Madam," returned Paul, gazing into the clear-cut features before him, glowing with the animation of the recital, "Kostopchin is ever open to misfortune—and beauty," added he, with a bow.

"Ah!" cried the lady, with a laugh in which there was something sinister; "I expect that misfortune would knock at your door for a long time, if it was unaccompanied by beauty. However, I thank you, and will accept your hospitality, but if evil come upon you, remember that I am not to be blamed."

"You will be safe enough at Kostopchin," returned Paul. "The police won't trouble their heads about me; they know that since the Emperor drove me to lead this hideous existence politics have no charm for me, and that the brandy-bottle is the only charm of my existence."

"Dear me," answered the lady, eying him uneasily, "a morbid drunkard, are you? Well, as I am half perished with cold suppose you take me to Kostopchin; you will be conferring a favour on me, and will get back all the sooner to your favourite brandy."

She placed her hand upon Paul's arm as she spoke, and mechanically he led the way to the great solitary white house. The few servants betrayed no astonishment at the appearance of the lady, for some of the serfs on their way back to the village had spread the report of the sudden appearance of the mysterious stranger; besides, they were not accustomed to question the acts of their somewhat arbitrary master.

Alexis and Katrina had gone to bed, and Paul and his guest sat down to a hastily-improvised meal.

"I am no great eater," remarked the lady, as she played with the food before her; and Paul noticed with surprise that scarcely a morsel passed her lips, though she more than once filled and emptied a goblet of the champagne which had been opened in honour of her arrival.

"So it seems," remarked he; "and I do not wonder, for the food in this benighted hole is not what either you or I have been accustomed to."

"Oh, it does well enough," returned the lady, carelessly. "And now, if you have such a thing as a woman in the establishment, you can let her show me to my room, for I am nearly dead for want of sleep."

Paul struck a hand bell that stood on the table beside him, and the stranger rose from her seat, and with a brief "Good night" was moving towards the door, when the old man Michal suddenly made his appearance on the threshhold. The aged intendant started backwards as though to avoid a heavy blow, and his fingers at once sought for the crucifix which he wore suspended round his neck, and on whose protection he relied to shield him from the powers of darkness.

"Blessed Virgin!" he exclaimed. "Holy Saint Radislas, protect me, where have I seen her before?"

The lady took no notice of the old man's evident terror, but passed away down the echoing corridor.

The old man now timidly approached his master, who, after swallowing a glass of brandy, had drawn his chair up to the stove, and was gazing moodily at its polished surface.

"My lord," said Michal, venturing to touch his master's shoulder, "is that the lady that you found in the forest?"

"Yes," returned Paul, a smile breaking out over his face; "She is very beautiful, is she not?"

"Beautiful!" repeated Michal, crossing himself, "she may have beauty, but it is that of a demon. Where have I seen her before?—where have I seen those shining teeth and those cold eyes? She is not like any one here and I have never been ten versts from Kostopchin in my life. I am utterly bewildered. Ah. I have it, the dying herdsman —save the mark! Gospodin, have a care. I tell you that the strange lady is the image of the white wolf."

"You old fool," returned his master, savagely, "let me ever hear you repeat such nonsense again, and I will have you skinned alive. The lady is high-born, and of good family, beware how you insult her. Nay, I give you further commands; see that during her sojourn here she is treated with the utmost respect. And communicate this to all the servants. Mind, no more tales about the vision that your addled brain conjured up of wolves in the marsh, and above all do not let me hear that you have been alarming my dear little Katrina with your senseless babble."

The old man bowed humbly, and, after a short pause, remarked:

"The lad that was injured at the hunt to-day is dead, my lord."

"Oh, dead is he, poor wretch!" returned Paul, to whom the death of a serf lad was not a matter of overweening importance. "But look here, Michal, remember that if any inquiries are made about the lady, that no one knows anything about her; that, in fact, no one has seen her at all."

"Your lordship shall be obeyed," answered the old man; and then, seeing that his master had relapsed into his former moody reverie, he left the room, crossing himself at every step he took.

Late into the night Paul sat up thinking over the occurrences of the day. He had told Michal that his guest was of noble family, but in reality he knew nothing more of her than she had condescended to tell him.

"Why, I don't even know her name," muttered he; "and yet somehow or other it seems as if a new feature of my life was opening for me. However, I have made one step in advance by getting her here, and if she talks about leaving, why all that I have to do is threaten her with the police."

After his usual custom he smoked cigarette after cigarette, and poured out copious tumblers of brandy. The attendant serf replenished the stove from a small den which opened into the corridor, and after a time Paul slumbered heavily in his arm-chair. He was aroused by a light touch upon his shoulder, and starting up, saw the stranger of the forest standing by his side.

"This is indeed kind of you," said she, with her usual mocking smile. "You felt that I should be strange here, and you got up early to see to the horses, or can it really be, those ends of cigarettes, that empty bottle of brandy? Paul Sergevitch, you have not been to bed at all."

Paul muttered a few indistinct words in reply, and then, ringing the bell furiously, ordered the servants to clear away the *debris* of last night's orgy, and lay the table for breakfast; then, with a hasty apology, he left the room to make a fresh toilet, and in about half an hour returned with his appearance sensibly improved by his ablutions and change of dress.

"I dare say," remarked the lady, as they were seated at the morning meal, for which she manifested the same indifference that she had for the dinner of the previous evening, "that you would like to know my name and who I am. Well, I don't mind telling you my name. It is Ravina, but as to my family and who I am, it will perhaps be best for you to remain in ignorance. A matter of policy, my dear Paul Sergevitch, a mere matter of policy, you see. I leave you to judge from my manners and appearance whether I am of sufficiently good form to be invited to the honour of your table————"

"None more worthy," broke in Paul, whose bemuddled brain was fast succumbing to the charms of his guest; "and surely that is a question upon which I may be deemed a competent judge."

"I do not know about that," returned Ravina, "for from all accounts the company that you used was not of the most select character."

"No, but hear me," began Paul, seizing her hand and endeavouring to carry it to his lips. But as he did so an unpleasant chill passed over him, for these slender fingers were icy cold.

"Do not be foolish," said Ravina, drawing away her hand, after she had permitted it to rest for an instant in Paul's grasp; "do you not hear someone coming?"

As she spoke the sound of tiny pattering feet was heard

in the corridor, then the door was flung violently open, and with a shrill cry of delight, Katrina rushed into the room, followed more slowly by her brother Alexis.

"And are these your children?" asked Ravina, as Paul took up the little girl and placed her fondly upon his knee, whilst the boy stood a few paces from the door gazing with eyes of wonder upon the strange woman for whose appearance he was utterly unable to account. "Come here, my little man," continued she; "I suppose that you are the heir of Kostopchin, though you do not resemble your father much."

"He takes after his mother, I think," returned Paul, carelessly; "and how has my darling Katrina been? he added, addressing his daughter.

"Quite well, papa, dear," answered the child, "but where is the fine white wolf-skin that you promised me?"

"Your father did not find her," answered Ravina, with a little laugh; "the white wolf was not so easy to catch as he fancied."

Alexis had moved a few steps nearer to the lady and was listening with grave attention to every word she uttered.

"Are white wolves so difficult to kill then?" asked he.

"It seems so, my little man," returned the lady, "since your father and all the serfs of Kostopchin were unable to do so," answered Ravina.

"I have got a pistol, that good old Michal has taught me to fire, and I am sure I could kill her if ever I got a sight of her," observed Alexis, boldly.

"There is a brave boy," returned Ravina, with one of her shrill laughs; "and now, won't you come and sit on my knee, for I am very fond of little boys?"

"No," I don't like you," answered Alexis, after a moment's consideration, "for Michal says——"

"Go to your room, you insolent young brat," broke in his father, in a voice of thunder. "You spend so much of your time with Michal and the serfs that you have learned all their boorish habits."

Two tiny tears rolled down the boy's cheeks as in obedience to his father's orders he turned about and quitted the room, whilst Ravina darted a strange look of dislike after him. As soon, however, as the door had closed, the fair woman addressed Katrina.

"Well, perhaps you will not be so unkind to me as your brother," said she. "Come to me," and as she spoke she held out her arms.

The little girl came to her without hesitation, and began to smooth the silken tresses which were coiled and wreathed around Ravina's head.

"Pretty, pretty," she murmured, "beautiful lady."

"You see, Paul Sergevitch, that your little daughter has taken to me at once," remarked Ravina.

"She takes after her father, who was always noted for his good taste," returned Paul, with a bow; "but take care, madam, or the little puss will have your necklace off."

The child indeed had succeeded in unclasping the glittering ornament, and was now inspecting it in high glee.

"That is a curious ornament," said Paul, stepping up to the child and taking the circlet from her hand.

It was indeed a quaintly fashioned ornament, consisting as it did of a number of what were apparently curved pieces of sharp-pointed horn set in gold, and depending from a snake of the same precious metal.

"Why, these are claws," continued he, as he looked at them more carefully.

"Yes, wolves' claws," answered Ravina, taking the necklet from the child and reclasping it round her neck. "It is a family relic which I have always worn."

Katrina at first seemed inclined to cry at her new plaything being taken from her, but by caresses and endearments Ravina soon contrived to lull her once more into a good temper.

"My daughter has certainly taken to you in a most wonderful manner," remarked Paul, with a pleased smile. "You have quite obtained possession of her heart."

"Not yet, whatever I may do later on," answered the woman, with her strange cold smile, as she pressed the child closer towards her and shot a glance at Paul which made him quiver with an emotion that he had never felt before. Presently, however, the child grew tired of her new acquaintance, and sliding down from her knee, crept from the room in search of her brother Alexis.

Paul and Ravina remained silent for a few instants, and then the woman broke the silence.

"All that remains for me now, Paul Sergevitch, is to

trespass on your hospitality, and to ask you to lend me some disguise, and assist me to gain the nearest post town, which, I think, is Vitroski."

"And why should you wish to leave this at all," demanded Paul, a deep flush rising to his cheek. "You are perfectly safe in my house, and if you attempt to pursue your journey there is every chance of your being recognized and captured."

"Why do I wish to leave this house?" answered Ravina, rising to her feet and casting a look of surprise upon her interrogator. "Can you ask such a question? How is it possible for me to remain here?"

"It is perfectly impossible for you to leave, of that I am quite certain," answered the man, doggedly. "All I know is, that if you leave Kostopchin, you will inevitably fall into the hands of the police."

"And Paul Sergevitch will tell them where they can find me?" questioned Ravina, with an ironical inflection in the tone of her voice.

"I never said so," returned Paul.

"Perhaps not," answered the woman, quickly, "but I am not slow in reading thoughts, they are sometimes plainer to read than words. You are saying to yourself. 'Kostopchin is a dull hole after all; chance has thrown into my hands a woman whose beauty pleases me; she is utterly friendless and in fear of the pursuits of the police; why should I not bend her to my will?' That is what you have been thinking, is it not so, Paul Sergevitch?"

"I never thought, that is——" stammered the man.

"No, you never thought that I could read you so plainly," pursued the woman, pitilessly, "but it is the truth that I have told you, and sooner than remain an inmate of your house, I would leave it, even if all the police in Russia stood ready to arrest me on its very threshold."

"Stay, Ravina," exclaimed Paul, as the woman made a step towards the door, "I do not say whether your reading of my thoughts is right or wrong, but before you leave listen to me. I do not speak to you in the usual strain of a pleading lover, you, who know my past, would laugh at me should I do so; but I tell you plainly that from the first moment that I set eyes upon you, a strange new feeling has risen up in my heart, not the cold thing that society calls love, but a burning resistless flood which flows down like molten lava from the volcano's crater. Stay, Ravina, stay, I implore you, for if you go from here you will take my heart with you."

"You may be speaking more truthfully than you think," returned the fair woman, as, turning back, she came close up to Paul, and placing both her hands upon his shoulders, shot a glance of lurid fire from her eyes. "Still, you have but given me a selfish reason for my staying, only your own self-gratification. Give me one that more nearly affects myself."

Ravina's touch sent a tremor through Paul's whole frame which caused every nerve and sinew to vibrate. Gaze as boldly as he might into those steel-blue eyes, he could not sustain their intensity.

"Be my wife, Ravina," faltered he. "Be my wife. You are safe enough from all pursuit here, and if that does not suit you I can easily convert my estate into a large sum of money, and we can fly to other lands, where you can have nothing to fear from the Russian police."

"And does Paul Sergevitch actually mean to offer his hand to a woman whose name he does not even know, and of whose feelings towards him he is entirely ignorant," asked the woman, with her customary mocking laugh.

"What do I care for name or birth," returned he, hotly. "I have enough for both, and as for love, my passion would soon kindle some sparks of it in your breast, cold and frozen as it may now be."

"Let me think a little," said Ravina, and throwing herself into an arm-chair she buried her face in her hands and seemed plunged in deep reflection, whilst Paul paced impatiently up and down the room like a prisoner awaiting the verdict that would restore him to life or doom him to a shameful death.

At length Ravina removed her hands from her face and spoke.

"Listen," said she, "I have thought over your proposal seriously, and upon certain conditions, I will consent to become your wife."

"They are granted in advance," broke in Paul, eagerly.

"Make no bargains blindfold," answered she, "but listen. At the present moment I have no inclination for you, but on the other hand I feel no repugnance for you. I will remain here for a month, and during that time I shall remain in a suite of apartments which you shall have prepared for me. Every evening I will visit you here, and upon your making yourself agreeable my ultimate decision will depend."

"And suppose that decision should be an unfavourable one?" asked Paul.

"Then," answered Ravina, with a ringing laugh, "I shall, as you say, leave this and take your heart with me."

"These are very hard conditions," remarked Paul. "Why not shorten the time of probation?"

"My conditions are unalterable," answered Ravina, with a little stamp of her foot. "Do you agree to them or not?"

"I have no alternative," answered he, sullenly; "but remember that I am to see you every evening."

"For two hours," said the woman, "so you must try and make yourself as agreeable as you can in that time; and now, if you will give orders regarding my rooms, I will settle myself in them with as little delay as possible."

Paul obeyed her, and in a couple of hours three handsome chambers were got ready for their fair occupant in a distant part of the great rambling house.

CHAPTER III

THE AWAKENING OF THE WOLF

The days slipped slowly and wearily away, but Ravina showed no signs of relenting. Every evening, according to her bond, she spent two hours with Paul and made herself most agreeable, listening to his far-fetched compliments and asseverations of love and tenderness either with a cold smile or with one of her mocking laughs. She refused to allow Paul to visit her in her own apartments, and the only intruder she permitted there, save the servants, was little Katrina, who had taken a strange fancy to the fair woman. Alexis, on the contrary, avoided her as much as he possibly could, and the pair hardly ever met. Paul, to while away the time, wandered about the farm and the village, the inhabitants of which had recovered from their panic as the white wolf appeared to have entirely desisted from her murderous attacks upon belated peasants. The shades of evening had closed in as Paul was one day returning from his customary round, rejoiced with the idea that the hour for Ravina's visit was drawing near, when he was startled by a gentle touch upon the shoulder, and turning round, saw the old man Michal standing just behind him. The intendant's face was perfectly livid, his eyes gleamed with the lustre of terror, and his fingers kept convulsively clasping and unclasping.

"My lord," exclaimed he, in faltering accents; "Oh, my lord, listen to me, for I have terrible news to narrate to you."

"What is the matter?" asked Paul, more impressed than he would have liked to confess by the old man's evident terror.

"The wolf, the white wolf. I have seen it again," whispered Michal.

"You are dreaming," retorted his master, angrily. "You have got the creature on the brain, and have mistaken a white calf or one of the dogs for it."

"I am not mistaken," answered the old man, firmly.

"And oh, my lord, do not go into the house, for she is there."

"She—who—what do you mean?" cried Paul.

"The white wolf, my lord. I saw her go in. You know the strange lady's apartments are on the ground floor on the west side of the house. I saw the monster cantering across the lawn, and, as if it knew its way perfectly well, make for the centre window of the reception room; it yielded to a touch of the forepaw and the beast sprang through. Oh, my lord, do not go in, I tell you that it will never harm the strange woman. Ah! let me——"

But Paul cast off the detaining arm with a force that made the old man reel and fall, and then, catching up an axe dashed into the house, calling upon the servants to follow him to the strange lady's rooms. He tried the handle but the door was securely fastened, and then, in all the frenzy of terror, he attacked the panels with heavy blows of his axe. For a few seconds no sound was heard save the ring of metal and the shivering of panels, but then the clear tones of Ravina were heard asking the reason for this outrageous disturbance.

"The wolf, the white wolf," shouted half a dozen voices.

"Stand back and I will open the door," answered the fair woman. "You must be mad, for there is no wolf here."

The door flew open and the crowd rushed tumultuously in; every nook and corner was searched, but no signs of the intruder could be discovered, and with many shame-faced glances Paul and his servants were about to return, when the voice of Ravina arrested their steps.

"Paul Sergevitch," said she, coldly. "Explain the meaning of this daring intrusion on my privacy."

She looked very beautiful as she stood before them; her right arm extended and her bosom heaved violently, but this was doubtless caused by her anger at the unlooked-for invasion.

Paul briefly repeated what he had heard from the old serf, and Ravina's scorn was intense.

"And so," cried she, fiercely, "it is to the crotchets of this old dotard that I am indebted for this. Paul, if you ever hope to succeed in winning me, forbid that man to enter the house again."

Paul would have sacrificed all his serfs for a whim of the haughty beauty, and Michal was deprived of the office of intendant and exiled to a cabin in the village, with orders never to show his face again near the house. The separation from the children almost broke the old man's heart, but he ventured on no remonstrance and meekly obeyed the mandate which drove him away from all he loved and cherished.

Meanwhile, curious rumours began to be circulated regarding the strange proceedings of the lady who occupied the suite of apartments which had formerly belonged to the wife of the owner of Kostopchin. The servants declared that the food sent up, though hacked about and cut up, was never tasted, but that the raw meat in the larder was frequently missing. Strange sounds were often heard to issue from the rooms as the panic-stricken serfs hurried past the corridor upon which the doors opened, and dwellers in the house were frequently disturbed by the howlings of wolves, the footprints of which were distinctly visible the next morning, and, curiously enough, invariably in the gardens facing the west side of the house in which the lady dwelt. Little Alexis, who found no encouragement to sit with his father, was naturally thrown a great deal amongst the serfs, and heard the subject discussed with many exaggerations. Weird old tales of folklore were often narrated as the servants discussed their evening meal, and the boy's hair would bristle as he listened to the wild and fanciful narratives of wolves, witches, and white ladies with which the superstitious serfs filled his ears. One of his most treasured possessions was an old brass-mounted cavalry pistol, a present from Michal; this he had learned to load, and by using both hands to the cumbersome weapon could contrive to fire it off, as many an ill-starred sparrow could attest. With his mind constantly dwelling upon the terrible tales he had so greedily listened to, this pistol became his daily companion, whether he was wandering about the long echoing corridors of the house or wandering through the neglected shrubberies of the garden. For a fortnight matters went on in this manner, Paul becoming more and more infatuated by the charms of his strange guest, and she every now and then letting drop occasional crumbs of hope which led the unhappy man further and further upon the dangerous course that he was pursuing. A mad, soul-absorbing passion for the fair woman and the deep draughts of brandy with which he consoled himself during her hours of absence were telling upon the brain of the master of Kostopchin, and except during the brief space of Ravina's visit, he would relapse into moods of silent sullenness from which he would occasionally break out into furious bursts of passion for no assignable cause. A shadow seemed to be closing over the House of Kostopchin; it became the abode of grim whispers and undeveloped fears; the men and maid-servants went about their work glancing nervously over their shoulders, as though they were apprehensive that some hideous thing was following on their heels.

After three days of exile, poor old Michal could endure the state of suspense regarding the safety of Alexis and Katrina no longer, and, casting aside his superstitious fears, he took to wandering by night about the exterior of the great white house, and peering cautiously into such windows as had been left unshuttered. At first he was in continual dread of meeting the terrible white wolf; but his love for the children and his confidence in the crucifix he wore prevailed, and he continued his nocturnal wanderings about Kostopchin and its environs. He kept near the western front of the house, urged on to do so from some vague feeling which he could in no wise account for. One evening as he was making his accustomed tour of inspection, the wail of a child struck upon his ear. He bent down his head and eagerly listened; again he heard the same faint sounds, and in them he fancied he recognized the accents of his dear little Katrina. Hurrying up to one of the ground-floor windows, from which a dim light streamed, he pressed his face against the pane, and looked steadily in. A horrible sight presented itself to his gaze. By the faint light of a shaded lamp, he saw Katrina stretched upon the ground; but her wailing had now ceased, for a shawl had been tied across her little mouth. Over her was bending a hideous shape, which seemed to be clothed in some white and shaggy covering. Katrina lay perfectly motionless, and the hands of the figure were engaged in hastily removing the garments from the child's breast. The task was soon effected; then there was a bright gleam of steel and the head of the thing bent closely down to the child's bosom.

With a yell of apprehension, the old man dashed in the window frame, and, drawing the cross from his breast, sprang boldly into the room. The creature sprang to its feet, and the white fur cloak falling from its head and shoulders disclosed the pallid features of Ravina, a short, broad knife in her hand, and her lips discoloured with blood.

"Vile sorceress!" cried Michal, dashing forward and raising Katrina in his arms. "What hellish work are you about?"

Ravina's eyes gleamed fiercely upon the old man, who had interfered between her and her prey. She raised her dagger, and was about to spring in upon him, when she caught sight of the cross in his extended hand. With a low cry, she dropped the knife, and, staggering back a few paces, wailed out, "I could not help it; I liked the child well enough, but I was so hungry."

Michal paid little heed to her words, for he was busily engaged in examining the fainting child, whose head was resting helplessly on his shoulder. There was a wound over the left breast, from which the blood was flowing; but the injury appeared slight, and not likely to prove fatal. As soon as he had satisfied himself on this point, he turned to the woman, who was crouching before the cross as a wild beast shrinks before the whip of a tamer.

"I am going to remove the child," said he, slowly. "Dare you to mention a word of what I have done or whither she has gone, and I will rouse the village. Do you know what will happen then? Why, every peasant in the place will hurry here with a lighted brand in his hand to consume this accursed house and the unnatural dwellers in it. Keep silent, and I leave you to your unhallowed work. I will no longer seek to preserve Paul Sergevitch, who has given himself over to the powers of darkness by taking a demon to his bosom."

Ravina listened to him as if she scarcely comprehended him; but, as the old man retreated to the window with his helpless burden, she followed him step by step; and as he turned to cast one glance at the shattered window, he saw the woman's pale face and bloodstained lips glued against an unbroken pane, with a wild look of unsatiated appetite in her eyes.

Next morning the house of Kostopchin was filled with terror and surprise, for Katrina, the idol of her father's heart, had disappeared, and no signs of her could be discovered. Every effort was made, the woods and fields in the neighbourhood were thoroughly searched; but it was at last concluded that robbers had carried off the child for the sake of the ransom that they might be able to extract from the father. This seemed the more likely as one of the windows in the fair stranger's room bore marks of violence, and she declared that, being alarmed by the sound of crashing glass, she had risen and confronted a man who was endeavouring to enter her apartment, but who, on perceiving her, turned and fled away with the utmost precipitation.

Paul Sergevitch did not display so much anxiety as

might have been expected from him, considering the devotion which he had ever evinced for the lost Katrina, for his whole soul was wrapped up in one mad, absorbing passion for the fair woman who had so strangely crossed his life. He certainly directed the search, and gave all the necessary orders; but he did so in a listless and half-hearted manner, and hastened back to Kostopchin as speedily as he could, as though fearing to be absent for any length of time from the casket in which his new treasure was enshrined. Not so Alexis; he was almost frantic at the loss of his sister, and accompanied the search daily until his little legs grew weary, and he had to be carried on the shoulders of a sturdy *moujik*. His treasured brass-mounted pistol was now more than ever his constant companion; and when he met the fair woman who had cast a spell upon his father, his face would flush, and he would grind his teeth in impotent rage.

The day upon which all search ceased, Ravina glided into the room where she knew she would find Paul awaiting her. She was fully an hour before her usual time, and the lord of Kostopchin started to his feet in surprise.

"You are surprised to see me" said she; "but I have only come to pay you a visit for a few minutes. I am convinced that you love me, and could I but relieve a few of the objections that my heart continues to raise, I might be yours."

"Tell me what these scruples are," cried Paul, springing towards her, and seizing her hands in his; "and be sure that I will find means to overcome them."

Even in the midst of all the glow and fervour of anticipated triumph, he could not avoid noticing how icily cold were the fingers that rested in his palm, and how utterly passionless was the pressure with which she slightly returned his enraptured clasp.

"Listen," said she, as she withdrew her hand; "I will take two more hours for consideration. By that time the whole of the house of Kostopchin will be cradled in slumber, then meet me at the old sundial near the yew-tree at the bottom of the garden, and I will give you my reply. Nay, not a word," she added, as he seemed about to remonstrate, "for I tell you that I think it will be a favourable one."

"But why not come back here?" urged he; "there is a hard frost to-night, and——"

"Are you so cold a lover," broke in Ravina, with her accustomed laugh, "to dread the changes of the weather? But not another word; I have spoken."

She glided from the room, but uttered a low cry of rage. She almost fell over Alexis in the corridor.

"Why is that brat not in his bed?" cried she, angrily; "he gave me quite a turn."

"Go to your room, boy," exclaimed his father, harshly, and with a malignant glance at his enemy the child slunk away.

Paul Sergevitch paced up and down the room for the two hours that he had to pass before the hour of meeting. His heart was very heavy, and a vague feeling of disquietude began to creep over him. Twenty times he made up his mind not to keep his appointment, and as often the fascinations of the fair woman compelled him to rescind his resolution. He remembered that he had from childhood disliked that spot by the yew tree, and had always looked upon it as a dreary, uncanny place; and he even now disliked the idea of finding himself there after dark, even with such fair companionship as he had been promised. Counting the minutes, he paced backwards and forwards, as though moved by some concealed machinery. Now and again he glanced at the clock, and at last its deep metallic sound, as it struck the quarter, warned him that he had but little time to lose if he intended to keep his appointment. Throwing on a heavily-furred coat and pulling a travelling cap down over his ears, he opened a side door and sallied out into the grounds. The moon was at its full, and shone coldly down upon the leafless trees, which looked white and ghost-like in its beams. The paths and unkept lawns were now covered with hoar frost, and a keen wind every now and then swept by, which, in spite of his wraps, chilled Paul's blood in his veins. The dark shape of the yew tree soon rose up before him, and in another moment he stood a few paces off, and by its side was standing a slender figure, wrapped in a white, fleecy-looking cloak. It was perfectly motionless, and again a terror of undefined dread passed through every nerve and muscle of Paul Sergevitch's body.

"Ravina!" said he, in faltering accents. "Ravina!"

"Did you take me for a ghost?" answered the fair woman, with her shrill laugh; "no, no. I have not come to that yet. Well, Paul Sergevitch, I have come to give you my answer; are you anxious about it?"

"How can you ask me such a question?" returned he; "do you not know that my whole soul has been aglow with anticipation of what your reply might be. Do not keep me any longer in suspense. Is it yes, or no?"

"Paul Sergevitch," answered the young woman, coming up to him and laying her hands upon his shoulders, and fixing her eyes upon his with that strange weird expression before which he always quailed; "do you really love me, Paul Sergevitch?" asked she.

"Love you!" repeated the lord of Kostopchin; "have I not told you a thousand times how much my whole soul flows out towards you, how I only live and breathe in your presence, and how death at your feet would be more welcome than life without you."

"People often talk of death, and yet little know how near it is to them," answered the fair lady, a grim smile appearing upon her face; "but say, do you give me your whole heart?"

"All I have is yours, Ravina," returned Paul, "name, wealth, and the devoted love of a lifetime."

"But your heart," persisted she, "it is your heart that I want; tell me, Paul, that it is mine and mine only."

"Yes, my heart is yours, dearest Ravina," answered Paul, endeavouring to embrace the fair form in his impassioned grasp; but she glided from him, and then with a quick bound sprang upon him and glared in his face with a look that was absolutely appalling. Her eyes gleamed with a lurid fire, her lips were drawn back, showing her sharp, white teeth, whilst her breath came in sharp, quick gasps.

"I am hungry," she murmured, "oh, so hungry; but now, Paul Sergevitch, your heart is mine."

Her movement was so sudden and unexpected that he stumbled and fell heavily to the ground, the fair woman clinging to him and falling upon his breast. It was then that the full horror of his position came upon Paul Sergevitch, and he saw his fate clearly before him, but a terrible numbness prevented him from using his hands to free himself from the hideous embrace which was paralysing all his muscles. The face that was glaring into his seemed to be undergoing some fearful change, and the features to be losing their semblance of humanity. With a sudden, quick movement, she tore open his garments, and in another movement she had perforated his left breast with a ghastly wound, and, plunging in her delicate hands, tore out his heart and bit at it ravenously. Intent upon her hideous banquet she heeded not the convulsive struggles which agitated the dying form of the lord of Kostopchin. She was too much occupied to notice a diminutive form approaching, sheltering itself behind every tree and bush until it had arrived within ten paces of the scene of the terrible tragedy. Then the moonbeams glistened upon the long shining barrel of a pistol, which a boy was levelling with both hands at the murderess. Then quick and sharp rang out the report, and with a wild shriek, in which there was something beast-like, Ravina leaped from the body of the dead man and staggered away to a thick clump of bushes some ten paces distant. The boy Alexis had heard the appointment that had been made, and dogged his father's footsteps to the trysting-place. After firing the fatal shot his courage deserted him, and he fled backwards to the house, uttering loud shrieks for help. The startled servants were soon in the presence of their slaughtered master, but aid was of no avail, for the lord of Kostopchin had passed away. With fear and trembling the superstitious peasants searched the clump of bushes, and started back in horror as they perceived a huge white wolf, lying stark and dead, with a half-devoured human heart clasped between its forepaws.

* * * * *

No signs of the fair lady who had occupied the apartments in the western side of the house were ever seen again. She had passed away from Kostopchin like an ugly dream, and as the moujiks of the villages sat round their stoves at night they whispered strange stories regarding the fair woman of the forest and the white wolf of Kostopchin. By order of the Czar a surtee was placed in charge of the estate of Kostopchin, and Alexis was ordered to be sent to a military school until he should be old enough to join the army. The meeting between the boy and his sister, whom the faithful Michal, when all danger was at an end, had pronounced from his hiding-place, was most affecting; but it was not until Katrina had been for some time resident at the house of a distant relative at Vitepsk, that she ceased to wake at night and cry out in terror as she again dreamed that she was in the clutches of the white wolf.

THE EYES OF THE PANTHER

I

ONE DOES NOT ALWAYS MARRY WHEN INSANE

A man and a woman—nature had done the grouping—sat on a rustic seat, in the late afternoon. The man was middle-aged, slender, swarthy, with the expression of a poet and the complexion of a pirate—a man at whom one would look again. The woman was young, blonde, graceful with something in her figure and movements suggesting the word "lithe." She was habited in a grey gown with odd brown markings in the texture. She may have been beautiful; one could not readily say, for her eyes denied attention to all else. They were grey-green, long and narrow, with an expression defying analysis. One could only know that they were disquieting. Cleopatra may have had such eyes.

The man and the woman talked.

"Yes," said the woman, "I love you, God knows! But marry you, no. I cannot, will not."

"Irene, you have said that many times, yet always have denied me a reason. I've a right to know, to understand, to feel and prove my fortitude if I have it. Give me a reason."

"For loving you?"

The woman was smiling through her tears and her pallor. That did not stir any sense of humor in the man.

"No; there is no reason for that. A reason for not marrying me. I've a right to know. I must know. I will know!"

He had risen and was standing before her with clenched hands, and on his face a frown—it might have been called a scowl. He looked as if he might attempt to learn by strangling her. She smiled no more—merely sat looking up into his face with a fixed, set regard that was utterly without emotion or sentiment. Yet it had something in it that tamed his resentment and made him shiver.

"You are determined to have my reason?" she asked in a tone that was entirely mechanical—a tone that might have been her look made audible.

"If you please—if I'm not asking too much."

Apparently this lord of creation was yielding some part of his dominion over his co-creature.

"Very well, you shall know: I am insane."

The man started, then looked incredulous and was conscious that he ought to be amused. But again the sense of humor failed him in his need, and despite his disbelief he was profoundly disturbed by that which he did not believe. Between our convictions and our feelings there is no good understanding.

"That is what the physicians would say," the woman continued—"if they knew. I might myself prefer to call it a case of 'possession.' Sit down and hear what I have to say."

The man silently resumed his seat beside her on the rustic bench by the wayside. Over against them on the eastern side of the valley the hills were already sunset-flushed and the stillness all about was of that peculiar quality which foretells the twilight. Something of its mysterious and significant solemnity had imparted itself to the man's mood. In the spiritual, as in the material world, are signs and presages of night. Rarely meeting her look, and whenever he did so conscious of the indefinable dread with which, despite their feline beauty, her eyes always affected him, Jenner Brading listened in silence to the story told by Irene Marlowe. In deference to the reader's possible prejudice against the artless method of an unpractised historian the author ventures to substitute his own version for hers.

II

A ROOM MAY BE TOO NARROW FOR THREE, THOUGH ONE IS OUTSIDE

In a little log house containing a single room sparely and rudely furnished, crouching on the floor against one of the walls, was a woman, clasping to her breast a child. Outside a dense unbroken forest extended for many miles in every direction. This was at night and the room was black dark: no human eye could have discerned the woman and the child. Yet they were observed, narrowly, vigilantly, with never ever even a momentary slackening of attention; and that is the pivotal fact upon which this narrative turns.

Charles Marlowe was of the class, now extinct in this country, of woodmen pioneers—men who found their most acceptable surroundings in sylvan solitudes that stretched along the eastern slope of the Mississippi Valley, from the Great Lakes to the Gulf of Mexico. For more than a hundred years these men pushed ever westward, generation after generation, with rifle and ax, reclaiming from Nature and her savage children here and there an isolated acreage for the plow, no sooner reclaimed than surrendered to their less venturesome but more thrifty successors. At last they burst through the edge of the forest into the open country and vanished as if they had fallen over a cliff. The woodman pioneer is no more; the pioneer of the plains—he whose easy task it was to subdue for occupancy two-thirds of the country in a single generation—is another and inferior creation. With Charles Marlowe in the wilderness, sharing the dangers, hardships and privations of that strange, unprofitable life, were his wife and child, to whom, in the manner of his class, in which the domestic virtues were a religion, he was passionately attached. The woman was still young enough to be comely, new enough to the awful isolation of her lot to be cheerful. By withholding the large capacity for happiness which the simple satisfactions of the forest life could not have filled, Heaven had dealt honorably with her. In her light household tasks, her child, her husband, and her few foolish books she found abundant provision for her needs.

One morning in midsummer Marlowe took down his rifle from the wooden hooks on the wall and signified his intention of getting game.

"We've meat enough," said the wife; "please don't go out today. I dreamed last night, O, such a dreadful thing!

I cannot recollect it, but I'm almost sure that it will come to pass if you go out."

It is painful to confess that Marlowe received this solemn statement with less of gravity than was due to the mysterious nature of the calamity foreshadowed. In truth, he laughed.

"Try to remember," he said. "Maybe you dreamed that Baby had lost the power of speech."

The conjecture was obviously suggested by the fact that Baby, clinging to the fringe of his hunting coat with all her ten pudgy thumbs, was at that moment uttering her sense of the situation in a series of exultant goo-goos inspired by sight of her father's racoon-skin cap.

The woman yielded: lacking the gift of humor she could not hold out against his kindly badinage. So, with a kiss for the mother and a kiss for the child, he left the house and closed the door upon his happiness forever.

At nightfall he had not returned. The woman prepared supper and waited. Then she put Baby to bed and sang softly to her until she slept. By this time the fire on the hearth at which she had cooked supper had burned out and the room was lighted by a single candle. This she afterward placed in the open window as a sign and welcome to the hunter if he should approach from that side. She had thoughtfully closed and barred the door against such wild animals as might prefer it to an open window —of the habits of beasts of prey in entering a house uninvited she was not advised, though with true female prevision she may have considered the possibility of their entrance by way of the chimney. As the night wore on she became not less anxious, but more drowsy, and at last rested her arms upon the bed by the child and her head upon the arms. The candle in the window burned down to the socket, sputtered and flared a moment, and went out unobserved; for the woman slept. And sleeping she dreamed.

In her dreams she sat beside the cradle of a second child. The first one was dead. The father was dead. The home in the forest was lost and the dwelling in which she lived was unfamiliar. There were heavy oaken doors, always closed, and outside the windows, fastened into the thick stone walls, were iron bars, obviously (so she thought) a provision against Indians. All this she noted with an infinite self-pity, but without surprise—an emotion unknown in dreams. The child in the cradle was invisible under its coverlet, which something impelled her to remove. She did so, disclosing the face of a wild animal! In the shock of this dreadful revelation the dreamer awoke, trembling in the darkness of her cabin in the wood.

As the scene of her actual surroundings came slowly back to her she felt for the child that was not a dream, and assured herself by its breathing that all was well with it; nor could she forbear to pass a hand lightly across its face. Then, moved by some impulse for which she probably could not have accounted, she rose and took the sleeping babe in her arms, holding it close against her breast. The head of the child's cot was against the wall to which the woman now turned her back as she stood. Lifting her eyes she saw two bright objects starring the darkness with a reddish-green glow. She took them to be two coals on the hearth, but with her returning sense of direction came the disquieting consciousness that they were not in that quarter of the room, moreover were too high, being nearly at the level of her eyes—of her own eyes. For these were the eyes of a panther.

The beast was at the open window directly opposite and not five paces away. Nothing but those terrible eyes was visible, but in the dreadful tumult of her feelings as the situation disclosed itself to her understanding she somehow knew that the animal was standing on its hinder feet, supporting itself with its paws on the window ledge. That signified a malign interest—not the mere gratification of an indolent curiosity. The consciousness of the attitude was an added horror, accentuating the menace of those awful eyes, in whose steadfast fire her strength and courage were alike consumed. Under their silent questioning she shuddered and turned sick. Her knees failed her, and by degrees, instinctively striving to avoid a sudden movement that might bring the beast upon her, she sank to the floor, crouched against the wall, and tried to shield the babe with her trembling body without withdrawing her gaze from the luminous orbs that were killing her. No thought of her husband came to her in her agony—no hope nor suggestion of rescue or escape. Her capacity for thought and feeling had narrowed to the dimensions of a single emotion—fear of the animal's spring, of the impact of its body, the buffeting of its great arms, the feel of its teeth in her throat, the mangling of her babe. Motionless now and in absolute silence, she awaited her doom, the moments growing to hours, to years, to ages; and still those devilish eyes maintained their watch.

Returning to his cabin late at night with a deer on his shoulders Charles Marlowe tried the door. It did not yield. He knocked; there was no answer. He laid down his deer and went round to the window. As he turned the angle of the building he fancied he heard a sound as of stealthy footfalls and a rustling in the undergrowth of the forest, but they were too slight for certainty, even to his practised ear. Approaching the window, and to his surprise finding it open, he threw his leg over the sill and entered. All was darkness and silence. He groped his way to the fireplace, struck a match, and lit a candle. Then he looked about. Cowering on the floor against a wall was his wife, clasping his child. As he sprang toward her she broke into laughter, long, loud, and mechanical, devoid of gladness and devoid of sense—the laughter that is not out of keeping with the clanking of a chain. Hardly knowing what he did he extended his arms. She laid the babe in them. It was dead—pressed to death in its mother's embrace.

III

THE THEORY OF THE DEFENCE

That is what occurred during a night in a forest, but not all of it did Irene Marlowe relate to Jenner Brading; not all of it was known to her. When she had concluded the sun was below the horizon and the long summer twilight had begun to deepen in the hollows of the land. For some moments Brading was silent, expecting the narrative to be carried forward to some definite connection with the conversation introducing it; but the narrator was as silent as he, her face averted, her hands clasping and unclasping themselves as they lay in her lap, with a singular suggestion of an activity independent of her will.

"It is a sad, a terrible story," said Brading at last, "but I do not understand. You call Charles Marlowe father; that I know. That he is old before his time, broken by some great sorrow, I have seen, or thought I saw. But, pardon me, you said that you—that you—"

"That I am insane," said the girl, without a movement of head or body.

"But, Irene, you say—please, dear, do not look away from me—you say that the child was dead, not demented."

"Yes, that one—I am the second. I was born three months after that night, my mother being mercifully permitted to lay down her life in giving me mine."

Brading was again silent; he was a trifle dazed and could not at once think of the right thing to say. Her face was still turned away. In his embarrassment he reached impulsively toward the hands that lay closing and unclosing in her lap, but something—he could not have said what—restrained him. He then remembered vaguely that he had never altogether cared to take her hand.

"Is it likely," she resumed, "that a person born under such circumstances is like others—is what you call sane?"

Brading did not reply; he was preoccupied with a new thought that was taking shape in his mind—what a scientist would have called an hypothesis; a detective, a theory. It might throw an added light, albeit a lurid one, upon such doubt of her sanity as her own assertion had not dispelled.

The country was still new and, outside the villages, sparsely populated. The professional hunter was still a familiar figure, and among his trophies were heads and pelts of the larger kinds of game. Tales variously credible of nocturnal meetings with savage animals in lonely roads were sometimes current, passed through the customary stages of growth and decay, and were forgotten. A recent addition to these popular apocrypha, originating apparently by spontaneous generation in several households, was of a panther which had frightened some of their members by looking in at windows by night. The yarn had caused its little ripple of excitement—had even attained to the distinction of a place in the local newspaper, but Brading had given it no attention. Its likeness to the story to which he had just listened now impressed him as perhaps more than accidental. Was it not possible that the one story had suggested the other—that finding congenial conditions in a morbid mind and a fertile fancy, it had grown to the tragic tale that he had heard?

Brading recalled certain circumstances of the girl's history and disposition, of which, with love's incuriosity, he had hitherto been heedless—such as her solitary life with her father, at whose house no one, apparently, was an acceptable visitor and her strange fear of the night, by which those who knew her best accounted for her never being seen after dark. Surely in such a mind imagination once kindled might burn with a lawless flame, penetrating and enveloping the entire structure. That she was mad, though the conviction gave him the acutest pain, he could no longer doubt; she had only mistaken an effect of her mental disorder for its cause, bringing into imaginary relation with her own personality the vagaries of the local myth-makers. With some vague intention of testing his new "theory," and no very definite notion of how to set about it, he said gravely, but with hesitation:

"Irene, dear, tell me—I beg you will not take offence, but tell me—"

"I have told you," she interrupted, speaking with a passionate earnestness that he had not known her to show— "I have already told you that we cannot marry; is anything else worth saying?"

Before he could stop her she had sprung from her seat and without another word or look was gliding away among the trees toward her father's house. Brading had risen to detain her; he stood watching her in silence until she had vanished in the gloom. Suddenly he started as if he had been shot; his face took on an expression of amazement and alarm; in one of the black shadows into which she had disappeared he had caught a quick, brief glimpse of shining eyes. For an instant he was dazed and irresolute; and then he dashed into the wood after her, shouting: "Irene, Irene, look out! The panther! The panther!"

In a moment he had passed through the fringe of forest into open ground and saw the girl's grey skirt vanishing into her father's door. No panther was visible.

IV

AN APPEAL TO THE CONSCIENCE OF GOD

Jenner Brading, attorney at law, lived in a cottage at the edge of the town. Directly behind the dwelling was the forest. Being a bachelor, and therefore, by the Draconian moral code of the time and place denied the services of the only species of domestic servant known thereabout, the "hired girl," he boarded at the village hotel, where also was his office. The woodside cottage was merely a lodging maintained—at no great cost, to be sure—as an evidence of prosperity and respectability. It would hardly do for one to whom the local newspaper had pointed with pride as "the foremost jurist of his time" to be "homeless," albeit he may sometimes have suspected that the words "home" and "house" were not strictly synonymous. Indeed, his consciousness of the disparity and his will to harmonize it were matters of logical inference, for it was generally reported that soon after the cottage was built its owner had made a futile venture in the direction of marriage—had, in truth, gone so far as to be rejected by the beautiful but eccentric daughter of Old Man Marlowe, the recluse. This was publicly believed because he had told it himself and she had not—a reversal of the usual order of things which could hardly fail to carry conviction.

Brading's bedroom was at the rear of the house, with a single window facing the forest. One night he was awakened by a noise at that window; he could hardly have said what it was like. With a little thrill of the nerves he sat up in bed and laid hold of the revolver which, with a forethought most commendable in one addicted to the habit of sleeping on the ground floor with an open window, he had put under his pillow. The room was in absolute darkness, but being unterrified he knew where to direct his eyes, and there he held them, awaiting in silence what further might occur. He could now dimly discern the aperture—a square of lighter black. Suddenly there appeared at its lower edge two gleaming eyes that burned with a malignant lustre inexpressibly terrible! Brading's heart gave a great jump, then seemed to stand still. A chill passed along his spine and through his hair; he felt the blood forsake his cheeks. He could not have cried out—not to save his life; but being a man of courage he would not, to save his life, have done so if he had been able. Some trepidation his coward body might feel, but his spirit was of sterner stuff. Slowly the shining eyes rose with a steady motion that seemed an approach, and slowly rose Brading's right hand, holding the pistol. He fired!

Blinded by the flash and stunned by the report, Brading nevertheless heard, or fancied that he heard, the wild, high scream of the panther, so human in sound, so devilish in suggestion. Leaping from the bed he hastily clothed himself and, pistol in hand, sprang from the door, meeting two or three men who came running up from the road. A brief explanation was followed by a cautious search of the house. The grass was wet with dew; beneath the window it had been trodden and partly levelled for a wide space, from which a devious trail, visible in the light of a lantern, led away into the bushes. One of the men stumbled and fell upon his hands, which as he rose and rubbed them together were slippery. On examination they were seen to be red with blood.

An encounter, unarmed, with a wounded panther was not agreeable to their taste; all but Brading turned back. He, with lantern and pistol, pushed courageously forward into the wood. Passing through a difficult undergrowth he came into a small opening, and there his courage had its reward, for there he found the body of his victim. But it was no panther. What it was is told, even to this day, upon a weather-worn headstone in the village churchyard, and for many years was attested daily at the graveside by the bent figure and sorrow-seamed face of Old Man Marlowe, to whose soul, and to the soul of his strange, unhappy child, peace. Peace and reparation.

CLEMENCE HOUSMAN

THE WERE-WOLF

The great farm hall was ablaze with the fire-light, and noisy with laughter and talk and many-sounding work. None could be idle but the very young and the very old—little Rol, who was hugging a puppy, and old Trella, whose palsied hand fumbled over her knitting. The early evening had closed in, and the farm servants had come in from the outdoor work and assembled in the ample hall, which had space for scores of workers. Several of the men were engaged in carving, and to these were yielded the best place and light; others made or repaired fishing tackle and harness, and a great seine net occupied three pairs of hands. Of the women, most were sorting and mixing eider feather and chopping straw of the same. Looms were there, though not in present use, but three wheels whirred emulously, and the finest and swiftest thread of the three ran between the fingers of the house mistress. Near her were some children, busy, too, plaiting wicks for candles and lamps. Each group of workers had a lamp in its centre, and those farthest from the fire had extra warmth from two braziers filled with glowing wood embers, replenished now and again from the generous hearth. But the flicker of the great fire was manifest to remotest corners, and prevailed beyond the limits of the lesser lights.

Little Rol grew tired of his puppy, dropped it incontinently, and made an onslaught on Tyr, the old wolf-hound, who basked, dozing, whimpering and twitching in his hunting dreams. Prone went Rol beside Tyr, his young arms round the shaggy neck, his curls against the black jowl. Tyr gave a perfunctory lick, and stretched with a sleepy sigh. Rol growled and rolled and shoved invitingly, but could gain nothing from the old dog but placid toleration and a half-observant blink. "Take that, then!" said

Rol, indignant at this ignoring of his advances, and sent the puppy sprawling against the dignity that disdained him as playmate. The dog took no notice, and the child wandered off to find amusement elsewhere.

The baskets of white eider feathers caught his eye far off in a distant corner. He slipped under the table and crept along on all-fours, the ordinary commonplace custom of walking down a room upright not being to his fancy. When close to the women he lay still for a moment watching, with his elbows on the floor and his chin in his palms. One of the women seeing him nodded and smiled, and presently he crept out behind her skirts and passed, hardly noticed, from one to another, till he found opportunity to possess himself of a large handful of feathers. With these he traversed the length of the room, under the table again, and emerged near the spinners. At the feet of the youngest he curled himself round, sheltered by her knees from the observation of the others, and disarmed her of interference by secretly displaying his handful with a confiding smile. A dubious nod satisfied him, and presently he proceeded with the play he had planned. He took a tuft of the white down, and gently shook it free of his fingers close to the whirl of the wheel. The wind of the swift motion took it, spun it round and round in widening circles, till it floated above like a slow white moth. Little Rol's eyes danced, and the row of his small teeth shone in a silent laugh of delight. Another and another of the white tufts was sent whirling round like a winged thing in a spider's web, and floating clear at last. Presently the handful failed.

Rol sprawled forward to survey the room and contemplate another journey under the table. His shoulder thrusting forward checked the wheel for an instant; he shifted hastily. The wheel flew on with a jerk and the thread snapped. "Naughty Rol!" said the girl. The swiftest wheel stopped also, and the house mistress, Rol's aunt, leaned forward and sighting the low curly head, gave a warning against mischief, and sent him off to old Trella's corner.

Rol obeyed, and after a discreet period of obedience, sidled out again down the length of the room farthest from his aunt's eye. As he slipped in among the men, they looked up to see that their tools might be, as far as possible, out of reach of Rol's hands, and close to their own. Nevertheless, before long he managed to secure a fine chisel and take off its point on the leg of the table. The carver's strong objections to this disconcerted Rol, who for five minutes thereafter effaced himself under the table.

During this seclusion he contemplated the many pairs of legs that surrounded him and almost shut out the light of the fire. How very odd some of the legs were; some were curved where they should be straight; some were straight where they should be curved; and as Rol said to himself, "They all seemed screwed on differently." Some were tucked away modestly, under the benches, others were thrust far out under the table, encroaching on Rol's own particular domain. He stretched out his own short legs and regarded them critically, and, after comparison, favourably. Why were not all legs made like his, or like his?

These legs approved by Rol were a little apart from the rest. He crawled opposite and again made comparison. His face grew quite solemn as he thought of the innumerable days to come before his legs could be as long and strong. He hoped they would be just like those, his models, as straight as to bone, as curved as to muscle.

A few moments later Sweyn of the long legs felt a small hand caressing his foot, and looking down met the upturned eyes of his little cousin Rol. Lying on his back, still softly patting and stroking the young man's foot, the child was quiet and happy for a good while. He watched the movements of the strong, deft hands and the shifting of the bright tools. Now and then minute chips of wood puffed off by Sweyn fell down upon his face. At last he raised himself very gently, lest a jog should wake impatience in the carver, and crossing his own legs round Sweyn's ankle, clasping with his arms too, laid his head against the knee. Such an act is evidence of a child's most wonderful hero worship. Quite content was Rol, and more than content when Sweyn paused a minute to joke, and pat his head and pull his curls. Quiet he remained, as long as quiescence is possible to limbs young as his.

Sweyn forgot he was near, hardly noticed when his leg was gently released, and never saw the stealthy abstraction of one of his tools.

Ten minutes thereafter was a lamentable wail from low on the floor, rising to the full pitch of Rol's healthy lungs, for his hand was gashed across and the copious bleeding terrified him. Then there was soothing and comforting, washing and binding, and a modicum of scolding, till the loud outcry sank into occasional sobs, and the child, tear-stained and subdued, was returned to the chimney-corner, where Trella nodded.

In the reaction after pain and fright, Rol found that the quiet of that fire-lit corner was to his mind. Tyr, too, disdained him no longer, but, roused by his sobs, showed all the concern and sympathy that a dog can by licking and wistful watching. A little shame weighed also upon his spirits. He wished he had not cried quite so much. He remembered how once Sweyn had come home with his arm torn down from the shoulder, and a dead bear; and how he had never winced nor said a word, though his lips turned white with pain. Poor little Rol gave an extra sighing sob over his own faint-hearted shortcomings.

The light and motion of the great fire began to tell strange stories to the child, and the wind in the chimney roared a corroborative note now and then. The great black mouth of the chimney, impending high over the hearth, received the murky coils of smoke and brightness of aspiring sparks as into a mysterious gulf, and beyond, in the high darkness, were muttering and wailing and strange doings, so that sometimes the smoke rushed back in panic, and curled out and up to the roof, and condensed itself to invisibility among the rafters. And then the wind would rage after its lost prey, rattling and shrieking at window and door.

In a lull, after one such loud gust, Rol lifted his head in surprise and listened. A lull had also come on the babble of talk, and thus could be heard with strange distinctness a sound without the door—the sound of a child's voice, a child's hands. "Open, open; let me in!" piped the little voice from low down, lower than the handle, and the latch rattled as though a tip-toe child reached up to it, and soft small knocks were struck. One near the door sprang up and opened it. "No one is here," he said. Tyr lifted his head and gave utterance to a howl, loud, prolonged, most dismal.

Sweyn, not able to believe that his ears had deceived him, got up and went to the door. It was a dark night; the clouds were heavy with snow, that had fallen fitfully when the wind lulled. Untrodden snow lay up to the porch; there was no sight nor sound of any human being. Sweyn strained his eyes far and near, only to see dark sky, pure snow, and a line of black fir trees on a hill brow, bowing down before the wind. "It must have been the wind," he said, and closed the door.

Many faces looked scared. The sound of a child's voice had been so distinct—and the words, "Open, open; let me in!" The wind might creak the wood or rattle the latch, but could not speak with a child's voice; nor knock with the soft plain blows that a plump fist gives. And the strange unusual howl of the wolf-hound was an omen to be feared, be the rest what it might. Strange things were said by one and other, till the rebuke of the house mistress quelled them into far-off whispers. For a time after there was uneasiness, constraint, and silence; then the chill fear thawed by degrees, and the babble of talk flowed on again.

Yet half an hour later a very slight noise outside the door sufficed to arrest every hand, every tongue. Every head was raised, every eye fixed in one direction. "It is Christian; he is late," said Sweyn.

No, no; this is a feeble shuffle, not a young man's tread. With the sound of uncertain feet came the hard tap tap of a stick against the door, and the high-pitched voice of age, "Open, open; let me in!" Again Tyr flung up his head in a long doleful howl.

Before the echo of the tapping stick and the high voice had fairly died away, Sweyn had sprung across to the door and flung it wide. "No one again," he said in a steady voice, though his eyes looked startled as he stared out. He saw the lonely expanse of snow, the clouds swagging low, and between the two the line of dark fir trees bowing in the wind. He closed the door without word of comment, and recrossed the room.

A score of blanched faces were turned to him as though he were the solver of the enigma. He could not be unconscious of this mute eye-questioning, and it disturbed his resolute air of composure. He hesitated, glanced toward his mother, the house mistress, then back at the frightened folk, and gravely, before them all, made the sign of the cross. There was a flutter of hands as the sign was repeated by all, and the dead silence was stirred as by a huge sigh, for the held breath of many was freed as if the sign gave magic relief.

Even the house mistress was perturbed. She left her wheel and crossed the room to her son, and spoke with him for a moment in a low tone that none could overhear. But a moment later her voice was high-pitched and loud, so that all might benefit by her rebuke of the "heathen chatter" of one of the girls. Perhaps she essayed to silence thus her own misgivings and forebodings.

No other voice dared speak now with its natural fullness. Low tones made intermittent murmurs, and now and then silence drifted over the whole room. The handling of tools was as noiseless as might be, and suspended on the instant the door rattled in a gust of wind. After a time Sweyn left his work, joined the group nearest the door, and loitered there on the pretence of giving advice and help to the unskillful

A man's tread was heard outside in the porch, "Christian!" said Sewyn and his mother simultaneously, he confidently, she authoritatively, to set the checked wheels going again. But Tyr flung up his head with an appalling howl.

"Open, open; let me in!"

It was a man's voice, and the door shook and rattled as a man's strength beat against it. Sweyn could feel the planks quivering, as on the instant his hand was upon the door, flinging it open, to face the blank porch, and beyond only snow and sky, and firs aslant in the wind.

He stood for a long minute with the open door in his hand. The bitter wind swept in with its icy chill, but a deadlier chill of fear came swifter, and seemed to freeze the beating of hearts. Sweyn snatched up a great bearskin cloak.

122

"Sweyn, where are you going?"

"No farther than the porch, mother," and he stepped out and closed the door.

He wrapped himself in the heavy fur, and leaning against the most sheltered wall of the porch, steeled his nerves to face the devil and all his works. No sound of voices came from within; but he could hear the crackle and roar of the fire.

It was bitterly cold. His feet grew numb, but he forebore stamping them into warmth lest the sound should strike panic within; nor would he leave the porch, nor print a foot-mark on the untrodden snow that testified conclusively to no human voices and hands having approached the door since snow fell two hours or more ago. "When the wind drops there will be more snow," thought Sweyn.

For the best part of an hour he kept his watch, and saw no living thing—heard no unwonted sound. "I will freeze here no longer," he muttered, and re-entered.

One woman gave a half-suppressed scream as his hand was laid on the latch, and then a gasp of relief as he came in. No one questioned him, only his mother said, in a tone of forced unconcern, "Could you not see Christian coming?" as though she were made anxious only by the absence of her younger son. Hardly had Sweyn stamped near to the fire than clear knocking was heard at the door. Tyr leaped from the hearth—his eyes red as the fire—his fangs showing white in the black jowl—his neck ridged and bristling; and overleaping Rol, ramped at the door, barking furiously.

Outside the door a clear, mellow voice was calling. Tyr's bark made the words undistinguishable.

No one offered to stir toward the door before Sweyn.

He stalked down the room resolutely, lifted the latch, and swung back the door.

A white-robed woman glided in.

No wraith! Living—beautiful—young.

Tyr leapt upon her.

Lithely she balked the sharp fangs with folds of her long fur robe, and snatching from her girdle a small two-edged axe, whirled it up for a blow of defence.

Sweyn caught the dog by the collar and dragged him off, yelling and struggling. The stranger stood in the doorway motionless, one foot set forward, one arm flung up, till the house mistress hurried down the room, and Sweyn, relinquishing to others the furious Tyr, turned again to close the door and offer excuses for so fierce a greeting. Then she lowered her arm, slung the axe in its place at her waist, loosened the furs about her face, and shook over her shoulder the long white robe—all, as it were, with the sway of one movement.

She was a maiden, tall and very fair. The fashion of her dress was strange—half masculine, yet not unwomanly. A fine fur tunic, reaching but little below the knee, was all the skirt she wore; below were the cross-bound shoes and leggings that a hunter wears. A white fur cap was set low upon the brows, and from its edge strips of fur fell lappet-wise about her shoulders, two of which at her entrance had been drawn forward and crossed about her throat, but now, loosened and thrust back, left unhidden long plaits of hair that lay forward on shoulder and breast, down to the ivory-studded girdle where the axe gleamed.

Sweyn and his mother led the stranger to the hearth without question or sign of curiosity, till she voluntarily told her tale of a long journey to distant kindred, a promised guide unmet, and signals and landmarks mistaken.

"Alone!" exclaimed Sweyn, in astonishment. "Have you journeyed thus far—a hundred leagues—alone?"

She answered "Yes," with a little smile.

"Over the hills and the wastes! Why, the folk there are savage and wild as beasts."

She dropped her hand upon her axe with a laugh of scorn.

"I fear neither man nor beast; some few fear me," and then she told strange tales of fierce attack and defence, and of the bold, free huntress life she had led.

Her words came a little slowly and deliberately, as though she spoke in a scarce familiar tongue; now and then she hesitated, and stopped in a phrase, as if for lack of some word.

She became the centre of a group of listeners. The interest she excited dissipated, in some degree, the dread inspired by the mysterious voices. There was nothing ominous about this bright, fair reality, though her aspect was strange.

Little Rol crept near, staring at the stranger with all his might. Unnoticed, he softly stroked and patted a corner of her soft white robe that reached to the floor in ample folds. He laid his cheek against it caressingly, and then edged close up to her knees.

"What is your name?" he asked.

The stranger's smile and ready answer, as she looked down, saved Rol from the rebuke merited by his question.

"My real name," she said, "would be uncouth to your ears and tongue. The folk of this country have given me another name, and from this"—she laid her hand on the fur robe—"they call me 'White Fell.'"

Little Rol repeated it to himself, stroking and patting as before. "White Fell, White Fell."

The fair face and soft beautiful dress pleased Rol. He knelt up with his eyes on her face and an air of uncertain determination, like a robin's on a doorstep, and plumped his elbows into her lap with a little gasp at his own audacity.

"Rol!" exclaimed his aunt; but, "Oh, let him!" said White Fell, smiling and stroking his head; and Rol stayed.

He advanced farther, and, panting at his own adventurousness, in the face of his aunt's authority, climbed up on to her knees. Her welcoming arms hindered any protest. He nestled happily, fingering the axe head, the ivory studs in her girdle, the ivory clasp at her throat, the plaits of fair hair; rubbing his head against the softness of her fur-clad shoulder, with a child's confidence in the kindness of beauty.

White Fell had not uncovered her head, only knotted the pendant fur loosely behind her neck. Rol reached up his hand toward it, whispering her name to himself, "White Fell, White Fell," then slid his arms round her neck, and kissed her—once—twice. She laughed delightedly and kissed him again.

"The child plagues you?" said Sweyn.

"No, indeed," she answered, with an earnestness so intense as to seem disproportionate to the occasion.

Rol settled himself again on her lap and began to unwind the bandage bound round his hand. He paused a little when he saw where the blood had soaked through, then went on till his hand was bare and the cut displayed, gaping and long, though only skin-deep. He held it up toward White Fell, desirous of her pity and sympathy.

At sight of it and the blood-stained linen she drew in her breath suddenly, clasped Rol to her—hard, hard—till he began to struggle. Her face was hidden behind the boy, so that none could see its expression. It had lighted up with a most awful glee.

Afar, beyond the fir grove, beyond the low hill behind, the absent Christian was hastening his return. From daybreak he had been afoot, carrying summons to a bear hunt to all the best hunters of the farms and hamlets that lay within a radius of twelve miles. Nevertheless, having been detained till a late hour, he now broke into a run, going with a long smooth stride that fast made the miles diminish.

He entered the midnight blackness of the fir grove with scarcely slackened pace, though the path was invisible, and, passing through into the open again, sighted the farm lying a furlong off down the slope. Then he sprang out freely, and almost on the instant gave one great sideways leap and stood still. There in the snow was the track of a great wolf.

His hands went to his knife, his only weapon. He stooped, knelt down, to bring his eyes to the level of a beast, and peered about, his teeth set, his heart beating—a little harder than the pace of his running had set it. A solitary wolf, nearly always savage and of large size, is a formidable beast that will not hesitate to attack a single man. This wolf track was the largest Christian had ever seen, and as far as he could judge, recently made. It led from under the fir-trees down the slope. Well for him, he thought, was the delay that had so vexed him before; well for him that he had not passed through the dark fir grove when that danger of jaws lurked there. Going warily, he followed the track.

It led down the slope, across a broad ice-bound stream,

along the level beyond, leading toward the farm. A less sure knowledge than Christian's might have doubted of it being a wolf track, and guessed it to be made by Tyr or some large dog; but he was sure, and knew better than to mistake between a wolf's and a dog's footmark.

Straight on—straight on toward the farm.

Christian grew surprised and anxious at a prowling wolf daring so near. He drew his knife and pressed on, more hastily, more keenly eyed. Oh, that Tyr were with him!

Straight on, straight on, even to the very door, where the snow failed. His heart seemed to give a great leap and then stop. There the track ended.

Nothing lurked in the porch, and there was no sign of return. The firs stood straight against the sky, the clouds lay low; for the wind had fallen and a few snowflakes came drifting down. In a horror of surprise Christian stood dazed a moment; then he lifted the latch and went in. His glance took in all the old familiar forms and faces, and with them that of the stranger, fur-clad and beautiful. The awful truth flashed upon him. He knew what she was.

Only a few were startled by the rattle of the latch as he entered. The room was filled with bustle and movement, for it was the supper hour, and all tools were being put aside and trestles and tables shifted. Christian had no knowledge of what he said and did; he moved and spoke mechanically, half thinking that soon he must awake from this horrible dream. Sweyn and his mother supposed him to be cold and dead-tired, and spared all unnecessary questions. And he found himself seated beside the hearth, opposite that dreadful Thing that looked like a beautiful girl, watching her every movement, curdling with horror to see her fondle Rol.

Sweyn stood near them both, intent upon White Fell also, but how differently! She seemed unconscious of the gaze of both—neither aware of the chill dread in the eyes of Christian, nor of Sweyn's warm admiration.

These two brothers, who were twins, contrasted greatly, despite their striking likeness. They were alike in regular profile, fair brown hair, and deep blue eyes; but Sweyn's features were perfect as a young god's, while Christian's showed faulty details. Thus, the line of his mouth was set too straight, the eyes shelved too deeply back, and the contour of the face flowed in less generous curves than Sweyn's. Their height was the same, but Christian was too slender for perfect proportion, while Sweyn's well-knit frame, broad shoulders and muscular arms made him pre-eminent for manly beauty as well as for strength. As a hunter Sweyn was without rival; as a fisher without rival. All the countryside acknowledged him to be the best wrestler, rider, dancer, singer. Only in speed could he be surpassed, and in that only by his younger brother. All others Sweyn could distance fairly; but Christian could out-run him easily. Ay, he could keep pace with Sweyn's most breathless burst, and laugh and talk the while. Christian took little pride in his fleetness of foot, counting a man's legs to be the least worthy of his limbs. He had no envy of his brother's athletic superiority, though to several feats he had made a moderate second. He loved as only a twin can love—proud of all that Sweyn did, content with all that Sweyn was, humbly content also that his own great love should not be so exceedingly returned, since he knew himself to be so far less loveworthy.

Christian dared not, in the midst of women and children, launch the horror that he knew into words. He waited to consult his brother; but Sweyn did not, or would not, notice the signal he made, and kept his face always turned toward White Fell. Christian drew away from the hearth, unable to remain passive with that dread upon him.

"Where is Tyr?" he said, suddenly. Then catching sight of the dog in a distant corner, "Why is he chained there?"

"He flew at the stranger," one answered.

Christian's eyes glowed. "Yes?" he said interrogatively, and, rising, went without a word to the corner where Tyr was chained. The dog rose up to meet him, as piteous and indignant as a dumb beast can be. He stroked the black head. "Good Tyr! Brave dog!"

They knew—they only—and the man and the dumb dog had comfort of each other.

Christian's eyes turned again toward White Fell. Tyr's also, and he strained against the length of the chain. Christian's hand lay on the dog's neck, and he felt it ridge and bristle with the quivering of impotent fury. Then he began to quiver in like manner, with a fury born of reason, not instinct; as impotent morally as was Tyr physically. Oh, the woman's form that he dare not touch! Anything but that, and he with Tyr, would be free to kill or be killed.

Then he returned to ask fresh questions.

"How long has the stranger been here?"

"She came about half an hour before you."

"Who opened the door to her?"

"Sweyn. No one else dared."

The tone of the answer was mysterious.

"Why?" queried Christian. "Has anything strange happened? Tell me?"

For answer he was told in a low undertone of the summons at the door, thrice repeated, without human agency; and of Tyr's ominous howls, and of Sweyn's fruitless watch outside.

Christian turned toward his brother in a torment of impatience for a word apart. The board was spread and Sweyn was leading White Fell to the guest's place. This was more awful! She would break bread with them under the roof tree.

He started forward and, touching Sweyn's arm, whispered an urgent entreaty. Sweyn stared, and shook his head in angry impatience.

Thereupon Christian would take no morsel of food.

His opportunity came at last. White Fell questioned of the landmarks of the country, and of one Cairn Hill, which was an appointed meeting place at which she was due that night. The house mistress and Sweyn both exclaimed,

"It is three long miles away," said Sweyn, "with no place for shelter but a wretched hut. Stay with us this night and I will show you the way to-morrow."

White Fell seemed to hesitate. "Three miles," she said, "then I should be able to see or hear a signal."

"I will look out," said Sweyn; "then, if there be no signal, you must not leave us."

He went to the door. Christian silently followed him out.

"Sweyn, do you know what she is?"

Sweyn, surprised at the vehement grasp and low hoarse voice, made answer:

"She? Who? White Fell?"

"Yes."

"She is the most beautiful girl I have ever seen."

"She is a were-wolf."

Sweyn burst out laughing. "Are you mad?" he asked.

"No; here, see for yourself."

Christian drew him out of the porch, pointing to the snow where the footmarks had been—had been, for now they were not. Snow was falling, and every dint was blotted out.

"Well?" asked Sweyn.

"Had you come when I signed to you, you would have seen for yourself."

"Seen what?"

"The footprints of a wolf leading up to the door; none leading away."

It was impossible not to be startled by the tone alone, though it was hardly above a whisper. Sweyn eyed his brother anxiously, but in the darkness could make nothing of his face. Then he laid his hands kindly and reassuringly on Christian's shoulders and felt how he was quivering with excitement and horror.

"One sees strange things," he said, "when the cold has got into the brain behind the eyes; you came in cold and worn out."

"No," interrupted Christian. "I saw the track first on the brow of the slope, and followed it down right here to the door. This is no delusion."

Sweyn in his heart felt positive that it was. Christian was given to day dreams and strange fancies, though never had he been possessed with so mad a notion before.

"Don't you believe me?" said Christian desperately. "You must. I swear it is sane truth. Are you blind? Why, even Tyr knows."

"You will be clearer-headed to-morrow, after a night's rest. Then come, too, if you will, with White Fell, to the Hill Cairn, and, if you have doubts still, watch and follow, and see what footprints she leaves."

Galled by Sweyn's evident contempt, Christian turned abruptly to the door. Sweyn caught him back.

"What now, Christian? What are you going to do?"

"You do not believe me; my mother shall."

Sweyn's grasp tightened. "You shall not tell her," he said, authoritatively.

Customarily Christian was so docile to his brother's mastery that it was now a surprising thing when he wrenched himself free vigorously and said as determinedly as Sweyn: "She shall know." But Sweyn was nearer the door, and would not let him pass.

"There has been scare enough for one night already. If this notion of yours will keep, broach it tomorrow." Christian would not yield.

"Women are so easily scared," pursued Sweyn, "and are ready to believe any folly without proof. Be a man, Christian, and fight this notion of a were-wolf by yourself."

"If you would believe me," began Christian.

"I believe you to be a fool," said Sweyn, losing patience. "Another, who was not your brother, might think you a knave, and guess that you had transformed White Fell into a were-wolf because she smiled more readily on me than on you."

The jest was not without foundation, for the grace of White Fell's bright looks had been bestowed on him—on Christian never a whit. Sweyn's coxcombry was always frank and most forgivable, and not without justifiableness.

"If you want an ally," continued Sweyn, "confide in old Trella. Out of her stores of wisdom—if her memory holds good—she can instruct you in the orthodox manner of tackling a were-wolf. If I remember aright, you should watch the suspected person till midnight, when the beast's form must be resumed, and retained ever after if a human eye sees the change; or, better still, sprinkle hands and feet with holy water, which is certain death! Oh, never fear, but old Trella will be equal to the occasion."

Sweyn's contempt was no longer good-humoured, for he began to feel excessively annoyed at this monstrous doubt of White Fell. But Christian was too deeply distressed to take offence.

"You speak of them as old wives' tales, but if you had

seen the proof I have seen, you would be ready at least to wish them true, if not also to put them to the test."

"Well," said Sweyn, with a laugh that had a little sneer in it, "put them to the test—I will not mind that, if you will only keep your notions to yourself. Now, Christian, give me your word for silence, and we will freeze here no longer."

Christian remained silent.

Sweyn put his hands on his shoulders again and vainly tried to see his face in the darkness.

"We have never quarreled yet, Christian?"

"I have never quarreled," returned the other, aware for the first time that his dictatorial brother had sometimes offered occasions for quarrel, had he been ready to take it.

"Well," said Sweyn, emphatically, "if you speak against White Fell to any other, as tonight you have spoken to me—we shall."

He delivered the words like an ultimatum, turned sharp round and re-entered the house. Christian, more fearful and wretched than before, followed.

"Snow is falling fast—not a single light is to be seen."

White Fell's eyes passed over Christian without apparent notice, and turned bright and shining upon Sweyn.

"Nor any signal to be heard?" she queried. "Did you not hear the sound of a sea-horn?"

"I saw nothing and heard nothing; and signal or no signal, the heavy snow would keep you here perforce."

She smiled her thanks beautifully. And Christian's heart sank like lead with a deadly foreboding, as he noted what a light was kindled in Sweyn's eyes by her smile.

That night, when all others slept, Christian, the weariest of all, watched outside the guest chamber till midnight was past. No sound, not the faintest, could be heard. Could the old tale be true of the midnight change? What was on the other side of the door—a woman or a beast—he would have given his right hand to know. Instinctively he laid his hand on the latch, and drew it softly, though believing that bolts fastened the inner side. The door yielded to his hand; he stood on the threshold; a keen gust of air cut at him. The window stood open; the room was empty.

So Christian would sleep with a somewhat lightened heart.

In the morning there was surprise and conjecture when White Fell's absence was discovered. Christian held his peace; not even to his brother did he say how he knew that she had fled before midnight; and Sweyn, though evidently greatly chagrined, seemed to disdain reference to the subject of Christian's fears.

The elder brother alone joined the bear hunt; Christian found pretext to stay behind. Sweyn, being out of humour, manifested his contempt by uttering not one expostulation.

All that day, and for many a day after, Christian would never go out of sight of his home. Sweyn alone noticed how he manoeuvred for this, and was clearly annoyed by it. White Fell's name was never mentioned between them, though not seldom was it heard in general talk. Hardly a day passed without little Rol asking when White Fell would come again; pretty White Fell, who kissed like a snowflake. And if Sweyn answered, Christian would be quite sure that the light in his eyes, kindled by White Fell's smile, had not yet died out.

Little Rol! Naughty, merry, fair-haired little Rol! A day came when his feet raced over the threshold never to return; when his chatter and laugh were heard no more; when tears of anguish were wept by eyes that never would see his bright head again—never again—living or dead.

He was seen at dusk for the last time, escaping from the house with his puppy, in freakish rebellion against old Trella. Later, when his absence had begun to cause anxiety, his puppy crept back to the farm, cowed, whimpering, and yelping—a pitiful, dumb lump of terror— without intelligence or courage to guide the frightened search.

Rol was never found, nor any trace of him. How he had perished was known only by an awful guess—a wild beast had devoured him.

Christian heard the conjecture, "a wolf," and a horrible certainty flashed upon him that he knew what wolf it was. He tried to declare what he knew, but Sweyn saw him start at the words with white face and struggling lips, and, guessing his purpose, pulled him back and kept him silent, hardly, by his imperious grip and wrathful eyes, and one low whisper. Again Christian yielded to his brother's stronger words and will, and against his own judgment consented to silence.

Repentance came before the new moon—the first of the year—was old. White Fell came again, smiling as she entered as though assured of a glad and kindly welcome; and, in truth, there was only one who saw again her fair face and strange white garb without pleasure. Sweyn's face glowed with delight, while Christian's grew pale and rigid as death. He had given his word to keep silence, but he had not thought that she would dare come again. Silence was impossible—face to face with that Thing—impossible. Irrepressibly he cried out:

"Where is Rol?"

Not a quiver disturbed White Fell's face; she heard, yet remained bright and tranquil—Sweyn's eyes flashed round at his brother dangerously. Among the women some tears fell at the poor child's name, but none caught alarm from its sudden utterance, for the thought of Rol rose naturally. Where was Rol, who had nestled in the stranger's arms, kissing her, and watched for her since, and prattled of her daily?

Christian went out silently. Only one thing there was that he could do, and he must not delay. His horror overmastered any curiosity to hear White Fell's glib excuses and smiling apologies for her strange and uncourteous departure; or her easy tale of the circumstances of her return; or to watch her bearing as she heard the sad tale of little Rol.

The swiftest runner of the countryside had started on his hardest race—little less than three leagues and back, which he reckoned to accomplish in two hours, though the night was moonless and the way rugged. He rushed against the still cold air till it felt like a wind upon his face. The dim homestead sank below the ridges at his back, and fresh ridges of snowlands rose out of the obscure horizon level to drive past him as the stirless air drove, and sink away behind into obscure level again. He took no conscious heed of landmarks, not even when all sign of a path was gone under depths of snow. His will was set to reach

134

his goal with unexampled speed, and thither by instinct his physical forces bore him, without one definite thought to guide.

And the idle brain lay passive, inert, receiving into its vacancy, restless siftings of past sights and sounds; Rol weeping, laughing, playing, coiled in the arms of that dreadful Thing; Tyr—O Tyr!—white fangs in the black jowl; the women who wept on the foolish puppy, precious for the child's last touch; footprints from pinewood to door; the smiling face among furs, of such womanly beauty—smiling—smiling; and Sweyn's face.

"Sweyn, Sweyn, O Sweyn, my brother!"

Sweyn's angry laugh possessed his ear within the sound of the wind of his speed; Sweyn's scorn assailed more quick and keen than the biting cold at his throat. And yet he was unimpressed by any thought of how Sweyn's scorn and anger would rise if this errand were known.

To the younger brother all life was a spiritual mystery, veiled from his clear knowledge by the density of flesh. Since he knew his own body to be linked to the complex and antagonistic forces that constitute one soul, it seemed to him not impossibly strange that one spiritual force should possess divers forms for widely various manifestations. Nor, to him, was it great effort to believe that as pure water washes away all natural foulness, so water holy by consecration must needs cleanse God's world from that supernatural evil Thing. Therefore, faster than ever man's foot had covered those leagues, he sped under the dark, still night, over the waste trackless snow ridges to the faraway church where salvation lay in the holy-water stoop at the door. His faith was as firm as any that wrought miracles in days past, simple as a child's wish, strong as a man's will.

He was hardly missed during these hours, every second of which was by him fulfilled to its utmost extent by extremest effort that sinews and nerves could attain. Within the homestead the while the easy moments went bright with words and looks of unwonted animation, for the kindly hospitable instincts of the inmates were roused into cordial expression of welcome and interest by the grace and beauty of the returned stranger.

But Sweyn was eager and earnest, with more than a host's courteous warmth. The impression that at her first coming had charmed him, that had lived since through memory, deepened now in her actual presence. Sweyn, the matchless among men, acknowledged in this White Fell a spirit high and bold as his own, and a frame so firm and capable that only bulk was lacking for equal strength. Yet the white skin was moulded most smoothly, without such muscular swelling as made his might evident. Such love as his frank self-love could concede was called forth by an ardent admiration for this supreme stranger. More admiration than love was in his passion, and therefore he was free from a lover's hesitancy, and delicate reserve and doubts. Frankly and boldly he courted her favour by looks and tones, and an address that was his by natural ease.

Nor was she a woman to be wooed otherwise. Tender whispers and sighs would never gain her ear; but her eyes would brighten and shine if she heard of a brave feat, and her prompt hand in sympathy fall swiftly on the axe haft and clasp it hard. That movement ever fired Sweyn's admiration anew; he watched for it, strove to elicit it and glowed when it came. Wonderful and beautiful was that wrist, slender and steel-strong; the smooth shapely hand that curved so fast and firm, ready to deal instant death.

Desiring to feel the pressure of these hands, this bold lover schemed with palpable directness, proposing that she should hear how their hunting songs were sung, with a chorus that signalled hands to be clasped. So his splendid voice gave the verses, and, as the chorus was taken up, he claimed her hands, and, even through the easy grip, felt, as he desired, the strength that was latent, and the vigor that quickened the very finger tips, as the song fired her, and her voice was caught out of her by the rhythmic swell and rang clear on the top of the closing surge.

Afterward she sang alone. For contrast, or in the pride of swaying moods by her voice, she chose a mournful song that drifted along in a minor chant, sad as a wind that dirges:

> "Oh, let me go!
> Around spin wreaths of snow;
> The dark earth sleeps below.

"Far up the plain
Moans on a voice of pain:
'Where shall my babe be lain?

"In my white breast
Lay the sweet life to rest!
Lay, where it can be best!

"'Hush! hush!' it cries;
'Tense night is on the skies;
'Two stars are in thine eyes.'

"Come, babe away!
But lie thou till dawn be gray,
Who must be dead by day.

"This cannot last;
But, o'er the sickening blast,
All sorrows shall be past;

"All kings shall be
Low bending at thy knee,
Worshipping life from thee.

"For men long sore
To hope of what's before—
To leave the things of yore.

"Mine, and not thine,
How deep their jewels shine!
Peace laps thy head, not mine!"

Old Trella came tottering from her corner, shaken to additional palsy by an aroused memory. She strained her dim eyes toward the singer, and then bent her head that the one ear yet sensible to sound might avail of every note. At the close, groping forward, she murmured with the high pitched quaver of old age:

"So she sang, my Thora; my last and brightest. What is she like—she, whose voice is like my dead Thora's? Are her eyes blue?"

"Blue as the sky."

"So were my Thora's! Is her hair fair and in plaits to the waist?"

"Even so," answered White Fell herself, and met the advancing hands with her own, and guided them to corroborate her words by touch.

"Like my dead Thora's," repeated the old woman; and then her trembling hands rested on the fur-clad shoulder and she bent forward and kissed the smooth fair face that White Fell upturned, nothing loath to receive and return the caress.

So Christian saw them as he entered.

He stood a moment. After the starless darkness and the icy night air, and the fierce silent two hours' race, his senses reeled on sudden entrance into warmth and light and the cheery hum of voices. A sudden unforeseen anguish assailed him, as now first he entertained the possibility of being overmatched by her wiles and her daring, if at the approach of pure death she should start up at bay, transformed to a terrible beast, and achieve a savage glut at the last. He looked with horror and pity on the harmless helpless folk, so unwitting of outrage to their comfort and security. The dreadful Thing in their midst, that was veiled from their knowledge by womanly beauty, was a centre of pleasant interest. There, before him, signally impressive, was poor old Trella, weakest and feeblest of all, in fond nearness. And a moment might bring about the revelation of a monstrous horror—a ghastly, deadly danger, set loose and at bay, in a circle of girls and women, and careless, defenceless men.

And he alone of the throng prepared!

For one breathing space he faltered, no longer than that, while over him swept the agony of compunction that yet could not make him surrender his purpose.

He alone? Nay, but Tyr also, and he crossed to the dumb sole sharer of his knowledge.

So timeless is thought that a few seconds only lay between his lifting of the latch and his loosening of Tyr's collar; but in those few seconds succeeding his first glance, as lightning-swift had been the impulses of others, their motion as quick and sure. Sweyn's vigilant eye had darted upon him, and instantly his every fibre was alert with hostile instinct; and half divining, half incredulous, of Christian's object in stooping to Tyr, he came hastily, wary, wrathful, resolute to oppose the malice of his wild-eyed brother.

But beyond Sweyn rose White Fell, blanching white as her furs, and with eyes grown fierce and wild. She leapt down the room to the door, whirling her long robe closely to her. "Hark!" she panted. "The signal horn! Hark, I must go!" as she snatched at the latch to be out and away.

For one precious moment Christian had hesitated on the half loosened collar; for, except the womanly form were exchanged for the bestial, Tyr's jaws would gnash to rags his honour of manhood. He heard her voice, and turned— too late.

As she tugged at the door, he sprang across grasping his flask, but Sweyn dashed between and caught him back irresistibly, so that a most frantic effort only availed to wrench one arm free. With that, on the impulse of sheer despair, he cast at her with all his force. The door swung behind her, and the flask flew into fragments against it. Then, as Sweyn's grasp slackened, and he met the questioning astonishment of surrounding faces, with a hoarse inarticulate cry: "God help us all!" he said; "she is a were-wolf!"

Sweyn turned upon him, "Liar, coward!" and his hands gripped his brother's throat with deadly force as though the spoken word could be killed so, and, as Christian struggled, lifted him clear off his feet and flung him crashing backward. So furious was he that, as his brother lay motionless, he stirred him roughly with his foot, till their mother came between, crying "Shame!" and yet then he stood by, his teeth set, his brows knit, his hands clenched, ready to enforce silence again violently, as Christian rose, staggering and bewildered.

But utter silence and submission was more than he expected, and turned his anger into contempt for one so easily cowed and held in subjection by mere force. "He is mad!" he said, turning on his heel as he spoke, so that he lost his mother's look of pained reproach at this sudden free utterance of what was a lurking dread within her.

Christian was too spent for the effort of speech. His hard drawn breath laboured in great sobs; his limbs were powerless and unstrung in utter relax after hard service. His failure in this endeavour induced a stupor of misery and despair. In addition was the wretched humiliation of open violence and strife with his brother, and the distress of hearing misjudging contempt expressed without reserve, for he was aware that Sweyn had turned to allay the scared excitement half by imperious mastery, half by explanation and argument that showed painful disregard of brotherly consideration.

Sweyn the while was observant of his brother, despite the continual check of finding, turn and glance where he would, Christian's eyes always upon him, with a strange look of helpless distress, discomposing enough to the angry aggressor. "Like a beaten dog!" he said to himself, rallying contempt to withstand compunction. Observation set him wondering on Christian's exhausted condition. The heavy laboring breath and the slack, inert fall of the limbs told surely of unusual and prolonged exertion. And then why had close upon two hours' absence been followed by manifestly hostile behavior toward White Fell? Suddenly, the fragments of the flask giving a clue, he guessed all, and faced about to stare at his brother in amaze. He forgot that the motive scheme was against White Fell, demanding derision and resentment from him; that was swept out of remembrance by astonishment and admiration for the feat of speed and endurance.

That night Sweyn and his mother talked long and late together, shaping into certainty the suspicion that Christian's mind had lost its balance, and discussing the evident cause. For Sweyn, declaring his own love for White Fell, suggested that his unfortunate brother with a like passion—they being twins in love as in birth—had through jealousy and despair turned from love to hate, until reason failed at the strain, and a craze developed, which the malice and treachery of madness made a serious and dangerous force.

So Sweyn theorized; convincing himself as he spoke; convincing afterward others who advanced doubts against White Fell; fettering his judgment by his advocacy, and by his staunch defence of her hurried flight, silencing his own inner consciousness of the unaccountability of her action.

But a little time and Sweyn lost his vantage in the shock of a fresh horror at the homestead. Trella was no more, and her end a mystery. The poor old woman crawled out in a bright gleam to visit a bed-ridden gossip living beyond the fir grove. Under the trees she was last seen halting for her companion, sent back for a forgotten present. Quick alarm sprang, calling every man to the search. Her stick was found among the brushwood near the path, but no track or stain, for a gusty wind was sifting the snow from the branches and hid all sign of how she came by her death.

So panic-stricken were the farm folk that none dared go singly on the search. Known danger could be braced, but not this stealthy Death that walked by day invisible, that cut off alike the child in his play and the aged woman so near to her quiet grave.

"Rol she kissed; Trella she kissed!" So rang Christian's frantic cry again and again, till Sweyn dragged him away and strove to keep him apart from the rest of the household.

But thenceforward all Sweyn's reasoning and mastery could not uphold White Fell above suspicion. He was not called upon to defend her from accusation, when Christian had been brought to silence again; but he well knew the significance of this fact, that her name, formerly uttered freely and often, he never head now—it was huddled away in whispers that he could not catch.

For a time the twins' variance was marked on Sweyn's part by an air of rigid indifference, on Christian's by heavy downcast silence, and a nervous, apprehensive observation of his brother. Superadded to his remorse and foreboding, Sweyn's displeasure weighed upon him intolerably, and the remembrance of their violent rupture was ceaseless misery. The elder brother, self-sufficient and insensitive, could little know how deeply his unkindness stabbed. A depth and force of affection such as Christian's was unknown to him, and his brother's ceaseless surveillance annoyed him greatly. Therefore, that suspicion might be lulled, he judged it wise to make overtures for peace. Most easily done. A little kindliness, a few evidences of consideration, a slight return of the old brotherly imperiousness, and Christian replied by a gratefulness and relief that might have touched him had he understood all, but instead increased his secret contempt.

So successful was his finesse that when, late on a day, a message summoning Christian to a distance was transmitted by Sweyn no doubt of its genuineness occurred. When, his errand proving useless, he set out to return, mistake or misapprehension was all that he surmised. Not till he sighted the homestead, lying low between the night-gray snow ridges, did vivid recollection of the time when he had tracked that horror to the door rouse an intense dread, and with it a hardly defined suspicion.

His grasp tightened on the bear-spear that he carried as a staff; every sense was alert, every muscle strung; excitement urged him on, caution checked him, and the two governed his long stride, swiftly, noiselessly to the climax he felt was at hand.

As he drew near to the outer gates, a light shadow stirred and went, as though the gray of the snow had taken detached motion. A darker shadow stayed and faced Christian.

Sweyn stood before him, and surely the shadow that went was White Fell.

They had been together—close. Had she not been in his arms, near enough for lips to meet?

There was no moon, but the stars gave light enough to show that Sweyn's face was flushed and elate. The flush remained, though the expression changed quickly at sight of his brother. How, if Christian had seen all, should one of his frenzied outbursts be met and managed—by resolution? by indifference? He halted between the two, and as a result, he swaggered.

"White Fell?" questioned Christian, breathlessly.

"Yes?" Sweyn's answer was a query, with an intonation that implied he was clearing the ground for action.

From Christian came, "Have you kissed her?" like a bolt direct, staggering Sweyn by its sheer, prompt temerity.

He flushed yet darker, and yet half smiled over this earnest of success he had won. Had there been really between himself and Christian the rivalry that he imagined, his face had enough of the insolence of triumph to exasperate jealous rage.

"You dare ask this!"

"Sweyn, O Sweyn, I must know! You have!"

The ring of despair and anguish in his tone angered Sweyn, misconstruing it. Jealousy so presumptuous was intolerable.

"Mad fool!" he said, constraining himself no longer. "Win for yourself a woman to kiss. Leave mine without question. Such a one as I should desire to kiss is such a one as shall never allow a kiss to you."

Then Christian fully understood his supposition.

"I—I—!" he cried. "White Fell—that deadly Thing! Sweyn, are you blind, mad? I would save you from her—a were-wolf!"

Sweyn maddened again at the accusation—a dastardly way of revenge, as he conceived; and instantly, for the second time, the brothers were at strife violently. But Christian was now too desperate to be scrupulous; for a dim glimpse had shot a possibility into his mind, and to be free to follow it the striking of his brother was a necessity. Thank God! he was armed, and so Sweyn's equal.

Facing his assailant with the bear-spear, he struck up his arms, and with the butt end hit so hard that he fell. Then the matchless runner leapt away, to follow a forlorn hope.

Sweyn, on regaining his feet, was as amazed as angry at this unaccountable flight. He knew in his heart that his brother was no coward, and that it was unlike him to shrink from an encounter because defeat was certain, and cruel humiliation from a vindictive victor probable. Of the uselessness of pursuit he was well aware; he must abide his chagrin until his time for advantage should come. Since White Fell had parted to the right, Christian to the left, the event of a sequent encounter did not occur to him.

And now Christian, acting on the dim glimpse he had had, just as Sweyn turned upon him, of something that moved against the sky along the ridge behind the homestead, was staking his only hope on a chance, and his own superlative speed. If what he saw was really White Fell, he guessed she was bending her steps towards the open wastes and there was just a possibility that, by a straight dash, and a desperate, perilous leap over a sheer bluff, he might yet meet her or head her. And then—he had no further thought.

It was past, the quick, fierce race, and the chance of death at the leap, and he halted in a hollow to fetch his breath and to look—did she come? Had she gone?

She came.

She came with a smooth, gliding, noiseless speed, that was neither walking nor running; her arms were folded in her furs that were drawn tight about her body; the white lappets from her head were wrapped and knotted closely beneath her face; her eyes were set on a far distance. Then the even sway of her going was startled to a pause by Christian.

"Fell!"

She drew a quick, sharp breath at the sound of her name thus mutilated, and faced Sweyn's brother. Her eyes glittered; her upper lip was lifted and showed the teeth. The half of her name, impressed with an ominous sense as uttered by him, warned her of the aspect of a deadly foe. Yet she cast loose her robes till they trailed ample, and spoke as a mild woman.

"What would you?"

Christian answered with his solemn, dreadful accusation:

"You kissed Rol—and Rol is dead! You kissed Trella—she is dead! You have kissed Sweyn, my brother, but he shall not die!"

He added: "You may live till midnight."

The edge of the teeth and the glitter of the eyes stayed a moment, and her right hand also slid down to the axe-haft. Then, without a word, she swerved from him, and sprang out and away swiftly over the snow.

And Christian sprang out and away, and followed her swiftly over the snow, keeping behind, but half a stride's length from her side.

So they went running together, silent, toward the vast wastes of snow where no living thing but they two moved under the stars of night.

Never before had Christian so rejoiced in his powers. The gift of speed and the training of use and endurance were priceless to him now. Though midnight was hours away he was confident that go where that Fell Thing would hasten as she would, she could not outstrip him, nor escape from him. Then, when the time came for transformation, when the woman's form made no longer a shield against a man's hand, he could slay or be slain to save Sweyn. He had struck his dear brother in dire extremity, but he could not, though reason urged, strike a woman.

For one mile, for two miles they ran; White Fell ever foremost, Christian ever at an equal distance from her side, so near that, now and again, her outflying furs touched him. She spoke no word; nor he. She never turned her head to look at him, nor swerved to evade him; but, with set face looking forward, sped straight on, over rough, over smooth, aware of his nearness by the regular beat of his feet, and the sound of his breath behind.

In a while she quickened her pace. From the first Christian had judged of her speed as admirable, yet with exulting security in his own excelling and enduring whatever her efforts. But, when the pace increased, he found himself put to the test as never had been done before in any race. Her feet indeed flew faster than his; it was only by his length of stride that he kept his place at her side. But his heart was high and resolute, and he did not fear failure yet.

So the desperate race flew on. Their feet struck up the powdery snow, their breath smoked into the sharp, clear air, and they were gone before the air was cleared of snow and vapour. Now and then Christian glanced up to judge, by the rising of the stars, of the coming of midnight. So long—so long!

White Fell held on without slack. She, it was evident with confidence in her speed proving matchless, as resolute to outrun her pursuer, as he to endure till midnight and fulfil his purpose. And Christian held on, still self-assured. He could not fail; he would not fail. To avenge Rol and Trella was motive enough for him to do what man could do; but for Sweyn more. She had kissed Sweyn, but he should not die, too—with Sweyn to save he could not fail.

Never before was such a race as this; no, not when in old Greece man and maid raced together with two fates at stake; for the hard running was sustained unabated, while star after star rose and went wheeling up toward midnight —for one hour, for two hours.

Then Christian saw and heard what shot him through with fear. Where a fringe of trees hung round a slope he saw something dark moving, and heard a yelp, followed by a full, horrid cry, and the dark spread out upon the snow— a pack of wolves in pursuit.

Of the beasts alone he had little cause for fear; at the place he held he could distance them, four footed though they were. But of White Fell's wiles he had infinite apprehension, for how might she not avail herself of the savage jaws of these wolves, akin as they were to half her nature. She vouchsafed to them nor look nor sign; but Christian on an impulse, to assure himself that she should not escape him, caught and held the back-flung edge of her furs, running still.

She turned like a flash with a beastly snarl, teeth and eyes gleaming again. Her axe shone on the upstroke, on the downstroke, as she hacked at his hand. She had lopped it off at the wrist, but that he parried with the bear-spear. Even then she shore through the shaft and shattered the bones of the hand, so that he loosed perforce.

Then again they raced on as before, Christian not losing a pace, though his left hand swung bleeding and broken.

The snarl, indubitably, though modified from a woman's organs; the vicious fury revealed in teeth and eyes; the sharp, arrogant pain of her maiming blow, caught away Christian's heed of the beasts behind, by striking into him close, vivid realization of the infinitely greater danger that ran before him in that deadly Thing.

When he bethought him to look behind, lo! the pack had but reached their tracks, and instantly slunk aside, cowed; the yell of pursuit changing to yelps and whines. So abhorrent was that fell creature to beast as to man.

She had drawn her furs more closely to her, disposing them so that, instead of flying loose to her heels, no drapery hung lower than her knees, and this without a check to her wonderful speed, nor embarrassment by the cumbering of the folds. She held her head as before; her lips were firmly set, only the tense nostrils gave her breath; not a sign of distress witnessed to the long sustaining of that terrible speed.

But on Christian by now the strain was telling palpably. His head weighed heavy, and his breath came labouring in great sobs; the bear-spear would have been a burden now. His heart was beating like a hammer, but such a dullness oppressed his brain that it was only by degrees he could realize his helpless state; wounded and weaponless, chasing that Thing, that was a fierce, desperate, axe-armed woman, except she should assume the beast with fangs yet more deadly.

And still the far, slow stars went lingering nearly an hour from midnight.

So far was his brain astray that an impression took him that she was fleeing from the midnight stars, whose gain was by such slow degrees that a time equalling days and days had gone in the race round the northern circle of the world, and days and days as long might last before the end—except she slackened, or except he failed.

But he would not fail yet.

How long had he been praying so? He had started with a self-confidence and reliance that had felt no need for that aid; and now it seemed the only means by which to restrain his heart from swelling beyond the compass of his body; by which to cherish his brain from dwindling and shrivelling quite away. Some sharp-toothed creature kept tearing and dragging on his maimed left hand; he never could see it, he could not shake it off, but he prayed it off at times.

The clear stars before him took to shuddering and he knew why; they shuddered at sight of what was behind him. He had never divined before that strange Things hid themselves from men, under pretence of being snow-clad mounds of swaying trees; but now they came slipping out from their harmless covers to follow him, and mock at his impotence to make a kindred Thing resolve to truer form. He knew the air behind him was thronged; he heard the hum of innumerable murmurings together; but his eyes could never catch them—they were too swift and nimble; but he knew they were there, because, on a backward glance, he saw the snow mounds surge as they grovelled flatlings out of sight; he saw the trees reel as they screwed themselves rigid past recognition among the boughs.

And after such glance the stars for a while returned to steadfastness, and an infinite stretch of silence froze upon the chill, gray world, only deranged by the swift, even beat of the flying feet, and his own—slower from the longer stride, and the sound of his breath. And for some clear moments he knew that his only concern was to sustain his speed regardless of pain and distress, to deny with every nerve he had her power to outstrip him or to widen the space between them, till the stars crept up to midnight.

A hideous check came to the race. White Fell swirled about and leapt to the right, and Christian, unprepared for so prompt a lurch, found close at his feet a deep pit yawning, and his own impetus past control. But he snatched at her as he bore past, clasping her right arm with his one whole hand, and the two swung together upon the brink.

And her straining away in self-preservation was vigorous enough to counterbalance his headlong impulse, and brought them reeling together to safety.

Then, before he was verily sure that they were not to perish so, crashing down, he saw her gnashing in wild pale fury, as she wrenched to be free; and since her right arm was in his grasp, used her axe left-handed, striking back at him.

The blow was effectual enough even so; his right arm dropped powerless, gashed and with the lesser bone broken that jarred with horrid pain when he let it swing, as he leaped out again, and ran to recover the few feet she had gained from his pause at the shock.

The near escape and this new, quick pain made again every faculty alive and intense. He knew that what he followed was most surely Death animate; wounded and helpless, he was utterly at her mercy if so she should realize and take action. Hopeless to avenge, hopeless to save, his very despair for Sweyn swept him on to follow and follow and precede the kiss-doomed to death. Could he yet fail to hunt that Thing past midnight, out of the womanly form, alluring and treacherous, into lasting restraint of the bestial, which was the last shred of hope left from the confident purpose of the outset.

The last hour from midnight had lost half its quarters, and the stars went lifting up the great minutes, and again his greatening heart and his shrinking brain and the sickening agony that swung at either side conspired to appal the will that had only seeming empire over his feet.

Now White Fell's body was so closely enveloped that not a lap nor an edge flew free. She stretched forward strangely aslant, leaning from the upright poise of a runner. She cleared the ground at times by long bounds, gaining an increase of speed that Christian agonized to equal.

He grew bewildered, uncertain of his own identity, doubting of his own true form. He could not be really a man, no more than that running Thing was really a woman; his real form was only hidden under embodiment of a man, but what it was he did not know. And Sweyn's real form he did not know. Sweyn lay fallen at his feet, where he had struck him down— his own brother—he; he stumbled over him and had to overlap him and race harder because she who had kissed Sweyn leapt so fast. "Sweyn—Sweyn —O Sweyn!"

Why did the stars stop to shudder? Midnight else had surely come!

The leaning, leaping Thing looked back at him a wild fierce look, and laughed in savage scorn and triumph. He saw in a flash why, for within a time measurable by seconds she would have escaped him utterly. As the land lay a slope of ice sunk on the one hand; on the other hand a steep rose, shouldering forward; between the two was space for a foot to be planted, but none for a body to stand; yet a juniper bough, thrusting out, gave a handhold secure enough for one with a resolute grasp to swing past the perilous place, and pass on safe.

Though the first seconds of the last moment were going, she dared to flash back a wicked look, and laugh at the pursuer who was impotent to grasp.

The crisis struck convulsive life into his last supreme effort; his will surged up indomitable, his speed proved matchless yet. He leapt with a rush, passed her before her laugh had time to go out, and turned short, barring the way, and braced to withstand her.

She came hurling desperate, with a feint to the right hand, and then launched herself upon him with a spring like a wild beast when it leaps to kill. And he, with one strong arm and a hand that could not hold, with one strong hand and an arm that could not guide and sustain, he caught and held her even so. And they fell together. And because he felt his whole arm slipping and his whole hand loosing, to slack the dreadful agony of the wrenched bone above, he caught and held with his teeth the tunic at her knee, as she struggled up and wrung off his hands to overleap him victorious.

Like lightning she snatched her axe, and struck him on the neck—deep—once—twice—his life-blood gushed out, staining her feet.

The stars touched midnight.

The death scream he heard was not his, for his set teeth had hardly yet relaxed when it rang out. And the dreadful cry began with a woman's shriek, and changed and ended as the yell of a beast. And before the final blank overtook his dying eyes, he saw the She gave place to It; he saw more, that Life gave place to Death—incomprehensibly.

For he did not dream that no holy water could be more holy, more potent to destroy an evil thing than the life-blood of a pure heart poured out for another in willing devotion.

His own true hidden reality that he had desired to know grew palpable, recognizable. It seemed to him just this: a great, glad, abounding hope that he had saved his brother; too expansive to be contained by the limited form of a sole man, it yearned for a new embodiment infinite as the stars.

What did it matter to that true reality that the man's brain shrank, shrank, till it was nothing; that the man's body could not retain the huge pain of his heart, and heaved it out through the red exit riven at the neck: that hurtling blackness blotted out forever the man's sight, hearing, sense?

In the early gray of day Sweyn chanced upon the footprints of a man—of a runner, as he saw by the shifted snow; and the direction they had taken aroused curiosity, since a little farther their line must be crossed by the edge of a sheer height. He turned to trace them. And so doing, the length of the stride struck his attention—a stride long as his own if he ran. He knew he was following Christian.

In his anger he had hardened himself to be indifferent to the night-long absence of his brother; but now, seeing where the footsteps went, he was seized with compunction and dread. He had failed to give thought and care to his poor, frantic twin, who might—was it possible?—have rushed to a frantic death.

His heart stood still when he came to the place where the leap had been taken. A piled edge of snow had fallen, too, and nothing lay below when he peered. Along the upper edge he ran for a furlong, till he came to a dip where he could slip and climb down, and then back again on the lower level to the pile of fallen snow. There he saw that the vigorous running had started afresh.

He stood pondering; vexed that any man should have taken that leap where he had not ventured to follow; vexed that he had been beguiled to such painful emotion, guessing vainly at Christian's object in this mad freak. He began sauntering along half-unconsciously following his brother's track, and so in a while he came to the place where the footprints were doubled.

Small prints were these others, small as a woman's, though the pace from one to another was larger than those which the skirts of women allow.

Did not White Fell tread so?

A dreadful guess appalled him—so dreadful that he recoiled from belief. Yet his face grew ashy white, and he gasped to fetch back motion to his checked heart. Unbelievable? Closer attention showed how the smaller footfalls had altered for greater speed, striking into the snow with a deeper onset and a lighter pressure on the heels. Unbelievable? Could any woman but White Fell run so? Could any man but Christian run so? The guess became a certainty. He was following where alone in the dark night White Fell had fled from Christian pursuing.

Such villainy set heart and brain on fire with rage and indignation—such villainy in his own brother, till lately loveworthy, praiseworthy, though a fool for meekness. He would kill Christian; had he lives as many as the footprints he had trodden, vengeance should demand them all. In a tempest of murderous hate he followed on in haste, for the track was plain enough; starting with such a burst of speed as could not be maintained, but brought him back soon to a plod for the spent, sobbing breath to be regulated.

Mile after mile he travelled with a bursting heart; more piteous, more tragic, seemed the case at this evidence of White Fell's splendid supremacy, holding her own so long against Christian's famous speed. So long, so long, that his love and admiration grew more and more boundless, and his grief and indignation therewith also. Whenever the track lay clear he ran, with such reckless prodigality of strength that it was soon spent, and he dragged on heavily, till, sometimes on the ice of a mere, sometimes on a windswept place, all signs were lost; but, so undeviating had been their line, that a course straight on, and then short questing to either hand recovered them again.

Hour after hour had gone by through more than half that winter day, before ever he came to the place where the trampled snow showed that a scurry of feet had come and gone! Wolves' feet—and gone most amazingly! Only a little beyond he came to the lopped point of Christian's bear-spear—farther on he would see where the remnant of the useless shaft had been dropped. The snow here was dashed with blood, and the footsteps of the two had fallen closer together. Some hoarse sound of exultation came from him that might have been a laugh had breath sufficed. "O White Fell, my poor brave love! Well struck!" he groaned, torn by his pity and great admiration, as he guessed surely how she had turned and dealt a blow.

The sight of the blood inflamed him as it might a beast that ravens. He grew mad with a desire to once again have Christian by the throat, not to loose this time till he had crushed out his life—or beat out his life—or stabbed out his life—or all of these, and torn him piecemeal likewise—and ah! then, not till then, bleed his heart with weeping, like a child, like a girl, over the piteous fate of his poor lost love.

On—on—on—through the aching time, toiling and straining in the track of those two superb runners, aware of the marvel of their endurance, but unaware of the marvel of their speed that in the three hours before midnight had overpassed all that vast distance that he could only traverse from twilight to twilight. For clear daylight was passing when he came to the edge of an old marlpit, and saw how the two who had gone before had stamped and trampled together in desperate peril on the verge. And here fresh blood stains spoke to him of a valiant defence against his infamous brother; and he followed where the blood had dripped till the cold had staunched its flow, taking a savage gratification from the evidence that Christian had been gashed deeply, maddening afresh with desire to do likewise more excellently and so slake his murderous hate. And he began to know that through all his despair he had entertained a germ of hope, that grew apace, rained upon by his brother's blood.

He strove on as best he might, wrung now by an access of hope—now of despair, in agony to reach the end, however terrible, sick with the aching of the toiled miles that deferred it.

And the light went lingering out of the sky, giving place to uncertain stars.

He came to the finish.

Two bodies lay in a narrow place. Christian's was one, but the other beyond not White Fell's. There where the footsteps ended lay a great white wolf. At the sight, Sweyn's strength was blasted; body and soul he was struck down grovelling.

The stars had grown sure and intense before he stirred from where he had dropped prone. Very feebly he crawled to his dead brother, and laid his hands upon him, and crouched so, afraid to look or stir further.

Cold—stiff—hours dead. Yet the dead body was his only shelter and stay in that most dreadful hour. His soul, stripped bare of all comfort, cowered, shivering, naked, abject, and the living clung to the dead out of piteous need for grace from the soul that had passed away.

He rose to his knees, lifting the body. Christian had fallen face forward in the snow, with his arms flung up and wide, and so had the frost made him rigid; strange, ghastly, unyielding to Sweyn lifting, so that he laid him down again and crouched above, with his arms fast round him and a low, heart-wrung groan.

When at last he found force to raise his brother's body and gather it in his arms, tight clasped to his breast, he tried to face the Thing that lay beyond. The sight set his limbs in a palsy with horror and dread. His senses had failed and fainted in utter cowardice, but for the strength that came from holding dead Christian in his arms, enabling him to compel his eyes to endure the sight, and take into the brain the complete aspect of the Thing. No wound—only blood stains on the feet. The great, grim jaws had a savage grin, though dead-stiff. And his kiss— he could bear it no longer, and turned away, nor ever looked again.

And the dead man in his arms, knowing the full horror, had followed and faced it for his sake; had suffered agony and death for his sake; in the neck was the deep death-gash, one arm and both hands were dark with frozen blood, for his sake! Dead he knew him—as in life he had not known him—to give the right meed of love and worship. He longed for annihilation, that so he might lose the agony of knowing himself so unworthy of such perfect love. The frozen calm of death on the face appalled him. He dared not touch it with lips that had cursed so lately, with lips fouled by a kiss of the Horror that had been Death.

He struggled to his feet, still clasping Christian. The dead man stood upright within his arms, frozen rigid. The eyes were not quite closed; the head had stiffened, bowed slightly to one side; the arms stayed straight and wide. It was the figure of one crucified, the blood-stained hands also conforming.

So living and dead went back along the track, that one had passed in the deepest passion of love, and one in the deepest passion of hate. All that night Sweyn toiled through the snow, bearing the weight of dead Christian, treading back along the steps he before had trodden when he was wronging with vilest thoughts and cursing with murderous hate the brother who all the while lay dead for his sake.

ELLIOTT O'DONNELL

MÈRE MAXIM

From WERWOLVES

In a village some three miles from Blois, on the outskirts of a forest, dwelt an innkeeper called Antonio Cellini, who, as the name suggests, was of Italian origin. Antonio had only one child, Beatrice, a very pretty girl, who at the time of this story was about nineteen years of age. As might be expected, Beatrice had many admirers; but none were so passionately attached to her as Herbert Poyer, a handsome youth, and one Henri Sangfeu, an extremely plain youth. Beatrice—and one can scarcely blame her for it— preferred Herbert, and with the wholehearted approval of her father consented to marry him. Sangfeu was not unnaturally upset; but, in all probability, he would have eventually resigned himself to the inevitable, had it not been for a village wag, who in an idle moment wrote a poem and entitled it

"Sansfeu the Ugly; or, Love Unrequited."

The poem, which was illustrated with several clever caricatures of the unfortunate Henri and contained much caustic wit, took live wildfire in the village; and Henri, in consequence, had a very bad time. Eventually it was shown to Beatrice, and it was then that the climax was reached. Although Henri was present at the moment, unable to restrain herself, she went into peals of laughter at the drawings, saying over and over again: "How like him—how very like! His nose to a nicety! It is certainly correct to style him Sansfeu—for no one could call him Sansnez!"

Her mirth was infectious; everyone joined in; only Henri slunk away, crimson with rage and mortification.

He hated Beatrice now as much as he had loved her before; and he thirsted only for revenge.

Some distance from the village and in the heart of the forest lived an old woman known as Mère Maxim, who was said to be a witch, and, therefore, shunned by everyone. All sorts of unsavoury stories were told of her, and she was held responsible for several outbreaks of epidemics —hitherto unknown in the neighbourhood—many accidents, and more than one death.

The spot where she lived was carefully avoided. Those who ventured far in the forest after nightfall either never came back at all or returned half imbecile with terror, and afterwards poured out to their affrighted friends incoherent stories of the strange lights and terrible forms they had encountered, moving about amid the trees. Up to the present Henri had been just as scared by these tales as the rest of the villagers; but so intense was his longing for revenge that he at length resolved to visit Mère Maxim and solicit her assistance. Choosing a morning when the sun was shining brightly, he screwed up his courage, and after many bad scares finally succeeded in reaching her dwelling—or, I might say, her shanty, for by a more appropriate term than the latter such a queer-looking untidy habitation could not be described. To his astonishment Mère Maxim was by no means so unprepossessing as he had imagined. On the contrary, she was more than passably good-looking, with black hair, rosy cheeks, and exceedingly white teeth. What he did not altogether like were her eyes—which, though large and well shaped had in them an occasional glitter—and her hands, which, though remarkably white and slender, had very long and curved nails, that to his mind suggested all sorts of unpleasant ideas. She was becomingly dressed in brown— brown woolly garments, with a brown fur cap, brown stockings, and brown shoes ornamented with very bright silver buckles. Altogether she was decidedly chic; and if a little incongruous in her surroundings, such incongruity only made her more alluring; and as far as Henri was concerned rather added to her charms.

At all events, he needed no second invitation to seat himself by her side in the chimney-corner, and his heart thumped as it had never thumped before when she encouraged him to put his arm round her waist and kiss her. It was the first time a woman had ever suffered him to kiss her without violent protestations and avowals of disgust.

"You are not very handsome, it is true," Mère Maxim remarked, "but you are fat—and I like fat young men," and she pinched his cheeks playfully and patted his hands.

"Are you sure no one knows you have come to see me?" she asked.

"Certain!" Henri replied; "I haven't confided in a soul; I haven't even so much as dropped a hint that I intended seeing you."

"That is good!" Mère Maxim said. "Tell no one, otherwise I shall not be able to help you. Also, on no account let the girl Beatrice think you bear her animosity. Be civil and friendly to her whenever you meet; then give her, as a wedding present, this belt and box of bonbons." So saying, she handed him a beautiful belt composed of the skin of some wild animal and fastened with a gold buckle, and a box of delicious pink and white sugarplums. "Do not give her these things till the marriage eve," she added, "and directly you have given them come and see me—always observing the greatest secrecy." She then kissed him, and he went away brimming over with passion for her, and longing feverishly for the hour to arrive when he could be with her again.

All day and night he thought of her—of her gay and sparkling beauty, of her kisses and caresses, and the delightful coolness of her thin and supple hands. His mad infatuation for her made him oblivious to the taunts and jeers of the villagers, who seldom saw him without making ribald allusion to the poem.

"There goes Sansfeu! alias Monsieur Grosnez!" they called out. "Why don't you cut off your nose for a present to mademoiselle? She would then have no need to buy a kitchen poker. Ha! ha! ha!" But their coarse wit fell flat. Henri hardly heard it—all his thoughts, his burning love, his unquenchable passion, were centred in Mère Maxim: in spirit he was with her, alone with her, in the innermost recesses of the grim, silent forest.

The marriage eve came; he handed Beatrice the presents,

and ere she had time to thank him—for the magnificence of the belt rendered her momentarily speechless—he had flown from the house, and was hurrying as fast as his legs could carry him to his tryst. The shadows of the night were already on the forest when he entered it; and the silence and solitude of the place, the indistinct images of the trees, and their dismal sighing, that seemed to foretell a storm, all combined to disturb his fancy and raise strange spectres in his imagination. The shrill hooting of an owl, as it rustled overhead, caused him an unprecedented shock, and the great rush of blood to his head made him stagger and clutch hold of the nearest object for support. He had barely recovered from this alarm when his eyes almost started out of their sockets with fright as he caught sight of a queer shape gliding silently from tree to tree; and shortly afterwards he was again terrified—this time by a pale face, whether of a human being or animal he could not say, peering down at him from the gnarled and fantastic branches of a gigantic oak. He was now so frightened that he ran, and queer—indefinably queer footsteps ran after him, and followed him persistently until he reached the shanty, when he heard them turn and leap lightly away.

On this occasion, the occurrence of Henri's second visit, Mère Maxim was more captivating than ever. She was dressed with wonderful effect all in white. She wore sparkling jewels at her throat and waist, buckles of burnished gold on her shoes; her teeth flashed like polished ivory, and her nails like agates. Henri was enraptured. He fell on his knees before her, he caught her hands and covered them with kisses.

"How nice you look today, my sweetheart," she said; "and how fat! It does my heart good to see you. Come in, and sit close to me, and tell me how you have fared."

She led him in, and after locking and barring the door, conducted him to the chimney-corner. And there he lay in her arms. She fondled him; she pressed her lips on his, and gleefully felt his cheeks and arms. And after a time, when, intoxicated with the joy of it all, he lay still and quiet, wishing only to remain like that for eternity, she stooped down, and, fetching a knot of cord from under the seat, began laughingly to bind his hands and feet. And at each turn and twist of the rope she laughed the louder. And when she had finished binding his arms and legs she made him lie on his back, and lashed him so tightly to the seat that, had he possessed the strength of six men, he could not have freed himself.

Then she sat beside him, and moving aside the clothes that covered his chest and throat, said:

"By this time Beatrice—pretty Beatrice, vain and sensual Beatrice, the Beatrice you once loved and admired so much —will have worn the belt, will have eaten the sweets. She is now a werwolf. Every night at twelve o'clock she will creep out of bed and glide about the house and village in search of human prey, some bonny babe, or weak, defenceless woman, but always some one fat, tender and juicy—some one like you." And bending low over him, she bared her teeth, and dug her cruel nails deep into his flesh. A flame from the wood fire suddenly shot up. It flickered oddly on the figure of Mère Maxim—so oddly that Henri received a shock. He realized with an awful thrill that the face into which he peered was no longer that of a human being; it was—but he could no longer think— he could only gaze.

H. WARNER MUNN

THE WEREWOLF OF PONKERT

They are neither brute nor human—
They are neither man nor woman—
They are Ghouls.
            POE: THE BELLS.

PROLOGUE

In the past, when I toured in France, invariably I made a point of never failing to stop at a certain tavern, about thirty miles from Paris. I will not give you more definite directions for reaching it, for it was a discovery of my own and as such I would share it with no one. The fact that the inn has very pretty serving maids is but incidental, the real reason for my visits being the superlative excellence of the wine.

Many a night have I and the old Pierre sat, smoked and drunk till the wee hours of the morning, and many have been the experiences we have exchanged of wild, eerie adventure in various parts of the globe. Pierre also was a great traveller and seeker after adventure before he drifted into the backwater of this placid village, to finish there the remainder of his days.

One night (or morning I should say), Pierre grew indiscreet under the influence of his nectar, and let fall a few words so pregnant of possibilities that I scented a mystery at once; and when he was sober I demanded an explanation. And, having said so much, seeing that he could not dissuade me, he brought forth proof of his dark hints in regard to a horrible occurrence in the annals of his family.

The proof was a book, bound in hand-tooled leather and locked by a silver clasp. When open it proved to be written in a crabbed hand in old Latin on what was apparently parchment, which was now yellow with age, but must when new have been remarkably white.

It comprised only four leaves, each a foot square and glued or cemented to a thin wooden backing. They were written on only one side and completely covered with this close, crabbed Latin.

On the back of the book were two iron staples, and hanging from each, several links of heavy rusted chain. Evidently, like most valuable books which were available to the public in the past, it had been chained fast to prevent theft.

Unfortunately, I cannot read Latin, or in fact any languages but French and English, although I speak several. So it was necessary for my friend to read it to me, which he did.

After I had recovered from the numbness which the curious narrative had thrown over me, I begged him to read it again—slowly. As he read, I copied; and here is the tale for you to judge and believe as you see fit. Told in Hungarian, transcribed in Latin, translated into modern French and from that into English, it is probably both garbled and improved. No doubt anachronisms abound, but be that as it may, it remains without dispute the only authentic document known of a werewolf's experiences, dictated by himself.

I

Having but a few hours in which to live, I dictate that which follows, hoping that someone thereby may be warned by my example and profit by it. The priest has told me to tell my story to him and he will write it down. Later it will be written down again, but I do not care to think of that now.

My name is Wladislaw Brenryk. For twenty years I lived in the village where I was born, a small place in the northeastern part of Hungary. My parents were poor and I had to work hard—harder, in fact, than I liked, for I was born of a languid disposition. So I used my wits to save my hands and I was clever, if I do say it myself. I was born for trading and bargaining, and none of the boys I grew to manhood with could beat me in a trade.

Time went on, and before I had reached manhood my father died in a pestilence. Although my mother was pestilence-salted (for she had the plague when she was a girl and recovered), she soon gave up, grew weaker and weaker, finally joining my father in the skies. The priest of our village said that it was the trouble in her lungs that killed her, but I know better, for they had loved each other much.

Alone and lorn for the first time in my life, I could not bear to remain longer amongst the scenes of my happy boyhood. So on a fine spring morning I set forth, carrying on my back those possessions which I could not bring myself to part with, and around my waist a well-stuffed money belt, filled with the results of my trading and the sale of our cottage.

For several years I wandered here and there, horse-trading for a time, then again a peddler of jewelry and small articles. Finally I came to Ponkert, and started a small shop in which I sold beautiful silks, jewels and sword hilts. It was the sword hilts that sold the best. They were highly decorated with golden filigree and encrusted with precious stones. Chiefs and moneyed nobles would come or send messengers for many miles to obtain them. I gained a reputation for honesty and fair dealing, likewise a less enviable notoriety for being a miser. It was true that I was careful and cautious, but I defy anyone to prove that I was parsimonious.

I had closed up the shop for the night and harnessed the horses for the long drive home, when for the first time I wished that I lived in the village instead of being so far away. I had always enjoyed the ride before; a man can think much on a ten mile ride and it gave an opportunity to clean my mind of the day's worries and bickering, so as to come to my dear wife and little daughter with thoughts of only them.

What made me look forward with anxiety to the long ride home that particular day was the many broad gold pieces secreted in my wallet. I had never been molested on that road, but others had been found robbed and partly devoured, with tracks of both man and beast about them in the snow. Obviously, thought I at the time, thieves had beaten them down, leaving them for the wolves.

But there was a disturbing factor in the problem: not only were the bodies horribly mutilated and the beast tracks about them extraordinarily large for wolf tracks, but the feet of the men were unprotected by any covering whatever! Barefooted men roaming through the forests, in the snow, on the slim likelihood of discovering prey which could be forced to yield wealth! The very idea was improbable. If I had only known then what I know now, my entire life might have been changed, but it was not so to be.

To return to my story: It was known that I had a large amount of money in my possession, for that afternoon the chief of a large Tartar caravan, which was passing through, had stopped at my shop and taken six of my best sword hilts with him, leaving their equivalent in gold. So I had cause enough to worry. I looked about for some sort of weapon, and found a short iron bar, which I tucked beneath the robes of the sleigh; then I spoke to the mares, and we were off on the long ride home.

For a long time we went creaking along, the sleigh runners squeaking on the well-packed snow. Frost was in the air, and the stars gleamed down coldly upon the dark forest, hardly lighting the road. As yet the moon had not risen.

I turned from the main travelled highway and took the river road. This left the forest behind, but the travelling was much worse. Exposed to the winds, the light snowfall of the morning had drifted, and the roadway was choked. I thought of leaving the road and taking to the smooth surface of the river which gleamed brightly to the left, but this would have meant a mile or more extra to travel, for the river curved in a great bend opposite our home, and there was an impassable barrier of small trees and brush for some distance.

The moon was now rising over the hill I had just quitted, and as the beams struck upon me, I was suddenly seized by a fit of the most unaccountable terror. This peculiar feeling held me rigid in my seat. It seemed as if a hand of ice had been suddenly laid upon the back of my neck.

The mares, it was evident, had felt this strange thrill also, for they imperceptibly increased their speed without urging of mine. Indeed, I could not have moved a muscle while that spell was upon me.

Soon we dipped down into the hollow at the hill's foot, and the power that had frozen me was removed. A strange feeling of exaltation and happiness swept over me, as if I had escaped from some terrible and unthinkable danger.

"Hai!" I shouted, rising in the sleigh and cracking my whip.

The mares responded nobly and we started to climb the next hill. As we did so, a fiendish howling came down the wind, but faintly, as if it were some distance away. I stopped the mares and stood up in the sleigh, the better to listen.

Faintly and far away sounded the cries, mellowed by distance. Then they grew louder and louder as the brutes came nearer and over the top of the hill I had just quitted swept the devilish pack! They were on my trail, and it was only too plain that before I could reach home they would be upon me.

There was only one chance, and I took it. I clucked to the horses and turned them on to the ice of the river where lay a straight smooth roadway. As long as the mares kept their feet, I was safe. But if one should stumble—!

Then that same spell of horror threw its icy mantle over me again; I sagged back; the mares took the bit in their teeth; and we rushed like a thunderbolt down the river.

Little puffs of diamond dust shot from the ice into my lap, as the steelshod hoofs rang and clicked. On we tore, while I sat in the sleigh like a stone, unable to move a muscle. Faster and faster we rushed between the banks of brush that fringed the icy causeway.

Fainter re-echoed the demoniac ululations behind me, until at last they ceased altogether and the horses gradually slackened their furious pace.

Here the spell left me, nor did it ever come again. Now we travelled at a trot, which slowed until the mares were but walking along, their panting breath paling their dark heaving sides to gray, in the frosty air.

Then we rounded the bend, and I saw black, open water ahead. Here progress, perforce, ceased. There was no way out, except to turn back and mount the bank where less underbrush grew, then into the smooth plain beyond and homeward.

So I tugged at the rein, and we swerved half-way around. In that moment of unpreparedness, all became confusion.

A gloating chuckle sounded evilly from the farther bank, and five great gray shapes charged at me across the ice.

To think was to act with me. I have always been a creature of impulse, and almost instinctively, I turned back, slashing the mares till they reared and we plunged straight forward into the onrushing mass of bodies. This resolute move took the beasts by surprise and halted them. They scattered, and I was through, with a clear road before me. But my escape was not to be so accomplished.

Silently, from the shelter of an overhanging rock, trotted two more of the creatures; a very giant of a beast, gaunt and gray, beside which moved a small black one. Roaring, the gray flung himself at the horses, which reared and plunged in terror; and the rest were upon me from the rear.

Then, turmoil of battle, pandemonium of sound, through which cut like a knife the scream of a horse. One was down! I felt the sleigh lurch to one side; heavy bodies struck at me, sharp teeth tore; but I kept my balance until one, such was his velocity, struck me and laid me flat in the bottom of the sleigh, himself rebounding and shooting over the side.

Something offered itself to my hand, something cold and metallic. I raised my arm, smote, felt steel bite bone, felt bone crunch beneath my stroke. I laid about me like a madman, with the bar, and cleared a space. I stood erect and waited for the attack.

But no instant attack followed. The menace of the bar was apparently too strong, and one by one they sank down on their haunches to rest or to wait. Jaws gaped wide and tongues lolled. Panting, they rested after the long run.

As I stood there in the sleigh, watching them, it seemed

as if they were laughing, ghoul-like, at my horrible plight. As I soon found, they were!

I became conscious of a noise behind me, a small noise, such as the wind might make blowing a dead leaf across the bare ice; a sound like dead twigs rustling in the breeze, a faint scraping of claws, a padding of feet; and turning, I looked straight into the red glaring dots which were the eyes of the black wolf!

I shouted hoarsely, swung up the bar and brought it down with every ounce of force that I possessed. Unfortunately for myself, the beast, and Hungary, the great gray creature which ran at his side swerved and took the blow instead, squarely between the eyes.

He grunted, choked; a stream of blood shot from his mouth and nostrils. His eyelids opened and closed convulsively. Then he collapsed. The bar had crashed halfway through his head.

I whirled, expecting to be overwhelmed by the six that still lived, but to my intense surprise the surge of bodies that I had seen from the tail of my eye, when I struck at the black wolf, had subsided and they were now loping round and round the sleigh.

As they moved, the stricken mare followed them with her pain-filled eyes, while the one that was unharmed struggled constantly to be free. As the black leader passed me in the circling rout, I, likewise, slowly turned to keep him always in sight. Instinct told me that from him would come my greatest danger.

Now I noticed a strange thing: about the necks of each of the five gray beasts there hung upon a thong a leathern pouch, about the size of a large fist. These pouches hung flat and flaccid as if they were empty. The black, examine as closely as I might, wore none.

Then, as with one accord, they stopped in their tracks, and sank on their haunches. That for which they had been waiting had at last occurred. There seemed to be some sort of silent signal given. Simultaneously they lifted their heads and loosed a long, low wail, in which seemed to hang all the desolation and loneliness of eternity. Thereafter none moved or uttered a sound.

Everything was deathly still. Even the wind, which had been sporting in the undergrowth, had now faded into nothingness and died. Only the laboured breathing of the two mares and the hoarse panting of the brutes was to be heard.

Little red eyes, swinish and glittering like hell-sparks, shone malevolently at me by the reflected light of the now fully risen moon.

In this unaccountable pause I had time to see the full beauty of the trap. As I have stated, the river formed a great bow, and while I was travelling on the curve between nock and nock, they had quitted the river and waited at the rapids, the line of their pursuit forming the string to the bow.

Also, for the first time, I could examine carefully and note what manner of beasts these were that held me in their power.

Far from being wolves, as my first thought had been, they were great gray animals, the size of a large hound, except the leader, who was black and more the size and shape of a true wolf. All, however, had the same general appearance, and the same characteristics. A high intelligent brow, beneath which gleamed little red piglike eyes, with a glint of a devil in their glance, which caused them to move with a rabbitlike lope when they ran; and most terrifying of all, they were almost hairless and possessed not the slightest rudiment of a tail!

The circle was so arranged that as I stood, wary of possible attack, I could see four of the six. The smaller black creature was directly in front of me, tongue hanging out, apparently chuckling to himself in anticipation of some ghastly joke to follow.

Two were behind me, in whichever way I turned, but the night was so still that I could have heard them approaching long before they could have rushed me.

As I watched the creatures, I suddenly noticed that they were no longer glaring at me, but at something behind and beyond me and on the ground. I whirled, fearing a charge, but not a move anywhere in the circle had taken place.

So I glanced with the tail of my eye for a rush at my back, and set myself to solve the mystery.

There was nothing before me, on the bare ice, but here and there a white line extended across the river, caused by the snow drifting into cracks. Now I noticed that across one of these there lay, inside the circle, the dead body of the thing that I had slain with the bar. The four creatures which I could now see were watching this intently. I did likewise, with senses alert for treachery. I glanced from one end of the warped, twisted and broken thing, to the other. Somehow it seemed more symmetrical than before; longer in a way, and of a more human cast of feature.

Then—God! Shall I never forget that moment?

I looked at its right forepaw, or where its right forepaw should have been and was not. A white hairless hand had taken its place!

I screamed, hoarsely and horribly, grasped my bar firmly, leapt from the sleigh and rushed into the pack, which, risen, was waiting to receive me.

Everything from that moment until my arrival home in the morning is a blur. I remember a black figure, standing erect before me, burning eyes which fixed me like a statue of stone, a command to strip and a sharp stinging pain in the hollow of my elbow, where the great vein lies.

Then more dimly, I seem to recall a moment of intense anguish as if all my bones were being dislocated and re-set, a yelping, howling chorus of welcome, a swift rushing over ice on all fours, and a shrill sharp screaming, all such as only a horse in mortal fear can give!

Then there is a clear spot of recollection in which I was eating raw flesh and blood of my own mare, with snarling creatures like myself gorging all around me.

How I reached home, I have not the slightest idea, but the next that I remember is a warm room and my dear wife's face bending over mine. All after that, for nearly a week, was delirium, in which I raved incessantly, so they told me, of wolves which were not wolves, and a black fiend with eyes like embers.

II

When I was well again I went to the scene of my adventure, but the ice had broken up in an early thaw; and only the swollen river rolled where I had been captured. At first, I thought that my half-remembered fancies were freakish memories, born of delirium, but one night in the early spring, as I lay in bed only half asleep, something occurred which robbed me of this hope. I heard the long, melancholy wail of a wolf! Calling and appealing, it drew me to the window in hopes of seeing the midnight marauder, but nothing was visible as far as I could see, so I turned to go back to bed again. As I moved away from the window it came again, insistently calling. A powerful attraction drew me. I silently opened the window and melted into the darkness outside.

It was a warm spring evening as I padded silently along on bare feet, through the forest, drawn in a direction that led toward the thickest portion of the wood. I must have gone at least for half a mile under the influence of a strange exhilaration that had come over me, like that of a lover who keeps a tryst with his beloved.

Then the wailing cry echoed again, but with a shock I realized that there was no sound in the wood save the usual night noises. I realized the truth! The sound did not exist in reality, but I was hearing with the ears of the spirit rather than my fleshly ones. I suspected danger, but it was too late to turn back.

A figure rose to a standing posture, and I recognized the master, as he called himself, and we also, later. Under a power not my own, I stripped off my night garments, concealed them in a hollow tree which the master showed me, and fell to the ground, a beast! The master had drunk my blood, and the old story that I had never quite believed, to the effect that if a vampire drinks one's blood, he or she has a power over that person that nothing can break, and eventually he also will be a *wampyr*, was coming true.

We raced off into the night, were joined later by the other five, and paused for a time, in the forest. Here the master transformed himself, and I also. We stood there, and for the first time I heard the master's voice.

"Look well!" it croaked. "Look well! Welcome you to the pack this man?" (From the tone and actions I judged that he was speaking by rote, and using set phrases for the occasion.) Here there arose a howl of assent.

"Look well!" he said to me. "Look well! Do you wish to be one of these?" pointing to the pack. I covered my eyes with my hands and shrank back. "Think well," he spoke again, catching my bare shoulder with one talon, and mouthing into my ear.

"Will you join my band of free companions, or will you furnish them with a meal tonight?" I could imagine that a death's-head grin overspread his features at this, though my eyes were still blinded.

"You have a choice," he said. "We do not harm the poor, only the rich, although now and then we take a cow or horse from them, for that is our due. But the rich we slay, and their jewels and fine gold are ours. I take none myself, all belongs to my companions. What do you say?"

I cried "No!" as loudly as I could, and stared defiantly into his face. Over his shoulder I noted that the pack was gradually moving in, stealthily with eager leering looks.

"Ha!" he cackled, as I paled before that menace; "where now is your bravery? Make your choice. Die here and now, or make a promise to obey me unswervingly, to deviate not a jot from any orders, no matter what they may be, and be my willing slave. I will make you rich beyond your wildest dreams, your people shall wear sables and ermine, and the king himself will be proud to acknowledge you as friend. Come, what do you say?" he asked.

I hesitated, temporizing. "Why do you single out me? I have never harmed you, do not even know you. There must be hundreds stronger than I and more willing, within easy reach. Why not use those you have or take someone else?"

"There must be seven in the pack," he answered simply. "You slew one, therefore must you take his place. It is but justice."

Justice! I laughed in his face. Justice, that a man fighting for his life should also perish if, slaying one of his enemies, he himself still lived!

My laughter infuriated him. "Enough delay!" he cried impatiently. "Come, decide! Death or life. Which? Do you promise?"

What a terrible choice I was offered! A horrible death beneath fangs of beasts which should never have existed, with no one ever to know that I had resisted the temptation of proffered life; or an even more terrible existence as one of these unnatural things, half man, half demoniac beast! But if I chose death, I should have a highly problematical hope of future life in the skies, and my wife and daughter would be left alone.

If I chose life, I should have high adventure to season my prosaic existence; I should have wealth with which I could buy a title. Besides, something might happen to save me from the fate which otherwise would sometime inevitably overtake me. Is it any wonder to you, why I chose as I did? Would you not do the same, in my predicament? Even if I had it all to do over again, knowing what I now know, I think I should say again that which I answered the master: 'I promise!'

But God, if I had only chosen death!

The things that I saw, heard, and did that night made a stain on my soul that all eternity will never erase. But finally they were over, and we separated, each returning to his home, and the master where no one knows.

I resumed my form by the tree, and as I did so, I remembered the events that had taken place that night. I fell prone on the grass, screaming, cursing, and sobbing, to think of my fate to come. I was damned forever!

Although I have called myself a *wampyr*, I was not one in the true sense of the word, at the time of which I speak. Neither were any of the rest of my companions, except the master, for although we ate human flesh, drank blood, and cracked bones to extract the last particle of nourishment therefrom, we did so to assuage our fierce hunger more than because it was necessary for our continued existence.

We ate heartily of human food also, in the man form, but more and more we found it unsatisfying appetite, which only flesh and blood would conquer.

Gradually we were leaving even this for a diet consisting solely of blood. This, in my firm belief, was that which the master lived upon. His whole appearance bore this out. He was incredibly aged, and I believe an immortal. (He still may be, for no one has seen him dead, although they tell me that he is.)

His face was like a crinkled, seamed piece of time-worn parchment, coalblack with age. His eyes glittered with youth, seeming to have an almost separate existence of their own. Gradually, very gradually, the expressions of our faces were changing also, and we were turning into true *wampyrs* when self-brought catastrophe overtook us.

I will not dwell long upon the year or so in which I was the master's slave, for our dark and bloody deeds are too numerous to mention in detail. Some nights we wandered about in fruitless search and returned empty-handed, but usually we left death and destruction behind us. Most times, however, we would be summoned on some definite foray, which culminated in each of us being, the next day, somewhat richer.

We delighted in killing horses and cattle. We went blood-mad on these occasions, sometimes even leaving our original trail to take up an attractive scent of ox or cow. For these, I do not condemn myself, in so far as no human souls were destroyed in these slaughters, to become *wampyrs* after death. But as I think of those who are ruined forever because of me, I shudder at the thought!

On one occasion when we dragged down humans, my conscience has always rested easily. We had set out on the track of a sleigh, loaded with wealthy travelers from foreign parts; an old man and his two grandsons about three to five years of age. We followed for several miles to find the sleigh lying on its side, the horses gone, and the three travelers, stiff and stark on the dark stained snow, which was churned by many footprints of horse and man. Enraged, not by the murder (for we ourselves had intended no less), but by the loss of our anticipated loot, we took up the trail which led away toward the mountains. Five men on horseback made up the party. They spurred their horses to the utmost when we sang the Hunger Song, baying as we ran, but they were too slow for us. One by one, we pulled them down, slew the slayers and despoiled the thieves, which was a grim and ghastly jest.

But not often could I console myself thus. Many were the helpless and harmless that we removed from existence, and more horrible did we become. Day by day we were growing hardened and inured to our lot, and only rarely did my soul sicken as at my first metamorphosis. At one of these times, I crept into the village church. It was late at night, and except for myself the building was empty.

I knelt at the altar and unburdened my soul. I confessed everything to the unhearing ears of the Greathearted One, abased myself and grovelled on the floor. For hours it seemed, I prayed and begged that I might be given a sign, some small hope, that I should not be damned forever— No sign!

I cursed, screamed and prayed; for a time I must have been mad.

Finally I left. At the church door I bared my head and looked up at the sky across which dark clouds were scudding, obscuring the stars. I rose on tiptoe, shook my fist at the racing clouds, cursed God Himself and waited for the lightning stroke, but none came. Only a light rain started to fall and I arrived home, drenched to the skin, with a heavier load on my heart than when I left.

Yet even then, so mysterious are the ways of an inscrutable Providence, my salvation was approaching in a horrible guise. For on that night I had the thought which was to result in annihilation for us all.

III

Sometimes, when I walked the village streets, I had met people who seemed to glance furtively at me with a wild look. These glances were quickly averted, but by them I had begun to decide within myself just who were the other members of the pack. Growing bolder and more certain, I had accosted certain of them, to find myself correct.

One by one, I sounded them out, but found only Simon the smith to be of my own sentiments toward our gruesome business. The rest all exulted in the joyous hunt, and could not, we were certain, be persuaded to revolt against this odious enslavement.

But gradually, as we became more hardened and unprincipled, more calloused to the suffering we caused, we had become yet more greedy and rapacious. Here Simon and I found a loophole to attack.

As I have said before, the master never took any of the money, jewels or other portable valuables which we found on the bodies or amongst the possessions of those whom we slew.

So I dropped a word here, a hint there, a vague half-question to one individual singly and alone, while Simon was doing the same.

The gist of all our arguing was, "What does the master take?"

This was a very pertinent question, for it was obvious to all of them that the master was not leader for nothing. He obtained something from each corpse when he went to it, alone, and we sat in the circle, waiting eagerly for the signal to rush in.

To me it was plain that this was nothing more material than the life blood of the slain unfortunates, which kept the master alive! Simon and I said nothing of this, gradually forming the opinions of the others to the effect that the immortal souls were absorbed into the master's being, giving him eternal life.

This staggering thought opened great possibilities in the minds of most, and as we thought, all; later I was to learn to my sorrow that not all were so credulous. But more and more they became dissatisfied, less patiently did they restrain themselves from leaping in ahead of their turn, on our bandit raids. For working in their minds, like worms in carrion, or smoldering sparks in damp cloth, which will presently burst into flame, was this: "Why not be immortal myself?"

So were discord and revolt fomented, and so was I the

unwitting cause of my further undoing and, strangely enough, my redemption.

Now, my wife was a good woman, and I am sure that she loved me as much as I loved her, but this very love worked our ruin. All people have a weakness in one way or another, and she was no exception to the rule. She was jealous—insanely jealous!

My frequent absences, which I thought had been unnoticed, since I had been careful not to make the slightest noise in opening the window and quitting the house, had been observed for weeks.

I found later that one had told the master what Simon and I had started, and it was the only female member of our pack. But he had already perceived, with his cunning senses, the almost imperceptible signs of revolt against his absolute power. Determining to crush this at the start, he decided to make an example of someone to bind the rest more closely to him by means of a new fear.

Why he chose me instead of Simon I have not the faintest idea, unless it was that I was more intelligent than the ignorant clods that made up the rest of the pack.

But so it was, I was chosen to be the victim, and this is the way he set about to bind me forever to him.

He enlisted the aid of old Mother Molla, who was regarded as a witch that had sold her soul to the devil. How she got into the house I was never able to discover, for the original excuse was either forgotten later, or merely left untold. But to the house she came one day, probably obtaining an entrance on some flimsy pretext of begging for cast-off clothing, or of borrowing some cooking utensil.

Before she left she casually mentioned that she had seen me in the early morning before sunrise, coming past her hut. There were only two houses in that part of the wood, Mother Molla's and the charcoal burner's, whose name was Fiermann. All would have yet been well, but the old hag insinuated that "Fiermann had a young and pretty daughter and that he himself was in town very often over night." And so the seeds of suspicion were planted in my wife's mind.

She said that she ordered the hag out, and helped her

across the threshold with a foot in the back, and when the old witch picked herself out of the mud she screamed, "Look for yourself, at half an hour before midnight," and hobbled away cackling to herself.

The mischief was done. At first my wife resolved to think nothing about the matter, but it preyed on her mind and gnawed at her heart. So to ease her suspicions she worked away a knot in the partition; and that night when I had gone to bed she waited and watched.

She saw me fling back the clothes and step out of bed, fully dressed, then walk silently across the floor and open the window slowly and carefully, vanishing into the moonlit night. At first, she told me later, she was horrified and heartbroken to think me unfaithful; then she resolved to go away or kill herself, so she would not be a hindrance to me any longer. But finally her emotions changed and vanished until only hate was left. She resolved to watch and wait to see what might befall. She sat by the knothole until I came back just as the cock crew; then she went to bed herself, to toss about sleeplessly until morning.

Night after night she waited, sometimes fruitlessly, for it was not every night that the silent call summoned us to the rendezvous. But when in a period of three weeks I had stealthily stolen out eight times, and she had satisfied herself that Fiermann had also been away, by artfully questioning his girl, her suspicions were aroused. He was with the pack, but neither knew that. So she decided to confront me with the facts and tell me to choose between the two, "herself, the mother of my child, or this upstart chimney-sweep" (I use her own words.)

All this time the master's mind was working upon hers to such effect, that although she thought she was choosing her own course of action, in reality she was following the plans which the master had made for her.

One night I heard the silent howl, which never failed, when I was in the man form, to send a chill down my back. I had been expecting this for several days, and had remained dressed each night until midnight, to be in readiness for the summons.

I stepped carefully to the window and released the catch that held it down, then lifted—. What was this? It stuck! I tugged harder with no better results.

Well, then, I should have to use the door. It was dangerous, but might be done. At all means, anything was preferable to going wild within the house. So I turned and was struck fairly in the eyes by a splinter of yellow light. Someone was on the other side of the partition door with a lighted candle, and the door was slowly opening!

Instantly I knew that I was discovered. I bounded toward the bed, intending to simulate sleep until she had gone away, but the door flew open with a crash, and my wife stood in the doorway with a scornful look on her face, and a candle held high, which cast its rays upon me. It was too late to hope for escape, so I attempted to brazen it out.

"Well, what is it?" I asked gently.

"What were you doing at the window?" she asked.

"It is so hot in here that I was going to let some air in," I replied.

"To let air in, or yourself out?" came, though spoken in a low tone, as a thunderclap to me.

I was struck dumb, and then she told me the whole story as she knew it. The mass of lies with which old Molla must have started her mind in a ferment poured into my consciousness in a heap of jumbled words.

Again came the howling cry, that only I could hear, and I thought I detected a note of anger in it at my delay.

"At first," she said, "I did not believe, but when I saw with my own eyes—"

"Silence!" I roared with such vehemence that the window rattled.

"I will be heard!" she cried. "I have nailed down the window and you shall not pass through this door tonight!"

She slammed the door, and stood dauntlessly before it! My heart went out to her in this moment. That blessed, bright little figure, standing there so bravely, made me forget why I must go. I took a step toward her—and that long eerie wail, which only re-echoed in my brain, sounded much more wrathfully—and nearer!

Torn between two desires, I stood still. My face must

have been a mask of horror and anguish, for she looked at me in amazement, which softened to pity.

"What is it, dear?" she whispered. "Have I wronged you after all? Won't you tell me, darling?"

Then I felt the pangs of change beginning and knew that the transformation would follow quickly.

I seized a heavy stool, and flung it through the window, following it as quickly myself. If I was to escape, not a second could be wasted.

With a swiftness I had never dreamed she possessed, she ran to me as I crouched in the window with my hands on the side, and one knee on the sill, drawing myself up and over.

She seized me by the hair and dragged my head back, crying meanwhile, "No! No! No! You shall not go. You are mine and I shall keep you! That slut Stanoska will wait long tonight!"

Then she pulled so mightily that I fell upon my back. All was lost! It was too late, for I no longer had any desire to leave! Although I still desired to leave! Although I still maintained the outward appearance of a man, I thought as a beast.

I have often thought that the change first took place in the brain and later in the body.

I shrieked demoniacally, and another cry arose outside the house, sounding loud through the broken window.

She paled at the sound and shrank back against the table, terrified at my wild and doubtless uncanny appearance. I sprang to my feet, tearing madly at my clothes, ripping them from my body in pieces. I had all the terror of a wild animal now for encumbering clothing or anything like a trap.

When completely stripped, I howled again loudly and fell upon all fours, a misshapen creature that should never have existed. I had become a wild beast! But it was not I, who slunk, bellying the floor, hair all abristle with hate, toward the horror-stricken figure by the table; it was not I—I swear before the God that soon will judge me—who crouched and sprang, tearing with sharp white fangs that beautiful white throat I had caressed so often!

At a sound outside, I turned, standing astride my victim, and ready to fight for my kill.

With forepaws on the window sill, through the broken pane a wolf's head peered. With hellish significance it glanced at the door of the next room wherein lay our little girl, asleep in her cradle, then turned its eyes upon me in a mute command.

It was I, the man spirit, who for a moment ruled the monstrous form into which my body had been transmuted. It was the man, myself, who curled those thin beastly lips into a silent, menacing grin, who stalked forward, stiff-legged, hackles raised and eager for revenge!

As swiftly as the head had appeared it withdrew and suddenly came again, curiously changing in form. Its outlines grew less decided, everything seemed to swim before my eyes. I grew giddy, and there visibly the wolf's head changed into that inscrutable parchment mask of the master. Those youthful eyes glared balefully into mine, with a smoky flame behind them.

I felt weak; again the beast was in the ascendant, and I forgot my human heritage. Lost was all memory of love or revenge. I, the werewolf, slunk through the door, over to the cradle, gloatingly stood anticipating for a moment while blood dripped from my parted jaws on my little girl's clean shirt. Then I clamped down my jaws on her dress, and heedless of her puny struggles, or her cries, I rose with a long clean leap through the broken window bearing my contribution to the ghoulish feast!

Then to my tortured memory comes one of those curious blank spots that sometimes afflicted me. I dimly remember snarls of fighting animals, and more faintly still, sounds of shots, but that must be the delirium of my wounds that speaks, for it could not be possible at that time of night that one might be wandering about armed with such an untrustworthy weapon.

Soon it was over. Over! I, the last of our line, took up the horrible hunt, blithe and rejoicing.

Down the valley roared the hellpack, and at the head the master. Foam from my bloody jaws flecked the snow with pink as we galloped along, and mounted the hill like a wave breaking on the beach. We were racing along at full speed with the master still ahead and the rest of the pack strung out at varying distances behind, when suddenly he turned in midleap, and alighting, confronted us.

The one who was directly in front of me, and behind the master, dug his feet into the ground and slid in order to avoid collision. I was going so swiftly I could not stop, and piled up on my mate. The next instant we were at the bottom of a struggling, clawing, snapping heap.

For a moment we milled and fought, while the master sat on his haunches, and lolled his tongue out of gaunt grinning jaws, breath panting out in white, moist puffs.

Then we scattered as if blown apart, and also settled into a resting position, a very sheepish-looking pack of marauders. At that moment I felt taking place within me the tearing, rending sensation that always preceded the transforming of our bodies from one form to another. My bones clicked into slightly different positions; I began to remember that I was human, and stood erect, a man again.

All of my companions had been transformed likewise, and were standing where they had stopped.

What a contrast! Six men, white men, each a giant in strength, bound till death and after (as the un-dead which walk but do not move with mortal life), bound to a thing which I cannot call a man. A black creature only four feet high, which physically the weakest of us might have crushed with one hand. But six men were slavishly obedient to his every order, and moved in mortal fear of him. The pity of it! Only two of us were still human enough to understand that we were damned forever and had no means of escape. To look at their faces made that plain, for deeply graven there were lines that brutalized them, marking our swift progress toward the beast.

I was changing also. I had been told frequently how bad I looked, and my friends thought I should rest more, for it was plain that I was overtaxing my energies; but I always changed the subject as soon as possible, for I knew the real reason for my appearance.

But now the master was advancing. An irresistible force urged me toward him, and as I moved the others closed in about me, so that he and I stood in the centre of a small circle.

Then he raised his hand, paw, or talon (I cannot say which, for it resembled all three), and spoke shrilly in a piping feeble voice, for the second and last time in my acquaintance with him.

"Fellow comrades." He leered at me, and I grew hot with rage but said nothing. "I have gathered you here with me tonight to give you a warning that you may use for your own profit. Leave me to do as I see fit and all will be well, but try for one instant to change my course of action or to attack me and you will curse the day you were born."

Then he lost control of himself.

"Fools," he shrilled; "cursed ignorant peasant fools, you who thought you could kill me, whom even the elements cannot harm! Idiots, clumsy dolts, who tried to plot against the accumulated intelligence of a thousand years, listen to me speak!"

Thunderstruck at this sudden outburst, we staggered and reeled under the revelation which came next.

"From the very first," he cried, "I saw through your stupid intrigue against me, and I laughed to myself. Every move you made, every word you spoke in the seeming privacy of your hovels, I knew long before you. This is nothing new to me. Eighty-four times has this been tried upon me, and eighty-four times have I met the problem in the same way. I have made an example of one of you to warn the rest, and there he stands!"

He whirled swiftly and thrust an ash-gray claw at my face. For some time I had been realizing now what he was about to say, and at this sudden blow I averted my eyes from his and sprang at his throat.

We went down together, and he would have died there and then, but they tore us apart. Poor blind fools! Again he stood erect, rubbing his throat where I had clutched it, and again he croaked, never glancing at me, as I was held powerless by three men.

"All of you have children, wives, or parents dependent upon you, and defenceless. I saw to this before I chose you, having this very thing in mind. I can at any time change any one of you to a beast by the power of my will, where-

182

ever I may be. Tomorrow, if you still resist me, I will change you, or you," darting his paw at each in quick succession.

From the circle rose cries of, "No! No! Do not do that! I am your man, and Master, you are our father; do with us as you like!"

Triumphant, he laughed, there in the snowy plain beneath the starry sky, then bent his gaze upon me.

Seizing my chin, he forced my eyes to meet his, and growled, "And you? What say you now?"

I could not resist those burning eyes.

"Master," I muttered, "I am your willing slave."

"Then get back to your den," he cried, giving me a push that sent me prone in the snow, "and wait there till I summon you again."

The pack changed from men back to brutes again, and raced off toward the forest, and though I tried to follow, I could not move until the sound of their cries had faded away into the distance. Finally I rose and went to my dreary home again.

I will pass over briefly what followed; I do not think I could repeat my thoughts as I stumbled along through the night, nearly freezing from lack of clothing and the exposure that resulted.

Dawn was just arriving when I came in sight of the four walls I had so recently called home. I staggered in, and sank into a chair, too listless to build a fire.

After a while, mechanically, I dressed myself, started a blaze in the fireplace, and bethought myself of hiding the body, which lay in the other room, until I could flee. Plan after plan suggested itself to my mind, but all were soon cast aside as useless. Tired out, I buried my head on my arms, as I sat by the table, and must have dozed away some little time.

Suddenly I was aroused from the dull apathy into which I had fallen by a small timid knock on the door. My first thought was that I was discovered. A fit of trembling overcame me, which quickly passed, but left me too weak to rise.

Again sounded the rap, followed by the rasp of frosty

gravel as footsteps haltingly passed down the clean-swept path.

Suddenly a plan had formulated itself in my poor distracted brain. I steeled my will to resolute action, hastened to the door, and threw it wide. No one was in sight.

Bewildered, I looked about, suspicious of more wizardry, and between two of the trees that fringed the road I spied a figure slowly travelling toward the village.

"Hai!" I shouted, cupping my hands at my mouth. "What do you want? Come back!"

As the figure turned and approached me, I recognized the halfwitted creature who limpingly traveled from village to village during the summer months, working when compelled by necessity to do so, but more often begging his food and shelter from more fortunate people.

"Why do you knock at my door?" I asked, as kindly as I could, when he had come near to me.

'I came last evening," he said, "and the lady that lives here said that she was alone and would not let me in or give me anything, but if later I would come when her husband had returned, she would let me have some old clothes, and something good to take with me. So I slept with the cows, and now I am come again."

I forced myself to speak composedly.

"You are a good lad, and if you will do something for me I will see that you receive new clothing, and much money. Here is proof that I mean well," and I tossed a broad gold piece to his feet.

Wildly did he scramble in the dust of the path, but I had no laugh, ridiculous as his action would have seemed at another time.

He whimpered in his eagerness to be off, looked into my face, and cowered as does a dog that expects a blow.

Some of my agony of spirit must have been reflected in my face, for he shrank away, all his joy vanished and he faltered fearfully, "What would you have me do, master?"

His pitiable aspect struck to my heart, and the words I had been about to speak died still-born on the end of my tongue. I shall never reveal to anyone what my intention had been, but something nobler and purer than I had ever known enlivened my soul. I drew myself to my full height, glared defiantly at the quivering wretch and cried, "Go you to Ponkert. Arouse the people and bring the soldiers from the barracks. I am a werewolf and I have just slain my wife!"

His eyes seemed starting from his head, his nerveless and palsied limbs carried him shakily down the path, the while he watched over his shoulder as if he expected to see me turn into a wolf and ravenously pursue him. At the end of the path he bethought himself of flight, threw the gold piece down and started with a curious reeling run toward the village.

A little wind was now rising, blowing flurries of snow and leaves about, and the round evil eye of yellow metal lay and blinked at the morning sun until a little whirlwind of dust collapsed on it and buried its gleam. But although I could not see it I knew it was there, the thing that all men slave, war, and die for, that all men desire, and obtaining are not satisfied, the struggle for which has maimed and damned more souls than any other one thing that had ever been. I went in, shut the door, and left it outside in the dirt, whence it came and where it belongs.

It might have been a minute or a year that I sat at the table, with my head buried in my arms, for any memory that I have of it, but so I found myself when I was roused by a dull roar of many voices outside. Opening the door, I stepped out and waited, expecting nothing less than instant death.

A crowd of about fifty persons came surging up the road, and seeing me standing there, passively waiting, milled and huddled together, each anxious to be in at the death, but none caring to be in the forefront and first to meet the dreaded werewolf.

Much coaxing and urging was given certain of the crowd to send them to me, but none was eager for fame.

Finally stepped out one tanner, clad only in his leather apron, and carrying a huge fish-spear in his right hand.

"Come," he shouted; "who follows if I lead?"

Just then sounded the pounding of hoofs, far down the road.

"He who comes must hasten," thought I, "if he would see the finish."

The tanner harangued the steadily growing mob without avail, none desiring to be the first.

At last I was out of the common rut in which the rest of the village was sunken. What a moment! Even in my hopeless situation I could not help but exult. Seventy-five or a hundred against one, and not a man dare move!

At last the tanner despaired of assistance and slowly moved toward me, now and then casting a glance behind to be assured of an open lane of retreat if such was necessary.

I believe, in that moment, that had I leapt forward at them, the whole flock of sheep would have fled screaming down the road; but I did nothing of the kind. I did not move, or even make any resistance when the tanner seized me by the shoulder, his spear ready for the deadly stroke. Why should I? Life had no longer any interest for me!

Finding that I stood passively, the tanner released my shoulder, grasped the spear in both hands and towered above me, his mighty muscles standing out like ropes on his naked arms and chest. The whole assemblage held its breath, the silence was that of death, and a loud clatter of hoofs twitched every head around as if they all had been worked simultaneously by a single string. Straight into the crowd, which broke and scattered before it, came a huge black horse, ridden by a large man, in the uniform of the king's soldiery.

As he came he smote swiftly, right and left with the flat of his long straight sword.

Down came the spear and down swept the sword full upon the tanner's head. He fell like a poleaxed steer, while the spear buried itself for half its length in the ground by the door.

"This man is mine!" he shouted. "Mine and the king's! He must go with me for trial and sentence; touch him at your peril."

The crowd murmured angrily, started for us, but disintegrated again before the rush of half a company of soldiers that had followed their captain.

IV

"And so, sirs," I was concluding my narrative in the prison barracks at Ponkert, "you see to what ends have I been brought by the machinations of this creature. I do not ask for life myself, for I shall be glad to die, and it is but just that I should; but give me revenge, and I will burn in hell for eternity most happily."

For a long time I thought that the officer would deny me, for he ruminated long before he spoke.

"Can you," he said, "entrap this hideous band, if I and my men will give you help?"

I leapt from my chair and shouted, "Give me a dozen men, armed, and not one of those fiends will be alive tomorrow morning!"

Carried away by my enthusiasm, he cried, "You shall have fifty and I will lead them myself," but then more gravely, "you realize that we cannot leave one alive? That all must die? All?"

I nodded, and looked him squarely in the eyes.

"I understand," I said. "When we have won, do with me as you will. I shall not resist, for I am very tired, and shall be glad to rest. But until then, I am your man!"

"You are brave," he said simply, "and I wish I need not do that which I must. Will you grip hands with me before we leave?" he asked almost diffidently.

I said nothing, but our hands met in a strong clasp, and as he turned away I thought I saw moisture fleck his cheek. He was a man, and I wish I had known him earlier. We could have been friends, perhaps; but enough of that.

Some distance from Ponkert there stands a wood, so dense that even at midday there in the center of the forest, only a dim twilight exists. Here sometimes laired the pack. At night we made it our meeting place, and now and again in the thickest recesses one or more of us would spend the day in seclusion. So, knowing this, I made my plans.

I tore my clothes, and dabbled them in blood, wound a bloody bandage around my head, and the soldiers tied my hands securely behind me, also putting a cord about my neck.

Toward evening we set out, about eighty of us in all, including the rustics who trailed along behind, carrying improvised arms, such as hay-forks, clubs, and farm implements which were clumsy, but deadly.

Straight through the heart of the wood we passed, I travelling in the midst, reeling along with head down as if worn out, which indeed I was. Now and then the soldier who held the other end of the cord would jerk fiercely, almost causing me to stumble, and on one of these occasions I heard a sullen, stifled growl from a thicket which we were passing. No one else apparently heard; I cautiously lifted my head, and saw a form slink silently into the darker shadows.

I had been observed, and the plan was succeeding!

We then passed from the forest and came into the sunlight once more. Between the wood and the hills flowed the river that before had served me so ill. Overlooking this there frowned a great castle that had once dominated the river and the trade routes which crossed the plain on the other side. But this long ago, so long that the castle builders had passed away, their sons, and theirs also, if indeed there ever were such, leaving only the castle to prove they had ever lived.

As the years went on, various parties of brigands had held this great stone structure, and wars had been fought around and within. Slowly, time and the elements had worked their will unchecked, until the central tower squatted down one day and carried the rest of the castle with it.

Still there remained a strong stone wall, which had enclosed the castle once, but now formed a great square, thirty feet in height, around a shapeless mountain of masonary in the centre. Under this imposing monument lay the last who had ever lived there, and some say that their ghosts still haunt the ruins, but I never saw any, or met one who had. At each side of the square, in the wall there stood an iron gate. These were still well preserved, but very rusty, so rusty indeed, that it was impossible to open them, and we were obliged to find an easier mode of entrance.

Finally we discovered a large tree, which, uprooted by a heavy wind, had fallen with its top against the wall, and so remained, forming a bridge which connected the wall and the ground by a gentle incline.

To gain the courtyard it was necessary to follow the wall around to where it faced the plain. Here a large section had fallen inward, leaving the wall but twenty feet in height at that point. Here we went down, by the rope which had tormented me so, and prepared our trap.

It was very simple; I was the bait and we knew that when the time came for the change, the pack would follow my trail unless the master was warned, and once inside the walls could not leap out. We could then slay them at our leisure, for we were more than ten to one, although many of the farmers had refused to enter the haunted castle and returned to the village.

At last it became near midnight, and faintly, far away, I heard the cries down below me in the wood.

"The time is near," I whispered to the captain as we stood in the enclosure. "I hear them gathering."

"Be ready," he warned the men. "Hide yourselves in the rocks. They come!"

Eagerly we waited, though none was visible now except the captain and two or three soldiers, standing by the pile of masonry.

As I waited near a large pile of stone blocks, I heard someone cry sharply, "Now!"

Shooting lights danced before my eyes, followed by black oblivion, and I fell forward on my face. I had been clubbed from behind.

When I became conscious again the stars still gleamed brightly overhead, but they no longer interested me. My sole thought was to escape from these two-legged creatures that held me prisoner. Again I was the beast!

For the first time I had not been aware of the transition when it took place. Now I had no recollection of my past, and for all I knew I might never have been anything but a quadruped.

Came swiftly the realization that I was being called insistently. From the tail of my eye I saw a man standing beside me, but a little distance away. Perhaps I might escape!

I drew my legs up, and my muscles tightened for the spring. I would leap the wall, I would flee for my life, I would . . . and then a tremendous weight came crashing down on my hind quarters, breaking both my legs.

The pain was excruciating! I gave vent to a scream of curdled agony which was answered by howls of mingled encouragement and rage from beyond the wall. Then down from the wall came leaping, one at a time, five great gray brutes. They had followed my trail and come, as they thought, to save me, not dreaming they were being led into a trap.

The soldiers had been wiser than I, for they had foreseen what I failed to see; that if my story was true, inevitably when my nature changed I would betray them to my comrades.

Between man and wild beast there can be no compromise, so they stunned me, and then toppled down a heavy stone, pinning me to the ground. Instead of warning the pack as I undoubtedly would have done had I but known earlier that they were present, I screamed for help, for the sudden pain drove any other emotion from my mind.

Now all was confusion. Howl of beast, and shout of man, mingled in chorus with clash of pike and fang. Now and again, but infrequently, a shot punctuated the uproar, but these new weapons are too slow to be of practical use, so it was a hand-to-paw, and cheek-to-jowl conflict.

The five were giving a far better account of themselves than I had dreamed possible. Springing in and out again, with lightning movements they could tear a man's throat out and be gone before he could defend himself. The confusion was so great, the press so thick, that a man might kill his comrade by accident. I saw this happen twice.

Now only four of the beasts were visible, springing to

and fro, fighting for their lives like cornered rats, and gradually forcing their way to the wall whence they had come. One must be down!

But no! I saw the missing one, old Mother Molla, rending with sharp white fangs at something which lay half hidden beneath her. A soldier stole silently behind her, and with a mighty display of strength thrust a pike completely through her body. But other eyes than mine had seen the stroke. The next instant the assailant went down and was buried from sight in the centre of the snarling pack. Now the pack was, for several seconds, in a tight knot of bodies, and while they thus remained the soldiers leapt in, pikes and clubs rising and falling. Before Mother Molla had reached the corner toward which she was slowly crawling, coughing out, meanwhile, her life in bloody bubbles, the remainder of the pack had avenged her, then died themselves.

It was at this critical moment that a head peered over the wall and two bright little red eyes took in the scene. Why the master had thus delayed his arrival I cannot explain. But whatever his faults he was at least no coward, for the first inkling the men had of his presence was the sight of a black wolf springing down and landing on the heap of dead bodies which had represented his former vassals.

With a bound he was in the midst of the soldiers, fighting with fang and claw. They scattered like sheep, but returned, forming now a close-packed circle around him, barring all egress. Now his only chance of life lay in motion so swift that it would be unsafe to aim a weapon at him for fear of injuring one of the men.

He saw now clearly that all was lost, and quite obviously perceived that flight was his only hope. He gave me a glance of encouragement as I lay there raving and frothing, snapping at, and breaking my teeth upon, the cold unyielding rock that held me down; and he rushed madly about the inside of the circle, searching for a weak spot in it.

So in the soldiers pressed, striking now and then as he passed, but harming him not.

With hot red tongue hanging from his slavering jaws,

he raced about the encircling cordon of foes. Soon was his plan of action made. He leapt in midstride straight at an ignorant yokel who wielded a hay-fork. The poor fool struck clumsily, instead of dodging, which mistake was his last, for he missed. Instantly the master had torn out his throat with a single snap and was streaking toward the castle wall.

Now the way was clear; puffs of snow rose behind, before him, and on either side, but apparently he bore a charmed life, for none of the missiles struck him. As he reached the wall he left the ground in the most magnificent leap I have ever seen, from either man or beast, hung by his forefeet twenty feet above the ground for the space of time in which a man might count ten; then, while bullets be-starred the ancient masonry all about him, he wildly scrambled with his hind feet to draw himself up, and was soon over the wall and gone!

His enemies rushed to the rusted gates, but their very haste defeated their efforts, and by the time they reached the open the plain was bare of life. But over the hill to the eastward floated a derisive mocking howl. The master's farewell! From that day to this he has never been seen in Ponkert. Thus ended the *wampyr's* rule.

So now is my ordeal ended, the master ousted, and the fear that held sway over the village is finished. I, out of all the pack that ravaged the land for many miles, alone am left alive.

Somewhere perhaps the master still roams silently, stealthily, in the cool darkness of our nights, but I am certain that never again will he return to Ponkert, for here is my assurance.

When his power crumbled to dust in the courtyard of that ancient castle, and he was forced to flee for his life, his last look and cry to me intimated that he would return and rescue me from my captors. There must have been some spark of humanity in that savage heart, something that would not allow him to leave those who had sworn allegiance to him; for witness that magnificent leap from the courtyard wall to the very midst of his foes, to save the one surviving member of his band.

He did return!

While I lay in the barrack dungeon, recovering from my broken bones and other injuries (for I must be in good health before I am permitted to expiate my crime), one night about a week after the fight I heard the old familiar silent cry.

I recognized the master's call and responded. I thought of all things I should like to tell him and could not through two feet of stone wall. I went over in my mind the whole series of actions by means of which I had escaped from his horrible enslavement.

Beginning with the involuntary murder of my wife and child, I related without uttering a spoken word that which I had done, and ended with the moment when I saw him leap the gap, a fugitive. I know he understood, for after a few seconds of silence, just outside the wall there arose the blood-chilling howl of a wolf. Higher and higher it rose, a long sobbing wail of hate, an undulating crescendo of sound; it thinned to a thread whose throaty murmur was drowned in the rushing trample of heavy feet overhead and the crash of exploding powder.

Flash after flash tore the velvet night, mingling with the shouts of the soldiers who were firing from the windows, and at some time in the tumult the master turned his back on Ponkert for the last time, I trust.

Utterly alone in the world, friendless and forlorn, I quit tomorrow this mortal form that had known such strange changes.

I go with no reluctance whatever, for I have nothing to live for, and the sooner gone, the sooner I shall expiate my sins, and at last win through to where I am expected. For I cannot believe that I shall suffer in torment forever.

Yet, I would even forego that bliss for the greater one of being a beast again and the master a man, so that I might feel my fangs sink into his black wrinkled throat, and feel the blood spurt warm into my mouth. Oh, to rip, to tear, to slash at that fiend, and have him utterly in my power! To feel his bones crunch beneath my powerful jaws, and to tear his flesh with them!

Yet—sometimes I think perhaps he was once as I, was

tempted, fell, sinking lower and lower. Perhaps he, too, was not wholly to blame, but even as I, was weak and doomed from the beginning. Is it the fault of the pot that it is misshapen in the making?

They tell me that every pang I suffer now will shorten my punishment in the future. What my pains on earth shall be I know not. I may be broken on the wheel or stretched upon the rack, but I am resigned and fortified against my fate.

But there is one thing of which I am positive, for they have told me, to add pang upon pang, that I shall be flayed, alive, my hide tanned like a beast's and dark and gloomy history written upon it for all to read who can!

I have never heard of these things being done before, but I have no doubt that they will be done to me. However, I care not. So much have I suffered in heart and thought that no bodily discomfort can surpass my other torments. I am resigned. May he who reads take warning. Farewell to all whom I know and have known. Farewell!

When the manuscript was finished I sat thinking for a little time. So this book was written on a human hide, which when occupied had enclosed Pierre's ancestor.

"I thought," said I to the old man, "that you told me that the person described in the narrative was your grand-père many times removed. But here it relates that his only child was murdered by himself. How do you explain that?" I asked.

"You will remember perhaps that he told how, after the flight from the cottage, immediately succeeding the act was a blank, save for a vague remembrance of shots. What is more probable than that someone aroused by the howling in the night should fire blindly at the noise, not once but several times. Granted that, it is probable that, frightened by the unexpected noise, the beasts would leave their prey. Such is the legend that has accompanied the book for centuries. Also it is said that this book has never been out of the possession of the Hungarian's descendants. Therefore, observing that I now possess the book, which was given to me by my father, as it was to him by his parent, I assume that in my veins courses the diluted strain of the werewolf."

"This may all be true," I said. "Surely in the weeks of his imprisonment he must have been informed that his little girl had not been devoured; yet he speaks consistently through the tale, as if he knew nothing about the rescue."

"Ah," he replied, "that puzzled me also when I first heard of this. But it is my sincere belief that this information was kept purposely from him to add mental torture to his physical punishment. Why should they trouble themselves to ease the spirit of a man that was responsible for so many crimes?" And such a cruel glitter lit his eyes, that I had nothing more to say.

After I had left I congratulated myself upon being so fortunate as to exist in the prosaic Twentieth Century, and not in the superstition ridden ones which we have just barely left. For even superstitions must have a beginning, and who knows how much truth may lie, after all, in this weird tale?

I never went back to the inn after that. I often meant to, but other business was more important, and procrastination finally made the journey useless.

Pierre is dead now, leaving no relatives or friends but myself. I now possess the book and it lies before me, as I write the story it contains for the world to read, and to laugh at in scorn.

SEABURY QUINN

THE WOLF OF ST. BONNOT

The house party with which Norval Fleetwood was celebrating the completion of Twelvetrees, his new country seat, was drawing to an inauspicious close. Friday and Saturday had been successful, and more than one luckless bunny had found his way into the game-bags and thence to the pot-pie, but with Sunday morning came a let-down which set the guests longing for the city, the theatre, the night clubs and the crowded, comfortable associations of the workaday world. Rain, lashed and driven by a northwest wind, opened the day, by mid-afternoon autumn gave up the fight and winter took possession of the world like a rowdy barbarian sacking a captured city. The late-November gale raced round the house, wrenching at doors and shutters, howling bawdy songs down chimneys and wrestling savagely with the twelve great oaks in the front lot from which the house took its name. The guests were wearied of each other as shipwrecked mariners might tire of their companions' faces, and to make matters more unbearable the line which fed electric current to the house went dead beneath the buffetings of the wind-storm and the radio ceased blaring forth its dancing jazz at the same instant every light in the house winked out and the motors of the big refrigerator in the pantry stopped humming.

Little spurts of flame here and there proclaimed lighted matches, a few candles were requisitioned and set alight, their feeble, trembling fingers doing little more than stain the pitch-black darkness with an indeterminate dusk, and host and guests settled down in gloomy contemplation of events to wait the opportunity of a reasonable excuse to say good-night and escape from each other's company.

"No one here can play dance music," grumbled one.

"No piano here to play, even if we had a musician,"

Fleetwood answered gloomily. "Dodson's are infernally slow getting the furniture out, it seems to me."

"Too dark to play bridge; can't see whether you're holdin' spades or diamonds."

"I shouldn't play if it weren't. Lost too much last night—lot more than I could afford."

"Grand service the electric company gives, I don't think. If I had my way——"

"Oh, *I* know what let's do!" Mazie Noyer, plump, forty and unbecomingly flirtatious, suddenly cried in the high, thin voice which seems the exclusive property of short, fat women. "Let's have a séance. This is just the night for it; cold and dark and spooky. Come on, everybody; I'll be the medium; I can make a dining-table take a joke any time!"

"But certainly," Jules de Grandin whispered in my ear. "Does she not do so three times each day, to say nothing of the enormous sandwiches she consumes between meals? Do not join them, Friend Trowbridge; he who puts his hands upon the table to summon spirits risks more than burned fingers. Yes. Let them have their foolishness by themselves."

Accordingly, while Fleetwood, his young wife and seven of their guests trailed into the dining-hall in the wake of Mazie's provocatively swishing skirts, de Grandin and I remained on the leather-upholstered settle before the blazing logs in the hall fireplace where we could watch the dim shapes circled round the table, yet be ourselves unobserved.

The ring was quickly formed. Each member of the party placed his hands flat upon the table's polished oak, his own thumbs touching, his extended little fingers in light contact with those of his neighbours to left and right.

"I think we ought to sing," suggested Mazie. "Madame Northrop always begins her séances with a hymn. What shall it be?" For a moment there was silence; then, in a high falsetto she began:

> "Behold the innumerable host
> Of angels clothed in light,
> Behold the spirits of the just
> Whose faith is changed to sight."

She concluded the verse with a dropping, pleading tremolo, then spoke in a still, awe-struck voice, as though she half believed her own mummery:

"Spirits of the departed, you from before whose eyes the separating veil has ben lifted, we are assembled tonight to commune with you, if any of you be here present." A short pause, then: "Are there any spirits with us? If so, signify your presence by rapping once upon the table."

Another pause, in which the crackling of a burning knot and the hissing of an imperfectly seasoned log sounded almost thunderously, followed her invitation.

Jules de Grandin snapped the flint of his pocket lighter and set a vile-smelling French cigarette aglow, then glanced impatiently through the archway leading to the room beyond. *"Insensée,"* he whispered contemptuously. "Had she but the sense with which the good God endowed the most half-witted of silly geese, she would know that her greatest success tonight would be a total failure to evoke——"

"Oh, how *nice!*" Mazie's high-pitched exclamation cut through his muttered observation. "Is it fine or superfine—I mean man or woman? Rap once for a man, twice for a woman, please."

The little Frenchman's sleek, blond head shot forward, his ear turned toward the doorway. All pretence of boredom was gone and every line of his small, sensitive face registered alert attention as it showed in sharp silhouette against the bright background of the firelight.

Through the dim, candle-lit dusk we caught the echo of a single sharp, incisive knock.

"A man!" Miss Noyer's voice came in an awed whisper. "Who are—I mean who were you? Where and when did you live? Strike once for A, twice for B, three times for C, and so on."

Another pause, then a slow, distinct rapping, as though the table had been struck sharply with a bent knuckle. Seven strokes, followed by nine, then twelve, another twelve, then five, continuing until *"Gilles Garnier—St. Bonnot—in the reign of King Charles,"* had been laboriously spelled on the resounding wood.

"Dieu de Dieu, 'Gilles Garnier of St. Bonnot,' it says!"

de Grandin exclaimed in a sharp, rasping whisper. "This is no longer a matter to amuse fools, Friend Trowbridge; we must intervene, right away, immediately, at once. Come."

He rose abruptly from the couch and took a step toward the dining-room, but paused in mid-stride, his head thrown back like a hunting dog sniffing the breeze for quarry. Almost, it seemed to me, the needle-sharp ends of his little, tightly waxed mustache quivered with excitement like the whiskers of an irritable and super-alert tom-cat. I, too, felt a sudden chill of nervous excitement—almost terror— run through me, for even as de Grandin paused, there came from far away, seemingly from the gloomy wooded hill, which lay a mile or more across the cleared pasture-land, a faint but steadily growing sound. So low it could scarcely be dissociated from the dismal skirling of the wind it was at first, but steadily it mounted and swelled in tone and volume, a long-drawn, ululant howl, rising to a shrill crescendo, sinking to a moan, then rising once again in a quavering, hopeless cry, poignant at the wailing of a lost soul seeking sanctuary from pursuing furies. And as the distant belling bay died once again amid the whistling chorus of the wind, there came an answering call *from the darkened dining-room*. It started with a choking, rasping moan, as though one of the sitters at the table had strangled and gasped for breath; then, as though torn from tortured flesh by torment too great to be resisted, it rose in answer to the distant howl: *"Ow-o-o-o-O-O-O!"* swelling with ever-increasing stress, then repeated once again with hopeless, mourning diminuendo: *"OW-O-O-O-o-o-oo!"*

Strangely, too, the half-reluctant, half-exultant cry was so quickly voiced that it was impossible to place its origin, save to say it emanated from the dining-room.

"Nom d'un chat noir, who makes this business of the monkey?" de Grandin challenged sharply. "I will not have it!" He burst into the dining-room, eyes ablaze, face working with unbridled fury. "Fools, *bêtes, dupes*, you know not what you do! To mock at them is to invite destruction of——"

He paused, fairly choking with savage anger, and as if to punctuate his tirade the electric current came on again, flooding the big house with sudden brilliance, limning the scene in the dining-hall like a *tableau vivant* on the stage. Fleetwood and eight others sat with hands still pressed upon the table, startled, rather foolish expressions on their faces as they blinked owlishly in the sudden deluge of light. Hildegarde, his six-months' bride for whom the house at Twelvetrees had been built, lay cheek-down upon the table, her heavy, dark-bronze hair unbound and cascading across the polished Flemish oak, her face pale as carven ivory, her lush red lips slightly parted, displaying twin lines of little milk-white teeth between them.

"Good Lord!" our host exclaimed, "she's fainted! That fool joke was too much for her." He glared angrily around the circle of startled faces. "Who let out that God-awful howl?" he demanded fiercely.

The little Frenchman cast an appraising look at the unconscious girl and a quick, venomous glance at Mazie Noyer. "See to her, Friend Trowbridge, if you please," he ordered curtly with a nod toward Hildegarde. *"Mademoiselle*, this is your work; I trust you are duly proud of it," he added coldly, glaring at Mazie again.

"I?" Miss Noyer returned in a scandalized voice. "Why, I never even *dreamed* of doing such a thing! I was as surprised as any one when that inhuman howl started —ugh, right in this room, too!" She shook her well-upholstered shoulders in a gesture of repugnance, then favoured de Grandin with a withering look. "I think you forget yourself, Doctor de Grandin," she reminded. "You owe me an apolo——"

"Mille pardons, Mademoiselle," he cut in acidly, "whatever my debt may be, this is no time for repayment. Me, I think an evening of *ennui* would have been preferable to your so stupid invocation of forces of which you know nothing. However, we can but pray that no great harm is done."

He turned his shoulder squarely on her and bowed to the company with frigid courtesy. *"Messieurs, Mesdames,"* he announced, "it grows late and we all have business in the city tomorrow. I suggest we seek our beds while this so temperamental light still holds." He turned on his heel and left the room without a single backward look at Mazie Noyer or any offer of apology for his hasty accusation.

"Am bringing Hildegarde to town for consultation. Please see me tomorrow.—Fleetwood."

I passed the telegram to Jules de Grandin and grinned in spite of myself at the sober expression on his face as he perused the terse message. "Why so serious?" I asked, helping myself to a fresh serving of griddle cakes and honey. "That sort of thing has been going on ever since Adam and Eve left the Garden to set up housekeeping. Norval and Hildegarde are excited, of course, but it's only a biological function, and——"

"*Ah bah!*" he cut in. "You annoy me, you vex me, you harass me, my friend. You say it is the coming of a happy event which brings Monsieur and Madame Fleetwood to town. I hope you are correct, but I fear you are in error. Would he telegraph if that were all? Must he see you right away, at once, immediately, about a matter which can not, in the course of nature, be either hurried or delayed? I doubt it. Indeed, I greatly doubt that it has anything to do with this"—he tapped the telegram with his breakfast fork—"but concerns something much more sinister. Yes, I have worried much concerning Madame Hildegarde since that accursed night when the senseless Mademoiselle Noyer played her monkey tricks in that darkened house. And——"

"You're absurd," I told him.

"I hope so," he admitted seriously. "We shall eventually see who laughs in whose face, my friend."

In deference to Fleetwood's message I stayed indoors most of the following day, but dinner-time came and went without further word from him. "Confound it," I grumbled, glancing irritably at my watch, "I wish they'd come, if they're coming. *King Lear's* playing at the Academy tonight, and I'd like to see it. If they'll only hurry I'll have time to get there before the middle of the first act, and——"

"*Eh bien*, be patient, my old one," de Grandin counselled. "Unless I am more mistaken than I think, you shall soon see a tragedy the like of which Monsieur

Shakespeare never dreamed. Indeed, I think the curtain is already rising——" He turned toward the consulting-room door expectantly, and as though evoked by his words Norval Fleetwood entered.

"Hildegarde's up at the Passaic Boulevard house," he answered my query as we shook hands. "It's such a wretched night, I thought I'd better leave her home, and——" He paused, as though the words somehow stuck in his throat; then: "And I thought I'd better see you before you see her, sir."

"*Ah?*" de Grandin's barely whispered comment had a ring of triumph in it, and I favoured him with a black look.

Fleetwood nodded shortly, almost as if in answer to the Frenchman. "I'm almost wild with anxiety about her, Doctor," he told me. "You remember that fool séance Mazie Noyer got up that Sunday night two weeks ago when the lights went out at Twelvetrees? It started right after that."

"*A-ah?*" de Grandin murmured.

"What seems to be the trouble?" I asked, casting another withering glance toward the little Frenchman.

"I—I only wish I knew, sir. Hildegarde was restless as a child with fever all that night, and dull and listless as a convalescent next day. I had to come to town and was delayed considerably getting back that night, and dinner should have been over an hour when I returned, but she hadn't eaten and said she had no appetite. That was strange for her, she's always been so well and healthy, you know. But"—he looked at me with the serio-comic expression every man uses in such circumstances—"well, you know how they are, sir."

This time it was my turn to register triumph, but I forbore to glance at de Grandin, waiting Fleetwood's next remark.

"It must have been something after eleven," he continued, "when out across the cleared land I heard the deep, long-drawn baying of a hound. Some one in the neighbourhood must have a pack of the brutes and let 'em run at night, for I'd heard 'em once or twice earlier in the evening, but not so near or loud as this time. Doctor Trowbridge——"

He paused again, swallowed once or twice convulsively, and drummed nervously on the edge of the desk with his finger-tips, averting his gaze like a shame-faced schoolboy about to make a confession.

"Yes?" I prompted as the silence lengthened embarrassingly.

"You remember that horrible, inhuman howl some one let out in my dining-room that Sunday night? Doctor de Grandin accused Mazie Noyer of it."

I nodded.

"It wasn't Mazie. It was Hildegarde."

"Nonsense," I objected sharply. "Hildegarde had fainted; it couldn't have been——"

"Yes, it was, sir. I know it, because the next night, when that devilish baying sounded under our window, she began to roll and toss restlessly in bed, as though suffering a nightmare; then"—he stopped again, then hurried on as though anxious to get the statement finished—"then she threw back the bed-clothes, rose to her knees *and answered it!*"

"*A-a-ah?*" Jules de Grandin placed his fingers tip to tip, crossed his knees and regarded the toe of his patent leather evening shoe as though it were a novel sight. "And then, *Monsieur*, if you please, what next?"

Fleetwood's voice trembled, almost as if with ungovernable anger. "That was only the beginning!" he shot back. "I shook her, and she seemed to wake, but for more than an hour she lay there as if on the borderline of consciousness, fingering the bedclothes, rolling her head on the pillow, and moaning piteously every once in a while. It must have been almost morning before she finally went to sleep. Once or twice while she lay in that odd semi-conscious state, that infernal howling sounded underneath the window, and each time she shook and trembled as if——"

"Of course. It frightened her," I interrupted soothingly.

"No! It wasn't like that. It was as if she were all eagerness to get out there with that devilish hound—fairly trembling to go, sir!"

I stared at him incredulously, but his next words left me fairly breathless:

"Next night she went!"

"What?" I almost shouted.

"Just that, sir. The howling started during dinner next evening, and Hildegarde dropped her knife and fork and almost went into hysterics. I went to the den and got out a gun to give the beast a dose of bird-shot, but when I opened the door there was nothing to be seen. I wandered round the house several times, and once I thought I saw it over by the wood lot—a big, white shaggy brute —but it was so far out of range I didn't even try a shot.

"I woke up a little after midnight with a queer feeling something was wrong, and when I looked at Hildegarde's bed she wasn't there. I waited nearly half an hour, then went to look for her. While I was going through the library I heard that dam' dog howling again, and when I went to the window and looked out I'll be hanged if I didn't see her out on the lawn—and a great, white, fuzzy-looking beast was fawning on her and leaping at her and licking her face! Yes, sir, there she stood in a temperature of thirty degrees with nothing but her nightdress on, fondling and playing with that beast as if it were a pet she'd had all her life!"

"What did you do?" I asked.

"Went out after her," he answered simply. "The ground was pretty well frozen and hurt my feet, and I must have looked away once or twice as I tried to pick my way across the lawn, though I tried to keep my eyes on her, for when I reached her the dog was gone and she was standing there alone, her teeth chattering with the cold. I called to her, and she looked—at—me——" the words came slowly, and there was a choke in his voice.

I waited a moment, then patted his shoulder gently. "What was it, boy?" I asked softly.

"She looked at me and *snarled*. You've seen the way a vicious cur curls its lips when you approach it? That's the way my wife looked at me, Doctor Trowbridge. And down in her throat she made a sort of savage growling noise, like a police dog when he's ready to spring. It frightened me almost senseless for a moment, but I kept on, and she seemed normal enough when I reached her.

" 'My dear, what are you doing out here?' I asked,

but she just looked at me in a dazed, half-frightened sort of way, and made no answer. I picked her up and carried her into the house, and put her to bed. She went to sleep immediately. Next morning she remembered nothing, and I didn't press matters, you may be sure. I didn't hear the dog again that night."

"Later?" de Grandin asked softly.

"Yes, sir. Next night, and the next, and every night since then it's howled around the house like a banshee, but though my wife has tossed in her sleep and risen to answer it once or twice, she hasn't gone out again—not to my knowledge, at any rate."

"Now, Norval," I soothed, "all this is very distressing, but I don't think there's anything to be really alarmed about. The other night when Hildegarde fainted and I was tending her, I made a discovery—has she told you?"

"You mean——"

"Just so, boy. Perhaps she's not aware of it, herself, yet, but you have a right to expect some one will be occupying a crib at Twelvetrees before next June. I'm violating no confidences when I tell you more than one patient I've had in similar conditions has been as erratic in behaviour as Hildegarde. One lady could not abide the smell of fish, or even their sight. Merely seeing a bowl of goldfish would make her violently sick. Another had an inordinate craving for dried herring, the saltier and smellier the better, and in several cases conditions were so bad they simulated real insanity, yet all came out right in the end, bore normal, healthy children and became normal, healthy women again. Zoöphilia—an abnormal love of animals—isn't as rare in such circumstances as you might suppose. I'm sure Hildegarde will be all right, son."

The young husband beamed on me, and to my surprise de Grandin concurred in my opinion. "It is so," he assured Norval. "I, too, have seen strange things at times like this. No woman is accountable for anything, however strange it be, which she may do while she bears another life beneath her heart. Assuredly Friend Trowbridge is correct. At present you have little to fear, but both of us will assist you in every manner possible. You have but to call on us, and I entreat you to do so the moment anything untoward appears."

"That was decent of you, backing me up that way, old chap," I thanked him as the door closed on Fleetwood. "I was in a perfect ague for fear you'd spring some of that occult hocus-pocus of yours and scare the poor lad so we'd have two of 'em to treat instead of one."

He regarded me solemnly, tapping the corner of my desk with the nail of a well-manicured forefinger for emphasis. "I played the unutterable hypocrite," he answered. "No word of what I said did I believe, for I am more than sure a very evil thing has been let into the world, and that much tears—blood, too, perhaps—must be shed before we drive it to its own appointed place again. All that you said concerning the manic-depressive insanity sometimes present in such conditions was true, my friend, but the history of this case differentiates it from those which you recalled. Normal young women may develop a morbid love for animals—I have seen them derive the keenest pleasure from running their fingers over the smooth back of a pussy-cat or the rugged coat of a sheep-dog—but they do not respond to wandering beasts' howling in kind. No. They do not run barefoot into the winter night to fondle wandering brutes; they do not greet their husbands with dog-snarls. These things are different, my friend, but as yet I fear we have seen but the prologue to the play. Still'"—he shrugged his shoulders—"trouble will come soon enough—too soon, *parbleu!*—let the poor young Fleetwood be spared as long as possible, for——"

The shrilling of the office telephone cut through his words.

"Doctor Trowbridge?" the tortured voice across the wire asked tremulously. "This is Norval—Norval Fleetwood. I just got home. Hildegarde's gone! Nancy, the coloured maid, tell me a dog began howling under the windows almost as soon as I left the house, and Hildegarde seemed to go absolutely wild—hysterical—laughing and crying, and shouting some sort of answer at the beast. Then she let out an answering bay and rushed out into the yard. She's not been back, and Nancy was frightened almost white. She's no idea which way Hildegarde went. What shall I do?"

"Wait a moment," I bade, then retailed his statement to de Grandin.

"*Mordieu*, so soon? I had not thought it!" the Frenchman cried. "Bid him wait for us, *mon vieux*, we come to him at once, right away, immediately!"

"*Tiens*, my friend, they fish in troubled waters who dabble in spiritism," he remarked as we hastened toward Fleetwood's town house in Passaic Boulevard. "Have I not said it before? But certainly."

"Bosh!" I answered testily. "What has spiritism to do with Hildegarde's disappearance? I suppose you're referring to the séance at Twelvetrees? When some smart Alec answered that hound's bay in the dining-room that night it gave the poor girl a dreadful shock. That was all that was needed to set her unbalanced nervous system running wild—she probably wasn't aware of her condition and hadn't taken any care of herself, and recurrent depressive insanity has resulted."

"Oh?" he asked sarcastically. "And since when has depressive insanity or any recognized state of aberration connected with birth made the patient sit up in bed and howl like a dog, or——"

"Of course!" I broke in triumphantly. "Norval gave us a typical symptom when he said she snarled at him. You know as well as I that aversion for the husband is one of the commonest incidents of this form of derangement. She's fought it as hard as she could, poor child, but it's overmastered her. Now she's run away. We may have to keep Norval out of her sight until——"

"What of the dog—as we persist in calling it—which follows her and whose howls she answers in kind?" he insisted. "Do you find it convenient to ignore him, or had he slipped from your memory?"

"Rats!" I scoffed. "The country's full of night-prowling dogs, and——"

"And the city, also?" he broke in. "Dogs which howl beneath ladies' windows the moment their husbands' backs are turned?"

"See here," I turned on him, "just what are you driving at, anyway, de Grandin? What has the dog to do with the case?"

"If it were a dog, little or nothing," he replied slowly. "We might dismiss it as a case of zoöphilia, as you suggested to the young Fleetwood, but——"

"But what?" I demanded. "Out with it. What's your idea?"

"Very well," he nodded solemnly. "Here is my opinion: the 'dog,' as we have called it, is no dog at all, but a wolf, or rather a *loup-garou*, what you call a werewolf, who has availed himself of the opportunity given him by Mademoiselle Noyer's so detestable séance to return and——"

I laughed aloud in spite of myself. "You *are* fantastic!" I told him.

"Let us hope so," he answered grimly. "Jules de Grandin fancies himself most excellently, but in this case nothing would please him more than to see himself proved a superstitious booby. Yes."

"Yas, suh," the colored maid replied to our hurried questions, "Miz Hildegarde done scairt me outa seven years' growth, a'most. Mistu Norval hadn't hardly turned his back on de house when de a'mightiest howlin' yuh ever *did* hear started right underneath Miz Hildegarde's winder, an' Ah like to fainted right where Ah wuz."

"What were you doing? Where were you at the time?" de Grandin asked.

"Well, suh, hit wuz like dis yere: We all'd come in from de country today, an' Miz Hildegarde an' me wuz 'most froze wid de cold. Ah done git me sumpin hot fo' to drink—jest a little gin an' lemon, suh—directly Ah got here, but she didn't want none, though she kep' shiverin' an' shakin' like a little dog that's been flung in de river an' jest swum out an' ain't dry yet. They—Mr Norval an' Miz Hildegarde—had dinner about seven o'clock, an' Ah had mine at de same time, 'cause Ah knowed Miz Hildegarde'd be wantin' me directly. Pore thing, she ain't been feelin' so pert lately. So, soon's they's finished Ah gits up to her room an' waits there fo' her. Ah'd helped her outa her dress an' jest got a black-chiffon negly-jay on her when Mistu Norval comes to say he's goin' over to see Doctor Trowbridge. Yessuh.

"'Bout five minutes later, Ah 'speck hit wuz, whilst Ah wuz brushin' Miz Hildegarde's hair, Ah hears all sudden-like, de awfulest hollerin' an' yellin' under de winder.

"'Nancy!' Miz Hildegarde says to me, does yuh hear dat?'

"'Certainly, Ah hears it, honey,' Ah says. 'Does yuh think Ah's deef?'

"She kinder walls up her eyes, like de pictures ob de saints 'bout to git kilt by de lions yuh sees, an' says, real fast-like, 'No, no; Ah won't; Ah won't, Ah tell yuh; Ah *won't!*' An' then she kinder breaks down an' shivers like she'd taken a chill or sumpin, an' sorter turns around to me an' says, 'It's no use, Nancy; he's got me; tell Mistu Norval Ah love——' An' wid dat she stops talkin', an' her lips sorter curls back from her teeth, an' her eyes goes all glassy an' stary, an' she sorter growls way down in her throat, an' her hands sorter balls up into fists, on'y de fingers is stretched out like she wuz goin' to scratch somebody, an'—jest about dat time Ah gits down behind de sofa over yonder, suh, 'cause Ah was pow'ful 'feared she wuz a-goin' to jump on *me.*"

"Yes, and then?" de Grandin asked, his little eyes shining.

"Lawd-a-massy, suh. Den de trouble *did* start. Like to scairt mah haid white! Miz Hildegarde done run over to de winder an' looked out at sumpin down there in de yard, an' yelled sumpin in some foreign words, an' den she took out an' run downstairs like de debbil hisse'f wuz after her, a-howlin' an' yellin' an carryin' on like she wuz a dawg her own se'f, suh. 'Deed, she did!"

"And can you recall what it was she said when she looked out the window, *Mademoiselle?*"

"Lawdy, no, suh. Ah don't speak no language 'ceptin' English!"

"Think, *Mademoiselle.* Much, a very great much, depends on it. Can you not say what the words sounded like, even though they conveyed no meaning to you?"

The woman rolled her eyes upward and inhaled deeply,

compressing her lips and puffing out her cheeks as though she would force memory by the very pressure of pent-up breath. At length:

"Hit sounded like she said 'jere raven,' suh," she replied, expelling the breath from her packed lungs with an explosive gasp. "Not perzackly 'raven,' suh, but sumpin like hit. Dat's de neares' Ah can come to hit. Yuh see, Ah wuz so scairt Ah wuzn't takin' no proper notice ob what she *said*. What she wuz gwine to *do* wuz what int'rested me, suh."

"Jere raven; jere raven?' de Grandin muttered musingly to himself. "Jere——

"*Barbe d'un porc*, I have it! *Je reviens*—I return—I come back! That was it; *n'est-ce-pas, Mademoiselle?*" he turned inquiringly to the maid.

"Yas, suh; dat's jes' what she said, like Ah done tole yuh. 'Jere raven;' dat's hit!"

He cast a swift, triumphant glance at me. "What have you now to say, my old one?" he demanded.

"Nothing, only——"

"*Très bon.* Say the 'nothing' now; the 'only' will wait till later. Let us first seek Madame Hildegarde."

A hurry call was put in to police headquarters, and for upward of three hours we patrolled the cold, deserted streets, but neither sight nor information of Hildegarde Fleetwood could we obtain. At last, cold, exhausted and discouraged, we turned back, dreading Norval's tragic eyes when we reported failure.

Beside the front portico of the house we paused a moment while I spread my lap-robe over the engine-hood, for I had not yet put on my winter radiator-front. As I turned toward the steps, a feeble, whimpering moan from the copse of dwarf spruce beside the porch attracted my attention. A moment later we had parted the evergreens, and de Grandin flashed the light of his pocket lamp into the shadow under them.

Hildegarde Fleetwood crouched huddled in a heap in an angle of the wall, the flimsy black-chiffon pajama negligée she wore torn to tatters, one black-satin mule hanging to her delicate, unstockinged foot by its heel-strap, the other only heaven knew where. Beneath the rents in her diaphanous costume cancelli of deep, angry scratches showed, her feet were bruised and bleeding and stained with red-clay mud above the ankles, other patches of earth-soil were on her knees and hands and arms, and the nails of every carefully-cared-for finger were grimy with fresh earth and broken to the quick. Earth-stains were on her face and clotted in her hair, too, as though she might have wiped her countenance and put back the flowing veil of her long, bronze hair with clayey hands while she performed some arduous task.

"Good Lord!" I cried, stooping to gather the all but frozen girl in my arms and bear her up the steps.

The little Frenchman aided me as best he could, lighting my way with his pocket torch, leaping before me to fling wide the storm- and vestibule-doors. "At last," he murmured softly, "at last, my friend, you do assume the proper attitude and call upon the Lord. We shall have much need of His aid before we finish—and of the aid of Jules de Grandin, likewise."

We hurried restorative treatment as much as possible. A sponge bath of chilled water, followed by a rubdown with alcohol and gentle massage with dry flannel cloths restored her circulation, and a cup of hot beef tea administered in spoonful doses brought some semblance of color to her pallid cheeks. We watched for any symptoms of congestion, but were at last satisfied that Hildegarde had suffered nothing worse than shock, and so we gave a bromide sedative and left, impressing Norval with the importance of calling us immediately if any change in her condition came.

I shook my head despondently as we drove toward my house. "This case appears more serious than I'd thought at first," I finally admitted.

"Much," de Grandin nodded emphatically. "Very much, indeed. Yes. Certainly."

"*Mordieu*, my worst fears are all confirmed! It is devilish, infernal, no less! Read, my friend, read and weep, then say whose diagnosis was wrong, who talked the words of the fool concerning poor, bedevilled Madame Hildegarde, if you please!" Jules de Grandin cried as he perused the *Morning Journal* next day at breakfast. He thrust the paper at me with hands which trembled with excitement, indicating the item in the upper right-hand angle of the first page:

GHOULS OPEN GIRL'S GRAVE

Remove body From Casket, Steal Lily From Dead Hands and Leave Remains Uncovered

Woman in Black Sought

Called at Cemetery Earlier in Night and Frightened Sexton

Ghouls, working in the silence of St. Rose's R.C. Cemetery, on the Andover Rd. two miles north of Harrisonville, it became known early today, dug up from a freshly made grave the body of Miss Monica Doyle, 16, daughter of Patrick Doyle, 163 Willow Ave., Harrisonville, who died last Wednesday and was buried yesterday morning.

From the slender hands crossed on the dead girl's breast, clasping a rosary and the stem of a white lily, the ghouls stole the flower and carried it away.

The corpse, with its shroud and burial clothing disordered and torn, was thrown back face down in the casket, the lid replaced and the grave left open.

The crime, with its weird settings and the added mystery of the visit to the cemetery earlier in the night of a strange black-robed woman accompanied by a monstrous white dog, who frightened the sexton, Andrew Fischer, was disclosed early this morning when Ronald Flander, 25, and Jacob Rupert, 31, grave-diggers, going to prepare a grave for an early morning funeral, noticed the fresh earth heaped up by the Doyle girl's violated grave and, going nearer, discovered the unearthed casket and corpse.

Desecration of Miss Doyle's grave forms one of the most remarkable crimes in the annals of New Jersey since the murder of Sarah Humphreys 5 years ago, the scene of which was the golf links of the Sedgemoor Country club which is slightly more than two miles distant from the cemetery and also abuts on the Andover Rd.

One theory advanced is that a person possessed of religious fanaticism, swayed by the superstition that a lily buried with a body will thrive on the corpse, committed the deed to remove the flower.

The police are now running down scores of clues in an effort to solve the mystery and an arrest is promised within 24 hours.

I finished the grisly account, then stared in wide-eyed horror at de Grandin. "This *is* terrible—devilish—as you say," I admitted. "Who——"

"*Ah bah,* who asks what overset the cream-jug when the cat emerges from the *salle à manger* with whitened whiskers?" he shot back. "Come, let us go. There is no time to lose."

"Go? Where?"

"To the cemetery of St. Rose, of course. Come, quick; haste, my friend. The police, in pursuit of the scores of clues so glibly talked of by our journalistic friend, may have already obliterated all that which would be useful to us. *Nous verrons.*"

"D'ye think they'll really make an arrest?"

"God forbid," he answered piously. "Come for heaven's love; hurry, *mon vieux,* I beseech you!"

A small egg-shaped stove, crammed with mixed soft coal and coke, and glowing dully red, heated the little cement-block office of St. Rose's Cemetery to mid-August temperature and made mock of the December wind whistling about the angles of the house and wrestling with the bare-limbed trees which dotted the dismal little burial park. Mr. Fischer, a round-faced, blue-eyed man in early middle age who looked as though he would have been more at home standing in white jacket behind a delicatessen counter, nodded us casual greeting from behind the copy of the *Morgen Zeitung* he was perusing with interest. "From the newspapers?" he inquired. "Can't tell you nothin' more'n you already know. Can't you fellers let me have no peace? I'm busy this mornin' an'——"

"So much is obvious," de Grandin cut in with a quick smile which took the edge from his irony, "but we will take but a moment of your time. Meanwhile, as your minutes are precious, perhaps you would accept a small compensation for a little information?" There was a flash of green, and a banknote changed hands with the rapidity of a prestidigitator's card disappearing. Mr. Fischer's slightly bored manner gave way to one of urbane alertness. "Sure, what can I do for you gents?" he wanted to know.

The little Frenchman produced his cigarette case, proffered it to Fischer and selected a smoke for himself with infinite care. "First of all," he replied, "we desire to know of the mysterious lady in black whose appearance has been commented on. You can tell us of her, perhaps?"

"Sure can," the other volunteered. "It was about half-past nine or ten o'clock she like to scared a lung out o' me. We close th' main gates at eight an' th' footpath gates at half-past nine, an' I'd just locked the small gate and gotten ready to hit th' hay when I heard it flappin' an' bangin' in th' wind. It was pretty bad last night, you know. I went out to see what th' matter was, an' darned if th' lock hadn't broken. It was kind o' old an' rusty, anyhow, but it oughtn't to have broken in an ordinary wind-storm. I tinkered with it awhile, but couldn't do nothin' with it, so I went to look for a piece o' rope or wire or somethin' to tie it shut.

"There's a tool shed over th' other end o' th' lot—other side o' th' consecrated ground, where suicides an' unbaptized children an' th' like o' that is buried, right by th' pauper section—an' I thought most likely I'd find what I was lookin' for there. Th' men dumps everythin' they don't happen to be usin' in it. Well, sir, just as I was cuttin' across to that shed, who should jump up out o' nowhere but a great, long, tall woman with th' biggest an' ugliest brute of a dog you ever seen standing right alongside her. *Gott in Himmel!*"—he dropped his idiomatic American for the language of his fatherland—"I was frightened!"

The Frenchman thoughtfuly flicked a half-inch of ash on the worn linoleum rug covering the room's cement floor. "And can you describe her?" he asked slowly, shooting me a quick glance, then regarding the curling smoke from his cigarette with careful scrutiny.

Mr. Fischer considered a moment. "I ain't sure," he replied. "It was so sudden, th' way she bobbed up from nowhere, an' I don't mind admittin' I was more anxious to run than stand there an' look at her. She was pretty tall, half a head taller than th' average woman, I'd say at a guess, an'—well, I suppose you could call her pretty, too. Kind o' thin an' straight, with great, long hair all blowin' round her face an' shoulders, dressed in some sort o' black robe with no sleeves, an'—an' kind o'—I don't just know how to say it, sir. Sort o' *devilish*-lookin', you might say."

"Devilish? How?"

"Well, she had a kind o' smile on her face, like she was pleased to meet me there, but more pleased I was alone—if you get me. More of a snarl than a smile, you'd call it; kind o' pleased an' savage-lookin' at th' same time.

"An' that dog! *Mein Gott!* He was big as a calf an' with a long, pointed snout an' great, red mouth hangin' open, an' long, narrow eyes, like a Chinaman's, an' they was flashin' in th' dark, like a cat's!"

"Did they move to attack you?"

"No, sir, I can't say that they did. Just stood there, th' dog with one foot raised, like he was ready to jump on me, an' th' woman standin' beside him with her hair all blowin' about her an' one hand on th' beast's back, an' *th' both of 'em growled at me!* So help me, th' beast growled first, an' th' woman did th' same.

"I didn't waste no time gettin' away from there, I can tell you!"

"You have no idea from whence they came?"

"None whatever."

"Nor where they went thereafter?"

"Not me. I got back here as fast as I could an' locked th' door an' moved th' desk against it!"

"U'm. And may one see the grave of the so unfortunate Mademoiselle Doyle?"

Racial antipathy flared in Fischer's eyes as de Grandin used the French title, but memory of recent largess was more potent than inherited hatred. "Sure," he agreed, with markedly lessened cordiality, and slipped a stained sheepskin reefer over his shoulders. "Come on."

Casket and earth had been replaced in the violated sepulchre, but the raw red earth showed like a bleeding wound about the place where Monica Doyle lay in everlasting slumber.

The little Frenchman observed surroundings carefully, sank to his knees to take a closer view of the trampled mud about the refilled grave, then rose with a nod. "And now, if you will be so good as to show us where you encountered the so strange visitants last night, we shall no longer trouble you," he told the sexton.

The cemetery was a small one, and obviously catered to a far from wealthy clientele. Few graves were properly mounded, and more briars than flowers evidently grew there in the summer. Now, in bleak December, it held an air of desolation which depressed me like a strain of melancholy music. Bare and desolate as the better portions of the park were, however, the section set aside for indigents and those who died without the pale was infinitely worse. No turf, save weed crab-grass, hid the bare, red clay from view, the graves were fallen in and those which sported markers were more pathetic than those unmarked, for mere white-painted boards or stones so crudely carved that any beggar might scorn to own them were all the monuments. Midway between the garden-plots of hopelessness the superintendent paused. "Here's where it was," he announced curtly, eyeing de Grandin with no friendly glance. "Make it snappy; I'm busy—can't stand here in th' cold all day."

Once more de Grandin surveyed the terrain. Sinking to his knees he looked minutely at the red and sticky mud where Fischer had been frightened, then rose, and with a queer, abbreviated stride, moved toward the lines of leafless Lombardy poplars which served as wind-break by the rear fence of the graveyard.

"Hey, I can't wait no longer," the superintendent warned. "Got a lot o' things to do. See me in my office if you want to ask me anything else," with which announcement he turned upon his heel and left us.

"*Sale caboche*," de Grandin muttered, casting a level stare of cold hatred at the sexton's retreating back. "No matter, you have served your turn; your absence is the best gift you can give us. Quick, Friend Trowbridge, stand before me, if you please."

From his waistcoat pocket he produced his cigarette lighter and set it flaring, and from the pocket of his top-coat he took a length of paraffin candle. "I thought we might have need of this," he explained as he proceeded to melt the grease and pour it carefully into the imprint of a tiny, slender shoe which showed in the wet clay.

"Whatever are you doing?" I asked, standing before him to shield him from the wind and the glance of any curious passers-by at once.

"Parbleu, I do construct a brick house in which to store your senseless questions!" he answered with a grin, tamping the hot paraffin daintily into the depression, then waiting anxiously for it to harden.

As soon as the impression had been made, he wrapped it carefully in two thick sheets of paper, then, with his find held tenderly as a day-old infant, proceeded methodically to pace across the graveyard, carefully obliterating every feminine footprint he could find. "I doubt the police have taken casts of these," he told me, "but if the good Costello comes into the case he may show more intelligence than most. He has associated much with me, you will recall."

When all had been accomplished to his satisfaction, he steered me toward the entrance. *"Merci beaucoup, Monsieur l'Allemand-transplanté!"* he called ironically as he lifted his green felt hat and passed from the cemetery.

"Dam' Frog!" returned Superintendent Fischer, with which exchange of amenities we parted company.

"Slowly, Friend Trowbridge, drive slowly, if you please," he ordered as we left the graveyard, and from his vantage-point beside me he peered from left to right at the scrub vegetation bordering the road. Once or twice at his request I stopped while he alighted and made forays into the undergrowth. Finally, when we had consumed the better part of an hour traversing a quarter-mile, he returned from an investigative trip with a smile of satisfaction. *"Triomphe!"* he announced, holding his find up for my inspection. It was a dainty, French-heeled black-satin bedroom mule, the strap designed to hold it to its wearer's heel torn loose from its stitchings at one end, and the whole smeared with sticky, red-clay mud.

"And now, if you will be so good as to put me down, I shall be very grateful," he informed me as we reached the central part of town.

Something like an hour later he entered my consulting-room, eyes shining with elation, a smile of satisfaction hovering beneath the needle ends of his diminutive, tightly waxed blond mustache. "Doubting Thomases must have their proof," he told me; *"c'est pourquoi* I bring you yours. *Regardez*:

"This"—he carefully unwrapped a parcel and laid its contents on the desk— "is the impression of the so dainty footprint which I did take at the cemetery. This"—from his overcoat pocket he fished the satin mule he had salvaged from the roadside—"is what we found near by the cemetery upon our homeward trip. And this"—from another pocket he produced the first satin slipper's mate —"is Madame Hildegarde's shoe which she wore last night when we did find her all unconscious outside her house. I did buy it from the *femme de chambre* whom we interviewed last night but one little hour ago. Yes. Now, attend me:

"You will observe the shoes are identical, save one is broken, the other whole. You will notice both are stained with identical red mud—the mud of St. Rose's Cemetery. Now, you will notice, each fits the impression I took among the graves. *Enfin,* they are each other's mates, the shoes of Madame Hildegarde which she wore last night —into the cemetery when she and that wolf-thing which companioned her dug up the corpse of Mademoiselle Doyle! She was the so mysterious 'woman in black,' my friend, and—*par pitié de Dieu!*—her companion was the revenant spirit of Gilles Garnier, the werewolf of St. Bonnot, which slipped through the door Mademoiselle Noyer let open at her never-to-be-enough-reprobated séance that Sunday night at Twelvetrees!

"Laugh, snicker, grin like a dog! I tell you it is so! *Plût à Dieu* it were otherwise!"

"I'm not laughing," I answered soberly. "I was inclined to think you were at your favorite game of phantom-fighting at first; but the developments in this case have been so strange and dreadful I'm willing to let you take full charge. We've seen some strange, terrible things together, de Grandin, and I'm not inclined to scoff now. But tell me——"

"Everything I can!" he cut in impetuously, holding out his hands. "What is it you would know?"

"If Hildegarde's animal companion really were a werewolf, why did they unearth the body of the Doyle girl? I've always heard werewolves attacked the living."

"And also the dead," he replied. "There are different grades among them; some kill dogs and sheep, but fight mankind only when attacked, some are like hyenas, and prey upon the dead, others—the worst—lust after human flesh, especially human blood, and quest and kill women, children, even men, when weaker game is not available. In this case, this vile Garnier perchance chose the helpless dead for victim for their raid because——"

"*Their* raid?" I echoed in horror. "*Their*——"

"Alas, yes. It is too true. Poor, unfortunate Madame Hildegarde has become even as her conqueror and master, Gilles Garnier. She, too, is *loup-garou*. She too, is of that multitudinous herd not yet made fast in hell. Recall how she cried out, 'No, no, I will not come!' last night, then, turning to her maid, said, 'It is no use, he has me!' Also how she charged the *femme de chambre* with a farewell message of love for her husband ere she ran howling from the house to join her ghostly master? Remember, too, how her nails were all mud-stained and broken when we found her? Assuredly, she had been digging in the grave beside that other one. Yes."

"Then why didn't they——" I began, but the question stuck in my throat. "Why didn't they—eat——" I stopped, nauseated.

"Because of what the dead girl's dead hands clasped," he answered. "The lily they could ravish away and tear to bits—I found shreds of it embedded in the mud beside the grave, though the police and others overlooked it—but the blessed Rosary and the body assoiled with prayer and incense and holy water—*ha, pardieu*, those defied them, and they could do no more than vent their futile, baffled rage upon the corpse and offer it gross insult and cast it back into its coffin. No."

He took a quick half-turn across the room, retraced his steps, snatched a cigarette from his case and set it aglow with savage energy. "Attend me," he ordered, seating himself on the corner of the desk and fixing me with a level, unwinking stare.

"You are familiar with the so-called 'new psychology' of Freud and Jung, at least you have a working knowledge of it. Very well, then, consider: You know there is no such thing as true forgetfulness. Every gross desire —every hatred, every passion, every lust the conscious, waking mind experiences is indexed and pigeon-holed in the recesses of the subliminal mind. Those whose conscious recollection is free from every vestige of envy, malice, hatred or lust may go to a séance, and there liberate all the repressed—the 'forgotten'—evil desires they have had since early childhood without being in anywise aware of it. We know from our study of psychology that fixed, immutable laws govern mental processes. There is, by example, the law of similarity, which evokes the association of ideas; there is the law of integration, which splits mental images into integral fragments, and the law of re-integration, which enables the subconscious mind to rearrange these split images into one complete picture of a past event or scene as one fits together the pieces of a jig-saw puzzle.

"Very good. Ten or a dozen people seat themselves in silence around a table, every condition for light hypnosis is present—lack of external attractions of the attention, darkness, a common focusing of thought upon a single objective, that of attracting spirits. In such conditions the sitters may be said to 'pool their consciousness'—the normal inhibitions of the conscious mind are relieved from duty. The sentry sleeps and the fortress gates are open! Conditions for invasion are ideal.

"*Eh bien*, my friend, do not think the enemy is slow to take advantage of his opportunity. By no means. If there be even one person at the séance whose subconsciousness locks up unholy desires—and who has been entirely free from thought-dominance by one of the Seven Deadly Sins throughout his life?—the Powers of Evil have a ready-made ally within the gates. That like attracts like is a dominant law of nature, and the law of similarity is one of the rules of psychology. The gateway of the *psyche* is thrown open to whoever may enter in.

"Now, who would be the easiest one attacked? Madame Hildegarde is not well. Her blood-stream, her whole system, must care for two instead of one, thereby lessening her powers of resistance.

"Very good. A sign? Consider what occurred. A rapping announces a man-spirit, seeking communication. His name is asked. He answers. *Eh bien,* I shall say he answers! He gives his real name, for there is little fear that any one present will recognize him. 'Gilles Garnier, who lived at St. Bonnot in the reign of King Charles,' he brazenly announces himself. Do you know him, perhaps?" He paused a moment, lifting his brows interrogatively.

"Why, no, I never heard of him," I answered.

"*Bien.* Neither had ony one there present. His name, his nationality, his epoch, all sounded 'romantic' to a circle of fat-headed fools; is it not so? Yes, decidedly.

"*Ha,* but Jules de Grandin knew him! As you have studied the history of medicine and anesthesia and of the recurrent plagues which have scourged the world, so I have studied the history of those other plagues which destroyed the body or the soul, sometimes both together. Listen, I will tell you of Gilles Garnier:

"In 1573, when Charles IX occupied the throne of France, there dwelt at St. Bonnot, near the town of Dôle, a fellow named Gilles Garnier. He was an ill-favoured churl, and those who knew him best knew little good of him. He dwelt alone, so that the country folk called him 'the hermit,' but the title carried with it no attribute of sanctity. Quite otherwise.

"Midsummer came that fateful year, and with it numerous complaints to the Parliament of Dôle. Farmers living near the city brought in accounts of sheep stolen from the fold at dead of night, or dogs killed as they watched the flocks, of little children found dead and horribly mangled along the roadside and beneath the hedges. Three wandering minstrels—all veterans of the wars and stout swordsmen—were set upon as they rode through the wood of St. Bonnot at night, and one of them was all but killed, though they resisted fiercely. The countryside was terrorized and even men-at-arms preferred to stay at home by night, for a *loup-garou,* or werewolf, the like of which had never before been known, had claimed the land for his own from sunset until dawn.

"On the evening of November 8, 1573, when the fields were all but nude of vegetation and the last leaves reluctantly parting company with the trees, three laborers were hurrying to their homes at Chastenoy by a woodland shortcut when they heard the screams of a little girl issuing from a dense tangle of vines and undergrowth. And with the child's cries mingled the baying of a wolf.

"Swinging their billhooks, they cut themselves a pathway through the wildwood, and hastened toward the sounds. In a little clearing they beheld this terrifying sight: Backed against a tree, defending herself as best she might with her shepherd's crook, was a little maid of ten, already bleeding from a score of wounds, while before her crouched a monstrous creature which never ceased its devilish baying as it attacked her tooth and nail.

As the peasants ran forward the thing fled off into the forest on all fours, disappearing instantly in the darkness. The men would have followed, but the fainting, sorely wounded child demanded their attention."

He paused to light another cigarette, then: "In court," he asked, "when there is contrariety of testimony, supposing all witnesses had equal opportunity of observation, which version would be believed?"

"Why, that supported by the greatest number of witnesses, I suppose," I answered.

"Very good. That seems logical, does it not? Consider then: Next day, when these peasants laid their story before the authorities, one swore the child's assailant had a man's body, though it was covered with hair and ran on all fours; the other two declared as positively it had the body of a gaunt, light-gray wolf, *but the eyes of a man.*

"You will recall, perhaps, the amiable Monsieur Fischer declared this morning that the brute which frightened him last night had 'eyes like a *Chinaman*'? Very well.

"November 14, 1573, a boy of eight disappeared. The

child had last been seen within a crossbow's range of the city gates, yet he had vanished as completely as though the earth had swallowed him. *Morbleu,* swallowed he had been, but not by the earth! No.

"Circumstantial evidence involved this so unsaintly hermit, Gilles Garnier. A *sergent de ville* and six arquebusiers went forth to arrest him and took him into custody shortly after noon on November 16. His trial followed quickly.

"It is a curious circumstance, often commented on, that those involved in such crimes seldom needed to be put to the question, but readily confessed when finally their sin had found them out. It was usually so in witchcraft trials; it was so in this. Garnier readily admitted making a compact with the Devil whereby he was given the power of transforming himself into a wolf at will, providing he willed it between darkness and cock-crow.

"Witnesses in flocks appeared against him. The *trouveurs* who had been attacked appeared, and so did many a farmer whose sheepfold had been raided: but the little maid the peasants saved near Chastenoy was strongest in her testimony, for she identified the prisoner *by his eyes.* Furthermore, when an impression of his teeth was taken, it matched precisely with the tooth-marks in her halfhealed scars. The werewolf keeps his human teeth, as well as eyes, while metamorphosized, it seems.

"Garnier admitted the attack and added tales of many others to it. On the last day of Michaelmas, near the wood of La Serre, while in his wolf-form, he had attacked with teeth and claws a little girl of ten or twelve, dragged her into a thicket and gnawed the flesh from her arms and legs. There were those who corroborated his story in part, by telling of the finding of the little mutilated corpse.

"On the fourteenth day after All Saints, also in the form of a wolf, he had killed and eaten a little boy. On Friday before the feast of St. Bartholomew he had seized and killed a lad of twelve near the village of Perrouze, and would have eaten him but for the appearance of some peasants. These men were found and corroborated the prisoner's story, and again conflict of testimony appeared.

Some swore he was in human form, though fur-covered and going on all fours; the others deposed he had a true wolf's form. All were agreed he howled and growled like any natural beast.

"By the way," he broke off, 'can you recall the date Mademoiselle Noyer convoked her séance at Twelvetrees?"

"Why—er"—I made a hasty mental calculation—"yes, of course. It was the twenty-sixth of November."

"Précisément," he nodded gravely. And it was upon November 26, 1573, that Gilles Garnier, forever after to be known as the werewolf of St. Bonnot, having duly been found guilty, was dragged for half a mile over a rough road by ropes attached to his ankles, bound to a stake and given to the flames."

"Coinci——" I began doubtfully, but:

"Coinci—devil!" he snapped. "Coincidences like that do not occur, my friend. For almost four and a half centuries this man's wicked, earthbound soul had hovered in the air, invisible, but very potent. Upon the anniversary of his execution his memory is strongest, for jealousy of life, and rage, and eagerness to return and raven once again are greatest then. He beats against the portal of our world like the wolf against the doors of *les trois petit cochons* in the nursery-story, and where he finds a door weak enough—*he breaks through!* Yes. Indubitably. It is so."

"But see here," I countered, "it's all very well to say he's seized Hildegarde's brain—I shan't dispute it with you—but how is he able to manifest himself physically? It might have been a vision or a ghost spectre, or whatever you wish to call it, that Fischer saw in the cemetery, or that Norval Fleetwood saw sporting with his wife on the lawn at Twelvetrees, but it was no unsubstantial wraith which dug the little Doyle girl from her grave and tossed her poor, desecrated body back into its casket. It won't do to say Hildegarde did it. Even granting she had the supernatural strength of the insane, the task would have been physically impossible for her to perform unaided."

"Incomparable Trowbridge!" he cried delightedly.

"Always when it looks darkest, you do show me a light in the blackness. To you I and Madame Hildegarde owe our salvation. No less!"

I stared at him open-mouthed. "What in the world——" I began, but he cut me short with a delighted gesture.

"Attend me carefully," he ordered. "You have resolved a most damnably complex problem into a most simple solution. Yes. You know—or at least I so inform you—that one of the common phenomena associated with spiritistic séances is the production of light. Numerous mediums have the power of attracting or emitting light, and even in small amateur circles where there is in all truth little enough 'light' in the psychic sense, such elemental phenomena are produced. Very good. What is this light? Some of it may be true spirit-phenomena, but mostly it is nothing but human mental energy manifested as light waves, and given off by the concerted thought of the circle of sitters at the séance. But at times this essence given off is something more substantial than the mere emission of vibrations capable of being recognized as light. There is indubitably proof of true materializations being made at séances. The British Society for Psychical Research and the *Société d'Etudes Psychiques*—both reliable associations of scientific men—have attested it. Very well, what makes such materializations possible?

"A spiritual being, whether it be the ghost of one once human or otherwise, possesses passions, but neither body nor parts to make them effective. Some 'ghosts' may show themselves, others may not, and it is these latter which visit séances in hope of materialization. Of themselves they can not materialize any more than the most skilled bricklayer can construct a house, but give the artizan materials with which to build, and *pouf!* the house is reared before you know it. So with these spirits. A form of energy is radiated by the sitters at the séance, something definite as radio waves, yet not to be seen or touched or handled. This is called psychoplasm. If enough of it be present, the hovering ghost spirit or demon can so change its vibrations, so compress it, as to render it solid and ponderable. In fine, he has built himself a body.

"In normal circumstances the psychoplasm returns to the bodies which gave it off, when once its work is done. *Ha*, but suppose the spiritual visitant is a larcener—one who so greatly desires once more to live and move and have his being in this world that he will not return that which furnishes him a corporeal body? What then?

"There lies the danger of the séance, my friend. It may unwittingly give bodily structure to a discarnate, evil entity. So it was in this case. Yes."

"Yes?" I answered. "Well, where's the solution of the problem you said you'd found?"

"Here, *pardieu!* I shall reassemble the sitters at that séance and make that thief, Gilles Garnier, give back what he stole from them. Yes, I shall most assuredly do that, and this very night."

All afternoon he was busy at the telephone, tracing down the ten members who composed the circle at Twelvetrees with Norval Fleetwood and his wife. When all had been reached and agreed to gather at Fleetwood's town house that night, he rose wearily. "Do not wait dinner for me, my friend," he told me sadly. "Rather would I lose a finger than forego the little young pig the so talented Nora McGinnis roasts in the kitchen for dinner, but something more precious than roast young pigs is involved here. I shall dine at an hotel in New York, *hélas.*"

"Why, where are you going?"

"To a booking agency of the theatre."

"A theatrical booking——"

"Precisely, exactly, quite so. I have said it. Meet me at Monsieur Fleetwood's at ten tonight, if you please, and as you value my friendship, see to it that no one of the party leaves before I come. *Au plaisir de vous revoir.*"

Half-past nine was sounding on the clock in Fleetwood's drawing-room when de Grandin arrived. Embarrassed and ill at ease, the sitters in the séance at Twelvetrees were grouped about the room, Norval doing his best to entertain them. Hildegarde, looking pale and haggard, but showing no serious physical results of her night's adventure, sat before the fire, and every now and then she shuddered slightly, though the room was warmed somewhat past the point of comfort. A frightened, half-expectant look was on her face, and once or twice as motor horns hooted mournfully in the street outside quick fear leaped into her eyes and she half rose from her seat with blenched cheeks and twitching, terrified lips.

With de Grandin came a tall, pale-faced young man in poorly fitting evening clothes, a virtuoso's mop of long, dark hair and deep-set, melancholy eyes. "Professor Morine, Doctor Trowbridge," de Grandin introduced the stranger. "Monsieur Fleetwood, Professor Morine."

"The professor is by profession a stage hypnotist," he explained in a lower tone. "At present he is without an engagement, but the gentlemen at the theatrical *bureau d'enregistrement* recommend his talents without reserve. His fee for tonight will be one hundred dollars. You agree, *Monsieur?*" he looked inquiringly at Fleetwood.

"If it will help cure Hildegarde it's cheap at twice the price."

"Very good, let us then say one hundred and fifty. Remember, the professor can secure no advertisement from tonight. Moreover, he has promised to forget all which transpires within this house."

"All right, all right," Fleetwood answered petulantly; "let's get started."

"*Très bien.* All is prepared in the farther room? Good. If you will kindly make excuse to have Madame Hildegarde leave the room a moment?"

Norval whispered something in his wife's ear, and as they left the apartment together de Grandin addressed the company:

"*Messieurs, Mesdames*, we are assembled here tonight in an endeavour to duplicate the conditions obtaining when Madame Fleetwood became first indisposed. Upon my honor I assure you no advantage will be taken, but it is necessary that you all submit to a state of light hypnosis. I shall stand by and personally see that all goes well. Do you agree?"

One after another the guests reluctantly acquiesced in the proposal until Mazie Noyer was reached. "I won't," she answered shortly. "I'll not be a party to any such ridiculous proceeding. You just want to get me in that man's power to make me a laughing stock. I know! No, indeed, I'll not consent!"

"Mademoiselle," de Grandin protested, "do you not care to see Madame Fleetwood restored to health? You assume a great burden by refusing."

"I don't care whether Hildegarde recovers or not. She can die before I'll consent to being hypnotized. You just want to make a fool of me!"

"Parbleu, nature has forestalled us in that!" he muttered, but aloud he answered: "Very well, *Mademoiselle,* as you wish. You will excuse us while we perform our work?" With a frigid bow he turned from her and motioned the others into an adjoining room.

All furniture had been removed from this apartment save a single round table and a dozen chairs. About the latter de Grandin traced a pentagram composed of two interlaced triangles, and in each of the five points he set a tall wax candle, a tiny, sharp-pointed dagger with tip pointing outward, and a small crucifix.

Norval led in Hildegarde, and as the sitters took their places round the table Professor Morine walked slowly round the circle, stroking each forehead and whispering soothingly. "All right, Doctor," he called softly as he completed the circuit. "What next?"

The Frenchman lighted the candles one by one, murmuring some sort of prayer or incantation as each took flame, surveyed the dimly lit room for a moment, then turned to the professor. "Bid them take orders from me, if you please," he answered.

While Professor Morine repeated the command, de Grandin drew forth five shallow silver dishes from beneath the table, poured some thick, dark fluid into each from a prodigious hip-flask; then from another flask he added some further liquor, dark like the first, but thinner and less viscid. As he recorked the second flask I became aware of the pleasant, heady odour of port wine.

Each of the five dishes he placed just outside one of the five points of the pentagram; then drawing something which jangled musically from beneath the table, he handed Morine and me each a small ecclesiastical censer and set the powdered incense glowing. "Keep them in motion, my friends," he ordered, "and should anything appear amid the darkness, swing your censers toward it without ceasing."

To the sitters round the table he ordered: "You will now concentrate with all your force on recovering that which is yours. No thought will you give to anything else, nor will you see or notice what may take place here, but ceaselessly you will say—*and feel*—'Gilles Garnier, give me back that which you withhold!' Begin!"

Like the muttering of a summer stormwind heard miles away, the low monotonous, whispered chorus began: "Gilles Garnier, give me back that which you withhold— Gilles Garnier, give me back that which you withhold!"

For upward of five minutes the murmured, monotonous chorus went on. The ceaseless repetition made me drowsy. I stared about the dim, candle-lit room in an effort to distract my attention from the unceasing monody, wondering when it would stop.

"Why did you bring in this professional hypnotist?" I whispered to de Grandin. "I've seen you do some wonderful work of that kind; do you think it advisable to bring in a stranger?"

"*Tiens*," he returned softly, "there were twelve of them to be subjected, counting the recalcitrant Mademoiselle Noyer. To put them all beneath the spell would have tired me greatly, and *le bon Dieu* knows I must be fresh and mentally alert this night. *Attendez;* it comes!"

A sensation of intense cold was spreading through the warm, closed room, and the five candles flickered and bent their flames as though a breeze blew on them, though the light silk-mesh curtains at the windows were still as though cast in metal. From one of the vessels by a starpoint there came a strange, soft sound, such a sound as a cat makes when it laps milk, and the rubescent liquid in the dish showed faint ripples, as though disturbed by a dabbling finger—or an invisible tongue. Lower, lower sank the liquid; the bowl was now all but empty.

Softly, swiftly, de Grandin moved, snatching one after another of the silver vessels, dragging them within the outline of the pentagram.

Again we waited, the monotonous, refrain, "Gilles Garnier, give me back that which you withhold!" dinning in our ears; then in a farther corner of the room showed a faint and ghastly phosphorescence. Brighter and brighter it glowed, took shape, took substance—a monstrous, shaggy white wolf crouched in the angle of the wall!

The beast was bigger than a mastiff, bigger than an Irish wolfhound, almost as big as a half-grown heifer, and from its wide and gaping mouth there lolled a gluttonous red tongue from which a drop of dark-red liquid dripped. But dreadful as the monster's size and aspect were, its eyes were more so. Incongruous as living orbs glaring through the eye-holes of a skull, they were, fierce, fiery malevolent and *human;* but human only to be vicious, cunning and wicked, as human intellect, perverted, is crueler than the instincts of the cruelest of brute beasts.

For a moment the monster glared at us; then with a bellowing cry of rage it rose upon its haunches, got to all four feet, and charged full-tilt upon us.

"Accursed of heaven, cast-off of hell, give back that which you withhold!" de Grandin cried, advancing to an angle of the pentagram to meet the werewolf's charge, swinging his censer toward it, so that clouds of incense floated forward, and returning the wolf-thing's glare with a stare of equal hatred and ferocity.

Where the narrow chalk-line of the pentagram traced across the floor the great beast stopped abruptly as though in contact with a solid wall, gave a bay of wild, insensate rage, and recoiled, choking and gasping from the cloud of incense.

"Accursed of heaven, give back that which you withhold!" de Grandin ordered yet again.

The great white beast eyed him questioningly, lowered itself till its bellyhairs scarcely cleared the floor, and slowly circled round the pentagram, whining half fearfully, half savagely.

"Accursed of heaven, give back that which you withhold!" came the inexorable command once more.

Oddly, the wolf-thing seemed losing substance. Its solidarity seemed dwindling; where a moment before it had been substantial as any terror of the forest, we could now plainly discern the outlines of the room through its body, as though it were composed of vapour. It lost its red and white tones and became luminous, like a figure traced in phosphorescent paint on a dark background. The head, the trunk, the limbs and tail became elongated, split off from one another, rose slowly toward the ceiling like little globes of luminosity, floated in mid-air a moment, then slowly settled toward the monotonously droning sitters round the table.

As each luminous globe touched a sitter's head it vanished, not like a bursting bubble, but slowly, like a ponderable substance being sucked in, as milk in a goblet vanishes when imbibed through a straw.

A single tiny pear-shaped globule of light remained, bobbing aimlessly against the ceiling, bouncing down again, as an imprisoned wasp may make a circuit of a room into which it has inadvertently flown.

"Accursed of heaven, give back that which you withhold!" de Grandin ordered, staring fixedly at the rebounding fire-ball, "give back that which——"

"Here, I've stood about enough of this—I want to know what's going on here!" Mazie Noyer burst into the room. "If you're doing anything mystic, I want to——"

"Pour l'amour de Dieu, have a care!" de Grandin's appalled shout cut her short. She had walked across an angle of the pentagram, oversetting and extinguishing one of the candles as she did so.

"I won't be bullied and insulted by you any longer, you miserable little French snip!" she announced striding toward him. "I'll——"

The fire-ball fell to the floor as though suddenly transmuted to lead. We could hear the impact as it struck the boards. For a moment it rolled aimlessly to and fro, seemed to shrink—compress itself—and quickly took on the shape of a tiny, white wolf.

Scarcely larger than a mouse it was, but a perfect replica of the great beast which had menaced us a few moments earlier, even to its implacable savagery. With a howl which was hardly more than a rat-squeak in volume, yet fierce and terrifying for all that, it dashed across the room, straight at the angle of the pentagram where the candle had been overturned.

"Pardieu, we meet on something like even ground, *Monsieur le Loup-garou,* I think!" de Grandin cried, seized one of the small, sharp-pointed daggers from the floor and impaled the advancing miniature monster with its keen blade.

The tiny, savage thing died slowly, writhing horribly. With teeth and claws it fought against the steel which pinned it to the floor, blood and futile, hissing, agonized squealing howls issuing from its gaping mouth. At last its struggles ceased, it quivered and lay still.

"Oh, you cruel, odious little wretch, you killed that poor little animal as heartlessly as——" Miss Noyer raged at him, then broke off her tirade abruptly and planted a resounding slap upon de Grandin's cheek.

A red and angry patch showed on his face where her palm and fingers struck, but the rest of his countenance went livid beneath the insult. *"Sorcière!* Witch-woman; ally of hell's dark powers!" he cried furiously. "Were it not that I must burn him to ashes in the fire, I would give you the carcass of your familiar for a keepsake. Be off, get gone, ere I forget your sex and——" He strode toward her, eyes blazing with such cold, concentrated fury that she recoiled from him as from a serpent. "You dare!" she challenged in a shrill frightened voice. "You just dare strike me!" then turned and raced through the door in fear of swift and condign punishment.

"Of course," de Grandin told me in my study some hours later, "we could neglect no precautions, my friend. The pentagram has at all times and in all ages been esteemed as a guard against the powers of evil; wicked spirits, even the most powerful, are balked by it. In addition, I placed in each of its five angles a blessèd candle from the church, a crucifix and also a dagger which had been dipped in *eau bénite*. Evil spirits of an elemental nature—those which have never been housed in human flesh—can not face pointed steel, probably because it concentrates radiations of psychic force from the human body which are destructive to them. In addition, I secured from the good *curé* who let me have the candles three censers filled with consecrated incense. *Mordieu*, he was hard to convince, that one, but once I had convinced him that the blessed articles were needed to combat a dread invader from the other world, he went the entire pig, as you Americans say. Yes. Incense, you must know, is highly objectionable to wicked spirits, whether they be the ghosts of long-dead evil men or ill-disposed neutrarians bent on doing mischief to mankind, whom they hate.

"*Eh bien*, I thought the grease was in the fire when that never-enough-to-be-abominated Noyer woman came into the room and overset the guardian candle. Her natural viciousness and her anger made a sad disturbance, she gave the one tiny remaining bit of psychoplasm as yet not reabsorbed the very nourishment it needed to become a ravening, preying, full-sized werewolf once more. Had I not killed it to death with the consecrated dagger when I did, it might have grown once more to its full stature— and it was already inside the protecting pentagram. *Cordieu*, I do not like to speculate on what might have happened then! No, we shall be far happier if we dismiss that thought from our minds."

"What was in those silver dishes?" I asked.

"Bait," he answered with a grin. "Blood and wine, my friend; wine and blood. The mixture of those liquids is especially pleasing to the hosts of evil. In the celebration of *la messe noire*—the black mass where Satan is invoked —by example, the chalice is filled with mingled wine and blood from the cut throat of a sacrificed babe. Therefore, I procured some fresh blood from the hospital and some fresh wine from a legger-of-the-boot this morning, and set my bait. The werewolf came to drink, but I would not let him lap his fill. No. When he had drank one bowlful I did move the others from his reach within the angles of the pentagram, lest he become too powerful for us. One does not nourish one's enemy before the encounter, my friend. Assuredly not. All of which reminds me——"

"Of what?" I asked, as he paused with one of his well-remembered, elfish grins.

"That wine unmixed with blood is very good to drink, and that I am most vilely thirsty. Madame Hildegarde's obsession is destroyed, she has no more to fear, for Gilles Garnier is deprived of bodily ability to do her harm. There is no immediate further need for the so great talents of Jules de Grandin, therefore"—he rose with a profound bow—"with your permission I shall proceed to drink myself into a state of blissful unconsciousness—and he who wakes me before noon tomorrow would be advised to have his *Pater Nosters* said beforehand!"

PETER FLEMING

THE KILL

In the cold waiting-room of a small railway station in the West of England two men were sitting. They had sat there for an hour, and were likely to sit there longer. There was a thick fog outside. Their train was indefinitely delayed.

The waiting-room was a barren and unfriendly place. A naked electric bulb lit it with a wan, disdainful efficiency. A notice, "No Smoking," stood on the mantel-piece; when you turned it round, it said "No Smoking" on the other side, too. Printed regulations relating to an outbreak of swine-fever in 1924 were pinned neatly to one wall, almost, but maddeningly not quite, in the centre of it. The stove gave out a hot, thick smell, powerful already, but increasing. A pale leprous flush on the black and beaded window showed that a light was burning on the platform outside, in the fog. Somewhere, water dripped with infinite reluctance onto corrugated iron.

The two men sat facing each other over the stove on chairs of an unswerving woodenness. Their acquaintance was no older than their vigil. From such talk as they had had, it seemed likely that they were to remain strangers.

The younger of the two resented the lack of contact in their relationship more than the lack of comfort in their surroundings. His attitude towards his fellow beings had but recently undergone a transition from the subjective to the objective. As with many of his class and age, the routine, unrecognized as such, of an expensive education, with the triennial alternative of those delights normal to wealth and gentility, had atrophied many of his curiosities. For the first twenty-odd years of his life he had read humanity in terms of relevance rather than reality, looking on people who held no ordained place in his own existence much as a buck in a park watches visitors walking up the drive; mildly, rather resentfully inquiring—not inquisitive. Now, hot in reaction from this unconscious provincialism, he treated mankind as a museum, gaping conscientiously at each fresh exhibit, hunting for the noncumulative evidence of man's complexity with indiscriminate zeal. To each magic circle of individuality he saw himself as a kind of free-lance tangent. He aspired to be a connoisseur of men.

There was undoubtedly something arresting about the specimen before him. Of less than medium height, the stranger had yet that sort of ranging leanness that lends vicarious inches. He wore a long black overcoat, very shabby, and his shoes were covered with mud. His face had no colour in it, though the impression it produced was not one of pallor; the skin was of a dark sallow, tinged with gray. The nose was pointed, the jaw sharp and narrow. Deep vertical wrinkles, running down toward it from the high cheek bones, sketched the permanent groundwork of a broader smile than the deep-set, honey-coloured eyes seemed likely to authorize. The most striking thing about his face was the incongruity of its frame. On the back of his head the stranger wore a bowler hat with a very narrow brim. No word of such casual implications as a tilt did justice to its angle. It was clamped, by something at least as holy as custom, to the back of his skull, and that thin questing face confronted the world fiercely from under a black halo of nonchalance.

The man's whole appearance suggested *difference* rather than aloofness. The unnatural way he wore his hat had the significance of indirect comment, like the antics of a performing animal. It was as if he was part of some older thing, of which homo sapiens in a bowler hat was an expurgated edition. He sat with his shoulders hunched and his hands thrust into his overcoat pockets. The hint of discomfort in his attitude seemed due not so much to the fact that his chair was hard as to the fact that it was a chair.

The young man had found him uncommunicative. The most mobile sympathy, launching consecutive attacks on different fronts, had failed to draw him out. The reserved adequacy of his replies conveyed a rebuff more effectively than sheer surliness. Except to answer him, he did not look at the young man. When he did, his eyes were full of an abstracted amusement. Sometimes he smiled, but for no immediate cause.

Looking back down their hour together, the young man saw a field of endeavour on which frustrated banalities lay thick, like the discards of a routed army. But resolution, curiosity, and the need to kill time all clamoured against an admission of defeat.

"If he will not talk," thought the young man, "then I will. The sound of my own voice is infinitely preferable to the sound of none. I will tell him what has just happened to me. It is really a most extraordinary story. I will tell it as well as I can, and I shall be very much surprised if its impact on his mind does not shock this man into some form of self-revelation. He is unaccountable without being *outré,* and I am inordinately curious about him."

Aloud he said, in a brisk and engaging manner: "I think you said you were a hunting man?"

The other raised his quick, honey-coloured eyes. They gleamed with inaccessible amusement. Without answering, he lowered them again to contemplate the little beads of light thrown through the iron-work of the stove onto the skirts of his overcoat. Then he spoke. He had a husky voice.

"I came here to hunt," he agreed.

"In that case," said the young man, "you will have heard of Lord Fleer's private pack. Their kennels are not far from here."

"I know them," replied the other.

"I have just been staying there," the young man continued. "Lord Fleer is my uncle."

The other looked up, smiled and nodded, with the bland inconsequence of a foreigner who does not understand what is being said to him. The young man swallowed his impatience.

"Would you," he continued, using a slightly more peremptory tone than heretofore,—"would you care to hear a new and rather remarkable story about my uncle? Its dénouement is not two days old. It is quite short."

From the fastness of some hidden joke, those light eyes

mocked the necessity of a definite answer. At length: "Yes," said the stranger, "I would." The impersonality in his voice might have passed for a parade of sophistication, a reluctance to betray interest. But the eyes hinted that interest was alive elsewhere.

"Very well," said the young man.

Drawing his chair a little closer to the stove, he began:

As perhaps you know, my uncle, Lord Fleer, leads a retired, though by no means an inactive life. For the last two or three hundred years, the currents of contemporary thought have passed mainly through the hands of men whose gregarious instincts have been constantly awakened and almost invariably indulged. By the standards of the eighteenth century, when Englishmen first became self-conscious about solitude, my uncle would have been considered unsociable. In the early nineteenth century, those not personally acquainted with him would have thought him romantic. To-day, his attitude toward the sound and fury of modern life is too negative to excite comment as an oddity; yet even now, were he to be involved in any occurrence which could be called disastrous or interpreted as discreditable, the press would pillory him as a "Titled Recluse."

The truth of the matter is, my uncle has discovered the elixir, or, if you prefer it, the opiate, or self-sufficiency. A man of extremely simple tastes, not cursed with overmuch imagination, he sees no reason to cross frontiers of habit which the years have hallowed into rigidity. He lives in his castle (it may be described as commodious rather than comfortable), runs his estate at a slight profit, shoots a little, rides a great deal, and hunts as often as he can. He never sees his neighbours except by accident, thereby leading them to suppose, with sublime but unconscious arrogance, that he must be slightly mad. If he is, he can at least claim to have padded his own cell.

My uncle has never married. As the only son of his only brother, I was brought up in the expectation of being his heir. During the war, however, an unforeseen development occurred.

In this national crisis my uncle, who was of course too

old for active service, showed a lack of public spirit which earned him locally a good deal of unpopularity. Briefly, he declined to recognize the war, or, if he did recognize it, gave no sign of having done so. He continued to lead his own vigorous but (in the circumstances) rather irrelevant life. Though he found himself at last obliged to recruit his hunt-servants from men of advanced age and uncertain mettle in any crisis of the chase, he contrived to mount them well, and twice a week during the season himself rode two horses to a standstill after the hill-foxes which, as no doubt you know, provide the best sport the Fleer country has to offer.

When the local gentry came and made representations to him, saying that it was time he did something for his country besides destroying its vermin by the most unreliable and expensive method ever devised, my uncle was very sensible. He now saw, he said, that he had been standing too aloof from a struggle of whose progress (since he never read the paper) he had been only indirectly aware. The next day he wrote to London and ordered the *Times* and a Belgian refugee. It was the least he could do, he said. I think he was right.

The Belgian refugee turned out to be a female, and dumb. Whether one or both of these characteristics had been stipulated by my uncle, nobody knew. At any rate, she took up her quarters at Fleer: a heavy, unattractive girl of 25, with a shiny face and small black hairs on the backs of her hands. Her life appeared to be modelled on that of the larger ruminants, except, of course, that the greater part of it took place indoors. She ate a great deal, slept with a will, and had a bath every Sunday, remitting this salubrious custom only when the house-keeper, who enforced it, was away on her holiday. Much of her time she spent sitting on a sofa, on the landing outside her bedroom, with Prescott's "Conquest of Mexico" open on her lap. She read either exceptionally slowly or not at all, for to my knowledge she carried the first volume with her for eleven years. Hers, I think, was the contemplative type of mind.

The curious, and from my point of view the unfortunate, aspect of my uncle's patriotic gesture was the gradually increasing affection with which he came to regard this unlovable creature. Although, or more probably because, he saw her only at meals, when her features were rather more animated than at other times, his attitude toward her passed from the detached to the courteous, and from the courteous to the paternal. At the end of the war there was no question of her return to Belgium, and one day in 1919 I heard with pardonable mortification that my uncle had legally adopted her, and was altering his will be in her favour.

Time, however, reconciled me to being disinherited by a being who, between meals, could scarcely be described as sentient. I continued to pay an annual visit to Fleer, and to ride with my uncle after his big-boned Welsh hounds over the sullen, dark-gray hill country in which—since its possession was no longer assured to me—I now began to see a powerful, though elusive, beauty.

I came down here three days ago, intending to stay for a week. I found my uncle, who is a tall, fine-looking man with a beard, in his usual unassailable good health. The Belgian, as always, gave me the impression of being impervious to disease, to emotion, or indeed to anything short of an act of God. She had been putting on weight since she came to live with my uncle, and was now a very considerable figure of a woman, though not, as yet, unwieldy.

It was at dinner, on the evening of my arrival, that I first noticed a certain *malaise* behind my uncle's brusque, laconic manner. There was evidently something on his mind. After dinner he asked me to come into his study. I detected, in the delivery of the invitation, the first hint of embarrassment I had known him to betray.

The walls of the study were hung with maps and the extremities of foxes. The room was littered with bills, catalogues, old gloves, fossils, rat-traps, cartridges and feathers which had been used to clean his pipe—a stale diversity of jetsam which somehow managed to produce an impression of relevance and continuity, like the débris in an animal's lair. I had never been in the study before.

"Paul," said my uncle as soon as I had shut the door, "I am very much disturbed."

I assumed an air of sympathetic inquiry.

"Yesterday," my uncle went on, "one of my tenants came to see me. He is a decent man, who farms a strip of land outside the park wall, to the northward. He said that he had lost two sheep in a manner for which he was wholly unable to account. He said he thought they had been killed by some wild animal."

My uncle paused. The gravity of his manner was really portentous.

"Dogs?" I suggested, with the slightly patronizing diffidence of one who has probability on his side.

My uncle shook his head judiciously. "This man had often seen sheep which had been killed by dogs. He said that they were always badly torn—nipped about the legs, driven into a corner, worried to death: it was never a clean piece of work. These two sheep had not been killed like that. I went down to see them for myself. Their throats had been torn out. They were not bitten, or nuzzled. They had both died in the open, not in a corner. Whatever did it was an animal more powerful and more cunning than a dog."

I said: "It couldn't have been something that had escaped from a travelling menagerie, I suppose?"

"They don't come into this part of the country," replied my uncle; "there are no fairs."

We were both silent for a moment. It was hard not to show more curiosity than sympathy as I waited on some further revelation to stake out my uncle's claim on the latter emotion. I could put no interpretation on those two dead sheep wild enough to account for his evident distress.

He spoke again, but with obvious reluctance.

"Another was killed early this morning," he said in a low voice, "on the Home Farm. In the same way."

For lack of any better comment, I suggested beating the nearby coverts. There might be some—

"We've scoured the woods," interrupted my uncle brusquely.

"And found nothing?"

"Nothing. . . . Except some tracks."

"What sort of tracks?"

My uncle's eyes were suddenly evasive. He turned his head away.

"They were a man's tracks," he said slowly. A log fell over in the fireplace.

Again a silence. The interview appeared to be causing him pain rather than relief. I decided that the situation could lose nothing through the frank expression of my curiosity. Plucking up courage, I asked him roundly what cause he had to be upset? Three sheep, the property of his tenants, had died deaths which, though certainly unusual, were unlikely to remain for long mysterious. Their destroyer, whatever it was, would inevitably be caught, killed, or driven away in the course of the next few days. The loss of another sheep or two was the worst he had to fear.

When I had finished, my uncle gave me an anxious, almost a guilty look. I was suddenly aware that he had a confession to make.

"Sit down," he said. "I wish to tell you something."

This is what he told me:

A quarter of a century ago, my uncle had had occasion to engage a new housekeeper. With the blend of fatalism and sloth which is the foundation of the bachelor's attitude to the servant problem, he took on the first applicant. She was a tall, black, slant-eyed woman from the Welsh border, aged about 30. My uncle said nothing about her character, but described her as having "powers." When she had been at Fleer some months, my uncle began to notice her, instead of taking her for granted. She was not averse to being noticed.

One day she came and told my uncle that she was with child by him. He took it calmly enough till he found that she expected him to marry her; or pretended to expect it. Then he flew into a rage, called her a whore, and told her she must leave the house as soon as the child was born. Instead of breaking down, or continuing the scene, she began to croon to herself in Welsh, looking at him sideways with a certain amusement. This frightened him. He forbade her to come near him again, had her things moved into an unused wing of the castle, and engaged another housekeeper.

A child was born, and they came and told my uncle that the woman was going to die; she asked for him continually, they said. As much frightened as distressed, he went through passages long unfamiliar to her room. When the woman saw him, she began to gabble in a preoccupied kind of way, looking at him all the time, as if she were repeating a lesson. Then she stopped, and asked that he should be shown the child.

It was a boy. The midwife, my uncle noticed, handled it with a reluctance almost amounting to disgust.

"That is your heir," said the dying woman, in a harsh, unstable voice. "I have told him what he is to do. He will be a good son to me, and jealous of his birthright." And she went off, my uncle said, into a wild but cogent rigmarole about a curse, embodied in the child, which would fall on any whom he made his heir over the bastard's head. At last her voice trailed away and she fell back, exhausted and staring.

As my uncle turned to go, the midwife whispered to him to look at the child's hands. Gently unclasping the podgy, futile little fists, she showed him that on each hand the third finger was longer than the second. . . .

Here I interrupted. The story had a certain queer force behind it, perhaps from the obvious effect on the teller. My uncle feared and hated the things he was saying.

"What did that mean?" I asked; "—the third finger longer than the second?"

"It took me a long time to discover," replied my uncle. "My own servants, when they saw that I did not know, would not tell me. But at last I found out through the doctor, who had it from an old woman in the village. People born with their third finger longer than their second become werewolves. At least" (he made a perfunctory effort at amused indulgence) "that is what the common people here think."

"And what does that—what is that supposed to mean?" I, too, found myself throwing rather hasty sops to skepticism. I was growing strangely credulous.

"A werewolf," said my uncle, dabbling in improbability without self-consciousness, "is a human being who be-becomes, at intervals, to all intents and purposes a wolf. The transformation—or the supposed transformation—takes place at night. The werewolf kills men and animals and is supposed to drink their blood. Its preference is for men. All through the Middle Ages, down to the seventeenth century, there were innumerable cases (especially in France) of men and women being legally tried for effences which they had committed as animals. Like the witches, they were rarely acquitted, but, unlike the witches, they seem seldom to have been unjustly condemned." My uncle paused. "I have been reading the old books," he explained. "I wrote to a man in London who is interested in these things when I heard what was believed about the child."

"What became of the child?" I asked.

"The wife of one of my keepers took it in," said my uncle. "She was a stolid woman from the North who, I think, welcomed the opportunity to show what little store she set by the local superstitions. The boy lived with them till he was ten. Then he ran away. I had not heard of him since then till—" my uncle glanced at me almost apologetically—"till yesterday."

We sat for a moment in silence, looking at the fire. My imagination had betrayed my reason in its full surrender to the story. I had not got it in me to dispel his fears with a parade of sanity. I was a little frightened myself.

"You think it is your son, the werewolf, who is killing the sheep?" I said at length.

"Yes. For a boast: or for a warning: or perhaps out of spite, at a night's hunting wasted."

"Wasted?"

My uncle looked at me with troubled eyes.

"His business is not with sheep," he said uneasily.

For the first time I realized the implications of the Welshwoman's curse. The hunt was up. The quarry was the heir to Fleer. I was glad to have been disinherited.

"I have told Germaine not to go out after dusk," said my uncle, coming in pat on my train of thought.

The Belgian was called Germaine; her other name was Vom.

I confess I spent no very tranquil night. My uncle's story had not wholly worked in me that "suspension of disbelief" which some one speaks of as being the prime requisite of good drama. But I have a powerful imagination. Neither fatigue nor common sense could quite banish the vision of that metamorphosed malignancy ranging, with design, the black and silver silences outside my window. I found myself listening for the sound of loping footfalls on a frost-baked crust of beech-leaves. . . .

Whether it was in my dream that I heard, once, the sound of howling I do not know. But the next morning I saw, as I dressed, a man walking quickly up the drive. He looked like a shepherd. There was a dog at his heels, trotting with a noticeable lack of assurance. At breakfast my uncle told me that another sheep had been killed, almost under the noses of the watchers. His voice shook a little. Solicitude sat oddly on his features as he looked at Germaine. She was eating porridge, as if for a wager.

After breakfast we decided on a campaign. I will not weary you with the details of its launching and its failure. All day we quartered the woods with thirty men, mounted and on foot. Near the scene of the kill our dogs picked up a scent which they followed for two miles or more, only to lose it on the railway line. But the ground was too hard for tracks, and the men said it could only have been a fox or a polecat, so surely and readily did the dogs follow it.

The exercise and the occupation were good for our nerves. But late in the afternoon my uncle grew anxious; twilight was closing in swiftly under a sky heavy with clouds, and we were some distance from Fleer. He gave final instructions for the penning of the sheep by night, and we turned our horses' heads for home.

We approached the castle by the back drive, which was little used: a dank, unholy alley, running the gauntlet of a belt of firs and laurels. Beneath our horses' hoofs flints chinked remotely under a thick carpet of moss. Each consecutive cloud from their nostrils hung with an air of permanency, as if bequeathed to the unmoving air.

We were perhaps three hundred yards from the tall gates leading to the stable yard when both horses stopped dead, simultaneously. Their heads were turned toward the trees on our right, beyond which, I knew, the sweep of the main drive converged on ours.

My uncle gave a short, inarticulate cry in which premonition stood aghast at the foreseen. At the same moment, something howled on the other side of the trees. There was relish, and a kind of sobbing laughter, in that hateful sound. It rose and fell luxuriously, and rose and fell again, fouling the night. Then it died away, fawning on satiety in a throaty whimper.

The forces of silence fell unavailingly on its rear; its filthy echoes still went reeling through our heads. We were aware that feet went loping lightly down the iron-hard drive ... two feet.

My uncle flung himself off his horse and dashed through the trees. I followed. We scrambled down a bank and out into the open. The only figure in sight was motionless.

Germaine Vom lay doubled up in the drive, a solid, black mark against the shifting values of the dark. We ran forward....

To me she had always been an improbable cipher rather than a real person. I could not help reflecting that she died, as she had lived, in the live-stock tradition. Her throat had been torn out.

The young man leant back in his chair, a little dizzy from talking and from the heat of the stove. The inconvenient realities of the waiting-room, forgotten in the narrative, closed in on him again. He sighed, and smiled rather apologetically at the stranger.

"It is a wild and improbable story," he said. "I do not expect you to believe the whole of it. For me, perhaps, the reality of its implications has obscured its almost ludicrous lack of verisimilitude. You see, by the death of the Belgian I am heir to Fleer."

The stranger smiled: a slow, but no longer an abstracted smile. His honey-coloured eyes were bright. Under his long black overcoat his body seemed to be stretching itself in sensual anticipation. He rose silently to his feet.

The other found a sharp, cold fear drilling into his vitals. Something behind those shining eyes threatened him with appalling immediacy, like a sword at his heart. He was sweating. He dared not move.

The stranger's smile was now a grin, a ravening comvulsion of the face. His eyes blazed with a hard and purposeful delight. A thread of saliva dangled from the corner of his mouth.

Very slowly he lifted one hand and removed his bowler hat. Of the fingers crooked about its brim, the young man saw that the third was longer than the second.

MANLY BANISTER

EENA

The she-wolf was silhouetted sharply against the moon-gilded waters of Wolf Lake. Silent as Death in the cover of a rotting log, Joel Cameron sighted along a dully gleaming rifle barrel. He squeezed the trigger.

The gray-tipped wolf leaped high, cavorted grotesquely in midair. The beast threshed in short-lived agony upon the ground and lay still. Joel ejected the cartridge from the smoking chamber.

"Five bucks, and all profit!" he grunted, anticipating the State bounty.

In the act of legging over the log, he stopped and swiftly raised his weapon. His attention had been so intent upon the she-wolf as she slunk from the forest edge, he had not noticed the whelp that followed her. Terrified, the whimpering wolf cub galloped toward the safety of the woods. Joel dropped his rifle and sprinted.

"I'll be darned!" he panted, scooping the wolfling up into his arms. "An albino whelp!"

In this manner, Eena the she-wolfling was introduced to the world and the ways of men.

Joel's cabin was a mile down the lake-shore, hidden in a wooded draw that protected it from wind and weather, and separated from the edge of the lake by a thin screen of timber.

Joel Cameron had been born and raised in the high pine woods. Later fortune, through the medium of a battered typewriter and a skilful ability to weave a fanciful yarn, had led him to life in the city. But each Spring he returned to the cabin he had built in the hills and stayed there until the crispness of early Autumn presaged the coming of snow.

It was an ideal life, one to which Joel's temperament

was ideally suited. When editorial favour inclined to the lean side, which it often did, he could depend upon the cabin in the mountains for refuge from the palsied palms of greedy landlords. The state wolf-bounty kept the figurative wolf from his door by inviting the literal one within.

Eena proved to be different from the usual wolfkind. Joel recognized this from the first. Even her albinoism was different. She lacked the red eyes usually associated with the lack of pigmentation. They were gray-hazel, and they gave Joel a weird sense of being somehow human. They were distinctly out of place in the snow-white, lupine visage of the wolflet.

Eena grew rapidly and prodigiously. At one time or another, every homesteader in the valley below passed by to see the albino. Some admired her look of intelligence, the growing strength of her. Some deplored the fact that a wolf so handy for killing should be allowed to live.

Pierre Lebrut, a trapper who had a tumble-down cabin a mile away, rubbed his palms on his greasy overalls and spat toward the caged wolf.

"Cameroon," said he, "I catch her, I keel her, you bet!" He scowled at the white wolf, and Eena's hackles raised in response. "She bad one, all right," Pierre growled. "She breeng bad luck. You see!"

The man went away, and Joel crouched by the chicken-wire fence of Eena's pen. He had got into the practice of talking softly to the animal.

"Kill you? Not you, my beauty!" He chuckled fondly. The half-grown wolf cocked her head at him and stared with unblinking, gray-hazel eyes.

"Sometimes I wonder if you'd let me scratch your ears?" He smiled through the fence. Eena lolled her tongue with a friendly grin. "On the other hand," Joel told her, "I need both my hands to type with! You're an independent she-cuss. Maybe that's why I like you!"

Eena furnished Joel with material for several stories that went over well. As the Summer drifted somnolently past, he regarded her with increasing fondness. By the time Fall came around, Joel considered himself on friendly terms with the wolf, though he never dared venture close enough to touch her.

By this time, too, the curiosity of the countryside was more or less satiated in regard to the albino wolf, and the traffic of visitors had long since returned to normal . . . one every two weeks.

Pete Martin worked the first homestead on the country road that led to Valley Junction. Pete Martin was the valley's pride as a wolf hunter.

"Sent three sons an' a daughter through college on wolf-hides!" he often asserted, referring to the monthly bounty-checks from the State.

"I'll give you fifty bucks fer that wolf-bitch," Pete told Joel. "You'll be winterin' in the city pretty soon, an' you can't take the hellion with you. I want to cross her with some o' my best dogs an' raise me a breed o' good wolf-hunters."

Eena, six months old now and as big as a grown wolf, snoozed in the shade of the kennel Joel had built for her. Joel frowned.

"If I could think of some way to keep her," he told the homesteader, "I'd never part with her. Under the circumstances, I'll take your offer. I'll be driving to the city within three days. I'll bring her by then."

The two men shook hands solemnly on the agreement.

That night, Eena burrowed under the chicken-wire fence of her enclosure. Like a silent wraith, she disappeared into the trackless wilds of the pine forest.

Joel drove his battered coupe back to the city, fifty dollars poorer than he might have been.

October winds rustled the waters of Wolf Lake. Deciduous trees turned red and gold and brown. The foothills blazed with Nature's paint-pot.

November skies were leaden. The frost giants awakened in the earth. Snow smothered the valley and the hills. Existence in the wild turned bleak and harrowing. On silent pads the wolfpack stole into the haunts of men. They followed the lead of a great, white she-wolf, the largest and most cunning wolf ever seen.

The wolves swept down from the hills and lurked in

the swirling skirts of the blizzard to strike and kill. They took a costly toll from the livestock that pastured in the valley. The homesteaders cursed the white she-leader of the pack. Joel Cameron's name was anathema on every tongue.

Eena was a year old the following spring. The handful of wolfling Joel Cameron had carried to his cabin a year before was now twice the size of the largest, sturdiest male in her pack. It was to this, and to her wise cunning, that she owed her leadership.

Eena regarded the black wolves lolling around her in the warm sun. These were her kind, yet not her kind. She knew she was different in more ways than size and the colour of her pelt. For weeks she had felt a recklessness stirring within her, an inexplicable thrilling of unknown significance.

Across the lake which glittered like a turquoise jewel in its setting of forest emerald, the sun sparkled upon the snowy mantilla of the mountain that thrust bare, stone shoulders up from a clinging bodice of pine woods.

Memory stirred the mind of the white she-wolf. She was thinking of a cabin hidden in a woody draw, hard by the waters of the lake. She remembered a clean-lined young face, a soothing voice that had spoken to her in pleasing, unintelligible syllables. She remembered kindness and something that amounted to friendship with a creature who was called man. Eena whimpered and got up.

The wolves rose with her and ringed around expectantly. A long moment Eena stood poised and silent, dwarfing the members of her pack. A thought, feeling ... a command ... went from her to them. The wolves sank back unto their haunches, tongues lolling. Eena turned and trotted alone into the forest.

The white wolf padded silently along sun-barred aisles of the forest. Her path led in an easy circle around the lake. Near sunset, she came unerringly upon the clearing occupied by Joel Cameron's cabin.

She crept into a thicket of elderberry trees and peered expectantly forth. Not toward the cabin, for that with the setting sun was at her back. Her questing glance winged

across the darkening blue waters of the lake and fixed
upon the glowing summit of the mountain.

Fascinated, Eena watched the fading beauty of it. The
sky turned smoky-hued. A star or two glittered diamond-
hard. A golden glow paled the sable sky beyond the
shoulder of the mountain.

Crouched in the voiceless shadows, Eena held her breath
and tingled with suspense. Instinct gave her thrilling
warning. She was about to witness the essence of her
difference from the wolfkind.

The moon came up full, a pumpkin-yellow disk, and
rested its chin upon the mountain to ponder the scene
thoughtfully before commencing its climb into the sky.
... And Eena *changed*.

The change shook her with ecstacy. Bubbling rapture
accompanied the smooth flowing of supple muscles, the
adjusting of bones in their sockets. An excitement of
sensual pleasure engulfed every nerve and sinew. Afterward, she lay for long supine, one arm flung across her
eyes to bar the eldritch glare of the moon, panting, trembling with remembered delight.

She sat up at last and thrilled to the shapely beauty of
her form. Eena knew she was a woman, and she was
content. She did not question how this had come about.

Eena crept down to the water's edge and surveyed her
reflection in the dark surface of the lake. A faint breeze
stirred the platinum tresses against round, golden
shoulders. Her face was eager, full-lipped with flaring
brows accenting her gray-hazel eyes. Her body was high
of breast and long of leg, and the moonlight caressed her
with a touch of mystery and magic.

The cabin was still, high-lighted and shadowed in the
moon-brimming canyon. Eena padded around it in a cautious circle. The air was dead, without scent. The man
with the kind face and soothing voice was not here.

Puzzled and hurt, Eena turned away. She swam a while
in the icy waters of the lake, revelling in the tonic effect
of the chill.

Later, she roamed aimlessly, enjoying the easy response
of her nerves and muscles. Once, her keen wolf-sense

detected a rabbit quaking in a patch of brush. She started it up. As the frightened animal ran out, she sprinted swiftly and seized it in her hands. The rabbit uttered a thin, terrorized shriek, and died.

Eena sank her teeth in the rabbit's throat and exulted to the gushing warmth of blood. She sat down upon the needled turf, methodically tore the animal to pieces and ate it.

From time to time in her wandering, Eena responded to her woman's nature and crept down to the lake to admire her reflection.

The night was short . . . too short. Eena's aimless peregrination brought her just before dawn to another cabin. Pierre Lebrut lived here. Eena's sensitive nose caught the trapper's reek strong upon the air. A sluggish memory stirred in her brain. Eena snarled without sound and retreated with the prickling of invisible hackles stirring the length of her spine.

A twig snapped under Eena's foot. Steel piano-wire sang, and a bent sapling straightened with a rush. Eena was flung to earth, one foot jerked high in the wire noose of a snare. She threshed in wild panic, clawing and snapping wolf-fashion at the searing pain in her ankle.

Within the musty cabin, Lebrut sat up in his tumbled bunk.

"By gar, she sound like bear in dat trap!"

He slipped into heavy boots—he slept in his pants and undershirt—seized his rifle and hurried outside.

Gray dawn lighted the east, reflected palely into the forest. Lebrut saw the woman caught in his snare, laid down his rifle, and hurried to release her.

"Sacre nom d'un loup!" he muttered, slackening the wire to remove the noose from Eena's threshing ankle. "Lady, you pick fine time an' place for peecneec—an' w'at you do wit' no clo'es on?"

Pierre was excited and his voice shrill. The scent of him was overpowering in Eena's nostrils. She bit him savagely on the calf.

Pierre yelled in sudden fright. He fell heavily on the wolf-girl, and she snapped and clawed in renewed terror.

The man grunted with anger and fought her, pinioned her arms.

"You wild one, *hein?*" Eena's body was closed, arched and quivering. Pierre grinned. "Maybe Pierre tame you wit' a kees, *hein?*"

The sun came up over the shoulder of the mountain and tinged the lake with blood. . . . And Eena *changed*.

It was no sensation of pleasure to return to the wolf. Eena felt the agony of the change in every muscle and nerve. She screamed with the horrid crunching and grinding of bones in her head, lengthening into the lupine muzzle. Albino fur sprouted like a million thorny barbs from her tender skin.

Pierre was still wide-eyed and frozen with horror when the fangs of the agonized wolf ripped the life from his terror-stricken body.

Pete Martin looked grim as he pried open the stiffened fingers of the dead trapper. The wind stirred a tuft of albino fur on the dead man's palm.

"Your albino bitch, Joel," the homesteader said.

Joel bit his lip.

"It's a devil of a thing for a man to come back to, Pete." He looked stolidly down at the dead man. "Poor Pierre! He died hard." Joel brought his glance up to meet the kindly stare of the homesteader. "I know the valley blames me for not killing Eena when she was a pup."

Martin shrugged. "It's too late now for blame, Joel. Maybe I'm to blame for not takin' her with me the day I offered to buy her. I dunno." He scratched his long jaw. "Well, we better see about gettin' Pierre properly planted, I guess."

Joel's expression was darkly stormy. "I feel responsible for the cattle . . . for Pierre." He wondered silently when and where the white wolf would kill again. He tongued dry lips. "I'll track her down and destroy her."

"There's a thousand dollars on her hide, Joel. Every homesteader in the valley chipped in."

"If I bring in her hide," Joel clipped, "it won't cost the homesteaders a cent!"

The homesteader's gray eyes lighted with a friendly gleam.

"Figured you'd look at it like that, Joel. I'll give you what help I can...."

Joel spent the following month in the hinterland, returning to his cabin at intervals only to replenish supplies. The wolves were wary. He seldom came upon wolf-sign, and saw no wolves at all. But he heard them. By night their lonesome song rang eerily through the forest and echoed from the mountains.

Joel made final return to his cabin, and that night drove his coupé down a moonlit road to the Martin homestead.

"Reckoned you wouldn't find her," the homsteader acknowledged Joel's aquiescence to defeat. "She knows she's hunted an' will always manage to be some place else. She was here night before last with her pack an' got my prize heifer."

Joel made a gesture of despair. "You see what I'm up against? Besides, I'm behind in my work. I came up here to finish a book. The publisher is yelling his head off for it. How can I write a book and hunt wolves, too?"

The homesteader spat a fine stream of tobacco juice. "You go ahead an' write your book, son. You've made your try, an' 'twarn't your fault you failed. Some of us are gittin' together in the mornin'. We'll take to the wolf-trail an' stick it out till we git her!"

Joel's heart felt heavy. He still had a fond memory of the white she-wolf he had nursed from babyhood. He remembered her attitude of sage intelligence, her qualities that had made her seem almost human. Then he remembered she had turned killer, and he peered into the moon-shadows as he drove along the country road, half afraid he might spy her lurking there.

He turned down the indistinct ruts that led to his lakeside cabin, and another mile of bumpy going brought him home. The wobbling headlights swept across the cabin front, revealed an open door.

Joel suffered mild panic. Had a bear forced entry? He could imagine the shambles the animal had made of the interior. He sprang out and approached the house cautiously, rifle ready. Everything inside was in order. He lit the mantle of the kerosene lamp, went out and shut off the car lights and re-entered the cabin.

Eena lay curled on a bearskin rug in front of the stone fireplace. Her platinum curls glistened silver contrast against the dull gold of her naked skin. She supported her chin with her hands and watched him with wide, wary eyes. A patch of full-moon brilliance, brighter than the lamplight, puddled the floor at her feet.

Joel stared. She was a dream come to life. The shock of seeing her there dismayed him.

"Who are you?" he essayed at last.

Eena stirred languidly. Her expression mimicked a wolfish grin. Hot blood surged into Joel's cheeks. He caught up a dressing gown and flung it to her.

"Put it on," he ordered.

Eena sobered, regarded the garment, and swung her level glance back to the man.

"Haven't you ever seen clothes before?" he asked sarcastically. He crossed over and adjusted the robe hastily about her shoulders. "Suppose one of the neighbours came by?"

The possibility was not likely, he knew. He said things simply to cover up his own shock and embarrassment. He sat down heavily in a leather club chair and stared at her. Eena stared back with friendly indifference.

Joel's mind boiled with fantastic questions. The girl remained silent. Only her eyes spoke, and their meaning was not quite clear to the beleaguered man.

He gave up trying to draw a word from her. Was she a deaf-mute? Who was she? Why was she here? He recalled stories he had heard of white savages; but those were found only in the wilds of the South American jungle, or in some hidden Shangri-La of Tibet. He tried to place her racial type, and was unsuccessful. There was something familiar about the shape and look of her eyes, but what it was eluded him.

He knew only that she was very beautiful, that he wanted her as he had never wanted another human being before. He could not know that Eena was not quite . . . human.

"I can't sit here all night, just looking at you," he said

at last. He grinned with wry humour. "It's an idea, though, at that!" He stood up. "Lady, if you will consent to occupy the guest room tonight, the hotel can accommodate you."

Joel held out his hand to help her rise. Eena moved like a flash, shaking off the encumbering dressing gown. She paused at the door and smiled at him. The lamplight made molten gold of her body, a tawny silhouette against the moon-silvered outdoors.

Then she was gone, like a wolf goes, on swift, silent pads.

And with her, the warmth went from the cabin. Joel felt a chill, followed by a helpless feeling of immeasurable loss.

In the cold, gray light of dawn, the cabin shivered to a thunderous knocking. Joel tumbled from bed, threw on a dressing gown, and greeted Pete Martin at the door. Martin was backed by half a dozen husky homesteaders.

"Thought I'd let you know we're headin' along the wolf-trail."

Joel grumpily asserted the idea was a fine one, he was glad to know it, and now would they go away and let him sleep?

"We wouldn't have stopped," Martin apologized, "except we wondered about your visitor last night."

Joel's jaw cracked in the middle of a yawn. He swallowed hard and flushed blackly.

"Visitor? What visitor?" he hedged.

The homesteader crooked a finger, and Joel followed out onto the porch. Martin pointed out the wolf-tracks that crossed and recrossed the yard.

"Those are the tracks of your white bitch, Joel. She came home last night. Didn't see her, did you?"

Joel closed his eyes. He felt a swimming sensation in his head.

"No. No, I didn't see her." Fantastically, he thought of the visitor he had seen, and thought of her body mutilated and torn by sharp wolf-fangs. He shuddered.

The homesteader shrugged. "Keep a look-out for her, Joel. She'll be back again . . . if we don't git her first!"

He gestured to his companions, and they filed off into the forest. Joel stood alone, looking down at the tracks ... at one track that had gone unnoticed by the others—the single print of a woman's shapely foot.

Joel Cameron was pleased with his own industry. He finished proofreading the final chapter of his book, gathered the manuscript together, and wrapped it for shipment. There, it was off his mind.

He took the manuscript down to the village post office, collected a few necessary supplies. Toward sunset, he legged into his car and chugged away up the country road toward home.

Night shadows fell quickly. The sky turned smoky, then sequinned. The moon came up full over the roof of the forest.

Joel turned into the ruts that meandered through the woods to his cabin. Wobbling headlamps bored a tunnel through the gloom. The night was eerily still throughout the pine woods. Joel slewed the machine around a bumpy turn. The wolf-woman stood starkly illuminated in the glare of the headlights.

Joel jammed a foot on the brakes. He scrambled from his seat, calling. Eena flashed into the shadows. After two minutes struggle with the whipping underbrush, Joel gave up and went back to his car.

He was suddenly lonesome and despondent. He ground the coupé through the final furlong and killed the motor in front of the cabin.

Eena sat quietly upon the porch.

Even with the lights off, Joel could see her there. Her form was tawny gold in the moonlight. Her hair was a flashing, silver aura enhaloing her laughing face.

Joel started toward her, thought better of it, and sat on the runningboard. Eena was less than ten feet away. Joel said nothing. Eena answered in kind.

After a while, Joel began to talk to her, softly. He mused and wondered aloud, letting his thoughts drift with the association of his words. Eena cocked her head attentively. She appeared to be listening, but he knew that his words held no meaning for her.

What language would serve him? What syllables would convey to her knowledge of the tumultuous beating in his breast her simple presence evoked?

He moved toward her, murmuring softly. He took the firm, golden flesh of her arm in his grasp. Eena looked up into Joel's strong kindly face. Her eyes spoke the thought her tongue could not.

Joel drew her gently to her feet. She swayed, and he caught her to him. Her lips were as tender and responsive as he had dreamed they would be. He took them, hungrily....

Eena prowled the forest resentfully. She hated to be hunted. Twice, now, the coming of the full moon had brought her only pangs of frustration. The hunters who swarmed in the woods prevented her going to the man she loved.

The pine woods shimmered in the heat of midsummer. Hunters from all over the state, attracted by the enormous price on Eena's hide, came to blunder among the hills. When they went away, defeated, others came instead of them.

Eena had no rest. She was hounded and harried. By night, the forest twinkled with campfires.

Once, a hunter reckless enough to hunt alone had cornered the she-wolf. Braving the fire of his weapon, Eena attacked and ripped the man to shreds of bloody ruin. The price of Eena's life doubled overnight.

Once, too, she had been trapped by a horde of hunters and their dogs at the lip of a precipice, overlooking Wolf Lake. The she-wolf leaped, and swam to safety through a hail of lead. The rock thereafter was called Wolf Leap, and Eena's character became legendary.

The swelling moon nightly presaged the approach of the change. Eena longed for it, longed for the pleasure of her human form, and gladly paid with the pangs of her return to the wolf. All the savage ferocity of her wolf nature rebelled at the restriction the presence of hunters imposed. Then cunning asserted itself.

Joel's cabin lay westward. Eeena turned her pointed muzzle into the east. On silent pads she fled through the silver and dross of the moonlit forest. At dawn, she rested.

Facing northward, she took up her way for a number of hours; then she turned into the west.

It was not easy running. The way led up steep mountainsides, down precipitous declivities. She swam mountain torrents, crossed ravines on fallen pines. When she hungered, she pulled down a white-tailed deer and gorged on the kill.

In mid-afternoon, Eena made her way southward. She had completely encircled the hunters that swarmed in the forest.

The white wolf came at last into familiar territory at the west end of the lake. She slackened her pace, although a frantic urge to hurry assailed her. She knew the limitations of her human form, and with moonrise tonight the Change would be visited upon her. She wanted to be close by the cabin when that came to pass.

She had slightly more than an hour to span the miles that yet lay between.

Eena skulked along in the shadowy underbrush, pausing at intervals to scent for danger. She soon paralleled the lakeshore, a hurrying white wraith in the green-gray shadows of the forest. The wind brought a smell of dampness off the lake, a formless breath of stale fishiness. The pines cast long shadows upon the water. The sky darkened in the east.

A rifle cracked. The whistling missile spent itself far out over the lake, and Eena gathered her muscles with the instant response of spring steel and lunged ahead. A man yelled, and dogs began to bark frantically. Eena doubled away from the lake, putting on a fresh burst of speed.

The wind had betrayed her. It had come to her nostrils from the sterile face of the water, while her danger lay on the other hand.

A rifle spat livid flame in the green gloom ahead. Eena leaped, snarling and snapping at the trenchant pain in her shoulder. Spurting blood reddened her muzzle, stained the snowy pelt of her side.

Other rifles cracked all around her. Rifle balls whined nastily through the woods. The yelping of dogs was bedlam.

The white wolf recovered her stride in spite of her searing wound. She ran with desperation and terror hounding her, her goal an idea interlocked with the memory of a kindly face and a soothing voice.

Eena fled for the protection of the one being in all the forest whom she loved, the one man among men who loved her.

Joel Cameron heard the flat racketing of gunfire, the distant shouting and yelping. A strange uneasiness held him motionless, listening. He caught up his rifle and hurried to the door.

The noise swelled louder by the moment. Twilight pressed down upon the forest, swirled into the clearing about the cabin. Joel saw the men, then, flitting silhouettes between the pines, limned against the tarnished silver of the lake. The forest trembled with the belling of the dog-pack.

His ears caught another sound, nearer . . . more terrifying. He heard the swift whisper or racing pads, the sound of a heavy body hurtling through the undergrowth.

The enormous, pale form of the wolf leaped from the forest edge, charged relentlessly toward him. A mental gong sounded in the man's clamouring brain. Joel's rifle snapped automatically into the hollow of his shoulder. The report ripped echoes from the hills.

The murderous shock of the ball lifted the white wolf, flung her with bleeding breast back upon her haunches. Gathering the last atom of her strength, Eena lunged and fell kicking at Joe Cameron's feet.

The man sighted carefully for the mercy shot that would send a bullet crashing into Eena's brain. The moon came up full over the shoulder of the mountain, bridged the lake with its golden track, thrust a questing beam through a gap in the pines.

The effulgent glow caressed Eena's wolf-form. Eena died with the ecstasy of the Change soothing the agony of her hurts.

Joel stared, uncomprehending. The rifle fell from his nerveless grasp. Slowly, his knees buckled. He dropped beside the huddled girl-shape, gathered limp, tawny shoulders against his chest and buried his face in the silver cloud of her hair.

He was holding her like that when the hunters burst into the moonlit clearing. He did not look up, even when they went silently away.

A. MERRITT

THE DRONE

Four men sat at a table of the Explorers' Club—Hewitt, just in from two years botanical research in Abyssinia; Caranac, the ethnologist; MacLeod, poet first, and second the learned curator of the Asiatic Museum; Winston, the archeologist, who, with Kosloff the Russian, had worked over the ruins of Khara-Kora, the City of the Black Stones in the northern Gobi, once capital of the Empire of Genghis Khan.

The talk had veered to werewolves, vampires, fox-women, and similar superstitions. Directed thence by a cabled report of measures to be taken against the Leopard Society, the murderous fanatics who drew on the skins of leopards, crouched like them on the boughs of trees, then launched themselves down upon their victims tearing their throats with talons of steel. That, and another report of a 'hex-murder' in Pennsylvania where a woman had been beaten to death because it was thought she could assume the shape of a cat and cast evil spells upon those into whose houses, as cat, she crept.

Caranac said: 'It is a deep rooted belief, and immeasurably ancient, that a man or woman may assume the shape of an animal, a serpent, a bird, even an insect. It was believed of old everywhere, and everywhere, it is still believed by some—fox-men and fox-women of China and Japan, wolf-people, the badger and bird people of our own Indians. Always there has been the idea that there is a borderland between the worlds of consciousness of man and of beast—a borderland where shapes can be changed and man merge into beast or beast into man."

MacLeod said: "The Egyptians had some good reason for equipping their deities with the heads of birds and beasts and insects. Why did they portray Khepher the

Oldest God with the head of a beetle? Why give Anubis, the Psychopomp, Guide of the Dead, the head of a jackal? Or Thoth, the God of Wisdom, the head of an ibis; and Horus, the Divine son of Isis and Osiris, the head of a hawk? Set, God of Evil, a crocodile's and the Goddess Bast a cat's? There was a reason for all of that. But about it one can only guess."

Caranac said: "I think there's something in that borderland, or borderline, idea. There's more or less of the beast, the reptile, the bird, the insect in everybody. I've known men who looked like rats and had the souls of rats. I've known women who belonged to the horse family, and showed it in face and voice. Distinctly there are bird people—hawk-faced, eagle-faced—predatory. The owl people seem to be mostly men and the wren people women. There are quite as distinct wolf and serpent types. Suppose some of these have their animal element so strongly developed that they can cross this borderline —become at times the animal? There you have the explanation of the werewolf, the snake-woman, and all the others. What could be more simple?"

Winston asked: "But you're not serious, Caranac?"

Caranac laughed. "At least half serious. Once I had a friend with an uncannily acute perception of these animal qualities in the human. He saw people less in terms of humanity than in terms of beast or bird. Animal consciousness that either shared the throne of human consciousness or sat above it or below it in varying degrees. It was an uncomfortable gift. He was like a doctor who has the faculty of visual diagnosis so highly developed that he constantly sees men and women and children not as they are but as diseases. Ordinarily he could control the faculty. But sometimes, as he would describe it, when he was in the Subway, or on a bus, or in the theatre —or even sitting tête-à-tête with a pretty woman, there would be a swift haze and when it had cleared he was among rats and foxes, wolves and serpents, cats and tigers and birds, all dressed in human garb but with nothing else at all human about them. The clear-cut picture lasted only for a moment—but it was a highly disconcerting moment."

Winston said, incredulously: "Do you mean to suggest that in an instant the musculature and skeleton of a man can become the musculature and skeleton of a wolf? The skin sprout fur? Or in the matter of your bird people, feathers? In an instant grow wings and the specialized muscles to use them? Sprout fangs . . . noses become snouts. . . ."

Caranac grinned. "No, I don't mean anything of the sort. What I do suggest is that under certain conditions the animal part of this dual nature of man may submerge the human part to such a degree that a sensitive observer will think he sees the very creature which is its type. Just as in the case of the friend whose similar sensitivity I have described."

Winston raised his hands in mock admiration. "Ah, at last modern science explains the legend of Circe! Circe the enchantress who gave men a drink that changed them into beasts. Her potion intensified whatever animal or what-not soul that was within them so that the human form no longer registered upon the eyes and brains of those who looked upon them. I agree with you, Caranac —what *could* be more simple? But I do not use the word simple in the same sense you did."

Caranac answered, amused: "Yet, why not? Potions of one sort or another, rites of one sort or another, usually accompany such transformations in the stories. I've seen drinks and drugs that did pretty nearly the same thing and with no magic or sorcery about them— did it almost to the line of the visual illusion."

Winston began, heatedly: "But—"

Hewitt interrupted him: "Will the opposing counsel kindly shut up and listen to expert testimony. Caranac, I'm grateful to you. You've given me courage to tell of something which never in God's world would I have told if it were not for what you've been saying. I don't know whether you're right or not, but man—you've knocked a hag off my shoulders who's been riding them for months! The thing happened about four months before I left Abyssinia. I was returning to Addis Ababa. With my bearers I was in the western jungles. We came to a village and camped. That night my headman came to me.

He was in a state of nerves. He begged that we would go from there at dawn. I wanted to rest for a day or two, and asked why. He said the village had a priest who was a great wizard. On the nights of the full moon the priest turned himself into a hyena and went hunting. For human food, the headman whispered. The villagers were safe, because he protected them. But others weren't. And the next night was the first of the full moon. The men were frightened. Would I depart at dawn?

"I didn't laugh at him. Ridiculing the beliefs of the bush gets you less than nowhere. I listened gravely, and then assured him that my magic was greater than the wizard's. He wasn't satisfied, but he shut up. Next day I went looking for the priest. When I found him I thought I knew how he'd been able to get that fine story started and keep the natives believing it. If any man ever looked like a hyena he did. Also, he wore over his shoulders the skin of one of the biggest of the beasts I'd ever seen, its head grinning at you over his head. You could hardly tell its teeth and his apart. I suspected he had filed his teeth to make 'em match. And he smelled like a hyena. It makes my stomach turn even now. It was the hide of course—or so I thought then.

"Well, I squatted down in front of him and we looked at each other for quite a while. He said nothing, and the more I looked at him the less he was like a man and more like the beast around his shoulders. I didn't like it— I'm frank to say I didn't. It sort of got under my skin. I was the first to weaken. I stood up and tapped my rifle. I said, 'I do not like hyenas. You understand me.' And I tapped my rifle again. If he was thinking of putting over some similar kind of hocus-pocus that would frighten my men still more, I wanted to nip it in the bud. He made no answer, only kept looking at me. I walked away.

"The men were pretty jittery all day, and they got worse when night began to fall. I noted there was not the usual cheerful twilight bustle that characterizes the native village. The people went into their huts early. Half an hour after dark, it was as though deserted. My camp was in a clearing just within the stockade. My bearers gathered close together around their fire. I sat on a pile of boxes where I could look over the whole clearing. I had one rifle on my knee and another beside me. Whether it was the fear that crept out from the men around the fire like an exhalation, or whether it had been that queer suggestion of shift of shape from man to beast while I was squatting in front of the priest I don't know—but the fact remained that I felt mighty uneasy. The headman crouched beside me, long knife in hand.

"After awhile the moon rose up from behind the trees and shone down on the clearing. Then, abruptly, at its edge, not a hundred feet away I saw the priest. There was something disconcerting about the abruptness with which he had appeared. One moment there had been nothing, then—there he was. The moon gleamed on the teeth of the hyena's head and upon his. Except for that skin he was stark naked and his teeth glistened as though oiled. I felt the headman shivering against me like a frightened dog and I heard his teeth chattering.

"And then there was a swift haze—that was what struck me so forcibly in what you told of your sensitive friend, Caranac. It cleared as swiftly and there wasn't any priest. But there was a big hyena standing where he had been—standing on its hind feet like a man and looking at me. I could see its hairy body. It held its forelegs over its shaggy chest as though crossed. And the reek of it came to me—thick. I didn't reach for my gun—I never thought of it, my mind in the grip of some incredulous fascination.

"The beast opened its jaws. It *grinned* at me. Then it walked—*walked* is exactly the word—six paces, dropped upon all fours, trotted leisurely into the bush, and vanished there.

"I managed to shake off the spell that had held me, took my flash and gun and went over to where the brute had been. The ground was soft and wet. There were prints of a man's feet and hands. As though the man had crawled from the bush on all fours. There were the prints of two feet close together as though he had stood there erect. And then—there were the prints of the paws of a hyena.

"Six of them, evenly spaced, as though the beast had walked six paces upon its hind legs. And after that only the spoor of the hyena trotting with its unmistakable sidewise slinking gait upon all four legs. There were no further marks of man's feet—nor were marks of human feet going back from where the priest had stood."

Hewitt stopped. Winston asked: "And is that all?"

Hewitt said, as though he had not heard him: "Now, Caranac, would you say that the animal soul in this wizard *was* a hyena? And that I had seen that animal soul? Or that when I sat with him that afternoon he had implanted in my mind the suggestion that at such a time and such a place I would see him as a hyena? And that I did?"

Caranac answered: "Either is an explanation. I rather hold to the first."

Hewitt asked: "Then how do you explain the change of the human foot marks into those of the beast?"

Winston asked: "Did anyone but you see those prints?"

Hewitt said: "No. For obvious reasons I did not show them to the headman."

Winston said: "I hold then to the hypnotism theory. The foot marks were a part of the same illusion."

Hewitt said: "You asked if that was all. Well, it wasn't. When dawn came and there was a muster of men, one was missing. We found him—what was left of him—a quarter of a mile away in the bush. Some animal had crept into the camp, neatly crushed his throat and dragged him away without awakening anybody. Without even me knowing it—and I had not slept. Around his body were the tracks of an unusually big hyena. Without doubt that was what had killed and partly eaten him."

"Coincidence," muttered Winston.

"We followed the tracks of the brute," went on Hewitt. "We found a pool at which it had drunk. We traced the tracks to the edge of the pool. But—"

He hesitated. Winston asked, impatiently: "But?"

"But we didn't find them going back. There were the marks of a naked human foot going back. But there were no marks of human feet pointing *toward* the pool. Also, the prints of the human feet were exactly those which had ended in the spoor of the hyena at the edge of the clearing. I know that because the left big toe was off."

Caranac asked: "And then what did you do?"

"Nothing. Took up our packs and beat it. The headman and the others had seen the footprints. There was no holding them after that. So your idea of hypnotism hardly holds here, Winston. I doubt whether a half dozen or less had seen the priest. But they all saw the tracks."

"Mass hallucination. Faulty observation. A dozen rational explanations," said Winston.

MacLeod spoke, the precise diction of the distinguished curator submerged under the Gaelic burr and idioms that came to the surface always when he was deeply moved:

"And is it so, Martin Hewitt? Well, now I will be telling you a story. A thing that I saw with my own eyes. I hold with you, Alan Caranac, but I go further. You say that man's consciousness may share the brain with other consciousnesses—beast or bird or what not. I say it may be that all life is one. A single force, but a thinking and conscious force of which the trees, the beasts, the flowers, germs and man and everything living are parts, just as the billions of living cells in a man are parts of him. And that under certain conditions the parts may be interchangeable. And that this may be the source of the ancient tales of the dryads and the nymphs, the harpies and the werewolves and their kind as well.

"Now, listen. My people came from the Hebrides where they know more of some things than books can teach. When I was eighteen I entered a little mid-west college. My roommate was a lad named—well, I'll just be calling him Ferguson. There was a professor with ideas you would not expect to find out there.

"'Tell me how a fox feels that is being hunted by the hounds,' he would say. 'Or the rabbit that is stalked by the fox. Or give me a worm's eye view of a garden. Get out of yourselves. Imagination is the greatest gift of the Gods,' he said, 'and it is also their greatest curse. But blessing or curse it is good to have. Stretch your consciousness and write for me what you see and feel.'

"Ferguson took to that job like a fly to sugar. What he wrote was not a man telling of a fox or hare or hawk—

it was fox and hare and hawk speaking through a man's hand. It was not only the emotions of the creatures he described. It was what they saw and heard and smelt and how they saw and heard and smelt it. And what they—thought.

"The class would laugh, or be spellbound. But the professor didn't laugh. No. After a while he began to look worried and he would have long talks in private with Ferguson. And I would say to him: 'In God's name how do you do it, Ferg? You make it all seem so damned real.'

"'It is real,' he told me. 'I chase with the hounds and I run with the hare. I set my mind on some animal and after a bit I am one with it. Inside it. Literally. As though I had slipped outside myself. And when I slip back inside myself—I remember.'

"'Don't tell me you think you change into one of these beasts!' I said. He hesitated. 'Not my body,' he answered at last. 'But I know my mind . . . soul . . . spirit . . . whatever you choose to call it—must.'

"He wouldn't argue the matter. And I know he didn't tell me all he knew. And suddenly the professor stopped those peculiar activities, without explanation. A few weeks later I left the college.

"That was over thirty years ago. About ten years ago, I was sitting in my office when my secretary told me that a man named Ferguson who said he was an old schoolmate was asking to see me. I remembered him at once and had him in. I blinked at him when he entered. The Furguson I'd known had been a lean, wiry, dark, square-chinned, and clean-cut chap. This man wasn't like that at all. His hair was a curious golden, and extremely fine—almost a fuzz. His face was oval and flattish with receding chin. He wore oversized dark glasses and they gave the suggestion of a pair of fly's eyes under a microscope. Or rather—I thought suddenly—of a bee's. But I felt a real shock when I grasped his hand. It felt less like a man's hand than the foot of some insect, and as I looked down at it I saw that it also was covered with the fine yellow fuzz of hair. He said:

" 'Hello, MacLeod, I was afraid you wouldn't remember me.'

"It was Ferguson's voice as I remembered it, and yet it wasn't. There was a queer, muffled humming and buzzing running through it.

"But it was Ferguson all right. He soon proved that. He did more talking than I, because that odd inhuman quality of the voice in some way distressed me, and I couldn't take my eyes off his hands with their yellow fuzz, nor the spectacled eyes and the fine yellow hair. It appeared that he had bought a farm over in New Jersey. Not so much for farming as for a place for his apiary. He had gone in for bee keeping. He said: 'I've tried all sorts of animals. In fact I've tried more than animals. You see, Mac—there's nothing in being human: Nothing but sorrow. And the animals aren't so happy. So I'm concentrating on the bee. A drone, Mac. A short life but an exceedingly merry one.'

"I said: 'What in the hell are you talking about?'

"He laughed, a buzzing, droning laugh. 'You know damned well. You were always interested in my little excursions, Mac. Intelligently interested. I never told you a hundredth of the truth about them. But come and see next Wednesday and maybe your curiosity will be satisfied. I think you'll find it worth while.'

"Well, there was a bit more talk and he went out. He'd given me minute directions how to get to his place. As he walked to the door I had the utterly incredulous idea that around him was a droning and humming like an enormous bagpipe muted.

"My curiosity, or something deeper, was tremendously aroused. That Wednesday I drove to his place. A lovely spot—all flowers and blossom-trees. There were a couple of hundred skips of bees set out in a broad orchard. Ferguson met me. He looked fuzzier and yellower than before. Also, the drone and hum of his voice seemed stronger. He took me into his house. It was an odd enough place. All one high room, and what windows there were had been shuttered—all except one. There was a dim golden-white light suffusing it. Nor was its door the ordinary door. It was low and broad. All at once it came to me that it was like the inside of a hive. The unshuttered window looked out upon the hives. It was screened.

"He brought me food and drink—honey and honeymead, cakes sweet with honey, and fruit. He said: 'I do not eat meat.'

"He began to talk. About the life of the bee. Of the utter happiness of the drone, darting through the sun, sipping at what flowers it would, fed by its sisters, drinking of the honey cups in the hive . . . free and careless and its nights and days only a smooth clicking of rapturous seconds . . .

" 'What if they do kill you at the end?' he said. 'You have lived—every fraction of a second of time. And then the rapture of the nuptial flight. Drone upon drone winging through the air on the track of the virgin! Life pouring stronger and stronger into you with each stroke of the wing! And at last . . . the flaming ecstasy . . . the flaming ecstasy of the fiery inner core of life . . . cheating death. True, death strikes when you are at the tip of the flame . . . but he strikes too late. You die—but what of that? You have cheated death. You do not know it is death that strikes. You die in the heart of the ecstasy . . .'

"He stopped. From outside came a faint sustained roaring that steadily grew stronger. The beating of thousands upon thousands of bee wings . . . the roaring of hundreds of thousands of tiny planes . . .

"Ferguson leaped to the window.

" 'The swarms! The swarms!'" he cried. A tremor shook him, another and another—more and more rapidly . . . became a rhythm pulsing faster and faster. His arms, outstretched, quivered . . . began to beat up and down, even more rapidly until they were like the blur of the humming bird's wings . . . like the blur of a bee's wings. His voice came to me . . . buzzing, humming . . . 'And tomorrow the virgins fly . . . the nuptial flight . . . I must be there . . . must . . . mzzz . . . mzzzb . . . bzzz . . . bzzzzzzz . . . zzzzmmmm . . .'

"For an instant there was no man there at the window. No. There was only a great drone buzzing and humming . . . striving to break through the screen . . . go free . . .

"And then Ferguson toppled backward. Fell. The thick

glasses were torn away by his fall. Two immense black eyes, not human eyes but the multiple eyes of the bee stared up at me.

"I bent down closer, closer, I listened for his heart beat. There was none. He was dead.

"Then slowly, slowly the dead mouth opened. Through the lips came the questing head of a drone ... antennae wavering ... eyes regarding me. It crawled out from between the lips. A handsome drone ... a strong drone. It rested for a breath on the lips, then its wings began to vibrate ... faster, faster ...

"It flew from the lips of Ferguson and circled my head once and twice and thrice. It flashed to the window and clung to the screen, buzzing, crawling, beating its wings against it ...

There was a knife on the table. I took it and ripped the screen. The drone darted out—and was gone—

"I turned and looked at Ferguson. His eyes stared up at me. Dead eyes. But no longer black ... blue as I had known them of old. And human. His hair was no longer the fine golden fuzz of the bee—it was black as it had been when I had first known him. And his hands were white and sinewy—and hairless."

AUGUST DERLETH

THE ADVENTURE OF
THE TOTTENHAM WEREWOLF

Very few of the problems which occupied the attention of my friend, Solar Pons, came to him through sources close to him, but at least one of them, the singular adventure of Septimus Grayle, the Tottenham Werewolf, I myself brought to his notice, however unwittingly. During Pons' absence on the Continent one summer, I had got into the habit of taking dinner at the Diogenes Club, and had observed there from time to time a porcine, well-muscled individual of middle-age, who made me uncomfortable by the forthright manner in which he examined me. In turn, I found myself wondering about him, and I determined to ask Pons to join me at dinner as soon as he returned from Prague.

Accordingly, one evening I ushered Pons to my table at the Club. "Ah, we are in luck, Pons," I said. "He is here."

I placed Pons so that he might obtain an excellent view of our fellow-diner in one of the mirrors which reflected the room beyond our table, and the keen grey eyes of my companion fixed upon the reflection in the glass, though his lean face was ostensibly turned toward me. The object of Pons' scrutiny was leisurely engaged in eating his meal, but he had observed our entrance and his expression had unquestionably quickened; yet he had returned to his meal with the assurance of a man who knows he will complete his dinner before you and be well on his way before you can take leave of your table. He was somewhat warmly clad this evening, but as always, he bore no evident clues about himself, and I was thus all the more interested in Pons' reaction.

"What do you make of him?" I asked presently.

"There is not much to be said," replied Pons, much to my satisfaction. "Though it is evident by his colour that he is an ex-colonial—Egypt, I should say, if the scarab ring he wears is any indication—that he has not long been back in England, that he is very probably not a member of the Diogenes Club but has a guest-card, that he is at present living outside London, since his visits here are periodic compared to yours, which are hardly regular, that he is a man of approximately fifty-five years of age, very clearly accustomed to administrative work—work, I submit, dealing in a large measure with native labour, that his interest in the Diogenes Club lies in something other than its cuisine, which is not exceptional."

"My dear fellow!" I protested. "I can follow most of your deductions with ease . . ."

"Dear me! how familiarity does breed contempt," murmured Pons.

"But how in the world do you arrive at the conclusion that his visits here have an ulterior motive?"

"You have not mentioned his interest in anything apart from yourself, Parker. I submit, therefore, that you are the object of his attentions."

"My dear Pons!"

"Because the gentleman has been observing you with a most definite purpose. Consider—he comes in from the country at regular intervals; you do not recall his interest in anyone else."

"You flatter me."

"Ah, do not say so, Parker. I fancy his interest in you is dictated by my absence from London."

"You, Pons!"

"I submit that our fellow-diner sought me some time ago, failed to find me—you will recall that Mrs. Johnson, too, spent these past weeks with her sister in Edinburgh, and then discovered your whereabouts either through the medical directory or by accident. He concluded that my return to London would be marked either by your absence from the Diogenes Club or by my appearance in your company. And now, if I am not mistaken, we shall have corroboration."

Our fellow-diner had finished his dinner, and was now coming to his feet. But instead of leaving the dining-room, he turned purposefully and came over to our table, beside which he stood in a few moments, a short, compact figure, bowing slightly.

"I beg your pardon," he said in a low, husky voice, "I believe I have the privilege of addressing Mr. Solar Pons, the private enquiry agent. I am Octavius Grayle, of Tottenham village, near Northallerton in Yorkshire."

"Pray be seated, Mr. Grayle," said Pons. "I believe you know Dr. Parker."

"By sight, yes. I fear I have been making a nuisance of myself by watching for your company. I could rouse no one at 7B Praed Street; so I concluded that sooner or later Dr. Parker's movements would give me some indication of your whereabouts."

"I have been out of London," said Pons. "But you are not interested in my itinerary."

"I have no doubt that you have already exercised those powers of yours which are so remarkable and correctly concluded that I am an ex-Colonial from Egypt, not too long—a year—back in England, and that I am not a member of the Club, but a guest on my brother's card. It is about my brother that I would like to consult you."

"By all means," answered Pons with a mirthful gleam in his eyes. "Your brother is Septimus Grayle . . ."

"The Tottenham Werewolf," finished our client, for manifestly such he had become. "I am afraid, Mr. Pons," he continued dryly, "that we must concede so much—my brother at least is convinced that he is a werewolf, very probably because he has certain extremely distressing compulsions, the most startling of which is a habit of loping about on all fours on moonlit nights and baying at the moon."

"Incredible!" I cried.

"But you apparently have some familiarity with the case, Mr. Pons," continued Grayle, as if oblivious to my exclamation. "You will then know that in the course of the past year a young man, William Gilton; a girl, Miss Miranda Choate; and our own uncle, Alexander Grayle, have been mysteriously slain, all discovered with their throats literally torn out. The last death, our uncle's, occurred only a month ago, and now my brother has been placed under what is called 'protective custody'. In short, he has been arrested, he has been all but charged and removed from the house. Mr. Pons, my brother may have the compulsion to believe that he is, and even in part to act like, a werewolf, but he is no murderer."

"What are your brother's circumstances, Mr. Grayle?"

"The three of us—my brother, my sister Regina, and I —live together. Each of us is independently wealthy, in a modest way, of course, and each of us lives rather independently of the other, though my sister and brother have naturally grown closer together during my long absence in Egypt. My brother, I should hasten to add, is aware of his affliction, but he is not more than ordinarily depressed by it from time to time, and he does not permit his knowledge of it to cloud his small pleasures. He is somewhat younger than I am, and our sister is younger than he. It is she who manages the servants and runs our household. My brother's situation is such that the mere fact of his arrest would precipitate a local scandal of great proportions, since our family is perhaps the oldest in Tottenham—and perhaps also the wealthiest. My late uncle was the largest landowner in the country, and his death has been widely chronicled, as you know. It is therefore implicit in the situation that the real murderer must be found. Detective-Sergeant Brinton is dogged and persistent, but he lacks any genuine acumen, and the county police are far more accustomed to dealing with traffic regulations infringements than with matters of this kind. Can I prevail upon you to join us at Grayle Old Place in Tottenham as soon as it is convenient for you to do so?"

"You may expect us in the morning, Mr. Grayle," said Pons.

Thereupon our client came at once to his feet, bowed with almost military precision, thanked Pons, and took formal leave of us.

Pons, his eyes twinkling, turned to me. "There is as engaging a fellow as I have laid eyes upon for a long time."

"A man like that would be capable of anything," I said.

"Precisely. You have done me a good turn, Parker; I

have been interested in the case ever since first I saw it in the papers. Indeed, I am carrying it with me."

So saying, he reached into his pocket and came forth with a neatly folded batch of clippings, through which he riffled without delay, selecting one finally, and drawing it forth.

"Ah, here we are. 'Murder of Prominent Landlord,' " he read. " 'Alexander Grayle, sixty-seven, of Tottenham, near Northallerton, Yorkshire, was found dead on a country lane not far from his home . . .' And so on. 'His death is the third in a series. Two previous victims were discovered in similar circumstances . . .' A curious, if somewhat gruesome, business, this. And clearly, I should venture to guess, intended to point to Septimus Grayle."

"The torn throat, yes," I agreed. "It would suggest the werewolf concept. Doubtless all the villagers are fully aware of Grayle's aberration."

"Unquestionably. All the deaths have been nocturnal; all have taken place on moonlit nights, when Grayle is known to yield to his strange compulsion. I submit, Parker, that this is no mere coincidence, but rather evidence of a design, which, if the facts are as Octavius Grayle has presented them, has already had the desired effect upon the local police who have proceeded, however deferentially, against Septimus. I fear there is devil's work afoot, Parker. Something dark and devious that troubles our client more than he has confided."

He looked up speculatively. "Can you go, Parker? Or is your practise too demanding?"

"I have a *locum tenens*," I answered. "You know I would be delighted."

"And your wife?"

"Constance is visiting her mother in Kent. She would urge me to go."

"Capital!" exclaimed Pons. "Wifely concurrence in these little adventures is always advisable. I have not looked up the railway timetable, but I believe we can entrain in the morning and arrive in good time. Let us have breakfast together and set out after."

Accordingly, early the following morning we met at

7B Praed Street in the familiar quarters which we had shared for so many years prior to my marriage, and partook of a hearty breakfast prepared by Mrs. Johnson, who served us with many assurances of her delight at seeing us together once again. Pons had already gone through the morning papers, and at the time of my arrival he sat in the midst of a host of newspapers around his chair.

"There is nothing further on the Tottenham puzzle," he said when at last Mrs. Johnson had left us. "The local police sergeant has given out the customary statements—fortunately in nothing like the volubility of his American counterparts. This time, however, I have no doubt that an arrest is imminent. There are delicate hints that the culprit is to be found in a high place, which presumably has reference to people of the Grayles' position in a village like Tottenham. Yet there has been no further outbreak."

"Do you expect one, then?"

"There will certainly be a fourth victim—possibly even a fifth," he said enigmatically.

"You sound very positive."

"Ah, Parker—how it used to annoy you! But it is not so. The speculation takes its rise in a logical deduction. Septimus Grayle either is guilty or he is not. Octavius does not believe him to be guilty. Supposing that he is correct, then I venture to guess that a fourth victim is inevitably meant to follow—obviously, that is Septimus himself. If he is not correct, there may well be another crime. And, remotely, yet one more beyond that. Contrary to the official position, there is very definitely a pattern in the crimes at Tottenham."

We set out directly after breakfast and were soon on the train en route to Yorkshire. It was a fine summer morning, with an early fog lifting rapidly before the sun, and the landscape, green and rolling, beyond the cars. But Pons was unaware of it: he sat throughout the journey with his hawk-like face turned away from the window, his chin sunk upon his chest, his eyes half-closed in an attitude of cogitation into which I did not break.

On our arrival at Tottenham, we sought rooms at the Boar's Head, the only local inn of any size. There we paused only long enough to enable Pons to set down and dispatch to the local sergeant of police a note informing him that Pons would appreciate the opportunity to discuss the Tottenham murders with him. Then we ventured forth in search of Grayle Old Place. We found our objective within a short time and without difficulty, for it was one of the two most imposing houses in the village, the other being the abode, until recently, of the third victim of the Tottenham murderer, Alexander Grayle. It was a house set well back into its grounds, with a gate at the driveway, and a sweep of lawns reaching to the Victorian building in which our client lived. Beyond the house lay gently rolling fields and woods. Its setting at the edge of the village was so idyllic that the very thought of the crime which Pons had come to look into seemed alien.

The massive door was opened to us by a dignified butler, hard upon whose heels came our client himself. He walked down a wide hall, the walls of which bore portraits of Grayle ancestors, his hands extended in welcome.

"You are just in time for tea, Gentlemen." To the butler he added, "Crandon, rooms for our guests."

"No," said Pons at once. "We have put up at the Boar's Head. It will give us greater freedom of movement."

An expression of disappointment crossed our client's face, but he said nothing. He turned on his heel and led the way into the drawing-room, where we were introduced to the other members of the family—Miss Regina Grayle, a woman whose dark, melancholy eyes belied her youth, a woman who clearly existed on a precarious line between youth and middle-age, and whose austerity of dress, black with a high collar relieved only by a cameo, and coiffure, her hair drawn tightly about her head, accentuated rather middle-age than youth; Randall Grayle, a brash young man, not long back from Canada, the son of yet another brother to our client's father; and Septimus Grayle, a tall, hawk-nosed man, lean almost to gauntness, who viewed us with frankly hostile eyes, in which brooded an unconcealed contempt. Septimus wore his hair long; it was greying now, but his face was still young, save for the scars of what appeared to be a fencing accident along his right cheek near his ear.

It was not readily evident whether our client had informed the household that he had retained Pons. Miss Regina made an inquiry as to whether Pons was assisting Sergeant Brinton to which Pons made an oblique reply; he was accustomed, he said, to lend the police all assistance within his modest power. This reply seemed to satisfy her. Not so Septimus, however; he continued to glower at Pons above the specious conversation which took place before the subject of the crimes in Tottenham was introduced.

"This terrible, terrible sequence of events," said Miss Regina passionately, clenching her hand about a handsome, old-fashioned back-scratcher she carried, "is all the more shocking when one considers that the police are actually concerned about our own Septimus, who would not harm a soul."

Septimus favored his sister with a wan smile.

"Our dear uncle was an almost saintly man," continued the lady, "and I could not imagine who would have wished him harm. And little Miranda Choate, while she has been known for sauciness, could hardly have inspired so heinous a crime. And Mr. Gilton, a young man of estimable character—indeed, it is not so many years since I went about in his company quite often—who could have desired his death? Oh, it is madness, Mr. Pons, madness."

At the mention of madness, Septimus Grayle underwent a ghastly alteration. His face greyed, became chalk-like, his lantern-jaw fell, and he drew his breath with a rushing sound through his quivering lips. But this transformation was soon again masked, though the unpleasant impression it had given us could not be concealed so easily. I observed Pons watching him surreptitiously, and, beyond him, young Randall Grayle, whose singular brawniness found no complements even in his cousin Octavius's manifest strength. The expression on Randall Grayle's features was puzzling; I could not determine whether he hid disgust or triumph, cunning or naivete.

"Forgive me, Septimus," said his sister quietly.

Our client looked over at Pons judiciously, as if to make certain that he had caught the interchange.

"Surely the police have not exhausted the avenues of inquiry," said Pons thoughtfully. "The press has set forth the lack of connection among the victims of the Tottenham murderer."

"There is none, Mr. Pons," said Octavius Grayle decisively.

"I submit that the choice of the victims may have a pattern."

"Homicidal mania reveals no pattern, Mr. Pons," said Miss Regina primly, reaching behind her to claw her back with the back-scratcher she was holding.

Pons inclined his head. Then he turned to Septimus Grayle. "Tell me, Mr. Grayle, did your late uncle leave a family?"

Septimus, who had hitherto not been directly addressed by Pons, was disagreeably startled. He gazed reproachfully at his brother, imploringly at his sister, and finally looked reluctantly at his inquisitor, who had not removed his eyes from him.

"No, no," he said hastily, with a marked uneasiness in his manner, "Uncle Alexander was not married. He was the one who wasn't, of the three brothers. Like us—none of us is married—except Randall; he's going to be, I think?" He looked to Randall for confirmation; the young man nodded and smiled. "We are all who are left. All the Grayles. We were never a large family. We have none of us married." A fine dew of perspiration made its appearance on his high forehead. Quite suddenly his voice changed. "And you know why, don't you, Mr. Pons? You know it. Everybody knows it!" he almost shouted. Then, biting his lip until it bled, he added almost in a whisper, "Madness! Madness! Madness!"

Abruptly he sprang to his feet and ran from the room.

Miss Regina rose, shot a punishing glance at her remaining brother, excused herself, and followed Septimus Grayle from the room.

"It was not what I would call a successful interview," said Randall Grayle dryly. "In Canada we do things differently—and perhaps more effectively."

Octavius looked angrily at his cousin. "May I remind you, Randall, that a gentleman always maintains the proper attitude toward guests?" He turned to Pons. "Pray excuse my impetuous cousin, Mr. Pons."

Pons lifted himself from the depths of his chair. "I fear we have exhausted our welcome, Mr. Grayle."

"Not at all, let me assure you," protested our client.

Randall Grayle said nothing at all. He had lit a cigarette and was watching curiously to see what Pons would do.

Pons began to walk from the room. "I am at your service at the Boar's Head, Mr. Grayle. Pray call on me there."

With this, we took our departure.

"What do you make of it, Pons?" I asked once we had got clear of the gate.

"A most interesting family, did you not think, Parker?"

"Oh, yes. But the murders?"

"Everything in good time, Parker. Do not be impatient. Let us just hurry along; unless I am greatly in error, Sergeant Brinton will be waiting for us."

Sergeant Brinton was indeed waiting for us at the Boar's Head. He was a young man, still, tall, big-boned, and sturdy in appearance. His manner was frank and cooperative, yet neither deferential nor condescending, though it was impossible for him to conceal entirely the impressiveness of this association with Solar Pons, whose reputation had long since spread the length and breadth of the British Isles.

"I was happy to have your note, Mr. Pons," he said without preamble. "I had learned from Mr. Octavius Grayle that he contemplated asking you to step into the case, rather than intercede with Scotland Yard. I am afraid, though, that there is little to be discovered."

"You are convinced it is Septimus Grayle?"

"I can conceive of no other solution. The crimes are very obviously the work of a homicidal maniac. All have taken place on moonlight nights, just such nights as those on which Septimus has his seizures. He imagines himself a dog, he bays at the moon . . ."

"Pray enlighten me," interrupted Pons. "For how long a time has Septimus Grayle been the victim of this strange compulsion?"

"For most of his life, I believe."

"It does not occur to you that this additional, shall we say, pastime, of his nocturnal repertoire—the tearing out of throats—is comparatively recent?"

"Obviously."

"You do not think it strange that this proclivity did not manifest itself before this?"

"Insanity, Mr. Pons, is unpredictable."

"Is it not, indeed? I should not have thought so; would you, Parker?"

"Certain forms, of course," I agreed. "But the majority of cases follow a fairly well-defined pattern. It is perfectly possible to predict a course of action."

The sergeant gazed at me thoughtfully and, I thought, a trifle impatiently, as if he thought I did not know what I was talking about. He forebore to say so, however.

"I submit that it is suggestive that this series of crimes took place within a relatively short time after the return of two of the Grayles from foreign parts," continued Pons.

Brinton gazed at him in candid astonishment. "You refer to Mr. Octavius and Mr. Randall." He did not wait for Pons' confirming nod. "But, of course, you do not mean to be serious. The suggestion is patently absurd—neither of them is a homicidal maniac."

"Ah, it is one of the characteristics of homicidal mania that it reveals no distinctive traits, such as those clearly associated with Septimus," said Pons. "But let us put aside this question for the moment. I would like to know something of the victims."

"I brought along photographs, Mr. Pons. If there is anything you would like to know, you have only to ask."

"Thank you, Sergeant. Let us just look at the photographs."

The sergeant opened a large manilla envelope and offered Pons a sheaf of pictures, the majority of which had been taken of the bodies at the scene of the crime. I bent over Pons' shoulder and looked, too, as he went rapidly through the prints, which had an unpleasantly harsh reality afforded by the glaring light which had been thrown upon the brutally slain victims.

They were not inspiring to look upon. The unhappy

victims of this fiendish attack were sprawled out beside rustic paths. Pictures taken at close range indicated that each had had his throat torn out, plainly as the amount of blood revealed while he still lived. The little girl was most pathetic and I could hardly bear to look upon the horrible scene so mercilessly revealed by the photographer.

Pons, however, appeared to have no such qualms. "Ah," he murmured, "Stunned, then slain."

"Exactly, Mr. Pons. The marks on the neck emphatically suggest some animal. May I point out that Mr. Septimus Grayle wears his nails unusually long?"

"I observed it," replied Pons grimly.

"The tears are deep, severing the jugular in each case. Death took place in a matter of minutes; the loss of blood was very great. In no case was any sound heard, though the victims were found on bypaths away from the better-illuminated thoroughfares. Only mania could explain such insensate and brutal slayings, Mr. Pons."

Pons had not lifted his eyes from the photographs. "Repeated attempts to sever the jugular, not just one gash," he said. He looked up at last. "Was this man Gilton married?"

"No, Mr. Pons. He was betrothed."

"His age?"

"Thirty-seven."

"He is financially comfortable?"

"Quite. He leaves only a sister, who inherits." Brinton paused and added, "I believe she is to be married to young Mr. Randall Grayle."

Pons closed his eyes and sat for a moment in silence. "And Mr. Alexander Grayle?" he asked presently.

"He was single, and wealthy. The four Grayles are his only heirs; they will divide his estate. But I must in duty point out to you that each of the Grayles is independently wealthy."

Pons turned this over in his mind. He did not comment on the wealth of the Grayles. "Let us return for a moment to Mr. Gilton," he said. "Was he not approximately of the same age as the youngest of the three Grayles?"

"I believe so, yes. He kept company with Miss Regina for some time. He was at that time rather indigent, but soon came into money through a series of fortunate investments."

"He was not favoured by Miss Regina Grayle?"

The sergeant shrugged. "I would not say precisely that, Mr. Pons. It was only that they simply drifted apart; perhaps they had been keeping company too long. They remained close friends, though I believe the brothers did not particularly fancy him." He cleared his throat uncertainly. "But I assure you, Mr. Pons, it is Septimus Grayle who holds the key to the riddle."

"And the child," continued Pons imperturbably.

"Poor Miranda Choate. She had been at a children's party and was returning home. She had been escorted for most of the way to her door by a party of young people with an older person who was their chaperone. There was a short distance just before her gate—by a coincidence, in the vicinity of the lane in which Gilton's body had been found; they had not walked that far, but stood at the other end until she had time to reach the gate. She was heard to call out a last goodnight. Evidence shows that she was struck down then, though her body was not found there, but down on a pasture path which led her away to one side of her home."

"An only child?"

"No, sir. One of a large family. She was a pert little thing."

The sergeant stood patiently waiting on Pons' next question. He seemed somewhat puzzled by the tenor and direction of Pons' inquiry, and quite clearly could not conceive what end Pons' pursued. He was no more mystified than I.

But Pons had no further inquiries. He gathered the photographs together and handed them to Brinton. "I am indebted to you, Sergeant. If I should need to send for you in some haste, I daresay you could be reached at the station?"

"Certainly, Mr. Pons, at any time. My home is in the same building."

"Capital, capital!"

After Sergeant Brinton had gone, Pons sat musing for

some little time. I waited patiently on his cogitation, and presently found his eyes dwelling on me in sardonic amusement.

"Is it not remarkable, Parker, how readily the human mind is blinded by the obvious?" he asked.

"I suppose it is the obverse of being too eager to shunt aside the obvious for the obscure."

"Well spoken, Parker," rejoined Pons, smiling. "But is there not something about this curious sequence of events which gives you the pause?"

"Nothing but the obvious," I replied firmly. "Here is the work of someone who is definitely unstable."

"Indeed," said Pons with heavy irony. "I submit that there is far more here than meets the eye. It does not seem to you that there is a pattern in these events?"

"None."

"Mr. Gilton was indigent; he became wealthy. His sister, who is to inherit his wealth, is engaged to marry Mr. Randall Grayle. The little Choate girl lived in the vicinity of the scene of Gilton's death. Alexander Grayle left no other heirs but the Grayles, who are wealthy and are now destined to become more so. Either these events are totally without connection, or they are the setting of a stage, and the return of Mr. Randall Grayle or our client served as the catalytic agent to precipitate them."

I could not help smiling. "I am afraid there is such a thing as looking too far afield for the solution of any puzzle," I said.

"I am delighted to hear you say so, Parker," said Pons, his eyes twinkling mischievously. "I am habitually distrustful of the obvious."

"But one need not be insistent on ignoring it. It is not beyond Septimus Grayle's malady to have led him to murder. There is an old adage that where there is smoke, there must be some fire."

"Ah, yes, but the fire may be of incendiary origin," retorted Pons. He looked at his watch and added, "I fancy we had better have a little supper, for, unless I am greatly mistaken, we shall need to return to Grayle Old Place before the night is far along."

"Why do you say so?"

"Is there not a moon tonight? I believe it is near the full. With both the moon and ourselves in Tottenham, the werewolf could scarcely resist the challenge. Moreover, it is past time for the final act of this gruesome little drama."

With this enigmatic statement, Pons led the way to the dining-room and we partook of a spare meal of beef and cabbage, Pons discoursing meanwhile on the lore of lycanthropy, with its roots in ancient beliefs of mankind, recalling many of the highly successful fictions in the genre as a parallel to references involving obscure and authenticated cases of diabolic cannibalistic acts associated with certain obscure crimes which bore at least a superficial resemblance to lycanthropic practises.

Our supper hour over, we retired to our quarters, where for some time Pons sat deep in thought, occasionally turning to the newspaper accounts of the Tottenham murders, which he had brought along from London. From time to time, he glanced at the clock, always with increasing restlessness.

"You are expecting someone?" I ventured at last.

"Now that darkness has fallen and the moon has risen, yes. I hope he will not disappoint me, or we may be too late to prevent another crime."

"Surely not!" I cried. "Who is it, then?"

"Our client. Who else? I submit that his next move must be to introduce us to Septimus by night."

He had no sooner spoken than there was a discreet, yet urgent tap on the door. Pons sprang at once to open it, disclosing Octavius Grayle.

"Mr. Pons, can you come?" he asked in a hushed voice.

"We are at your service, Mr. Grayle. I take it your brother has had a seizure?"

Our client nodded. "He has just left the house. I know the paths he will take. For the time being he will confine himself to the grounds and to the woods and byways outside the village; he seldom ventures the village itself until past midnight—and he does not always remain away from the house for more than an hour, so that he seldom invades Tottenham."

Octavius Grayle led the way rapidly to Grayle Old Place, where we entered the grounds not by the central gate, but by means of a small garden gate which opened through a hedge out of sight of the principal entrance. At once the perfumes of flowers and herbs invaded our nostrils, rising with cloying insistence in the humid evening. The moon shone high overhead, now near the full, a great luminous satellite laving all the earth in its unterrestrial radiance. Beyond the garden, the house loomed spectrally, with but little light showing in its windows, save where the moon reflected from the panes.

Our client made his way by a devious route around the house and plunged into the shadowed paths on the far side. It was patent presently that his goal was a small eminence not far ahead and yet a considerable distance from the house. Octavius Grayle moved with an agility which was remarkable in one of his years, for soon we were mounting the slope through a glade toward an open place beyond.

At that instant there burst upon our ears a weird and horrible sound—the simulated howling of a wolf or baying of a dog in human voice. Before me, our client, who had reached the top of the knoll, turned and caught hold of Pons' arm as my companion came up.

"You hear?" he whispered harshly. "Now watch—over there."

Below, the moonlit landscape rolled gently away in grassy valleys and dark woods. Our client pointed to a valley not far distant, plainly part of the Grayle estate. Even as he spoke, a shadowy figure loped on all fours across the moonlit glade, out of one dark wood into another, and through it to emerge on the far side, once again in the moonlight, where it rose half way and once again gave voice to that horribly suggestive ululation which so closely resembled the howling of some wild beast.

"He began it as a child," whispered Octavius Grayle. "Will he ever cease, I wonder?"

"That is in Parker's department," murmured Pons.

"If one finds the cause," I said. "There is a reason hidden deep in his subconscious for compulsions such as this."

"I hope you are right, Doctor," said our client fervently. "I do not relish living out my life to this, every moonlit night. Now mark him; he has begun to move again; he will follow the line of that valley, plunge into the wood over there, and when he emerges from it he will begin an arc which will bring him either through the copse at the foot of this knoll, or on this other slope and across part of the knoll itself. We shall watch both courses; if you, Mr. Pons, will watch the slope itself, with Dr. Parker, I will descend to the copse."

"And by what signal shall we communicate?" asked Pons.

"If his baying does not suffice, let us say the crying of a screech owl to signify that he has passed."

"Agreed," murmured Pons.

Thereupon Octavius Grayle vanished into the shadows on the far side of the slope, leaving Pons and myself in possession of the knoll. But Pons had no intention of remaining; he paused only long enough to instruct me.

"Pray hold the fort, Parker," he whispered. "I am not interested in that afflicted man. Guard yourself; we have been followed."

Then he was gone on the path taken by our client.

I looked uneasily around, but was reassured by the expanse of unbroken moonlight holding to the top of the knoll. No one could creep upon me unseen without the protection of shadows, which did not begin for some distance down the slope on all sides. I gazed once more along the route defined by our client as that customarily taken by his unfortunate brother; but Septimus Grayle was nowhere to be seen. Perhaps he had varied his route; perhaps he lingered on the edge of a wood out of range of my vision.

Suddenly his voice sounded once more, raised in that eerie crying. Small wonder that Tottenham looked upon him with fear and suspicion! Even as I thought so, even while the echoes of that fearful cry still resounded in the valleys, I heard and recognized another voice.

"Parker! Parker! Here—at once."

It was Pons. Casting discretion to the winds, I sped down the slope in the direction of his voice as fast as I could run through that unfamiliar country. Down out of the moonlight into the dense trees of the slope; through one grove and past another patch of moonlight, finding a dim, winding path; and, at the foot of the slope, into another, even denser copse. In my headlong rush, I almost fell over Pons.

He was crouched on the ground in deep shadow. In a moment I saw that he held our client in his arms. Octavius Grayle lay ominously still.

"For God's sake!" I cried. "What has happened?"

"My flashlight is in the grass beside me, just out of my reach," said Pons. "It fell from my hand. His throat has been cut; I cannot determine how badly, but his pulse is still strong."

It was the work of but a few moments to recover Pons' flashlight, to turn it upon our client, and to ascertain that, though he was unconscious from the blow which had struck him down and bleeding profusely from his throat, his jugular vein had not been severed, no important artery had sustained any injury, and, unless the blow were more serious than it appeared, he would recover.

"What happened?" I asked again.

An exclamation of disgust escaped Pons. "I was only just too late," he said bitterly.

"I should have said you were just in time," I answered. "Was it an animal?"

"The Tottenham werewolf," murmured Pons. "It is unforgiveable; I anticipated this and was not fast enough to prevent it. Our pursuer was closer than I thought."

"The attack perhaps you did not prevent; his death you certainly did prevent. Come, let us get him to the house. I can staunch this wound here."

"We shall want Sergeant Brinton," said Pons. "There is still time for us to catch a late train back to London."

"Poor Septimus," I murmured.

"Oh, it was not Septimus," said Pons lightly. "But no less obvious, for all that."

He did not explain this cryptic announcement.

The Grayle family, with Pons and myself, were gathered about our client's bedside, when Detective-Sergeant Brinton came into the room from an examination of the house and grounds. He carried the blood-stained back-scratcher which had belonged to Miss Regina Grayle.

"Just as you thought, Mr. Pons—it was in Septimus's quarters," he said.

"Oh, no, not Septimus!" cried Miss Regina in anguish.

Randall Grayle looked at Pons with distrust plain on his handsome features.

Octavius Grayle opened his eyes and regarded the tableau before him. He met Pons' steady gaze.

"You know now, Mr. Pons?" he whispered.

"Indeed, sir. I knew from the time of our initial visit here."

The sergeant stepped reluctantly toward Septimus.

"But no, Sergeant," interposed Pons. "Miss Regina is right. It is not Septimus. The charge must be placed against Miss Regina herself."

For a moment there was an arresting silence.

Then Miss Regina Grayle's placidity dropped from her; her prim face underwent an awesome transformation. Glowing with the agility and speed of a cat, she leaped forward, snatched the back-scratcher from the sergeant's hands, and struck at Pons, who caught her arm and twisted it unceremoniously behind her back. In this manner he held her.

"Your prisoner, Sergeant."

"Mr. Pons, I am afraid . . ." began the sergeant uncertainly, looking on with dismay.

"I think, if you will examine into the status of the family fortunes, you will find ample evidence, Sergeant," said Pons crisply. "Mr. Gilton should have repaid the money she lent him, unsecured though it was; it would have saved his life; it would have saved the life of the little girl who witnessed something which might have trapped Miss Regina; it would have saved the life of Alexander Grayle, whose bequest was necessary to conceal the loss of the money in her care she took from Septimus. Except for the bequest from Alexander, Miss Regina and Septimus are both without more than the most vitally necessary funds. If Octavius had not begun to suspect something amiss, her diabolic plan might well have carried through—he would have been the fourth victim, and Septimus, as the planned and perfect suspect, the fifth."

"The problem turned on an elementary factor," said Pons out of the darkness of our compartment, as the late train sped toward London and the welcome security of our respective quarters. "There was no obvious motive, as the puzzle was presented to us, and there were too many suggestions of homicidal mania, which would rule out motive. However, of the three victims, two were possessed of means, the younger man having come by wealth somewhat recently, the older wealthy by long standing. Now, Parker, I submit that when a man of wealth is slain, the motive which at once presents itself is gain. The primary consideration at Tottenham which obscured every other was the curious behaviour of Septimus Grayle; yet to the observer untroubled by the affliction of the so-called Tottenham werewolf, the motive for gain immediately appeared."

"Ah, but it was generally believed that the Grayles were themselves wealthy," I put in.

"It is elementary that a premise is either true or not true. No one had any question but that Miss Regina Grayle was independently wealthy, and that she had therefore no need of a bequest such as her uncle left. You know my methods, Parker; I could not accept the assumption, and proceeded on the precise opposite. Though everyone stated without equivocation that the Grayles were wealthy, there was no evidence to support the premise, apart from the specious fact of their ownership of Grayle Old Place. On the hypothetical assumption that the generally accepted belief was unfounded, I could conceive of the reasonable motive and its instant application to one of the four who stood to gain by Alexander Grayle's death.

"Proceeding in this fashion, then, it followed that there was a reason for each crime. If the motive for Alexander Grayle's death were gain, then the young man and the girl might have been slain solely to confuse any investigation with the suggestion of homicidal mania. Yet a secondary motive was not inadmissible, and I had to look for it. It was perfectly plain at our meeting in the Diogenes Club that Octavius Grayle had certain apprehensions he did not reveal. Clearly, too, he was both observant and intelligent, and it was patent from the beginning even as he had hinted that the murderer was deliberately planning for the arrest and imprisonment of Septimus Grayle as the climax to the events which had taken place at Tottenham. This implied a secondary motive.

"I had to ask myself who but some member of his own family could possibly have motive for desiring Septimus to be found guilty. I confess that for a short time I was thrown off the track by the fact that both Octavius and Randall had but recently returned to England; there was thus presumptive evidence that their return was connected with the events at Tottenham, and the primary assumption, of course, was that one or the other of them was guilty. And yet I could not deny that anyone encountering the problem could be expected to reason in this manner. If neither were guilty, only Miss Regina remained. Therefore, either one of the prodigals was guilty, or the return of one or both set in motion a chain of events which culminated in the wanton crimes at Tottenham.

"Our brief visit at Grayle Old Place this afternoon confirmed my suspicion of Miss Regina. She spoke of the first victim, you will remember, with passing regret and carefully concealed animosity, which was surely nothing more than the hatred of a woman scorned—she had kept company with him, but he was now betrothed to someone else. She spoke of Miranda Choate as naughty and saucy, as if to salve her conscience. She spoke of her murdered uncle with something akin to remorse, which was as genuine as her conviction of the necessity of his death. Finally, she herself levelled at her brother Septimus by suggestion as the only possible explanation for the crimes the charge of homicidal mania.

"I had my murderer; I had then to find the motive. Sergeant Brinton supplied it. He said of Gilton, if you recall, that at the time he was keeping company with Miss Regina, he was 'rather indigent, but soon came into money with a series of fortunate investments.' Now, I submit, Parker, that in order for young Gilton to have made investments he must have received money from some source. What source more obvious than Miss Regina, who in her infatuation showered him with all the money he demanded, using not only her own funds but also those of her brother, Septimus, which were in her care? Indeed, one feels bound to ask whether Gilton's fortunate investments were an actuality or whether they were simply his canny accumulation of the money he had obtained from that infatuated woman.

"Surely, then, the obvious first victim of her counterfeiting homicidal mania might as well be the young man who had spurned her as well as robbed her. The selection of the child was purely happenstance; a little girl had seen her in the vicinity at the time Gilton had been slain. Miss Regina accordingly feared her, and she became the second victim. The stage was then set for Alexander Grayle's death, and he, too, died as the others—stunned by a blow from the leaded handle of her back-scratcher, and calmly dispatched while unconscious by what must certainly be regarded as one of the most unusual lethal weapons in a long roster of adventures.

"Having proceeded thus far, it was only logical to assume that if Octavius had not already arrived at the same conclusion he must must soon do so. It followed, therefore, that his death must occur with as little delay as possible, in order that Miss Regina's purpose might be accomplished. I had only to wait upon events. Our entrance on the scene would surely precipitate her violence, even as Octavius's arrival in England and his subsequent inquiry into the state of Septimus's finances set in motion the events which were the final acts in the concealed tragedy which was Miss Regina's life.

"All in all, an interesting if gruesome diversion. I am indebted to you, Parker."

BEVERLY HAAF

MRS. KAYE

My neighbour's voice was strained as she asked, "Jane have you ever known a person so frightening it was like knowing you were having a nightmare, yet you could not awaken?"

I stared at Karen. Nightmare? Unable to awaken? What an odd question, but then, she was an artist and exceptionally sensitive to moods and auras. At the time, I thought of myself as practical and unimaginative.

My answer came quickly: "No, Karen. I never met anyone who made me feel that way."

As soon as the words left my mouth, I shuddered. My sentence had a mocking echo that was ominously significant—as if someday I would recall my reply with horror, wondering how I could have been so blind. Hastily I reached for the coffee Karen pushed across the table, glad she was busy with her own thoughts and unaware of my strange premonition.

Her yellow-brown eyes held a vague stare as she spoke again, more to herself than to me. "Mrs. Kaye makes me feel I'm living a nightmare."

I waited uneasily for her to continue, considering what an odd person she was. She specialized in portraits; however, ceramics was a hobby, and she'd made the cups we drank from—black cups. On the lustrous jet sides were painted curious flower designs: designs which on close inspection proved to be miniature portraits of a child, a girl with masses of petal-like fair hair.

Suddenly I had the mad impulse to snatch up my small daughter, Beth, from the next room and run home. My senses seemed sharpened: the coffee too bitter, the doughnut too sweet, the very air of the room charged with menace. But I heard myself ask calmly, "Why does this Mrs. Kaye give you so horrible a feeling?"

I had to strain forward to hear the whispered answer. Her pale lips moved slowly, as if speaking caused her pain. "I met Mrs. Kaye before moving here. She upset me badly, yet I would have found it impossible to explain just why. Then, a few days ago I saw her again. I'd been shopping, and as I glanced into a store window I caught her reflection. She moved closer to me, and I was helpless —I could see her advancing and I wanted to run away— yet I was paralysed, held as if by invisible hands, forcing me to stay and listen to her." Karen's eyes widened, recreating the panic she'd felt. "Jane—she claimed she was a werewolf."

Werewolf! Something grotesque and unworldly was dredged up at the mention of that name, and then dissipated.

I tried to laugh. "But—this woman was joking with you —trying to frighten you with a weird joke. She had to be!"

Karen smiled without humour. "No, she was deadly serious. She claimed she had been afflicted with the malady since childhood and bore the mark."

"The mark? Come now, Karen. Certainly you don't . . ."

She cut me off with a voice as thin and sharp as the blade of a knife.

"Don't argue about legends. My grandmother was from Germany, and while she pretended to take the old tales lightly, I had to promise never to be without my gold cross. You see, if a child was unprotected by this emblem, a werewolf might pad up softly from behind and sink its teeth into the nape of the child's neck, dooming it to carry on the curse."

"And you believed this?" It was sickening to imagine a little girl forced to brood on such horrors.

"Of course I didn't believe it—not really. I sometimes went without it for days before Grandmother noticed and fastened it back."

I fought with the illogic of her statement until a thought cleared my puzzlement. "Could you be so upset because this Mrs. Kaye recalled your childhood guilt at deceiving your grandmother?"

302

My neighbour shook her head furiously. "No, no! Don't you understand? I'm afraid of this woman! Her eyes have such a strange light—you could see it even in the reflection. I think a wolf must glow like that when remembering something it killed. It makes me wonder if she too had a grandmother who gave her a cross, but she took it off while playing, and something crept behind her . . ."

"Stop it, Karen!"

My shrillness shocked me, and my neighbour threw back her head as if struck, tears springing into her eyes. Immediately I softened. How could I have forgotten she was preparing for an important art show in New York? She was capable of feverish intensity in her work, and was no doubt near exhaustion.

I set about soothing her in a sympathetic but brisk way. Surely the eerie situation she spoke of was greatly exaggerated because of the high pitch of her nerves, I said, and my efforts were rewarded by a wan smile. By the time Beth and I left, she was calm, and I was sure her bad experience would fade quickly.

Despite my sureness, I half expected to dream of werewolves myself that night. I am a widow (but not alone, for I have my dear Beth) and my temperament is steady; however, there was something terribly unnerving in the manner Karen had told her story. Thankfully, my dreams were all of a fair haired child dancing in a meadow ringed with a lush forest. Even during my sleep I smiled in misty recognition of the child—the one whose image was upon the black ceramic cups.

It was not until very late at night, a week later, that I saw Karen again. Since I must work (leaving Beth in the care of Agnes, my housekeeper) I have little chance to meet with my neighbours during the week, and so I was startled when Karen's frantic knock pounded at my door.

I let her in, surprised at her appearance. Never had she appeared less than fastidious, but when she stumbled into the room I saw her hair hung in tangled strands, and her hands, which clutched at me, were smeared with oil colours.

"I saw her—I saw her again," she moaned, holding me

with surprising strength. "It happened at the train station. No one was there but me—and then—Mrs. Kaye!"

I helplessly tried to soothe her, managing to get her into a chair despite her wild sobbing. And all the while I murmured comforting things I was aware of a coldness in the air. It was warm outside, the windows were open, but the chill crept about the room like an uninvited guest.

I patted Karen's shoulder. "Perhaps Mrs. Kaye didn't see you," I fumbled.

Karen gave a short laugh and looked up. Her yellow-brown eyes were clear and unswollen, the tears slipping down as coolly as drops from an icicle. A shudder wracked her thin body. "Yes, she saw me. I was all alone—the train had gone—and when I passed the phone booth on the station wall, something moved. When I turned, there she was."

There she was. My hand fell from Karen's shoulder as I stepped back. Her tone made the experience sound inevitable, as if nothing could change what was happening . . . I shook my head with confusion. Did I believe Karen was being threatened? And even if she was, why did I feel I was also involved?

"Did she ask where you lived?" I said, and then, before I could halt the words I rushed on, "You didn't tell her, did you? You didn't tell her where you lived?"

The answer was slow, almost measured. "I think that she already knows."

Her words died away as a terrible vision crept over my mind.

I could see Mrs. Kaye, her features indistinct except for the gleam in her eyes and the white edge of teeth which showed between parted moist lips. Coarse gray hair fell across her narrow shoulders, and while her form was that of a woman, it was distorted so that she could glide on all fours. I saw her lope with malevolent grace through the shadowed streets, sniffing at each path: sniff, sniff, sniffing, hunting for the trail which led to the house next door. And most horrible of all, I saw her pause, not at Karen's—but at my house, at my door . . .

"I think you'd better go home," I said to Karen, trying

to hide the tremor in my voice. "It's late and you're upset. Things will look better in the morning."

She did leave, thanking me for my kindness. I wanted to tell her to call me if she became frightened during the night, but I couldn't. I didn't want her to call—no matter what—I just wanted things to go on as they had always, Beth and me together—with no fears, no threats.

The next few days were blurred. As I had predicted to my neighbour, things did look better in the morning, but there lingered a haunting sensation of uneasiness. Then, when I returned from work one afternoon and Karen greeted me with a cheerful airy wave, I relaxed. I saw she was spraying fixative on paintings lined against the fence, apparently involved in nothing but her work. She certainly had recovered from her upsetting experiences, so why should the matter trouble me?

I was humming happily when Agnes met me at the door. She looked over my shoulder and into the yard. "Did you see the weird pictures out there?" she asked.

I smiled at my housekeeper. I knew well what she thought of what she called my neighbour's "queer paintbrushings". I'd tried to tell her it was the modern way to paint, but Agnes always insisted no one with normal eyes could choose the colour combinations Karen did.

"You may not care for them," I replied tolerantly, "but since they're for a show in New York, they must be good."

"A show? Well, I hope she don't end up where I heard she went after the last show of hers."

"What do you mean?"

Agnes shrugged. "They say her nerves got her. She was sent to an asylum, but of course they prettied it up by calling it a 'rest home'. She was only put away a few months, but when I saw the crazy pictures she carried into the yard, I wondered if maybe she shouldn't have been kept locked up."

As wonderful as my housekeeper was, she was inclined to prattle. "I didn't know you were a gossip," I said sharply. A woman alone in the world has enough problems without loose tongues making trouble. This rest home which conveyed such dark meaning was probably a health resort where Karen vacationed after the exhaustive strain of her show. "Gossip is harmful," I added. "I've often left Beth with Karen when I've gone out unexpectedly. Would I do that if I had doubts?"

Agnes flushed at my scolding, and feeling sorry that I spoke so sharply, I changed the subject, asking about her married daughter, who was expecting a baby.

By the time Agnes's son-in-law arrived to drive her home, we were again on excellent terms. But in the back of my thoughts was my statement about leaving Beth with Karen. I'd said I had no doubts . . . was it true? The vision of Mrs. Kaye hunting for Karen, yet stopping before my house, taunted me. Then I shrugged the mood away and strolled to Karen's yard to look at the paintings.

My neighbour seemed proud of the display, and justly so. All the work was beautiful: if not in line, then in colour. And what colours! On some, brilliant hues exploded with jagged force across the canvas as if by an electrified brush, while others were dreamlike with haunting misty shades blended with a touch as light as a breath. I stopped before a square showing a delicate girl with hair like gossamer petals.

"This is the same child as on the cups," I said with recognition.

Karen shook her head. "No, that's your Beth."

I stared. It was Beth—but the hair, the fairy-like colours . . . The sweet vulnerability in the fair painted face was unreal in its perfection. Was this what Karen called "capturing a soul?"

"It does resemble the child on the cups," said Karen. "I did them from an old snapshot of me. The photo was faded, giving me the idea for the treatment of the hair. I find it surprisingly effective. It gives a defenceless look, like a newly opened flower."

I returned to my house feeling vaguely upset. Perhaps it was surprise at finding a picture of Beth. Or was it—a necklace with a small gold cross?

Would I leave Beth with Karen? I did not know. I honestly did not know.

When a week of poor weather struck, leaving me no occasion to meet with my neighbour, my uneasiness ebbed and I shook my head at my earlier foolishness. And it was in this mood that I accepted the dinner invitation of a co-worker. A hasty call to Agnes assured she would fix supper for Beth, and with a clear conscience I stayed in town. The evening was pleasant and it was not until several hours later that I caught the train for home.

By the time I arrived at my station, it was dark, but the night air was clear. I glanced up at the moonlit sky, wondering why my contentment had fled. The lifting of the heavy rain clouds should hardly seem an omen of danger—yet it did. I shivered and walked on quickly, stepping on the wavering legs of my own shadow.

Then I saw it! From the corner of my eye *something moved!* A shape, a shape with a pale face and long hair. I recalled Karen's words, "I was all alone . . . then, there she was." *Mrs. Kaye?* My pulse pounded as a dreadful pressure rose in my ears. My lips parted to scream—then I saw what it was. Not Mrs. Kaye, but my own frightened reflection staring back at me dimly from a mirror placed on the station wall near the phone booth.

Relief winged through me. Then I paused, realizing Karen might have been stricken by the same experience. Poor Karen. I gave a helpless laugh of pity and the image in the mirror bared her teeth to laugh with me. Suddenly my hand flew to my mouth in dread. Karen had seen Mrs. Kaye on two occasions—seen her in a mirror!

I recoiled, then whirled and dashed to my car. The starter whined, the motor caught, the car spun into the street. My racing thoughts were a jumble of images which mixed the gray loping shape of a werewolf with the misty face of a child with petal-like hair. An urgent fear pressed me on.

I must get home to Beth!

As the car roared into my street the thudding panic within me exploded. My house was dark. There was a note on the side door: *"My daughter's baby came early. I've gone to the hospital with her. Beth is with the woman next door."*

I looked from Agnes's scrawled signature and across to Karen's house. A full moon glinted on the roof, but her house was as dark as mine.

Beth!

I slammed through Karen's unlocked door and through the kitchen, pressing on the light as I ran. "Karen!" and louder, "Beth, Beth, where are you?"

My frantic footsteps rang in the cruel emptiness of the rooms. I swept down the hall and flung open the door of Karen's workroom. My hand caught the edge of the light switch and brightness flooded the scene. I stared, then gasped as sickness struck me.

The room was filled with paintings—all of Beth!

Over and over Karen had painted my child. They were done in the style copied from her own childhood photograph, as if in Karen's mind, Beth's and her own childhood were intermingled. But as I looked about the room I saw the sweet face become more abstract, the petal hair flowing more wildly. The colours remained delicate and misty, but I could see the menace coming as the pictures changed. A menace coming nearer. The tiny face was thrown to a sun which tinged the petal hair blue—a blue coldness curling inward, reaching like jagged teeth towards the cheeks and eyes. The pale throat was bare in the final picture, the cross remembered only in a breath of yellow thrown at the canvas edge. Mad. Crazy mad!

Beth. Where was my Beth?

I flung against the last door. Karen's bedroom—locked.

"Beth! Beth!" My hands pounded against the wood. Then I stopped. There was a difference in the house. The chill within the walls wafted away and I heard sounds from behind the door.

"Jane?" asked Karen as she unlocked the door. Her eyes were blank and glazed.

"Where's Beth?" I pushed past Karen as she turned on the light. There was Beth upon the bed, a sleepy smile about her lips. Her warm arms slipped about me as I gathered her to me.

"I'm sorry," murmured Karen. "You must have been frightened to find the house dark." I lifted Beth and my neighbour moved behind me, hurrying me from the room, talking rapidly as she led me down the hall. "I was tired when Agnes brought her, so I got her to lie down with me. I locked the door so she couldn't wander out if I dozed, but I had no idea we would both sleep until dark."

"It's all right—all right," I said, resenting the fast explanation, but still so glad to be leaving the house and her. I saw she had gotten her coat and was slipping it on as we walked.

She noticed my glance and nodded. "I'm going out—really—I'm leaving for awhile." She laughed. It was an ugly hoarse sound, ending on the wrong note. "I've got to leave. I know now that Rena is back."

"Rena?" I wondered why the chill crept round me.

"Yes, Mrs. Kaye, Rena Kaye."

I murmured something which had no meaning and stumbled from the doorway, holding Beth tightly as I ran to my porch. Then, with my child still pressed against me, I turned to see Karen come from her house.

The dull illumination from the moon showed everything in muted colourless tones, and as my enighbour limped toward her car I was startled by the grayness of her—the shaggy hair, the skin, the clothes, all were gray—all but the eyes, which seemed to glow with a fire of their own. It all happened in a matter of seconds, but I stood transfixed, seeing the limping loping walk, the eyes, the grayness—and most ungodly of all, the last terrible look she flung at me before she drove away. Will I ever forget the way her head threw back as she smiled, her teeth gleaming like polished quartz in the moonlight?

My numb lips moved, repeating, "Rena Kaye, Rena K, Rena-K-Rena, K-Rena, K-rena, Karena . . . Karen!"

Then I understood. *Karen was Mrs. Kaye!*

And what of the hideous transformation I'd seen, the thing which turned my blood to ice and sent my control reeling? I fought against the word, but it came unbidden, screaming within my brain: *Werewolf! Werewolf!*

I managed to get Beth inside the house, where I undressed her with trembling hands. She was sleeping, her flushed face innocent of Karen's mad obsessions. How her sweet slumber made her resemble the child of the black cups. Had this resemblance caused the insanity Karen showed in the horrible portraits of my child?

But insanity was not the word. I thought of the asylum

Agnes told me about. Karen suffered from something far more loathsome than a shattered mind—it was an unspeakable disease, an incredible sickness passed through the centuries, attacking the innocent and driving them to lives of agony and doom.

The moon waiting outside seemed to send back an echo of my voice from long ago, a mocking whisper: "Nightmare." Almost sobbing, I slipped Beth's rounded arms into the sleeves of her nightgown and lifted her, smoothing down the fabric. She whimpered faintly and her drowsy head fell forward against my arm. Then I looked down...

Beth's soft hair parted on either side of her small head, falling down like drooping petals. "No—" I cried. *"It is a nightmare!"*, and my tears fell to wash the smooth nape which showed a small oval of red with the barest trace of blood about the edges. A small angry oval where something had recently bitten her.

DALE C. DONALDSON

PIA!

I wasn't too enthused about the party, particularly as it was a wet, stormy night, typical of Portland's winter season. But Mathilde wanted to go, and after all, I'm only the husband.

Thirty thousand a year in the advertising business allowed me a staff of a dozen artists and writers, the right to bellow and dictate thereto, the privilege of a late-in-the-morning-early-home existence, and bed and board in my ten-room house in the Irvington district. There my authority ceased and Mathilde took over. I was only a husband. And I loved it.

Hutch gave the party. Under the spousely thumb like myself, Hutch was an old war buddy, fast climbing into the top brackets of the publicity field. His apartment in the Bell Manor Arms gave evidence that he was ready to settle down and build ulcers. His wife, Ruth, was the most beautiful woman I have ever seen. I mused over her delightful figure as I guzzled my Tom Collins.

The apartment held the eight of us nicely. Old man Dunton—with ever a roving eye for feminine loveliness—was Hutch's boss, and was eternally ducking the displeasure of his young, tight-lipped wife, Pia. It was public knowledge that Pia had married old Dunton for his money, and that she gave him nothing but a bad time. He countered by using his wealth in the pursuit of other, more willing women, but Pia remained virtuous. I know.

Paul and Jill Montgomery were still young enough to be completely in love with each other, and had joined our group only for the business contacts afforded. Paul did something in insurance, and Jill was a model . . . hats and dresses in a downtown department store.

". . . and so I told him that he was off his rocker, and

asked him why he didn't go back to the old country." Old man Dunton giggled nervously, and leered at Ruth.

Ruth, self-appreciative of her charm, smiled as she served him a Martini. "And then what did he say?"

"He said that it was old fools like myself who maligned the truth by ridicule, thus affording the evil a surety of safety." Dunton continued, "And that he was sure that I would be among the first to go." He burst into a cackle of laughter. "I'll see him six feet under before my turn comes."

I groped for Mathilde's hand on the couch beside me. "What's he prattling on about?" I asked.

Mathilde clucked disapprovingly. "Climb out of that Collins, boy, and lend an ear." Then, aware that I really hadn't heard, she explained. "Dunton stopped off at the floor above before coming to the party. He knows a Doctor Chives—or Cheeves . . ."

"And Chives told him that he'd have to stop living so fast?"

"Uh-uh. Chives—Cheeves told Dunton that the goblins would get him if he didn't change his attitude."

"How nice. Ruth!" I called, waving my empty glass. "Play hostess!"

Mathilde pulled my arm. "No. Seriously, Chet, it seems that Cheeves is an occultist. He was at one time a Doctor of Psychology, but left it for the study of black magic when he became convinced that a majority of hallucinations conform to a pattern. Then he went all the way, and devoted his life to the protection of us more skeptical mortals."

"S'fine. Ruth!" I got my empty glass into the air again.

Mathilde shook me. "Listen, goof. Cheeves is no quack. He told Dunton that tonight was the night of the full moon. And that Dunton should be careful. And that . . ."

"And that a great big, bloody vampire would fly in the window and suck up what blood old Dunton has left in his alcoholic veins. Could a drunken vampire fly, I wonder?"

Mathilde frowned prettily, and moved away. I could see that I was in for one of her martyred moods of silence.

"Look, kitten. You don't really believe in all this business of ghouls, and werewolves. Why the concern?"

She thawed a little. "No, Chet. I don't think I do. But I do believe . . ."

". . . seems he can sense vibrations." Hutch's deep voice boomed into our conversation. "He says that he has become somewhat psychic, and can tell when one of the elementals is due to appear."

"But why the emphasis on Mr. Dunton?" Jill Montgomery asked. "And why tonight, of all times?"

"Tonight is the night of the full moon," Hutch answered, glancing at all of us apologetically. "Dr. Cheeves says that he has sensed the vibrations gathering in this apartment for a long time."

I stood, and walked over to where Hutch was holding the group enthralled. "Hutch," I said, "you sound as if you believe this pile of spook tales."

Ruth pushed me gently to a chair. "You haven't heard the full story, Chet," she reproved softly. "Listen before you talk."

Hutch ran his fingers worriedly through his hair, and sat down on the edge of the table. From then on, his tale was directed mostly to me.

"I met Dr. Cheeves about a year and a half ago when we moved into this apartment," Hutch related, "and it just so happens that Ruth studied under him at the University." He glanced at his lovely wife, and she nodded her head in agreement. "Since he already knew half of the family, the three of us got well acquainted. He told us that he had left teaching to do some deeper research in the field of the occult. He didn't mention the subject much, and it wasn't until three months ago that he brought up this business about 'vibrations'. I laughed when I first heard it, and put it down to overwork. I thought maybe he needed a rest." He paused and quickly drained his glass. Ruth took it from his hand as I settled back comfortably to hear a nice ghost story.

"All of you, each and every one, has been to our apartment many times." Hutch looked each person in the eye, stopping when he got to me. "When Dr. Cheeves has come down the next day, or later, he senses the vibrations of the elemental. But the traces are nebulous. He can't identify the exact person responsible. And thus the little gathering tonight."

Pia Dunton rose slowly to her feet. "Do you mean that it is suspected that one of us is an . . . elemental?"

Hutch nodded. "To be more precise, a werewolf!"

Old man Dunton went off into a peal of laughter. "Hutch, m'boy," he gasped, at the end of his cackle, "I knew you needed a vacation. Consider yourself with two weeks off, beginning tomorrow." He chortled gleefully.

No other voice broke the dead silence. I looked thoughtfully at the other members of the group, people I had heretobefore considered quite sane and normal. Both Hutch and Ruth were still and solemn-faced, Paul and Jill, young and impressionable, Pia, white-faced, possibly because of her dark European background, and even Mathilde, quiet and reserved. The only spot of normalcy rested with old Dunton, who was gazing hungrily at the twin points of Ruth's satin blouse.

And then the lights flickered and went out.

Of course. A game. I had just enough gin in my system to go along with the gag. Silently, I tiptoed over to the door while the others were gasping with varied fears. I turned the key to lock the door, bent, and slipped the key under the sill, out into the hallway. Better make this good, I cautioned myself, and stealthily slipped over to the phone box on the wall. I jerked, and felt the wires part. On my way back to my seat, I became aware of a sharp, sangy odour, and flicked on my cigarette lighter to see Pia standing directly before me, her eyes huge and dark. She had always used the damnedest perfume!

I broke into the babbled, half-panicked conversation. "Why doesn't someone light a candle?" I asked. "I don't want to get chewed up by some monster when I can't see who's chewing."

Dunton chuckled delightedly.

As Ruth moved toward the kitchen to get a candle, the lights again flickered, then came on in bright intensity. Of the eight, only Ruth, Pia and I had moved. And of the faces, six were drawn and worried. Only Dunton's was mischievous.

Glancing apprehensively at the light globes, Paul Montgomery addressed the silent Hutch. "Let's approach this with science," Paul said. "Assuming for the moment that there is a . . . werewolf in the group . . . he, himself, knows that he is not human."

"Or she," suggested Hutch, drily.

"Or she. Now, I've always understood that there are definite facts concerning lycanthropy, such as a longer ring finger, hair on the palms of the hands, an aversion to silver, and so on. Am I correct?"

The group nodded solemnly, even Dunton, who had evidently decided to play along. So I nodded solemnly too.

"O.K. So assuming the werewolf is here . . ." Paul moved over and picked up a heavy silver ashtray upon which was a mounted a model airplane with sharp wings and tail section, ". . . I think it would be wise to have a little hand inspection to see if we can't locate those identifying marks."

Hutch shrugged. "Good idea, but impractical. The palm of the hand can be shaved, and the offending finger shortened by surgery, or even lengthened by plastic."

"Let's have an inspection anyway," said Jill as she moved over to join her husband.

Old man Dunton cleared his throat. "Let's talk a minute more first. Agreeing that there's a beastie here— I don't, but let's pretend—and if this beastie is indeed a werewolf, it's quite dreadfully dangerous. It would never submit to inspection. That ashtray . . ." Dunton indicated the heavy silver piece that Paul held, ". . . would be less than useless. From all the reading that I've ever done, it seems that only a silver bullet in the heart can stop a lycanthrope. Anybody got a gun with silver bullets?"

"Yes," Hutch answered. "Dr. Cheeves, upstairs."

"Then I suggest that you get it," said Dunton.

Strangely and totally without valid reason, doubt grew. Wives moved closer to their husbands, and I felt Mathilde's fingers clutch my sleeve. This, I thought, was silly.

I held up my hand. "Wait," I said. "We're really frightening one another." I turned to Hutch. "Tell them that it's a game, and let's get back to our drinking."

Hutch looked at me gravely. "It's not a game as far as I'm concerned."

I felt a little of my reason slipping. "But it must be. Even if it is the night of the full moon, the monster couldn't see it. There's a storm outside, and the moon is covered."

No one answered.

"And if we do have a beast here, why didn't it attack when the lights were out a few moments ago? No. We've all known one another for a long time. Call off the game, Hutch."

Ruth pushed him toward the door. "Go on, Hutch. Get Dr. Cheeves."

"Wait!" I demanded, angrily. "If there's a wolf in here do you think he's going to let you get to Cheeves?"

The room was filled with a strange silence, and I suddenly felt all eyes directed toward me.

"Methinks he doth protest too much," Jill said softly. I felt Mathilde move away from me.

"Dunton . . ." I pleaded.

Slowly, the group formed across the room. Seven of them, even my wife. I found myself at bay.

The humour of the situation got the best of me, and I collapsed into a chair, chuckling. "Go get the Doctor," I said.

Keeping both eyes on me, Hutch sidled over to the door. Then I remembered. "You can't get out, Hutch," I called. "I locked the door and threw the key under the sill!"

The tableau froze. There was no longer question in their eyes; they looked at me in fear. I saw Ruth fumbling behind her.

"And, Ruth," I continued, "I tore the phone out by the roots."

By this time the seven of them were as far away from me as they could get. And the fear was turning to terror. Paul swallowed, and hefted the silver ashtray.

At last Pia stepped slowly forward—ten hesitant steps, which placed her exactly between the group and myself. "What . . ." she asked, voice shaking, ". . . do you want?"

316

Thoughtfully, I reached out my hands, fingers extended, and slowly turned my palms upward. "Look closely, Pia," I requested. "Do you see any stubble of hair? Are any of my fingers the wrong length?"

She advanced fearfully, watching me with those dark, troubled eyes. Quite carefully, she scrutinized my hands, and then she met my eyes.

"No," she murmured. "They look all right."

I stood up quickly. Pia flinched, but I grabbed her by a soft forearm. "I'm not your wolf," I said to the others in a loud, clear voice. "There's no wolf here."

"But why the door—the phone . . ." Hutch mumbled helplessly.

"It was part of the game I thought you were playing," I answered. "Now if Ruth will get your extra key, you can go after Doctor Cheeves. And I'm quite sure that the beast won't tear you to pieces on the way." My hand slid down Pia's arm, and I took her hot, moist hand. I could feel her relax.

"There's no other key," said Ruth. The group was breaking up now, but at her words, they tensed.

"How about the window?" asked Paul. "Can we get to the next apartment?"

They crowded to the window, all but Mathilde, who stood alone, watching my hold on Pia.

"Thanks for the confidence, partner," I remarked. "Do you think you'll be able to live with me from here on out?"

Mathilde walked slowly toward me, and I could feel Pia releasing her hand. I let her go. After all, she belonged to Dunton. I would have liked to have had her, though; she was soft and sweet, except for her hands, which were always tightly clenched. A sign of her virtue, I suppose.

". . . can't do it. Not wide enough. And eight floors down." I caught a mumble from the group at the window as Mathilde came into my arms. ". . . have to break the door. Hey, Chet!"

Hutch strode over to me and thrust out his hand. "I'm sorry, chum, but you certainly acted suspicious."

I waved aside the hand and the apology. "And what about the window?" I asked.

"Only a five-inch ledge," he answered. "Can't get to

the next apartment that way. We'll have to break down the door."

Now that the tension was over, there were eager queries for drinks. People circulated into other rooms, and I left Mathilde to find Dunton. What had made him change his attitude so quickly?

As I crossed the bedroom on the way into the bathroom, the lights flickered again, and went out. There was a moment of intent, black silence, and then the rustle of people as they searched their pockets for matches.

I reached into my coat for my lighter, and a heavy body struck me. It was moving fast, and the impact knocked me over onto the bed. I swore violently as I disentangled myself, but stopped abruptly at the sound of a vicious animal snarl. And then a scream! A woman's voice in high-pitched terror, shrill and—cut off with a blubbering moan. It came from the bathroom.

I leaped to my feet and, regardless of the blackness, rushed for the door. Again the rasping snarl, and a heavy fetid odour of wildness. As I reached the bathroom door, the body again collided with me, and the weight threw me to the floor. And I was sickeningly aware that I had touched moving wet fur!

I would have lain there, frozen, had I not heard the moans from the woman in the bathroom. I crawled to my hands and knees, and thrust my head into the room. Laboriously, I flicked the wheel on my lighter, and, as the wick caught, the electric current came back, flooding the bathroom with light.

For a moment I couldn't move, and then, as my eyes forwarded what they saw to my brain, I staggered to the basin and retched, violently and lengthily. I was aware of Pia as she came running from the bedroom, aware of her sharp gasp, and aware of her immediate collapse into unconsciousness. I heard the drumming of other feet, and moved to the bathroom door, quickly closing it and turning the latch. Whoever was in the lead slammed head first into the panel.

"What is it? What happened? Who's in there? Open the door! Open, I say!" Frantic fists beat against the wood.

They were all out there now, all but Pia and I, the

woman moaning on the floor, and the awful thing sprawled over the tub. I leaned my forehead against the wall while I collected my wits.

At last I pounded on the door for silence. As the babble of voices died away, I called quite clearly, "There's been an accident. Everybody into the front room except Hutch. I'll let Hutch in!"

"What happened in there?"

"Everybody go but Hutch! Go on! Get away! Only Hutch!"

There was a murmur of voices, among which I could hear Mathilde calling, "Chet, Chet, let me in!" and then a gradual withdrawal. Hutch rapped on the panel. "O.K., Chet, I'm alone."

I opened the door, carefully keeping my back to the tub. Hutch's flushed face peered over my shoulder, and I saw his eyes widen, and heard the gasp of nausea. My hand steadied him.

As he entered, I again locked the door, then turned and steeled my quaking stomach.

Ruth, the initial shock now over, was on the floor, her face buried in her hands. She was sobbing wretchedly. Hutch was bent over her, awkwardly caressing her trembling shoulders. Flung backward over the tub was Dunton—what was left of him. His face was a gory mess, completely unrecognizable. It was as if some monstrous claw had torn his features away, only white cartilage, stringing, gave evidence as to where his nose had been. One eyeball hung loosely from a gaping socket; the other was gone, leaving only a raw blood-filled hole. His lower jaw had been bodily torn away from the skull, and sharp white bone protruded from the aperture.

The claw had torn again at his waistline, and he lay disembowelled. And above all, over everything else, was the hot, rich stench of freshly spilled blood.

Crooning a wordless tune, Hutch got Ruth to her feet, and we left the bathroom, I carrying Pia in my arms. The other three met us at the living room entrance, and the babble of questioning began.

"What happened? What's the matter? Where's Dunton?"

Laying Pia on the couch, I held up my hand for silence. Mathilde was on my arm again.

"It's no longer a game," I began. "Dunton's in the bathroom, ripped to pieces."

Ruth sat upright on Hutch's lap. "I saw it!" she gasped hysterically. "It was a wolf—big as a mountain!" She shuddered spasmodically against Hutch's chest, and her fingers clutched his coat lapels. He soothed her hair. "Don't talk about it, honey."

"Yes, I must!" She looked around wildly, with nearly vacant eyes. With a tremendous effort, she got herself under control.

"I had gone to the bathroom to put—on some—lipstick," she continued. "Dunton came in and began—pawing me." She looked at Hutch for reassurance. He nodded. She wet her dry lips. "And then the lights went out. I moved away, but he followed, and I felt his hands on me. I asked him to light a match, and he did, and I could see by the flare that he meant to make the most of his opportunity. And then it came!" Her voice broke again, and she put her hands over her face.

"And then . . . ?" Paul prompted.

"And then it hit him. By the flare of the match I saw—it. It was as big as the bathroom door, and it—lunged—out of the darkness—big, red eyes, and teeth—like—daggers . . ." A spasm shook her body.

"A wolf?" I asked.

She nodded. "So big—I saw—I saw its jaws close over his face as it struck him, and he fell against me, and knocked me to the floor. The match went out, and then it —it—I could hear the sound of the—tearing, and—the—Oh, God!" She moaned and buried her face in Hutch's coat.

There was silence. At last I cleared my throat. "It knocked me down twice," I said. "In the bedroom. Coming and going."

Paul spoke sharply. "Then there *is* a werewolf. And he's here. One of us." He still had his silver ashtray.

"And if the lights go out again . . ." Pia, who had regained consciousness, spoke from the couch.

Hutch stood swiftly, placing Ruth on her feet. "Let's

get Cheeves." He moved toward the door. "C'mon, Chet, let's break it down!"

Quickly, Ruth was in front of him. "If that thing's in here," she said, "it'll kill you when you touch the door!"

Tension mounted in the room. One of us was a beast. And the rest of us were helpless. It could strike at will, and we had no defence. Stark terror filled Mathilde's eyes, and Jill's, and Ruth's. We men looked at one another cautiously. And Pia. *Where was Pia?*

Of one accord, we rushed to the window. Out on the narrow five-inch ledge stood Pia, slowly edging her way to the next window. Her dark eyes were enormous, but her lips parted in a sickly smile as she saw us. "I'll get Cheeves," she murmured.

We watched her hanging perilously on that ledge until she had gained the next window and disappeared into the room. Then we drew in our heads.

Hutch ruffled his hair distractedly. "Six of us here now," he said, "and one a killer. Chet, what if the lights go out?"

I looked around the room. Of the girls, only Mathilde was there. "Where are Ruth and Jill?" I asked.

"In the kitchen," Mathilde said. "Ruth's going to brew a pot of coffee."

Silently, I ran across the apartment to the kitchen door. Blessing the expensive fixtures of a high-priced apartment, I quietly shut the kitchen door, and turned the latch. The others looked at me in amazement.

"Now there are only four of us," I said. "And if Mathilde and I lock ourselves in the coat closet, there will be only two. That way the beast can have only one more victim, and will be forced to expose himself."

"What good will that that do?" asked Paul.

"Can you think of anything better? And it's only until Cheeves gets here with . . ."

The apartment was ripped with a shrill scream of utter terror. Emanating from the kitchen, the scream grew in crescendo to an unbearable pitch, then abruptly stopped. I beat the other two men to the locked door. As I spread-eagled myself against its surface, I could hear a rasping, snuffling sound from within. We had our wolf!

"Let me in, damn you!" Hutch raged, clawing at my arms. "That's Ruth in there!"

"And Jill!" Paul was beating at my face with his free fist.

Using the door as a leverage for my back, I managed to throw them both from me. Sobbing, Paul raised the heavy ashtray. "Get away," he cried, "or I'll kill you!"

"Wait!" I raised my hand to fend off the blow. "If we open this door, the wolf will come out. Shall we all die?"

They paused momentarily, and I continued. "What's done in there is done. We can't change it. And we have to live long enough to kill the beast. Wait for Cheeves!"

Paul dropped his hand, and Hutch looked at me out of dull eyes. "Ruth's dead," he said. "She can't be the thing because she saw it kill Dunton in the bathroom." He turned his head bleakly to Paul. "Your Jill. A monster."

Stupidly, Paul's chin began to quiver. I glanced over Paul's shoulder to reassure Mathilde. And my heart stopped still!

There on the living room floor crouched Mathilde, my wife of eight years. She was on her hands and knees, swaying from side to side. Her head was turned in our direction, but it was no human head. Huge, red-rimmed eyes stared balefully at us, and her face was a horror of canine hatred. She snarled threateningly, and white fangs glittered. Even as I watched, her lovely hands turned to clawed pads, and her sleek thighs to muscled haunches. And then she leaped!

One bound carried her to the living room entrance, and at that moment the hall door opened. The beast was already in mid-air in her second leap, but twisted frantically, and landed at our feet, snarling, facing the open door.

A small, partially bald man stood in the doorway, and in his blessed hand was the sparkle of a gun. Cheeves!

With a rumble of vicious rage, the wolf lunged at the little man. Without a tremor, he lifted the gun and fired. Calmly and coolly. One shot.

The impetus of the monster carried it halfway through the living room, where it collapsed in a lifeless heap. It lay still on the carpet, cavernous jaws agape.

As we moved toward it, the re-transition began. The frenzied expression of the muzzle turned again to the smooth patrician nose of my wife. The slavering jaws disappeared, to be replaced by sweet, warm lips. And the canine body became an outline of adorable womanhood. It was again Mathilde.

Mathilde!

Hutch laughed nervously. "Doc, you got here just in time."

The Doctor came into the room and closed the door behind him. "Are you all here?" he questioned.

Staring apathetically at the slowly flowing death wound above Mathilde's left breast, I heard Hutch answer. "Yeah. All of us. Except—except Pia. Doc, where's Pia?"

"I did not see her. Why do you ask me?"

"But she went after you. The window—the window—the window goes to the kitchen. The kitchen! The animal! Ruth! Ruth!" Hutch sprang away to the kitchen door, closely followed by Paul.

"Stop 'em, Doc," I mumbled. "There's something in the kitchen."

Doctor Cheeves fired his silver gun again, and a bullet splattered on the kitchen door moulding. "One moment, please," the Doctor commanded. Hutch and Paul came to a standstill.

"What about this kitchen, and this—Pia?" he asked me.

"Pia went out the window to the next apartment so that she could get to you."

"I saw no Pia. I came down because I was worried that you had not come after me. And the kitchen?"

"Pia went out the window, and Ruth and Jill went to the kitchen," I told him. "And I locked them in. And they screamed. And we heard an animal. In the kitchen. And then—Mathilde."

The Doctor stationed himself in the centre of the floor, his gun pointing at the doorway. "Open, if you please."

Neither Hutch nor Paul was over-eager. There was no indication of what might emerge. As for myself, I didn't much care. How could it be? My Mathilde—dead.

"Mr. Montgomery. If you will please come back into

the living room," the Doctor directed. "And you," he indicated Hutch, "open the door and step behind it."

After a moment's hesitant pause, Hutch walked to the door and turned the lock. Cautiously, he put a hand on the knob, then jerked the door violently open, scrambling out of the line of fire.

Pia stood in the doorway. Her eyes were big and black, and her fists tightly clenched. "I heard," she whispered.

Hutch and Paul rushed into the kitchen, pushing her aside. Soon they returned, carrying the women in their arms. "They're just unconscious," Hutch said to me. "Thank the Lord!"

The Doctor had not taken his eyes off Pia, nor had I. His gun was still lifted, pointing at her heart. She watched silently as the men lay the girls down and forced liquor between their lips.

"I was afraid," she said at last. "I couldn't make it to the next apartment. I went in the kitchen window. I—don't know what happened."

"You lie!" My voice was hoarse and heavy. "I heard the . . ."

"Doctor Cheeves!" It was Ruth, struggling to consciousness.

The Doctor glanced at Ruth quickly. And the moment his eyes left Pia, the room was filled with raging werewolf. Her transition was immediate, and she was 200 pounds of slashing fury, bearing the Doctor to the floor. The gun flew across the room. The sound of the chomping jaws mingled with the agonized screams of the Doctor.

Hutch scrambled for the gun, turned, and pumped two shots into her maddened body, causing her to leap high into the air. Hutch fired again, and the third bullet snapped her spine. She fell limply to the rug.

Again transition was rapid and it was Pia who lay with a broken back, bleeding from three wounds. With an effort, she opened her lips, and raised a bloody finger to point at me.

"Get him!" she gasped. "A traitor! Shoot him!"

Awed, but with gun hand steady, Hutch looked from the woman to me.

"Get him! He's one of us!" Blood gushed from her

throat and Hutch bent to her aid. "Quickly—look at his hands. The fur . . . The fingers . . ."

Hutch raised, bringing the gun up quickly.

But I was gone. I howled as I loped down the hallway, around the corner out of range of the deadly silver bullet. I howled in glee, for the scent of fresh blood was in my nostrils and there were humans to be slaughtered in the dark, rainy streets of the city below.

The Compleat Werewolf

ANTHONY BOUCHER

A splendid collection of short stories that include amongst their subjects...

WEREWOLVES...

DEMONS...

DOPPELGANGERS...

ANDROIDS...

ALIENS...

And other delights for the reader who dares to dabble in the rich world of Anthony Boucher's imagination.

Sphere Books   35p

The Following Horror Titles Are Also Available From Sphere Books

THE YEAR'S BEST HORROR STORIES No. 2	Richard Davis (Ed.)	30p
THE WILD NIGHT COMPANY	Peter Haining (Ed.)	40p
THE SCARS OF DRACULA	Angus Hall	25p
THE EXORCISM	Ronald Pearsall	30p
THE POSSESSED	Ronald Pearsall	30p
THE CASE AGAINST SATAN	Ray Russell	30p
A MAN CALLED POE	Sam Moskowitz	35p

All Sphere Books are available at your bookshop or
newsagent, or can be ordered from the following address:

Sphere Books, Cash Sales Department,
P.O. Box 11, Falmouth, Cornwall.

Please send cheque or postal order (no currency), and allow
7p per copy to cover the cost of postage and packing
in U.K. or overseas.